THE
TORCHBEARERS

For John, Jack, Tom and Kate

ONE ROAD LEADS TO HEAVEN
BUT MANY LEAD TO HELL

THE
TORCHBEARERS

BAIRBRE HIGGINS

A THRILLER

MINARD PRESS

First published in 2018 by
Minard Press
Clontarf
Co. Dublin
Ireland
www.bairbrehiggins.com

Paperback   ISBN: 978-1-78846-039-2
eBook – mobi format   ISBN: 978-1-78846-040-8
eBook – ePub format   ISBN: 978-1-78846-041-5
CreateSpace paperback   ISBN: 978-1-78846-042-2

Produced by Kazoo Independent Publishing Services
222 Beech Park, Lucan, Co. Dublin
www.kazoopublishing.com

Kazoo Independent Publishing Services is not the publisher of this work. All rights and responsibilities pertaining to this work remain with Minard Press.

Kazoo offers independent authors a full range of publishing services.
For further details visit www.kazoopublishing.com

Cover design by Andrew Brown
Printed in the EU

About the Author

Born in Cork, Bairbre Higgins lives in Dublin, Ireland, with her husband, three kids and two dogs. Having studied economics, she worked in the Irish financial services industry for many years but is now focused full time on writing.

A hurry through which known and strange things pass
That catch the heart off guard and blow it open.

from "POSTSCRIPT" *by* SEAMUS HEANEY

Chapter One

ENDURANCE

"And let us run with endurance the race God has set before us."

— HEBREWS 12:1

He would still be alive if he had been with her instead of me. If I hadn't pressed him to come to the house, he would never have seen the lights. He wouldn't have followed them down into the desert's dark embrace.

Images of Mike's final moments keep playing in my mind. Sleeping pills help at night, but the daytime is a struggle. Like a junky in withdrawal, I have become obsessed with self-distraction, and this has given me a new appreciation of the limits of human endurance. That tipping point in a long run when the world fades and emotional pain evaporates. Stride over stride, breath after breath. A kind of hypnosis. My daily runs are my anesthetic, my means of escape, all that is left between me and a precipitous descent into despair.

I pass the halfway point, pounding out the miles. Thirty is today's goal. A loop, starting and finishing in Deming. Having left the hard shoulder of Interstate 10 four miles east of town, I backtrack in a wide westward arc through the Chihuahuan Desert wilderness. The parched earth is peppered with clumps of tobosa grass, mesquite and creamy blooming yucca. As far as the eye can see, imperceptible gradients create a palette of pale green, mustard and the odd spray of mauve. In the cloudless sky a buzzard glides lazily along invisible corridors of warm air.

I adjust my bandana in an attempt to stem the perspiration without having to stop. All long runs have peaks and troughs of ecstasy and agony, and right now I am in the zone. My hands appear in front of me in metronomic regularity, and my feet deliver a satisfying crunch as they grip and propel. The intermittent throb along the line of sutures in my scalp has escalated into a radiating aura of pain. The doctor advised against exertion for two weeks, but I find the discomfort oddly pleasing.

Nineteen miles. Now running due south. The I-10 emerges through the haze like a quivering thread of mercury. I cross the railroad tracks, turn back east toward town along the highway and soon come to the diamond interchange for Exit 67. This is the junction for Old County Road, the desolate, sixty-mile ribbon of asphalt where I have lived during these past seven months of self-imposed exile.

Behind a green mile marker on the hard shoulder rests the decaying red hulk of a Chevy Beauville van and a skeletal water tower. The words "Danni's Desert Tours" are printed on the side of the van in faded script. The same pathetic pairing caught my eye eight days ago through the window of the police vehicle on the way back from Deming Medical Center and struck me then as chance installation art depicting the death of a dream.

My trip to the center earlier that morning had been by ambulance. Several police cars followed behind, sirens blaring, heralding an emergency that didn't exist. Minutes after the small cavalcade had left my house, the chatty young paramedic carefully lifted my head from my hands to loosen the makeshift turban-style bandage. When he released my ponytail, the whole mess slid off in one big wad. "Oooh, that's a messy one, all right," he said, wincing. "Ten to fifteen stitches, I'm guessing." Then he sponged the caked blood out of my ear.

Sergeant Marge Newlands shifted uncomfortably in the jump seat beside the ambulance door, muttering into a radio or phone for most of the journey. We hadn't made eye contact since our little exchange at dawn, when we heard that the bodies had been found.

The moment I clapped eyes on her, Newlands reminded me of Sadistic Sister Sauerkraut, the horse-faced mother superior in my Catholic elementary school in Queens. She never ever smiled, that woman, not even when the kindergarten kids carried the baby Jesus up to the crib on Christmas Eve.

After the doctor in the triage theater had treated the four-inch gash in my head, I was tended to by a kindly nurse who insisted on privacy while with her patient.

"It's past ten. You need to come with us. Now!" It was the third time the sergeant's angry head had appeared through the gap where the cubicle curtain met the IV drip, and her tone had acquired a world-is-about-to-end urgency.

The nurse shot her an exasperated look and continued to apply antiseptic to the thirteen staples in my head. "As I told you already, Officer, we'll be with you when I'm finished and not one second before that." She raised her eyes to heaven and murmured "ridiculous" under her breath.

The journey from Deming to Prospero Police Station took

forty-five minutes. I had been in a police car only once before, and that was a fake. "A flashy blue tour of the Strip" was how the travel agent had sold it to my friend Natalie the week before my thirtieth birthday celebration in Vegas a few years ago. The driver was buck naked apart from his police cap, aviators and a gem-encrusted jock strap. He switched on the roof lights and sirens only when we gave him a tip.

The sirens were silent on our journey from the hospital that morning. There was no talking, either, after the driver had communicated to base that we were on the way. Exhausted and raw from the sharp slap of sudden loss, everyone stared blankly out the window. The hospital staff had given me a pale-gray sweat suit to replace my blood-stained clothes (taken in evidence) and I sat stock still in the back like a posed mannequin, sandwiched between Newlands and another officer. I remember sensing the hatred welling up around me in that quiet car. When we passed the sad-looking Chevy at the Old County Road junction, the enormity of the situation had begun to sink in.

I wasn't sure I was being arrested until they sat me down in a small interview room in the basement of the police station and Newlands read me my rights. "I am arresting you, Ariel R. Mignolet, under reasonable suspicion of having committed a crime," was how she put it to me, as opposed to charging me with the murder of the three people found dead a mile from my house the night before.

"There was a group. They tried to kill me, too," I think I muttered while being manhandled through the mug shot and prints process. I'm not entirely sure. My memories of that morning are pretty patchy.

The clamoring pack of journalists, shooed out of the car's path to allow us to pass under the boom barrier into the station's rear parking lot, seemed to know much more about what was going on than I did. In a few moments they had the police car surrounded. The officer sitting to my left leaned back as far as he could to facilitate the onslaught of lenses thrust violently at the car window like rifle sights. One lucky shot yielded an unflattering image of me that subsequently appeared nationwide, for twenty-four hours, across every news medium in every bulletin concerning the SAN FRANCISCO HEDGE FUND PARTNER ARRESTED FOR MURDER IN FUNDAMENTALIST BAPTIST TOWN IN NEW MEXICO.

I didn't get sight of that picture myself until three days later, last Tuesday, the morning before Mike's funeral. A folded newspaper slipped out of the front pocket of my mother's suitcase while I was lifting it onto the guest bed. It might seem strange to get picky about a stupid mug shot, but it struck me that the shadows accentuated the size of my nose and the shocking streak of tangerine antiseptic conveniently distorted my image into the mold of maniac or monster.

I have no doubt that a psychologist, had there been one within the ranks of the Prospero Police Department, would not have passed me fit for interrogation that morning. By the time the sergeant and three of her minions began questioning me, I had been awake for thirty-six hours and was still in the stupefying grip of profound shock. The sergeant led the two sessions, each one two hours in duration and each beginning at the beginning. That is to say, the beginning as defined by Marge Newlands.

"Officer Mike Argyll noticed the strange lights at approximately ten-twenty last evening, the evening of Friday, September ninth? At your home? At The Bank, Old County Road?" This was her lead-in on a few occasions. No mention, of course, of what had gone before.

"That is correct," I replied.

"At approximately ten-twenty-five, he looked through the night-vision telescope in your house to get a better look at the lights you say you saw moving about in the Playas Valley?"

"He did. Yes," I said.

"You say he departed and drove down onto the Playas plains in a southeasterly direction toward Big Hatchet Peak at approximately ten-thirty-five and that's when you called the station and spoke to me, having been unable to get through to Officer van Kanz?"

"That is what happened. Yes."

"And you admit to following Officer Argyll out onto the desert plateau in front of your property?"

And on we went in that stuffy little room. Question by painstaking question through my shaky, eyewitness testimony of how things had unfolded the night before. There were blanks, mistakes, revisions. I don't recall being definite about anything.

All purveyors of financial products become very familiar with the body language of mistrust early in their careers. Little signals across the desk. Subtle eye movements or a particular pattern of seat-shifting that suggest your sales pitch has already failed. I didn't need to draw heavily on such skills eight days ago as I recounted the events of Friday night. The incredulity on the officers' faces was clear to see as I offered my version of the bizarre truth. The frustration was excruciating as my words were met with disbelief that rapidly matured to scorn.

When they switched off the recording device after session two, I had recovered enough common sense to use my phone call to contact my best friend, Sunil Narine, a rising star in

San Francisco's legal scene. It turned out he had been trying to make contact all day and was already armed with a plan. I was to immediately invoke my right to silence and demand a local lawyer while he hired the best criminal counsel money could buy. He assured me he would have someone there within twenty-four hours and would follow on himself the day after that.

Having already sung like a canary for four hours, I resisted his advice not to answer any questions but refused to add to my existing statements until my nominated local attorney, Henry Marsling, Esq., arrived. They produced all seventy-four years of him within minutes, fresh from his afternoon bridge game in the nearby church hall. He wore a chunky hearing aid, only slightly more advanced than an ear trumpet, and never made any attempt to disguise the fact that he was merely going through the motions.

My third account of how Mike had discovered the two bodies, the lead-up to his subsequent murder and the attackers' attempt on my own life took all of five hours, across two extended sessions, mostly because the device attached to Henry's left lobe continually malfunctioned. It would randomly emit a series of high-frequency pips like blasts of Morse code from a sinking ship and these alarming interruptions would be followed by an "I'm sorry, could you repeat that?" and several minutes of tweaking before we could proceed.

I slept fitfully that night, in a surprisingly comfortable holding cell, with the aid of generous quantities of painkillers and sleeping pills prescribed to me by the doctor in Deming. I awoke in the fetal position on the narrow cot, my mouth open wide in a silent scream.

That morning I had to account for various pieces of evidence found at the scene or taken from my home. They placed the tagged exhibits, one by one, on the table in front of me. Although I didn't raise the issue, I was much more surprised by the absence of certain items than the presence of others.

This session was followed by a short break for lunch, during which Henry informed me that the attorney my friend had engaged was due to land in El Paso at five-thirty that afternoon. Henry was impressed.

"Martha Gratton. Really? Defended Senator Taylor in Washington, if I'm not mistaken? Indeed, I very much look forward to making her acquaintance," he whispered to me in an aside, and I noticed a fresh gob of blue sticky tack affixed to the battery pack behind his ear.

It was at that point I told my interrogators that I was not prepared to answer any more questions until my newly engaged legal counsel was present.

"Why stay silent when you have nothing to hide?" Sergeant Newlands countered immediately.

The sheer audacity, I thought. Only a matter of hours earlier, she herself must have broken every known law relating to the preservation of a crime scene and concealment of evidence. Just after dawn, with pink-and-yellow, full-of-promise sunshine washing into the house as though nothing earth-shattering had taken place the night before, I had watched her gloved hands move through my living room with the efficiency of a fruit picker at harvest's end. At that point, of course, I wasn't aware that she was actually *lifting* evidence. Our half-drunk bottle of Burgundy, those two Waterford Crystal long-stem glasses, the throw and several other items were inserted into Ziploc bags and ferried out to her trunk in a blue cardboard box—never, it seems, to be seen again.

And she had only needed minutes to make the decision. A short spell of contemplation after the news about Mike came through over the radio. Enough time to observe, to take everything in, collect herself and execute a potentially life-altering plan.

If I am honest, I admire her for it, really. Admire the speed and clarity of thinking, like a financial trader reacting instantaneously to a massive market shock. She knew what needed to be done to protect Mike's memory and had grabbed the whole shit show by the scruff of the neck.

What I don't understand is why, even at that early stage, she was already so sure I would not stand in her way or blow her cover, no matter at what personal cost. What gave her the confidence to sit across the table from me later that morning in Prospero Police Station, in front of witnesses, and baldly suggest that it was *I* who might have something to hide?

Hapless Henry Esq. did manage to hear her jibe about why I was choosing to remain silent and had just begun a pat legal reply. "Pardon me, Sergeant Newlands, my client has the right not to be coerced in a manner prejudicial to ..." when he was cut off mid-flow by the sudden entrance of the officer who had sat beside me in the car the day before. He stood half in, half out of the room, waving a sheet of paper.

"Sergeant, sorry to interrupt, but you need to read this. Immediately."

Sergeant Newlands took to her feet and read the letter's contents, her face turning red as the seconds ticked by. She then read it aloud to myself and Henry, who didn't catch its import and kept trying to pull me back to my seat for several seconds after the announcement was over and I had stood up to leave.

> Ariel R. Mignolet, on behalf of the State Police of New Mexico, I am in a position to inform you that due to new evidence supplied to us by the El Paso

offices of the Federal Bureau of Investigation, you are no longer a suspect in the case of the murders of State Police Officer Mike Argyll, Sr. Miguel Hernandez and Sr. Fernando Luiz. Official public communication of this fact will be made forthwith. Notification of your clearance will be made to the Arrest and Criminal History Section at State Police Headquarters and records of your arrest will be expunged. A deposition stating that all charges against you have been dropped will be submitted by the State Police of New Mexico to the Criminal Justice Information Services Division. You are free to leave with immediate effect and we apologize unreservedly for all inconvenience caused.

"Must have some friends in high places," the sergeant concluded bitterly before skimming the memo toward me across the table.

I wasn't at all sure my legs would be strong enough to carry me out the door. I had to stop for a minute or two in the corridor to ride out a wave of nausea. None of the uniformed officers apologized, and it was clear throughout the discharge process that their suspicions remained intact despite my dramatic formal reprieve. They handed me back my phone and I called Sunil to cancel my counsel, left a message for my mother to tell her I was okay and e-mailed my business partner, Ben, to summarize the situation.

Through gritted teeth, Sergeant Newlands advised that she would make contact in the coming days in the hope that I could provide them with further assistance with their investigations. Then, without having been offered an alternative plan, I walked alone out the back door, into the parking lot, around the building into a feeding frenzy of news-hungry hacks in the midst of whom my taxi waited, meter running.

*

Compared with the current chaos, last year, for all its problems, now seems a distant dream of routine and order. Days crammed with tasks, deadlines and social appointments and all with the comforting veneer of decadence. Every hallmark of so-called success, apart from marriage or kids, and I had followed the fastest of fast tracks to arrive there. Stanford graduate school, progressing to a bulge-bracket financial giant on the East Coast before establishing my own hedge fund in San Francisco seven years ago in partnership with people I count as genuine friends.

Cardinal Nine Capital, named for Ben's favorite football team and the espresso bar on 9th Street in New York, where we first concocted the plan to set up the company and move out West, has been a big success. We are pair-trade specialists, seeking to identify two traded assets like stocks or currencies that tend to move in tandem over a long period, simultaneously buying one and selling the other whenever they diverge in an abnormal way. Also known as statistical arbitrage, it is a brand of investing that works equally well in bull and bear markets. It involves attention to detail bordering on obsessive, drilling deep to identify when subtle divergences in a long-held pattern are a trend or simply a temporary aberration and making profits by getting more of these calls right than wrong.

Building the business has been all consuming and over the years our unflinching dedication has yielded life-changing financial dividends. But it has also brought a raft of negative consequences for our personal lives and ultimately, in my case, delivered me to this remote, arid corner of New Mexico and a valley of pain.

"There must have been a latent weakness," Dr. Carter said

the first time I sought help. "Severe mental wear and tear," she opined as though I were some class of an implement. Barely detectable fractures in the thoughts, feelings and sensibilities that make up my being, like an imperceptible web of hairline cracks in a china cup. It hadn't taken a major life tremor to widen them either, it seems—just quiet passage beyond some tipping point.

Even now, at this remove, I haven't gained much in the way of new perspective on what exactly led to my unexpected *turn for the worse*. The only symptoms of mental fatigue I had experienced seem altogether too subtle to classify as simmering portents of gloom.

Apathy was one. There is no denying that, as far back as two years, my enthusiasm for work had waned, replaced by an omnipresent low-level unease preventing me from deriving joy from my successes. Upcoming conferences, meetings with company management and important new client pitches had all begun to feel like looming chores rather than challenges to relish. Around the same time, and much to my embarrassment in a world where aircraft cabins regularly double as one's office, I had developed a significant fear of flying. It began with a quietly anxious grip of the armrest during a particularly precipitous descent into LaGuardia but, over a matter of months, rapidly escalated to dropping a Xanax an hour before every takeoff, a practice I had often warned others off and that severely compromised my ability to complete any work during the flight.

Another straw in the wind was the gradual erosion in my powers of concentration. For all my years in college and business, I held a reputation for being able to absorb information while excluding all manner of distractions—a core strength in an industry where fine print and attention to minuscule detail can make a difference to the bottom line. I could digest research documents and complicated accounts while around me a cacophony of brokers and traders worked their phones like a cloud of screeching gulls shadowing a trawler.

Some time at the start of last year, these powers noticeably receded and I became easily side-tracked. Even in the quietude of my own office, I would regularly spend hours surveying the streetscape below, watching the progress of random passersby on mid-morning shopping expeditions or casually dressed lunchtime loiterers leisurely sipping their coffees in the Starbucks across the street. Like a pet dog cocking its ear at the distant howl of a wolf, some part of me yearned to escape from the place at which I had worked so long and hard to arrive.

There were outside voices, too. In the years spent building up the client base and grinding out the company's results, Ben was twice divorced while, for me, casual liaisons, some of which might have loosely qualified as relationships, came and went with the frequency of the seasons. It reached the point of extreme cynicism where I knew with confidence that I was merely going through the motions, predicting failure from the outset, secretly ticking off the key turning points of each affair all the way to its inevitable grizzly end. The dating phase, the physical phase and, finally, the analysis phase, at which point I was usually searching for the exit if the other half of the union hadn't already glimpsed the rot and abandoned ship.

In two cases, both involving men who, on paper at least, would have made perfect life partners, I was given unpalatable feedback after hastening the end. Suitor one delivered an eloquent but highly indignant postscript speech on the limestone steps of my apartment building followed six months later by suitor two, who sent a searingly honest letter that made me blush on the cable car on the way to work. Differing only in tone, both impolitely suggested that I possessed a core fault line, a missing piece rendering me incapable of placing my trust completely in another human being outside of a tiny inner circle. I didn't have to reflect too deeply to know that this assessment was, in large part, correct.

Soon the chinks widened to cracks. The first rupture appeared over a year ago in the form of a vivid recurring dream after an unremarkable trip to a photographic exhibition depicting scenes from San Francisco's great earthquake and fire of 1906. The exhibition took place in UC Berkeley's Bancroft Library, a veritable treasure trove of eight million reference photographs, from which the curator had selected and smartly displayed a few hundred of the most interesting along somber marble halls.

I had taken the ferry across the bay with my secretary, Bess, in the afterglow of a few post-work martinis in the plush surrounds of the bar at the Four Seasons Hotel. We spent most of the journey on the windy deck, drinking in the spring evening air and admiring the kaleidoscope that is San Francisco's nightscape, congratulating ourselves for carving out the time to enjoy a cultural outing.

It was the opening night, and fifty percent of sales from prints and merchandise were to benefit the San Francisco Firefighters Benevolent Fund. The best of Californian wines, artfully constructed canapés, and scented tea lights circulated on silver trays as the organizers primed their wealthy patrons.

Hung as a pair, two of the photographs depicted scenes

of the disaster from the point of view of Nob Hill, the street where I live. The lower one was titled: *A View from Nob Hill looking South East after Great Fire of Apr. 18th to 20th 1906, San Francisco, Calif.* It was a ten-inch-square sepia stereographic print depicting the utter devastation wreaked by the flames that burned on for days after the earthquake.

It wasn't a particularly disturbing or violent image and I couldn't say it was in any way more or less remarkable than its thirty-eight sister stills in that section of the exhibition. Perhaps it struck a chord simply because the perspective was so familiar to me. In the foreground, debris from flattened homes lay strewn about like piles of smoldering matchsticks. Behind, the hollowed-out carcasses of office blocks and government buildings were reduced to a row of pathetic conical trellises set starkly against the smoky sky. A line of burnt trees, like black skeletons frozen in dramatic poses, divided the scene.

But even if it was no more or less remarkable, I was in thrall to it. Transfixed. Rooted to the spot three feet in front of it in the corridor until Bess alerted me to the fact that I had become a roadblock in the exhibition's recommended circuit.

"They're gonna call in the removal guys, Ariel."

A set of beautifully manicured burgundy nails alighted gently on my sleeve and her silky British accent crept into my trance.

"They're selling prints of these ones at the main reception if you like them," she whispered. "Four hundred dollars, but they're beautifully framed in rosewood with gold trim. Kind of like an old legal document. Might work with some of your more traditional stuff, or perhaps hang them in a downstairs loo or something. As a curiosity for visitors maybe? You seen enough?" She had mentioned when we planned the outing that she had a very early start the next day.

"Yeah, let's get the ten-thirty," I replied and we left minutes later after I had purchased the two Nob Hills.

Packed in bubble wrap, brown paper and tied with string with a loop for carrying, the prints found a new home propped up against the wall in the hallway of my apartment, to be hung when I found the time. I thought no more about them until exactly one week later when I woke at four in the morning in a feverish sweat shouting for help, having dreamt that my apartment was on fire.

Descent into madness is how it is generally described. Starting in one comfortable lofty location and then dropping toward somewhere unpalatable far below, as through a trap door or over the edge of a cliff. An ungraceful shunt from sanity into a pit of anxiety. Sliding actually better describes my progress. Slow to begin with before momentum took over and I quickly lost control. That first fire dream marked the start of a downward trajectory in my mental health that seemed to come out of nowhere. No known sleep or relaxation remedy would shake it off. Like Swiss clockwork, it woke me in a state of distress at three or four o'clock each morning and left me too agitated to return to sleep. I began to dread the night and, after two weeks, started obsessing about the dream during the day, visualizing it as a clever beast stalking me, biding its time to make its move under cover of darkness.

Exhausted, I soon became too distracted to concentrate through a full day's work and felt overwhelmed at the thought of travel. Next, some long-since under-control obsessive-compulsive behaviors I had suffered with at university resurfaced like maggots from a rotting wound.

I tried to excise the cancer by FedExing the two prints, still in their wrapping, back to the exhibitors, suggesting they could resell them for their worthy cause. After three sleep-starved weeks, my doctor referred me to a psychotherapist who advised that my recurring nightmare was a textbook case of a stressed-to-the-max dream. Apparently, to the dreaming mind, your house is you, or rather your state of mind, your personality construct. He said the dream was not necessarily connected to a particular stressor but was a warning sign that I was operating on complete overload and possibly at high risk for developing full-blown depression. "Your dreaming mind can't scream any louder than this," he warned.

My mother, whose lilting Irish brogue is substantially diluted after thirty-two years of exposure to the great American twang but who has managed to maintain an impressive mental back catalog of every old wives' tale and *seanfhocal* ever uttered throughout Ireland's long history, assured me I was simply experiencing a period of *lionn dubh*, a Gaelic expression that translates as "a touch of black." I, on the other hand, sensed a more fundamental unraveling, a coming apart at the seams, and I harbored a growing fear that the space between the unappealing somewhere I was headed and the successful life I knew was growing inexorably wider.

Five miles farther, only four left to Deming, my rate of progress has slowed to a shuffle and nausea sweeps over me in waves. I have entered the realm of pain where every mile feels like a full marathon. My inner thighs are chafing and warm acidic sweat stings where the top layers of skin have rubbed off. I have commenced a full-blown verbal debate with myself over whether to stop and rest to ease the throbbing in my right calf that has moved from spasm to permanent cramp. Twenty-six miles. Stop in half a mile and walk it home. The marathon was *the* target two months ago, so that's progress. Do twenty-seven and walk out the last three. What's the problem? Walk out the last three. No, keep it up. Come on, you've been here before. The cramp will ease. Keep running to the finish.

The internal wrangle continues as I run. Come on. Must stop. No, hydrate and go on. Take three sips from the fluid pack and twenty strides, three sips and twenty strides, and keep on going like that. Three sips. One, two, three, four. Come on, breathe, I tell myself, but it feels as though a cinch has been pulled tight across my torso, leaving only the tiniest pocket for incoming air at the back of my throat. My GPS says through twenty-eight miles now. Less than two home. I can make it. Breathe, five, six, seven. Sip. Eight. Breathe, swallow. The heat is overpowering and I have lost the ability to focus and apply any useful mental recitations.

"Jesus wept." I barely wheeze out the words as I pull to a stop at the edge of the road a mile and a half from town. The line of passing cars on the parallel interstate slows down noticeably. Faces flash by looking curiously on at my predicament. Bent over, hands on hips, mouth gasping like a dying fish, I drop my head to my knees and slide my sunglasses over my bandana. My focus quickly adjusts to the microscopic details of the dusty roadside debris beside my shoes. Tiny insect trails crisscross a patch of sand, circumnavigating spatters of oil. A shard of gray rubber, so dried and worn by time and the elements that it resembles the gnarled bark of a tree, commands my full attention in that briefest moment of calm before the inexorable heave coats it all, tsunami-like, with a cascade of watery, bile-tinged vomit.

The first retch expels fluid with such force that much rebounds off the road to knee height, spattering a nearby wooden fence. Subsequent gushes contain thin streaks of acidic sputum accompanied by a strangulated sound from the back of my throat like the squeal of a stuck piglet. The last waves are empty but no less violent as my digestive system tries to kick-start itself. Finally a lull as some primeval off switch is flicked. My knees are wobbling, foal-like. Mucus drips from my nostrils and this combined with the tightness in my chest is making it very difficult to draw any breath into my lungs in my doubled-over position.

Rhythm's spell sundered, death's pale facsimile of Mike's pulchritude steals into my mind's eye. A kind of waxwork nestled between puffed-up pleats of yellow satin. Even the practiced hand of the undertaker could not completely disguise the livid line on his right cheek where stone and bone had collided. I had filed past with the other mourners and the procession afforded me a fleeting last look. His fair hair was swept to one side in an unfamiliar style, to hide what must have been a grisly seam from that first merciless blow.

"You okay there?" comes a voice alongside. "Need a ride into town?"

I raise my head to see a Stetson-wearing Samaritan smiling broadly through the open passenger window of a red Ford pickup.

A well-rehearsed debate commences in my head, complete with subconscious finger wagging. Quitting prematurely. Leaving behind unfinished business. It was the pig-iron element within me that was most drawn to the challenge of ultra-running. An attempt to dispel the spirits of capitulation that possessed all areas of my life apart from work.

"No thank you, sir, but I really do appreciate you stopping. I'm fine. Really," I say unconvincingly, casting my eyes up at him from knee level and waving to suggest he drive on.

"If you're sure, then," says the driver with a wry smile as the four-liter engine roars back to full tilt in a cloud of dust.

With the afternoon temperature touching ninety-six, legs shaking and the monotonous drone of cars on the nearby interstate for company, my heart rate soon normalizes and my stomach settles. I walk the final stretch to Deming.

Deming was the first New Mexican town I stopped in seven months ago on the drive from El Paso Airport, where I picked up my navy BMW SUV after paying a courier company a thousand bucks to transport it across three states. I wouldn't have brought it with me at all except Bess threatened a monumental blowup if I left it behind. I know nothing about cars and had given her the task a year ago to find me one that I could squeeze a few friends and a beer cooler into for the few days a year I might venture out to Sonoma or down to L.A. to visit Natalie. She called me up three weeks later from Sunset Boulevard and told me she had found me the perfect vehicle. State-of-the-art, German engineering (the price of a coastal condominium) bedecked with gaudy Beverley Hills plate-frames that I keep forgetting to have removed.

The journey from the airport had taken one and a half hours, past the Florida Mountains, through an area known as Snowbirds' Heaven, with scenery so stunning I had called the office to boast.

My lower leg muscles burn as I approach the center of town and pass the boxy bungalows with white-washed walls and roof tiles in shades of pink or paprika that contrast beautifully with the clear blue sky. I had parked earlier in the lot of a Quality Inn next to a mall just off the interstate adjacent to Cedar Street. As I take the key from its hiding place behind the front left tire, I notice red-haired Sprite lady sitting on the partially subsided boundary wall between Walgreens and Denny's.

I first encountered her on that journey from the airport, when I pulled in to the drugstore to buy a few essentials. She was sitting on the exact same spot, dressed to the nines in a calf-length tartan skirt, a crisp cream blouse and the kind of white pantyhose and black pumps combo you might see in the posh Catholic areas of Boston. Her legs were crossed daintily at the knees and she gazed wistfully into the middle distance while draining a two-liter bottle of Sprite Zero and chain smoking cigarettes.

Having noticed her several times on subsequent trips to the mall, I asked the checkout guy in Walgreens about her. He told me she lived in a state-subsidized community care program and received a weekly allowance, which was just enough to finance her soda and cigarette habit.

She comes to the wall six days a week for about two hours at a time and consumes the entire two litres, as well as a good portion of the twenty Camels, which she lights one from the other with the urgency of a death row prisoner being trussed up for the chair. In between puffs, she confabs with some internal companion who sometimes makes her laugh out loud.

Mike later told me her name was Bertha Walton, but he had nothing to add to the back story my friend at the cash register had given me. I became curiously drawn to seeing her on the wall and, for reasons I don't fully understand, have sometimes even taken deliberate detours, if I have business in or around Deming, so that I can drive by and see her puffing and drinking and chatting to nobody in particular.

"Excuse me. Hello? Excuse me."

A shrill voice blares through the SUV's partially open window as I wait to pull out into the line of traffic. In the rear-view mirror, I see Bertha. Now on her feet, she is lumbering awkwardly in my direction; her pencil skirt curbs her stride as she shouts aloud and waves a cigarette frantically in the air to the surprise of several passersby. With less than twenty feet still between her and the back of my car, I put my foot to the gas and accelerate onto the freeway's feeder lane.

Chapter Two

THE HOUSE

The faint blue glow from my laptop in the small office adjoining the kitchen catches my eye as I whisk up eggs for an omelet to gently reintroduce food to my traumatized stomach. It took me a week to muster up the resolve to open the screen, but I haven't touched it since because I fear that reengaging with the real world will pierce my bubble of grief and the new routine I have established within it. Whisk and bowl in hand, I stand at the central island, staring into the frothy yellow emulsion. Listening.

This kitchen is perfect for listening as there is nowhere for sound to hide. All work surfaces are matte, moss-green concrete, accented with highly glazed white tiles and stainless-steel cabinets. There is little softness either in the cavernous living area, apart from the giant navy couch and the black-and-white hearth rug where Mike and I made love that night.

Milky soapstone dining and occasional tables give the room the air of a modern art gallery. I drew this comparison the very first time I saw a video of the interior, so I was not at all surprised to learn the owners' occupations.

In the course of our initial conversation, during a

FaceTime walk-through of the property, Felix Metcalf, of Metcalf and Els Real Estate, Deming, New Mexico, had offered up the couple's details with pride and, I felt, a lack of discretion when trying to tempt me into signing up for the year. He explained how the remote location of the house on this stretch of the Old County Road known as The Bank, ten miles from Prospero and with only one neighboring property as far as the eye could see, suited them both perfectly.

The wife is an abstract artist whose recent success at one of New York's top galleries had prompted their move to a beach house in the Hamptons. Now acting as his wife's manager, the husband had been a high-ranking officer among the legions of Border Patrol agents in this part of New Mexico whose numbers have swelled dramatically in recent years with the government's renewed interest in homeland security.

This factoid was relayed to me by the nauseatingly enthusiastic Felix while he trained the iPad's lens on the panoramic views of the Chihuahuan Desert afforded by the house's floor-to-ceiling windows. A sophisticated-looking telescope, balanced precariously on a tripod like a top-heavy stick insect, stood out in the scene. "This baby extends your view all the way to the *old* Mexico," he boasted, as though it might clinch the deal.

Early-evening shadows creep toward me across the floor as dusk gathers. Listening. The monotonous hum of the fridge is the loudest sound, but now and then there is a submarine-like ping from my Mac when an e-mail lands in the inbox. Ping. I close my eyes as if to tune in telepathically to the pleading and sympathizing voices I know dwell behind the liquid crystal display. I set the omelet mixture down very softly so as not to break the spell of the room.

In the far corner to the left of the fireplace stands Letterhead, a six-foot-tall, hollow-frame sculpture of a man's head fashioned from thousands of matchbox-sized yellow letters soldered together in a random pattern. Letterhead is the only work I allowed myself to bring from my art collection. I have positioned him with great care, for his own benefit, to gaze uninterrupted through the center of the room upon the desert vista. As evening descends, I am pleased to discover that, rather like the *Mona Lisa*, he also casts a kindly sideways glance in my direction when, wine glass in hand, I recline senatorially on the daybed end of the couch.

The plash of golden liquid against crystal is comforting in the silence as I drain the last of the bottle and the slow seep of inebriation pulses pleasantly in the mind space at the top of my head. As I replace the glass carefully on the floor beside me, my phone shudders to life on the side table, vibrating like a giant housefly in the throes of death. I put it out of its misery but don't say anything, just listen for the caller's voice, my finger at the ready on the End Call icon.

"Ariel? Are you there, love?"

She sounds slightly breathless.

"Yes, Mom. I'm here. Sorry. I got your messages. Apologies. It's just that I've been lying low. Trying to … I, well … to clear my head, I guess."

Right at this moment, my head feels anything but clear, and just sounding sober is a strain.

"You sound strange, love. Are you lying down?"

My mother finds it hard to hold a phone conversation unless she can visualize the exact physical position of the person on the other end of the receiver.

"Yeah, I'm just having a glass of wine on the couch here. Probably shouldn't really after a long run, but I figure it might help me sleep."

"No one could sleep after what you've been through, love. Did you try those tablets I sent you? Just a half, mind you. They'd take down a water buffalo for six hours."

"Yeah, thanks. I tried them the last few nights and they worked great. I've been meaning to ask you how many I would need to take to achieve a more permanent outcome?" I regret my poor attempt at humor the moment the words leave my mouth. My mother knows my survival story.

A month after the first fire dream, I talked Ben through the problem and he agreed with my decision to take the psychotherapist's advice—a longer-than-usual vacation to try and stop the rot. I settled on skiing in the hope that snowy peaks, blue skies and pristine alpine air might quell the flames. As it was almost May, my options were very limited and I decided on the Hintertux Glacier in the Austrian Tyrol.

In hindsight, I should have gone with a friend. My logic for traveling alone was that I felt I couldn't inflict my, by then, slightly unstable self on another person, soaking up their precious time off work with matters melancholy.

Everything went well for the first few days. The weather at the glacier was uncharacteristically cloudy and cool for the time of year and, with almost no wind, it was near-perfect ski conditions. I slept soundly for the first five nights and this, combined with the fresh air and exercise, lured me into thinking that I may have landed on a cure.

But six o'clock on the seventh morning, the ghost flames of the great fire of 1906 licked up the walls of my subconscious once again and I awoke drenched in sweat.

I called Sunil and wept in despair. He encouraged me to think positively and suggested that a week free of the night terrors was a sign things were improving. He proposed that I ski to the point of exhaustion that day and get up extra early the next to try and head off the fresh advance at the pass.

Taking his advice, that morning I rode the Gletscher gondolas three thousand two hundred meters to the glacier's peak and completed two runs from top to bottom, before heading for quieter valleys. At the base of the Tuxer Joch lift station, a heavy-set bearded man clad in fire-engine-red salopettes and a white turtleneck gave a friendly smile as he shuffled into position alongside and we were swept up in the four-man chair. We glided to the gush of an Alpine stream, the odd swoosh of skiers below and the steady hum of the pulley and cable above. Rays of sunshine broke through, illuminating the snow-capped peaks in the surrounding valleys.

Only two or three hundred feet from the top, having just passed under the last supporting tower, the bull wheel in the station ahead ground to a halt and the chair stopped, leaving momentum to sway us forward and back seventy feet above a steep ravine. Perhaps someone tripped or missed their seat. Such scenarios ran through my mind as I peered down from our lofty swing.

Stark against the icy edge of the gully, a stray black glove sat proud like the only evidence of an avalanche victim's final reach to escape their snowy grave. What grumblings its owner must have uttered in that moment when it fell.

It was an innocuous train of thought and, even now, it's hard to view it as some kind of trigger, but as though reigniting some base instinct, those five forlorn fingers seemed to beckon to me and I suddenly had a nagging urge to jump.

Bitten by the very thought, I sat bolt upright and took a few exaggeratedly deep and rapid breaths while gripping the lift's safety bar. Furtive eye contact with my lift partner exposed my heightened state of agitation and I recall him looking somewhat bemused. His expression changed dramatically moments later when my urge escalated to an overwhelming compulsion and I made a determined attempt to raise the bar as our seat continued to rock back and forth.

"Nein! Stop!" He shouted frantically and pressed his skis down on the footrest to counteract my efforts to remove the only thing that stood between us and certain death. I remember straining against him for a few minutes, every ounce of strength focused on pulling up the rail in a desperate bid to escape. That exit blocked, I used my poles to snap open the bindings on my skis, taking a moment to watch them fall silently to earth, one spearing the ice lancet-like just as the lift shuddered back to life and we resumed our ascent.

Gunther Metzl was my savior's name, I later learned. An unfortunate local bus driver randomly paired off with a crazy Yank while enjoying his day off. The medical clinic in Tux gave me his details and I sent him a note and a bottle of expensive rowanberry brandy the next day by way of inadequate thanks for saving my life. How he held on to me for the time it took for us to reach safety, I don't know. It was probably less than a minute, but I was dogged in my efforts. With my knees up under me on the padded seat, I had fought hard to free myself from his desperately clasping arms, the ski poles around his wrists flicking and flailing awkwardly like giant chopsticks as he grappled with my squirming Gore-Tex limbs and heavy ski boots.

The aging Austrian medic who treated me after my ignominious descent to Tux, accompanied by three humorless lift guards, had perfect English but looked and sounded like a caricature Sigmund Freud. He prescribed a heavy sedative and advised me to fly home and seek immediate medical attention because, in his opinion, some psychological affliction was blocking the normal mechanisms controlling the cauldron of impulses bubbling away in my subconscious. In his opinion, there was a high probability that my stunt on the ski lift was a presage of similar events to come.

"You need to come home, Ariel." My mother's tone has instantly switched from light banter to deadly serious and I sense the onset of a rehearsed speech.

"Look, Mom, I ..."

"Please just listen, love. Come and stay with me. Get up early tomorrow and take the lunchtime flight I took from El Paso last week. What's stopping you? Even just a few days will set you right and then you can head back there and tie up any loose ends. Here is where you should be, Ariel. For ... for, to take stock and all. I didn't say it when I was there because I knew you had enough going on with the trauma of everything on top of the grief and coping with the press and so on. But my fear now is that ... I mean my experience of patients I have nursed who suffered shock is that ... is that things can deteriorate once the dust of an event has settled. Kind of like aftershocks more powerful than the actual earthquake. Now I really don't want you out there in the middle of nowhere should that happen, so could you please get a flight tomorrow and just hang out here for a while? Do it for me, Ariel, if not for your own health and sanity. I'm really begging you here, love. Please, please come home."

Still lying flat, I grab a throw cushion and plant it over my head to cover half my face, leaving just enough room for words to escape. "I know, Mom. I hear what you're saying, but I can't leave yet. For one thing, there will be further questioning by the police here in the next few days. My first meeting is scheduled for tomorrow and, as their key witness, I ... like ... I feel I at least owe it to Mike to help. All that will take a few days, but I absolutely promise a trip home after that. The press have moved on as well, so I'm not under siege anymore, which is a major improvement."

The silence on the other end of the phone is laden with doubt.

"Honestly. I'm talking days not weeks. I promise you."

"Look, love, I know you're hurting. I know you loved him and then there's the sheer brutality of what happened ... to both of you. But I've seen a lot of life and I have to tell you I have never experienced anything like the naked hostility of some of the people we met at his funeral. I mean, you must see how utterly strange their lives are, under the cosh of that church. And God forgive me for speaking ill of the dead, but I'm not saying this out of badness, love, I just want to make sure I am understanding the situation fully ..."

I can hear her mind ticking over as she trawls for the right words and I press the cushion harder over my eyes to steel myself.

"He was lying to you, Ariel. There it is, love. He was living a lie. If he was really the one for you, you have to ask yourself would he have been living a lie? Look, you saw her there, too. His fiancée. At the church. At his graveside?

Right in the heart of it all. It's clear to—"

"Please stop," I say a little more forcefully than intended as my head spins with the effects of the alcohol and the sting of truth. "It's hard enough. You would have to have known him to understand how complicated things were. I'm trying to figure it out myself, and also deal with the reality that he would still be alive if it weren't for me. I drew him here that night. As far as I'm concerned, I lured him to his death and that's something I'm finding hard to process right now."

"Ariel, love, I'm going to keep saying this until it sinks in. Mike would still be alive if it weren't for the murderers who took his and those other poor unfortunate people's lives. He was doing his job. And you? You tried to save him, love. That was you who ran out there in the desert night.

"You must understand, love, my main worry stems from the fact that all this is coming on top of your problems last year. If you had let me stay on, I'd be able to keep an eye out for you. You've been through so much and the thought of you rattling around in that giant fish tank doesn't sit well. I'm sleeping so badly myself these days, even I might have to go and consult the lovely Ms. Weiss. Have you still got her details?"

Her lightening of the mood is appreciated. Paloma Weiss is the flaky, so-called dream expert I consulted with over a year ago in the throes of my nervous collapse and whose advice, ultimately, led me to New Mexico.

"Please don't be worried, Mom. I'm not going to do anything stupid here. The house is like Fort Knox and the runs are really helping. In fact, I strongly recommend you and your pals in the medical profession should prescribe distance running as a cure for all ills. It's the one thing getting me through. I'll send you my travel plans in a few days and we'll go to Mamma Soliso's the night I get back. Okay? Thanks for your concern, Mom, really, but I'm fine. I'll see you very soon. Okay?"

"I'll be waiting, Ariel. *I won't be ignored, you know.*" I have to smile as she signs off with an actor's flourish, embellishing her favorite Glenn Close line from the movie *Fatal Attraction.*

Two unread texts catch my eye in the unbroken column of green icons. The first is from Sunil and is typically succinct: *Visit? Read my e-mail. S.*

The second is a reminder notice of my meeting with Sergeant Marge Newlands, scheduled for tomorrow, Monday, Sept. 19th, 2016, at 10:45 a.m. The venue is Meeting Room Two, Prospero Police Station, Main Street and the sender suggests I allow up to four hours.

The patter of raindrops on the window begins to intensify and feels like welcome company. One of the things that attracted me to this location at the far reaches of the southwestern US monsoon area was the prospect of frequent biblical downpours and the grandstand enjoyment of them that this house affords. My first experience of these spectacular sky bursts came several months into my New Mexican adventure, in early July, when a tumultuous torrent of water pounded the glass for hours before stopping abruptly to reveal a riot of rainbows, as though nature were flaunting some of her best tricks.

Although now late enough in the monsoon season, the descent of dusk this evening brought with it a dense bank of clouds that crept ominously over the peaks of the Big Hatchet Mountains to the east, before billowing across the sky, filling every corner with a sweep of gun-metal gray clouds so pregnant with rain they hung unfeasibly close to the earth. With the moon shrouded, I watch the last slivers of light disappear and the cloak of darkness descend.

Chapter Three

CALEB FREETH

This will be my fifth nightly vigil in what is becoming a firmly entrenched routine. After the funeral ended and I had returned from dropping my mother to the airport, I used the night-vision setting on the telescope to scan the expanse in front of the house in the hope of catching any glimmer of light in the dark valley. It makes me feel useful. I only search at night and all the lights in the living room must be off to eliminate reflections in the huge expanse of glass.

To turn off all the overhead lights, I must perform the on/off wall switch ritual. This compulsive behavior has not left me despite the fire dream ending months ago. I seem unable to let go of the fear of what might happen should I stop.

Click the switch off, then back on, off, then on and, finally, off. Relief.

I gaze into the gloom, panning the fateful lens. I have become quite the expert now and can sweep quickly from nearest to farthest range and zoom in on any sign of life. A lone coyote on the prowl entered my field of vision two nights ago. I watched it for a while, envious of the nonchalant way it meandered through the creosote, sniffing air and earth. All business with no notion of being admired from afar.

Forty fruitless minutes later, I close my eyes, rest my neck on the back of the couch and blink slowly to release the strain of being fixed in the spy position for so long. Restfulness is short-lived, however, as untamable thoughts transport me back to the night of Mike's murder. Running. Sprinting for my life across the plain. Torchbearers weaving in my wake. Lungs burning. Adrenalin coursing. The sounds of footfall drawing closer.

Spurred on by these imaginings, my heartbeat races into an anxiety-driven tachycardia, frighteningly rapid and unpredictable. The gush and suck of my heart pounds violently within my chest, reverberating behind my ears like a taut drum. I try the *Kapalbhati* or "breath of fire" exercise Sunil taught me during our final exams, pressing my hand into my stomach to push out the waste air, then inhaling sharp, energetic drafts through my nostrils. I repeat this process twenty to thirty times and, just as the rush of oxygen begins to relax my mind, I hear the slam of a door outside. The blinding glare of two 300-watt security beams explode into my living room like giant vaudeville spotlights.

On the few occasions Mike confronted my next-door neighbor on my behalf about the light pollution, Caleb Freeth always maintained that the powerful lights mounted on the side of his house were directed only toward the road. He didn't offer any reason and aggressively objected to inquiries as to their purpose, arguing that it was a free country, he paid his taxes and had every right to protect his property as he saw fit. But, as Mike made plain to him, for all the good it did, the outsize bulbs are housed within aluminum and glass casings that cast the glow at a wide angle and, with no curtains or blinds to shield me and the giant glass frontage of my house situated closer to the road than his, the lights suffuse my entire living space with overpowering fluorescence.

Not wanting to run the risk of a face-to-face showdown, I had left it to Mike to plead my case in an official capacity. Apart from my dramatic encounter with my neighbor in his driveway on the night of the murders—of which I have incomplete recollection—the only interaction we have had these past seven months has occurred when our paths just happened to cross either coming and going from our houses or on the sidewalk in Prospero. On these occasions he has never been anything other than brusque and monosyllabic.

Caleb Freeth is one of those people who carries a natural air of menace, a negative aura like an aged, wounded tiger on the prowl for easy prey. His eyes are shrouded beneath bushy fair brows that make him look much older than his early middle age. Yellowing teeth contrast starkly with snow-white hair, cropped Army short. His body is all lean muscle and he cinches his shabby jeans with an oversized leather belt that resembles a horsewhip.

I often remarked to Mike that there was a curious contrast between my neighbor's disheveled, almost beggar-like appearance and the scrupulously tidy state of his property and machinery. It is hard to reconcile the gruff, aggressive character with the artistic and tasteful layout of the landscape around his home. The entire border of his two-acre plot, including the machine yard to the rear of the house, is lined with carefully planned combinations of Joshua trees and cactus. Raised, symmetrically aligned beds of native drought-resistant plants, set against black lava rock and boulders, grace both sides of the property's entrance, and his driveway to the front and side are covered in gold-and-pewter quarry dust bordered with terracotta brick.

His house, a plain two-story structure with small windows and a slated roof, is painted the purest white and its only distinguishing feature is a slightly creepy, gigantic wooden crucifix, about thirty feet in height, which sits in a custom-built concrete casing to the right of the eastern gable.

When I first viewed my rental home on Google Earth, I remember making positive soundings to the agent about the neighboring grounds and remarking that I was looking forward to meeting the person who could create such beauty in this barren place. I now have a better understanding of why his response was so half-hearted, his change of subject so swift.

One encounter with Caleb Freeth, early into my New Mexican odyssey, set the tone for our relationship. Walking out my front gates to my car, parked roadside, I heard the lazy clop of Caleb's horse's hooves. As far as I can gather, he rides out every second day, usually between the hours of four and six, when the sun has finished baring its teeth.

My car was no more than a few feet away, but instead of going for the door, I decided to wait at the entrance and salute him, to catch his eye as he passed by, maybe strike up conversation in the spirit of neighborliness. Like his garden, his rangy bay quarter horse is always beautifully turned out, with a burnished coat groomed to perfection and ruler-straight black mane and tail. It approached at a leisurely walk along the dusty verge, past the last of the wiry, windswept Joshua trees. I stood just outside its line of progress and fixed my gaze on Caleb, awaiting any flicker of acknowledgment like a dog gazing at its owner's back door.

It was clear to me that he knew I was there but was studiously avoiding eye contact, looking down, either upon the saddle pommel or left across the road. When he was close enough for me to hear the horse breathing and see the dust rising ahead of its hooves, he fixed his eyes on mine for an instant and urged his steed to veer sharply right so that its shoulder and then flank forced me to retreat. Then, with a squeeze of his legs, his mount sprang off its haunches into a slow canter. Caleb threw the words, "Real sorry 'bout that," over his shoulder and I knew with absolute certainty that he wasn't.

Mike told me Caleb Freeth was basically a good man saddled with a string of demons, very possibly compounded by post-traumatic stress disorder as a result of postings to Afghanistan and Iraq at times when the fighting was at its most ferocious. Apparently he had returned from his first tour in 2002 to find that his wife and two-year-old twins had left. He started again from scratch, buying his house on the Old County Road years before the house I am renting was built. He trained as an Army mechanic during a further tour in 2004 and has lived a solitary, almost hermit-like existence since then, eking out a living from the heavy machine repairs and rental business he runs out of the yard at the rear of his house.

He has a reputation as a straight-dealing, reliable man to do business with but as someone not to be crossed. He famously once chased a poor credit down the road with a shotgun held to his head before removing the tires from the man's car and not replacing them until he came with the payment two weeks later. Mike had testified as a character witness to prevent Caleb incurring a jail term for the incident and said he got to know a softer side to the man in the run-up to the court case. But the story grew legs and reinforced his reputation in Prospero as a man to be wary of. He became a subject of fear and scorn with local children, who could be heard singing about him:

Caleb Freeth, Caleb Freeth
Snow-white hair and yellow teeth
Chases cheats with his old shotgun
He won't stop 'til he kills someone.

In keeping with his benign view of the world, Mike always maintained that the man's travails must have stunted his emotional development and rendered him antisocial, seemingly preferring the company of his horse over any human being. Mike felt people should make allowances for his gruff behavior, to which I responded that that was easy for him to say as he didn't have to live next door to him.

In any case, after many incidents of being visually assaulted by the glare of his security lights and having had Mike pay him official police visits on at least three occasions to try and reason with him, the agreement we had reached was that he would only switch them on after eleven o'clock or when my living room had been in darkness long enough for him to conclude that I was either out or asleep in my bedroom at the back of the house. Since September sixth, he has had them on a timer switch for eleven o'clock. However, tonight it is only seven-thirty and the blinding beams are impossible to ignore. Perhaps he assumed I was out because the house has lain in darkness since I began my vigil.

I turn on all the lights in a vain attempt to let him know that I am here, but they are drowned out in the wall of illumination. Alcohol and adrenalin carry me outside into cool evening air cleansed by the recent rain. As I approach my neighbor's house under the eerie shadow of the towering cross, I use my hand to shield against the glare until I get close enough to bring me inside the scope of the bulbs. Before I reach the front door, I look through the window and am surprised to see another man standing in the middle of the living room.

The weak glow from a single low-wattage central pendant is enough for me to recognize the distinguished, almost presidential-looking Pastor Seb Funchess, spiritual leader of Prospero's Independent Resurrection Baptist Church and chief celebrant at Mike's funeral last week. He stands proud, unspeaking, staring steadily ahead at the wall in the center of Caleb Freeth's empty front room.

Curious, I edge closer, now conscious of myself and taking care not to be seen or for the crunch of the gravel beneath my shoes to betray me. There's Caleb. He kneels in front of the pastor and uses some kind of cloth to wash his feet. He immerses what looks like a strip of muslin in an aluminum bucket and wrings out the excess water before carefully spreading it over the full breadth of his hand and cleaning Seb Funchess's bare feet from toes to calf. He repeats the process three or four times while the tall preacher stands stock still, trousers rolled up past his knees, hands resting by his side.

I instinctively find the scene disturbing. It strikes a discordant note even though I know that in some other context or with another set of actors it could be a tender act of humility, an ancient symbol of atonement like the poignant news item my mother directed my attention to a few years ago showing a plain-clothed archbishop washing the feet of clerical sexual abuse victims beneath the Gothic arches of a cavernous Irish cathedral. How powerful the message of apology that dignified ceremony delivered.

But here, tonight, there is a look on the pastor's face that utterly jars with that ideal. As he stands there near the center of the room, a yellow murk illuminating his thick thatch of silver hair, he occasionally casts his eyes down upon the washer. He is smiling and his smile unmistakably reeks of triumph. Triumph and, possibly, something worse—pleasure.

A few minutes pass and I resolve to leave without knocking on the door, reluctant to interrupt the ritual in the front room. As I take a step backward, the giant lights extinguish and the front yard of Caleb Freeth's home is suddenly plunged into darkness. With the fright of the unexpected alteration in my surroundings, I make an unplanned lunge away from the window and know instantly that the scrape of gravel will not go unheard.

The pastor looks directly toward me, eyes squinting and smile fading. When he identifies me, his look matures to defiance. As I scramble a few more steps backward, Caleb Freeth's face rises up directly behind the window pane and his features contort with raw anger. Knit brows leave two black shadow-wells for eyes, and lips curl. I turn and run the short distance home, glancing over my shoulder as I go, my mind filled with what that face might be capable of. As I lock my front door, the children's rhyme whispers itself to me.

Chapter Four

PROSPERO

Despite clear blue skies the next morning, there is a coolness in the air hinting at the season's turn. My legs are stiff from the previous day's exertions, but I squeeze in a fast-paced ten-miler for the feel-good factor, running due east from my house. On the advice of police, I no longer run any southerly routes but track east or west along the Old County Road's edge or drive to Luna County to run the trails. Five miles out at a fast pace, then backtrack at a more moderate clip, passing only one car and a few startled jack rabbits along the way.

I try not to look south though I know no traces of the atrocity remain. Ever-shifting sands will have airbrushed the skids and scars from the earth's surface and three days of forensic experts traipsing back and forth across the area swept up all other remnants. I spent hours tracking their distant movements from my window chair. A legion of white-clad experts combed the scene on foot, adhering to some kind of grid-reference methodology, like a slow-moving chorus line.

For me, the area remains a glistening, blood-soaked shroud. An impression of the violence resides in my memory like a latent virus. Sometimes I cannot resist the urge to imagine the sound that accompanied what I witnessed. Dull crack or rip as his skull split when the first blow was delivered? Every horrific detail is condensed into a vivid mental snapshot, equal and opposite of that perfect holiday photograph we have all taken the trouble to mount. That one where everyone is captured in some unscripted playful pose with bright smiles. But in this case, the image is shockingly violent and the fear it ignites is heightened by the fact that I know the perpetrators probably still lurk close by.

After a quick shower, the nine-mile drive to Prospero takes fifteen minutes and the temperature has risen to a pleasant seventy-eight degrees with little or no humidity. On the approach into town, I pass the enormous billboard signage, one of three identical hoardings positioned at each artery into town.

WELCOME TO PROSPERO. OF THE LORD, WITH THE LORD, FOR THE LORD. NOW AND FOREVER AMEN.

The New Mexican morning sunshine provides a dazzling show of refracted light bouncing off the southerly shop windows, like a heavenly runway down Main Street. But even nature's warm embrace fails to open Prospero's arms to me. Officially registered as an abandoned site or ghost town in the 1970s, when the last of what was once an army of copper mine workers boarded up their homes and left for good, it was repopulated in the mid-eighties when a successful industrialist named Clayton Marron purchased the entire town and a good portion of the wilderness surrounding it for $501,000.

He opened a wire-fencing factory thirty miles up the

highway near the border with Arizona and offered jobs to those willing to come and live in the town. His social experiment was kick-started with the refurbishment and conversion of the old Methodist church and school and the installation of two Baptist pastors from Indiana who, I learned after googling them, appear to have come as a tag team of Bible-thumping evangelists.

Information dating back to the eighties describes Seb Funchess and Anthony Blount as independent fundamentalist Baptist preachers and two of the earliest graduates of Galen Johnson College, Indiana. One site, with the dubious title of God's American Army, described them as inspirational, charismatic preachers in the mold of the now-deceased firebrand preacher Fred Galen.

In 1986 Funchess and Blount named their newly minted ministry the Resurrection Baptist Church and attached an invitation to join the congregation to every piece of promotional literature aimed at growing the town. Dated 1988, the last reference to Blount had the curious headline of PASTOR BLOUNT'S FIRST TRUTH FLOCK DEPARTS, but I was unable to access the associated newspaper article from a now-defunct website.

More recent postings from the nineties relate only to Seb Funchess. It is clear his beliefs evolved into a radically conservative fundamentalist interpretation of the King James Version of the Bible from the 1600s. Under Funchess's leadership, the tenets of Prospero's Resurrection church came to include separation from other faiths, living one's life according to a strict interpretation of the Bible, shunning alcohol and extramarital sex, and adopting an ultraconservative dress code.

Mr. Marron financed the reinstatement of the post office,

converted the town's only hotel into a police station and built convenience stores and houses to accommodate the new arrivals. His attempts at rural renewal and expanding church membership succeeded, in part, because they coincided with a strengthening in homeland security efforts in the United States and, with it, a sharp increase in the number of newly graduated Border Patrol officers being deployed in areas close to the Mexican border. There was a shortage of accommodation at the time in towns along the interstate, such as Lordsburg and Deming, and the resulting overflow was enough to steadily breathe new life into Prospero, whose population has now reached 2,300 mostly young and almost entirely white-faced souls. And souls, that immaterial part of a human being that defines us, best describes what the denizens of the town seem to be, in a very discerning way, in the business of collecting.

From behind the walls of my à-la-carte Catholic upbringing, I had had no prior exposure to such an extreme traditionalist Christian belief system and, based on my experience since I first set foot in Prospero, have no desire for further encounters in the future.

I park my car halfway along Main Street, thirty minutes early for my meeting with Sergeant Newlands. Donning aviator sunglasses with my still-wet hair air drying loosely around my shoulders, I wait for the familiar cold stare behind the counter at The Fairfield newsstand where I collect my pre-ordered copy of *The Wall Street Journal*. I head, as usual, for the Cuppa Jo coffee shop on the corner between Main and Francisco Streets. There are three orders ahead of me so I choose not to queue and instead take one of only twelve chairs in the cozy café's seating area, positioning myself with my back to the window to avoid the shards of sunlight needling in beneath the too-short yellow blind.

I've been studying the currency section closely for about ten minutes when a familiar voice whispers in my ear, "The yen is diving south. Time to buy the Nikkei? You doin' okay?"

My only friend in town gently squeezes my shoulder. "Back in a mo," she says before breezing off to wipe down the table of the other seated customer as he prepares to depart. I shake my head in disbelief at another accurate on-the-spot analysis by Miranda Vasquez.

The graph she commented on is today's slightly more mature version of a chart Ben e-mailed me in March during one of his many ploys to tempt me back to the office with attractive pair-trading opportunities.

When government policies in Tokyo are aimed at weakening the yen, this generally proves good for Japanese company profits and, thus, an inverse correlation develops between the Japanese currency and the Nikkei 225 index. This trend began back in 2013 and, on and off since then, Ben has profited from the pattern by buying the Nikkei 225 index while selling the JPY versus the US dollar. If it's appearing in the *Journal* as a good investment opportunity, I have no doubt that he has already walked away, pockets bulging.

Nonetheless it is no mean feat that it took a seventeen-year-old student, part-time barista, and short-order cook all of three seconds to identify the trade, which might be old news on Wall Street but I doubt has made the business section of the *Hidalgo County Herald* in recent weeks.

This isn't the first time, either. You could say we met over a pair trade on my first visit to the Cuppa Jo, last March. During the first few weeks away from the office, I found that the business pages were like a comfort blanket, a whiff of the familiar, softening the sharpest edges of exile.

Equities are the asset class of most interest to me: tracking two companies whose prices have moved in lockstep over long periods and researching them intensively to understand the impact of every new scrap of information coming to the market. Every sneeze or change in body language by senior management matters. Every number and word in every quarterly report of industry peers must be parsed. Shifts in the trading pattern of put-and-call options and changes in the share register are relevant. Once I have paddled up the river of facts, I wait for the inevitable opportunity to open up. A misstep in performance or possibly a time lag in data flow of one of the companies can bring about a change in the pattern and an opportunity to capitalize.

Four weeks into my New Mexican adventure, while sipping coffee and perusing a graph on the back page of the *Financial Times*, a surprising remark came out of left field.

"From where I'm sitting, I'm thinking to sell XOM and buy COP."

I swiveled around to see my young server sitting on the counter between a pile of scones and the church charity collection box. Wiping her hands in the folds of her green-and-white gingham apron, she raised her eyebrows and gave an unapologetic teenage shrug.

"Sorry, like, for disturbing you," she said with a cheeky smirk. "Only that's what I'd do if I were on that trade."

"In fact, that's exactly what I did myself twelve months ago," I replied, scrambling to reconcile her youth with the insight. "Made a tidy profit. Are you in the market for a second job by any chance?"

"Sorry, no. Too busy growing this franchise."

A royal sweep of her arm indicated that she was referring to the four paprika-washed walls and a collection of mismatched wooden chairs tucked under blue Formica tables.

"Where did you learn about pairs trading?"

"My dad. He worked in construction for Powell Homes a long time ago and a guy in his bank got him into trading the stock against another homebuilder called Lennox. Made enough to buy his first car. He showed me the gist of how it works two years ago when we were reading up on statistics."

"Wow. Mind if I check that one out here?" I said, tapping the PHL-LNX tickers into my phone to call up their price graphs. "I didn't cover it until second year in business school. Cool dad. Does he still trade?"

"Naw. He wouldn't have time for all that now, I'd say. More coffee?"

We chatted for hours, like we had known each other for years. We made each other laugh.

I don't know any teenagers in my real life, having no connections to their world through my circle and so no preconceived notions or reference points as to how they should behave beyond what I see in the media. In the main, I treat her exactly like any other grownup or peer and I'm sure this has helped us form a firm friendship. She told me as much and, as the months went by, I learned that the mutual respect that we shared was in utter contrast to the typical relationships between adults and young people in the town of Prospero.

"How are you getting on?" she whispers sympathetically in my right ear while depositing my coffee on the table and sitting down on the chair opposite.

She is one of those tiny, lithe people who moves about

like a will-o'-the-wisp and her face is a pleasure to dwell on, with an unvarnished beauty of the almost other-worldly kind you see imitated on the cover of fashion magazines. Her jet-black hair frames a perfectly symmetrical face with healthy, honey-toned skin so smooth and pore-less that while we talk I find myself subconsciously scanning it over and over to detect even the tiniest of flaws, but there are none. A rose-colored, V-shaped angel's kiss birthmark between her brows is her only blemish, but it's visible only when she laughs hysterically or gets very annoyed, neither of which extremes I get to see very often.

"Getting there," I reply first before deciding to admit the truth. "Not great, really."

"You in town to see my mom?" she inquires.

Miranda is the only child of Sergeant Marge Newlands and her husband, Gonzalo Vasquez, whom I saw at Mike's funeral.

"Yeah, I'm heading there in a minute. Still helping with the investigation. They're hopefully making progress, but I'll know more tomorrow. How about you? Still mulling over business colleges?"

I am merely trying to steer the conversation away from the topic of Mike, but Miranda smiles and wags her finger in response to what she knows is a tease. I had dragged her top-percentile ACT scores out of her a few weeks ago and that information, combined with the patently obvious talent she has for all things financial, has led me to advocate strongly for her to apply to Stanford to study finance or something else on the business spectrum.

"For the last time, Ariel. Finance is not my bag. Veterinary is the only thing I have any real interest in but I couldn't afford it, even if I was accepted. Following your passion is for people with money. I'd settle for anything at this stage, just to get out of town. The church leaders say they'll sponsor me to do law, so that's another possibility, but to be honest it's all becoming a bit of a drag. My parents are completely *obsessed*." She imbues the word with a demonic quiver.

"Veterinary is great," I say, stifling a fake yawn. "All that vocational endeavor. Helping the poor sick animals. Admirable stuff. But Miranda Vasquez (my speech calls for a Gandalf-the-Druid-style voice), I have come here to this tiny hamlet in the asshole of nowhere on a mission. I, Ariel R. Mignolet, minion of the great Lord Buffet and broken-down disciple of Dow, have been sent from the daaaaaark side to tell you that the world of capitalist vultures needs *you*. We think that you may be our *Speccciaaaal Ooooooooone.*"

I leave the café to the sound of her giggling.

Chapter Five

Unspoken Conspiracy

A hundred feet farther along Main Street, I arrive at the police station and retreat a few steps to the edge of the sidewalk to take a wider-angle look at the building whose rear entrance I was dragged into nine days ago. Its enormous entrance doors are studded with diamond-shaped hinges and circular iron handles the size of dinner plates that hang beneath a Gothic over-arch in a style redolent of a European medieval castle. Having once housed a four-star hotel, its fanciful frontage serves as a monument to more frivolous times in this mecca of prudence.

A small buxom lady with gray hair and tiny gold-rimmed glasses mutters quietly into a phone. The light from clear blue skies filters through an imposing stained-glass window halfway up the stairwell behind her desk. Crimson beams create a kaleidoscope effect on today's newspapers, strewn across the round table in the center of the room. I strain my neck to read.

MYSTERY STILL SURROUNDS DESERT MURDERS blares the front-page headline above a color photograph of Sergeant Newlands standing on a podium, hand raised, index finger pointing, mouth open, beckoning the next question from the array of heads in the foreground of the photograph.

While I wait for the receptionist, banter and laughter frequently break the stillness as police officers and Border Patrol agents, mostly in pairs, cross the ten feet from the front door to the elevator to access the business end of the building.

"Sergeant Newlands will see you now," she says, peering over her spectacles. "Stairs to the second floor, halfway down the corridor. The meeting rooms are numbered one to four and yours is number two. Second on your right."

The sergeant doesn't stand or welcome me when I enter the office after my soft knock elicits a curt "yes." Sitting rigidly upright behind an old-fashioned writing desk, her head seems disproportionately big for her slim shoulders, an impression not helped by a thick nest of highly coiffed, wiry, ochre hair knitted together in a single unmoving mass with no escaping tendrils. She casts a glance at the space opposite her to indicate where she wants me to go.

A barely detectible flicker of her swimming-pool blue eyes as I take my seat betrays a note of scorn at my clothing choice of Lycra running capris and a lime-green cotton hoodie. Something in how she is positioned, like a cannon taking aim, reminds me again of Sadistic Sister Sauerkraut and a tremor of nervous energy nudges the pit of my stomach.

"Thank you for coming in. I had hoped that we would be joined at today's meeting by Agent Paul Pitcavage from the FBI's domestic counterterrorism arm and Officer Branson of the Border Patrol's tactical unit, but Agent Pitcavage had to postpone until tomorrow and I felt there was little point in having one here without the other. Consequently, we are a bit limited in the progress we can make today. Can you make yourself available again the same time tomorrow to meet them?"

"Be happy to. So the big guns have arrived? The investigation must be progressing well?" I ask but am not surprised to be ignored.

"Agent Pitcavage wants two things from his meeting with you tomorrow. First, the FBI have sent over one of their most experienced sketch artists from Houston to sit down with you today and try and come up with a good likeness for this 'ring leader' you said you had a good look at. She's all set up and waiting for you in the office next door.

"Agent Pitcavage is also very interested in the timeline of events on the day in question—like the chronology of your communications with Officer Argyll in the hours leading up to his death. His arrival time at your property. The time at which he set off in pursuit and, of course, the timing of your nine-eleven call. All items you and I have covered several times over.

"This morning, I simply want to … you know … clarify or, if you like, unify our responses to his questions tomorrow so there are no gray areas or disparities and we can save time and move on to other more important aspects of the investigation. Are you happy to do that now?"

"Sure," I respond hesitantly and we stare silently at one another for longer than would normally be considered polite. "That's fine," I say, injecting more conviction to bring an end to the staring match.

As though she has drawn some additional, unsavory conclusion about me from our visual joust, her scornful gaze drifts away and she shuffles through papers on her desk to find my earlier statements.

"So I have here your first statement dated Saturday

the tenth of September, the morning after the murder of Officer Argyll and Messrs. Hernandez and Luiz. I'm just going to run back through the timeline, if I may. You stated here that you called Officer Argyll on the evening of the sixth of September and he arrived at your property on the Old County Road at ten-zero-five p.m. He was there to attend to your concerns regarding the unusual lights in front of your property?" A slight rise in her intonation is the only indication she is asking me a question because she never looks up from the script. "This tallies with Officer Argyll's official call-out records so can we both agree about the description?"

"Yes, Sergeant," I reply warily. "Although, as I believe I explained to yourself and the other officers in prior statements, I wanted Mike's, sorry, Officer Argyll's help to deal with what I could reasonably describe as unusual lights beaming onto my property from next door. That's the matter I called him about that evening and he attended to it when he called at ten-oh-five p.m. I hadn't seen the other strange lights you are referring to on the plain on the sixth."

"Okay," she says tersely. "I will let the official record show that your call on the sixth was in relation to your spat with Mr. Freeth. However, would I be correct in saying that you had seen strange lights on the plain in front of your home on various dates prior to the night of the murder and that you had mentioned the mysterious appearance of these lights to Officer Argyll on several occasions during the course of other phone conversations? Can we establish that as a matter of fact?"

"Yes, it would be true to say that we had spoken about them both in previous phone conversations and in person."

"You see, Agent Pitcavage has queried the specific

details of this other phone call." The nib of her pen hovers over one line of a lengthy cell phone record and then she repeatedly circles the relevant numbers while speaking. "This short one. The one you made to Officer Argyll at six-fifty-six p.m. on the evening of September ninth? The evening he was murdered? Now I would like to firm up on … or at least … get an understanding of the context around that call so we can be clear with the agent tomorrow. There will be a lot of ground to cover, so clearing this up now will save time. Did you make that call to Mike to talk about the issue of the strange lights on the plateau the night before? Or to complain about Mr. Freeth?"

She needs either one of these answers. I know it and she knows I know it. But I am not quite ready to roll over.

"Not really, Sergeant. I called him to see how he was doing. You know, as a friend? I did mention to you before that we had become friends, right? I was just calling to … to check in, I suppose you could call it."

Before I finish, she looks down as though distracted by some pressing piece of paperwork on her desk. If it's a ploy to maintain the upper hand in our discussion, it works to great effect.

"To … check … in." She repeats each word with a kind of robotic inflection. "Okay," she continues, trying another tack. "Is it fair to say that the regular communications you had with Officer Argyll concerning the strange lights in the Playas Valley as well as Mr. Freeth's security lights were how you two became well acquainted?"

"Sergeant Newlands, as I explained before, Mike and I met in Phoenix and *that* is where I made his acquaintance."

The furrow between her eyes deepens to resemble a thick stroke of indelible marker. "It is irrelevant where you first met each other. My question stands. In the weeks leading up to his death, Officer Argyll filed a series of reports about your sightings of lights moving in the distance near your property and he detailed how he paid several visits there during the course of his investigation into *that* matter." She holds aloft a blue file as though revealing a key exhibit to a jury. "In all his official entries into the file relating to your property, which is thorough and meticulously detailed, Mike never once mentions any problems you claim to have had with Caleb Freeth and there is sure as hell no mention of *chats* and *check-ins*. Now, I am only interested in giving Mr. Pitcavage clear responses to the questions he is going to ask you tomorrow. So, once again, did you call Officer Argyll at six-fifty-six p.m. on the ninth to talk about your concerns regarding unusual lights on the plateau in front of your house and is it fair to say that the friendship between yourself and Mike Argyll developed during the course of his investigation into this matter?"

I try to recall the moment our unspoken conspiracy began. That is, the precarious pact between Detective Sergeant Marge Newlands, engaged in the biggest case of her career, and me, Ariel Mignolet, first a suspect, now the main witness assisting with the investigation of a triple murder. It is hard to pinpoint the exact moment because my recollections of the morning after the murders remain distorted, a collection of sensory snapshots, some perfectly detailed, others opaque and misleading. I have since learned that memories tethered to trauma are sylph-like and unclear, and the head injury I received no doubt accentuated this.

I recall the short walk from my neighbor's front garden to my house in the company of Sergeant Newlands and a junior officer. Blue lights blared and shrank like lighthouse beacons through the cool morning air as we weaved between vehicles parked at every angle. There's the tang of iron on my tongue when a droplet of blood escaped the head bandage, and radios bursting to life here and there with crackly voices machine-gunning snippets of information. By the time we reached the house, the sun was peeking over the horizon and, at one point, I remember beseeching the young officer who was accompanying the sergeant and me to take me back out there. Permission denied, they ushered me inside and we had just reached the top of the stairs when the report about Mike came through.

"We found him, Sarge," came the voice over the airwaves. "Half-covered. Two more bodies here. Look Mexican. Hard to say. Christ." A long pause. "Mike." Then the abrupt electrical suck of a two-way radio over and out.

Pinched throat, hot tears, buzzing radios, muffled voices, shouts, car engines firing.

I remember the sergeant shrinking silently into my giant navy couch. Head bowed, her black-and-gray uniform enveloped by voluminous inky cushions. Meanwhile, her sidekick had seethed, pacing up and down beside the window in youthful frustration, uttering strings of expletives promising revenge to no one in particular. Having passed it by a few times, he eventually stopped at the telescope and panned across the brightening vista.

"This thing's not working," he proclaimed at first, before, "Hang on, I have it," as he flicked the switch at the base of the rangefinder from night to day vision, the same switch Mike and I had discovered the night before. "I can see them all perfectly out there, Sarge," he shouted across the room. "They could be standing here next to me. They're putting the cover over his body now. I see his truck. It's badly smashed up, Sarge. Take a look. It's unbelievable." He sounded giddy.

It was around then I noticed the sergeant studying me, watching tear follow tear. Why would I be crying like that, she must have asked herself. Then she surveyed the room in more detail, her investigative instincts springing to life despite the emotion of the moment. I saw her gaze fall on the two half-filled wine glasses by the fireplace. I watched her stare panning over the collection of tea lights and candles on the coffee table and fire hearth. By that point in the morning, all the flames were extinguished apart from one scented beeswax stump, which infused the room with the faintest note of Turkish delight.

Springsteen's *Tunnel of Love* album, Mike's favorite, was still playing on a loop in the background. The throw he was wrapped in the night before lay in a soft heap near the window, cast off casually and in haste, a beacon of reckless abandon in contrast to the meticulous tidiness of the rest of the house.

She stood for a moment at the iPod speaker dock beside the fireplace before aggressively twisting the volume dial to zero. Then she looked directly at me and I saw the dawn of realization in her eyes. A new reality was being foisted upon her there in my living room. A rapid reassessment of assumptions.

"Steve, get Eliza on the phone for me," she instructed the officer who was still engrossed with the lens. "We need to let her know as soon as possible before she hears it from someone else. You know Eliza?" She addressed me directly then. "Mike's fiancée? Eliza Marron?" A pause. Long enough to assess my reaction. "Have you met her?"

She didn't have to look too closely to see that, up until that moment, I had never heard of the woman. A new class of pain sidled in beside the grief and shock. I stared into Marge

Newlands' watery eyes and it was her turn to witness dawning realization.

That was the moment our unspoken pact began.

"Yes, Sergeant. It was concerning the strange lights on the plain that I called Mike on the ninth," I reply, my words betraying little of the emotional heat rising in my chest.

Her only reaction is a slight rounding of her shoulders, as stiff as epaulettes since I entered the room. "Good. Before you leave town, Mr. Pitcavage will also want to talk to you in more detail about your encounter with the chief suspect. By way of preparation for that meeting, as I mentioned to you earlier, they have arranged for you to have a session with the sketch artist, Ms. Pamela Gregan. She is waiting in the office next door and I am very hopeful that with your cooperation, we—"

"Pardon me, Sergeant. You said *before you leave town*. What do you mean by before I leave town? Do you mean before I leave Prospero or before I leave New Mexico? What makes you think I'm planning to leave town?"

"Mike mentioned to me a few weeks ago that you only planned to stay for three-quarters of the year until some long-distance race or other. In December, I think he said? He mentioned it in passing when we were discussing your file."

Her words strike a painful chord. Downgraded now to his water-cooler topic.

"I have revised my plans. My lease is good up to next February, and who knows after that?"

"What's here for you?"

I sense this question has been on the tip of her tongue since we first met.

"You're not among your own here. You're a tropical fish in a tiny cold creek and my strong advice to you would be to help us out today and tomorrow and then head back west to recuperate. I will keep you posted, of course ... on developments ... and call if we have any follow-up questions. Why linger?"

All my dealings with the sergeant up to now have involved aggressive body language, minimal eye contact and a thinly veiled contempt, so her more up-front approach actually comes as a relief, as though a boil has been lanced.

"Okay. Let me help you with that, Sergeant. I am planning to stay around as long as it takes to witness the arrest of the crazy, sand-dwelling fucking psychos who murdered my friend, those other two men, and tried very hard to kill me, too. I frankly don't care what you or anyone else in this Jesus-freak shithole think of me. The fact is, you and I both know that you are consumed with hiding the true nature of my relationship with Mike and, while I am happy to go along with you on that, up to a point, please make no mistake about where I am coming from here. What I want, in fact what I *need* from the system loosely called justice here in Prospero, is closure on this issue and, until I get that, you better get used to seeing my tropical face. Does that help you any? You know? In your *understanding* of me and all?"

After a protracted pause, she leans over the desk to the point where I can see every shiny pore. Her voice is so laden with emotion that the words come slow and shakily at first like the burst and sputter of water from a long-dry faucet. Then they speed up until she is firing them at me like a high-pressure hose.

"I am sorry. Maybe I didn't catch that correctly. Did I actually just hear you say that you need closure? Closure then. How melodramatic. How very Californian of you. Let's see, you knew Mike how long, ten weeks? And you were what, friends? Closure you say? I'm sorry, but you simply don't qualify. *You!"* she bellows, prodding an index finger toward me. "You are too far back in line for that. Did you know that his parents up in Silver City are my best friends? Next-door neighbors for twenty years, we were. Or did I happen to mention at all that I carried him, my godchild, in my arms when his body was so tiny I could lay it out flat along one forearm, his tiny velvet head here in my palm? Or that I taught him how to cross the road? Eight years old, he was. We used to play the blind old lady game. *Take me by the arm, Mike. You're all I have,* I'd say to him. Then I was there to cheer him on from the sidelines at his college football games and was his mentor when he joined the force. I even introduced him to his fiancée, here in Prospero.

"Closure? Pardon me, but Mike has lots of friends who will be real happy to stand on the necks of those murderous sons-of-the-devil hiding out there like snakes under rocks, but you, Ariel Mignolet from San Francisco, you just don't make the cut.

"If you …" she is picking her words carefully now, trying to reestablish her earlier note of calm, "if you did come to respect Mike's many fine qualities within the short time you made his acquaintance and, more importantly, if you truly respect his legacy now, then you will stay as long as it takes to assist this investigation without sullying his memory and then quietly slink back to rejoin the rest of your money-changer friends in the temple. Now if you don't mind, I am real busy here and you are late for your meeting next door. I will see you again tomorrow with Officer Pitcavage." Her shaking hands grip the edge of the desk and she doesn't look up again as I depart.

Chapter Six

The Sketch

I knock softly on the half-open door of Meeting Room One and Ms. Pamela Gregan bids me to enter. "Hi there. Hiiii," she says, holding the *i* all the way through our handshake before gesturing for me to take a seat with all the flourish of a cheerleader. "How are you doing today?" she chirps.

"Great, thanks," I reply a little curtly, only vaguely disguising my objection to casual chitchat given the sobering business at hand.

Pamela takes the hint and shifts to a more matter-of-fact, if still very sweet, tone to explain how the process will work. She fits the image of a newly graduated kindergarten teacher with her bobbed, strawberry-blonde hair, open face and light-blue spectacles. and a way of explaining things in a deliberate, step-by-step manner, as though reeling off the classroom rules to a group of preschoolers.

"Now, I'm just here to articulate a drawing based on everything you can remember of the suspect. Is that okay? I understand from Sergeant Newlands that it was dark when you saw this person, but I'm very hopeful that we can recreate a good image by piecing together your memories of that visage. I have some tools here, catalogs and books of faces and isolated facial features, and we will go through these together, systematically selecting those you feel are the closest fit. As we go, I will add the reference numbers of each feature to this other sheet until we have filled in all these boxes here, see? Now this part of the process will take between two and four hours. Are you okay with that timeline?"

She continues before I have a chance to reply. "The thing is that it is always best to conduct this part of the process in one sitting to keep the … to keep a flow going, if you can understand. The second part of the process is where I will sketch up our image, trying to capture all the key traits of the suspect using the completed sheet. This will likely take me about twenty to thirty minutes and then, hopefully, we will just be tweaking the drawing at the edges at that point. The key thing, really, though, is that you try and relax at the outset and let your memory work for you. Do you think you can do that? Have you any questions at this point?"

I feel myself shrinking into the role of a small child who needs to be reassured and nursed along. The other me, that person people look to for answers, seek out for advice, defer to, is once again completely lost in this process and is someone I have been unable to resurrect for many days.

I reply that I have no questions and just want to get this over with as quickly as possible. I only saw his face briefly and it was in the flickering glow of firelight, so I'm pretty sure my memory was cheated of a clear impression by the dance of the flame.

Ms. Gregan takes me methodically through thousands of images of noses, eyes, jaw lines, ears, hair and then head shapes and full head shots, all the while gently guiding and deftly picking up on all my subtle signals of recognition before moving ahead in line with a well-honed plan.

Going into the meeting, all I had in my head was a vague impression, a fleeting image of youth and beauty imbued with coldness. Ninety minutes later, Ms. Gregan has filled in all her boxes with reference numbers and begins sketching the visual while I gladly take up her suggestion to stroll around to the coffee shop. As I leave, she asks me to flick on the light switch as the late-afternoon sun has begun to wane. I stand in the doorway and press the switch to the on position. Ten seconds later, I still haven't left and my trembling hand hovers an inch from the shiny brass panel. The compulsion to perform the ritual is overwhelming.

Ms. Gregan looks up from her sketch book, tilting her head to one side in the kind of cute pose puppies make when confused. "You okay?" she asks, sounding genuinely concerned. "I'm all set here now so you can head out for your walk or take a seat outside and relax for about thirty minutes. There's a vending machine directly above us on the next floor if that's of any use? Can I help?"

My loitering is clearly making her feel uncomfortable. Beads of perspiration prickle my forehead despite the air conditioner. It has to be done. I flick the switch off and then repeat on, off, on, off, delivering instant relief. I depart without looking back. She must be staring after me, but I am past caring.

I return to the Cuppa Jo to while away time. It is twenty minutes before closing and Miranda is mopping up around empty chairs. She nods toward a corner table at the back, pours herself a Coke and joins me with a small carafe of strong Colombian.

"Heck, that nearly took all day," she says. "You want

something to eat? I just wrapped up the salads but I could make you a ham sandwich, if you like. You seriously look like you could use it, Ariel. It's no trouble. Honest." She gnaws on a jagged nail still tenuously attached to her index finger, extracting it deftly with her teeth. She bites her nails constantly so that the tips of her fingers are round pink stubs.

"Can't eat," I reply. "Sugary coffee, maybe. I know I need food, but my stomach is in knots. Your mother had arranged a sketch artist and I feel like I've been mentally assaulted."

"Did they get a good likeness?" she whispers with wide-eyed fascination and I immediately regret drawing someone so young into something so morbid. As I start rolling back on the conversation with a change of subject to my coming week's training plan, the ding-a-ling of the old-fashioned doorbell heralds the entrance of Pastor Seb Funchess and Clayton Marron.

As I came to understand in the aftermath of the murder, Clayton Marron, the man who financed the rebirth of Prospero, was Mike's soon-to-be father-in-law. His status as the local big-cheese industrialist appears to afford him a great deal of respect in town, and Miranda has told me that people defer to him on most major decisions. I have never seen him out of the pastor's company and, within that relationship, it is plain to see that he is the junior partner. Seb Funchess appears to have such control over his important friend, the only thing missing is a leash.

As I experienced at the funeral, the pastor emits a kind of energy, like faint tremors from a distant earthquake, invisible waves that make you sit up a little straighter and take notice in the expectation that something important is about to happen. A tall man, about six foot four, he has the groomed silver hair and handsome face that would not look out of place on a country-and-western album. He has a peculiar habit of walking around with his hands buried deep in the pockets of his suit trousers and, when he's in conversation, has a tendency to tilt his upper body back and thrust his hips forward while his fingers jangle whatever loose change he is carrying.

Both men cast disapproving looks in my direction.

"Everything okay here, Miranda?" asks Clayton Marron.

"I expect you're nearly ready to head home right about now, young lady, that right?" says the pastor. "We're just collecting our tea before evening sermon, but I'd be happy to bring you along straight, if you like. Or if you want to head on home first, Clayton here would be glad to take you. That so, Mr. Marron?" Pastor Funchess looks at his companion, who is so intent on staring a borehole into the side of my head that he has barely progressed from the door.

"Thank you, Pastor, I'll get that for you now," Miranda says, moving back behind the counter. "It's all wrapped up and ready to go, but I'll make fresh coffee for you. I'm fine for a ride, though, thanks. My mom is picking me up on her way home at five-thirty."

"Marge must be busy with all this terrible business," says Funchess. "I saw her pulling out of the driveway very early yesterday morning. We were flying over your house, weren't we, Clayton?" he adds loftily.

"Saw that new colt of yours from overhead, too. Noise of the chopper blades frightened the hind quarters off him, I'm sorry to tell you, but he sure showed himself off with all the commotion. Beautiful animal you've got there, young lady. Careered around the paddock at a hundred miles an hour, like a bronco with a stuck burr. You planning on breaking him any time soon?"

"Have done already, Pastor. I'm riding trails now to build stamina. He's as smooth as silk," Miranda replies.

Clayton emerges from his trance to insinuate himself into the space between the back of my chair and the pastor. Miranda takes the opportunity to commiserate. "How is Eliza bearing up, Mr. Marron? I'm sure it must be very hard for her. Please tell her again we are all praying for strength and that God will help us punish the people who did this. Ariel here tells me they are sketching up the main suspect now so it seems things are progressing."

Clayton Marron makes no reply and his silence weighs heavily on the atmosphere. He picks up the steaming coffee cup, hastily secures its plastic lid and storms out under the tinkling bell in the doorway.

The pastor's hands plunge into his pockets for the comfort of coins. He rocks slightly back on his heels, stomach pushed against the counter, eyes trained on Miranda's crestfallen face. "I think you need to be a bit more careful with the company you keep, young madam," he says, looking pointedly toward me. "And I'm sure your mother wouldn't appreciate any loose talk about the details of the case. If you're going to be a lawyer, you need to develop a better sense of discretion," he adds brusquely while gathering up the paper parcels from the counter. "Have you firmed up your college plans yet, by the way? I've been talking to Reverend Chitty over there in Wessborough. Says he has a place waiting for you next September and he'd love to show you around personally, early next year if you'd like. He can tell you all about the course. Big potential for someone like you in the church, Miranda Vasquez. All those brains!

Why don't I tell him you'll head down there in January to have a look around? You do well there the first year and Resurrection church will sponsor you to study law in a fancy college. We need good lawyers on the side of righteousness.

"And be not conformed to this world: but be ye transformed by the renewing of your mind, that ye may prove what is that good, and acceptable, and perfect, will of God." He recites the verse as though channeling the Lord Himself. "That's Romans 12:2, young lady. Your Lord is calling you now."

Extracting an arthritic-looking hand from his pocket, he reaches across the counter to grip Miranda's arm near her shoulder and it conjures up an image I have seen somewhere of a hawk's talons clenching down on a young rabbit. "The time has come for you to live the next part of His plan for you, and I'll be guiding you to start by clearing this café and calling in to your mother right this minute. You hear me now?"

As the door of the café closes slowly in his wake, Miranda stares out after him, the expression on her face a mix of resignation and fear. "I need to go," she says, staring out at the quiet street, and I am not sure if she is talking about her imminent departure from the café or a more permanent exit from Prospero and its dead weight of expectations.

"Where are the church leaders proposing you study law?" I have to ask. "It's a great platform degree but where you study it really matters. You should talk to my friend Sunil Narine about it. He works as a deputy district attorney in Northern California, specializing in civil rights. He'd be a great guy to give you the lowdown on law degrees."

She seems coy, as though she is betraying someone just by discussing the issue. "Their plan is for me to take

Religious Studies and Legal Philosophy in Wessborough, near San Diego, and do a law degree afterward. Apparently, other churches have sent students on a similar path and it's been really successful. Anyway, I'm talking it all through with Mom and Dad right now. To be honest with you, I'm not that pushed about the idea of studying law. My dream is to become a vet. But beggars can't be choosers, right?"

"Is it normal for the church to get so involved in a member's career path?" I ask, aware that I am straying into territory outside the light-hearted boundaries within which our friendship has grown. "What about your school friends? Any of them getting a similar degree of interest from the powers that be?"

"I'm really not sure, Ariel. Can't speak for most of the other kids in town coz I was educated at home. I do have one friend with college plans, but I think her parents enrolled her way back … in Galen Johnson College, Indiana. Ever heard of it?"

I cannot disguise how taken aback I am by the fact that this incredibly bright young woman, whose fields of knowledge range from the Classics to sophisticated financial analysis, has never been to public school. "Is your dad your educator?"

"Yeah, my dad's pretty much stuck at home twenty-four-seven. A car accident put him in a wheelchair twelve years ago. He still does some woodturning and stuff, but he's an amazing teacher. My ever-present bookmobile."

"Certainly did an amazing job with you, Miranda. I was a selfish pain in the ass when I was seventeen, and my mom didn't have the money to send *me* to college either. But I got lucky. Really lucky. With a bit of hard work and my mother's iron will, I scored a scholarship and that one break changed the course of my life. Education is important, Miranda. And, okay, I know I've been kidding you about doing finance and all that, but if there is one thing I've learned over the years, it's that the happiest people are those who follow their passion. If veterinary studies is what you are passionate about, then that is what you should do."

She looks toward the window again. At her own reflection this time, I think.

"I'm at a point now where I want to give back, if I can use that awful phrase," I say. "This past year has … I guess I've started to look at things differently. Anyway, I want you to know that if funding is a barrier to you following your chosen path, then I'd be more than happy to subsidize you, no matter the cost. I have the resources, Miranda. And I can't think of anything better to do with it than invest in your talents.

"Call it a loan if you prefer. You can pay me back when you patent some medical device for cats or something. Run it by your parents but, please, do give it serious thought and let me know. I'd truly like to help. Let's talk more about it in the next few days." I put my change for the coffee on the table and open the door to leave.

"That's an awesome offer, Ariel. Too generous, really, but, well, thank you. Sincerely."

Ms. Gregan's completed sketch rests face down between us on the green pleather desktop when I return. "You full sure you're all set?" she asks, her voice tinged with concern. "You know it might just be a good idea for you to collect yourself. Maybe take a few deep breaths or just a quiet moment of contemplation to envision what you are going to see and how it might impact you. It's just that I have a lot of experience with the aftereffects of trauma and people

can sometimes be overwhelmed when they see, well …
when they are reminded visually of—"

"Please!" The word leaves my mouth spontaneously like
a cry for help. Her voice feels like an aggravating drone
and I have the strangest sensation that I have vacated my
seat and am looking in from outside, watching her prattling
endlessly on and on to someone else in my place. I want to
shout "just turn the damn thing over" but manage to strike
a more diplomatic note. "I'm sorry. I'm just tired. Could we
get on with it, if you don't mind?"

A little taken aback, she turns over the page, glancing
quickly at me for any response. For what seems like a long
time, but minutes really, I sit still and say nothing until
eventually a few incoherent words escape under my breath.
The cheerleader has done something very strange because
there in front of me is an image I wasn't fully sure I had
actually witnessed. She has conjured it up or painlessly
extracted it from a place inside I didn't know existed.

The face illuminated in front of me ten nights ago is staring
up with the same dark, cold eyes. Ms. Gregan's impression is
accurate enough to kick-start my memory, enabling me now
to recall the scene exactly as though looking at a photograph.
She has reached into recesses and disturbed, if not fully
unearthed, something my subconscious had perhaps buried
for my own safety.

I am suddenly aware that my hand is covering my mouth
and she is standing behind me, touching my shoulder,
asking me if I am okay, when it is clear that I am not. In
the dark room of my mind's eye, there is also now another
image emerging alongside hair and skin and eyes. There are
his hands. One holds a fiery torch, above which clusters of
orange embers melt wispily into the night sky. The other

holds a blunt stone-headed axe, and even in the dim light, I can clearly see the glistening blood.

Chapter Seven

It wouldn't be correct to say that the night of Mike's murder began just like any other. I lured him to the house after previous attempts failed because of his obsession with secrecy. We were still at that early, exhilarating stage of a relationship when everything qualifies as a milestone. Each meeting has special significance and then, afterwards, each new discovery or deepening of understanding will be ruminated upon and replayed over and over in self-directed dreams designed to prolong the pleasure.

Viewed through this lens, I can say that the first act of the tragedy that played out on this lonely stretch of the Old County Road on the ninth of September was, in fact, the most passionate few hours of my life. Exquisite in its intensity.

I had called him toward the end of his shift, the first Friday he had worked since we met. I now know, of course, that it was exactly 6:56 p.m. After a brief exchange of greetings, I said three words, "Mine at nine," before hanging up. It was a dare, really, I suppose, because I knew he was so reluctant to meet there. Up to that point, he had only set foot in my house on three occasions and always in an official police capacity while attempting to resolve the situation with Caleb Freeth's lights. He never crossed the threshold when stopping by to collect me on his days off. The routine was that he would call from his pickup outside and I came out and hopped in.

Mike never had to spell out for me why he was so keen to keep our relationship a secret. In eleven weeks, I never once asked him to explain it. I have never been one for making personal demands on my lovers—a fact that has in the past been mistaken for indifference. In any case, when I left that voicemail on September ninth, I hadn't seen him for three days and had taken a chance that he might be missing me a fraction as much as I ached to see him. My hope was that he would set aside whatever concerns he had for a few hours and stay a while with me at the house.

His last visit had been the night of the sixth. He pulled up at around 10 p.m. in a police vehicle and we went to make a third appeal to Caleb to leave his security lights off, either until it was clear to him that I had gone to bed or until eleven o'clock each night. That was when he had reluctantly conceded to a timer switch for eleven o'clock and I could live with that. It was a breakthrough.

Three nights later, by nine o'clock everything was ready. I switched off all the lights and descended into blissful calm in my window chair, bare toes pressed against the glass, sipping a vintage Burgundy. It was the kind of balmy early fall night that invites you out to rest in its embrace. The cicadas were singing their chorus and there was so little movement in the air that the tiny tea-light flames along the stairwell and around the hearth hardly flickered despite the open windows at the front and back of the house. This was a very unusual tranquility, as there is almost always wind in the Playas Valley between the Animas and Hatchet ranges. The prevailing southeasterly can blow hard and straight for days on end such that you have to brace yourself every time you leave the house, covering your face with your jacket just to get to the car without feeling the whip and prick of airborne particles.

Mini sandstorms sometimes swirl uninterrupted through the channel and I like to watch them approach. They start many miles away as barely visible puffballs, but by the time they mount the embankment, cross the road and hit the house's facade, the sylph-like shapes have built up such a head of steam they can suck open windows shut and shunt them ajar again a few minutes later, sprinkling sand onto the inside sill like a sedimentary calling card.

The very last streaks of daylight on the horizon had faded an hour ago, giving way to the spectacular celestial show that is the desert sky at night. I recall thinking for the first time that this whole crazy adventure was delivering on its promise. I was sleeping like the dead, without medication; it was months since my last panic attack and, most importantly, for someone so used to being in control of every facet of my life, there was an invigorating freedom in how out of control I felt in the throes of this affair.

I missed the approach of his pickup due to a temporary abandonment of my lookout post to throw on a shirt, refill my glass and change the music. Returning to my seat, I looked down to see Mike staring steadily up at me from the front porch, his face revealed in the blue mist of the security lantern. He looked serious, like someone preparing to deliver important news, and I remember feeling a gnarl of worry in the pit of my stomach. When I opened the front door, no words passed between us and our embrace felt born of desperation. Hands covered ground greedily, almost violently. Fingers knitted into hair before sliding down, lingering briefly on bands of muscle beneath the skin, shifting like a climber over a rock face, stealing across the smooth to search out grooves and dwelling in hollows that fit the palm. Arms took hold and clung for an instant before shifting up or down to other silky sub-cotton territory.

My lips and cheeks traveled slowly to those barely detectable goose bumps on Mike's chest. I don't ever remember sweat on his skin, even on the hottest of days. He seemed hewn from some other-worldly marble-like material designed more for beauty than mere function.

Four feet shuffling and eyes out of focus, we moved in clumsy unison away from the open front door and up the stairs as though welded together, hitting either side of the stairwell in a precarious balancing act that progressed us slowly upwards, mouth pressed on moist mouth or tongue or eye or warm neck or cool forehead. Shedding our clothes Houdini-like, wanting no interruption to the dance until skin finally met skin on the hearth rug.

Then we lay in each other's arms beside the blue heatless flames, surrounded by candles and sipping wine with the *Tunnel of Love* album playing on a loop. Mike sang along to "Two Faces" in a nasal, comedic, country-and-western drawl and we whiled away time playing a game I had invented over many weeks spent living with only Letterhead for company. The uplight in front of his giant, hollow, alphabet-soup skull created shadows on the far wall with some projected letters more elongated or prominent than others. We cobbled words and messages out of the jumbled mess like children finding creatures in the passing clouds.

When the first song on the album played for the second

time, I checked my watch and reminded Mike to enjoy the darkness now before my neighbor's lights turned the place into a runway in another forty minutes. Mike said something about needing to head home soon before his attention was drawn to a flicker in the abyss outside. Since his arrival, a rising wind had swept a sheet of clouds across the moon and a draft of cool air came through the open windows. Draped in a cotton throw, he stood and walked toward the window, one hand holding a gather of material and the other raised to his right temple like a saluting Roman senator before he pressed it right up against the pane.

"Are those the same as the lights you've seen before?" he asked, feeling his way along the expanse of the window in semi-darkness.

"Yeah. Looks like them," I replied from the floor where my elbows and hands were propping up my chin, following his line of sight to the ten or so small yellow orbs zigzagging in the distance like fireflies.

"They look like flame torches to me. The Harry Potter kind," he added while removing the cap on the telescope. "Do you know anything about this thing, Ariel? Have you used it much? It looks like a German kit. Military standard," he muttered, using his phone as a flashlight, pressing his right eye to the scope and twisting the largest dial on top.

"I guessed from all the knobs and screens it's fairly high tech," I said, "but I haven't spent much time using it. The homeowner was in the Border Patrol. Maybe it was his lookout equipment?"

"Nope. This sure as hell isn't standard issue," Mike said, still bent over with his right eye on the eyepiece. "This baby is top of the range. I'd say ten thousand bucks' worth at least. He must have paid for it himself. It's a Schmidt and Bender sight. You'd usually find these on long-range telescopic rifles and I'm talking about the kind reserved for special forces." Still tweaking, he turned briefly to look at me when imparting that piece of information before settling his eye back into position. "You know? The likes of CIA or sharpshooters in Afghanistan? I've only ever seen one in officer training college. See? This bit at the end is some kind of accessory."

That was the last thing I remember him saying before he found the switch, twisted a few dials and the whole situation started to shift. I now know he had managed to turn on and fine-tune a Hensoldt night-sight that had been added on to the end of the lens. Turns out this is one of the most powerful pieces of night-vision equipment in the world of optronics and once he had zoomed in on the lights and finely tuned the magnification and focus of the telescopic sight, he had given himself a ringside view of the happenings over a mile away on the desert plain.

Mike's demeanor changed utterly in the few minutes it took him to take in the scene where the lights still danced. He panned the lens back and forth within a very narrow angle for a while and I remember his jaw muscles tensing as every fiber fixed itself into place for total concentration.

"What are you seeing out there?" I asked casually.

He didn't reply, but stood abruptly upright, as though recoiling, before resuming his watching pose again for another few minutes.

"What can you see out there? What is it?" Alarm was creeping into my voice.

From that moment on, Mike moved at emergency response speed. He spared no time to explain anything, only asked me over and over again, in the matter of seconds it took him to dress and grab his keys, to call the police station in Prospero and ask for two units to come as fast as possible and follow him about a mile southeast of my house onto the Playas Valley. As he ran down the stairwell, he kept reciting the phone number to me and when he reached the still-open front door, he shouted up to check if I had written it down or put it in my phone.

"Yes, I'm dialing it. What the hell did you see out there?" I shouted down only to hear his pickup door slam and its engine fire into life. I crossed the room to see the tail lights drop out of view as he descended the embankment across the road onto the inky plateau below.

The number Mike had given me was that of Peter van Kanz, a colleague of his in the Prospero Police Station who he knew was on duty. Unfortunately it was his direct line and went straight to his answering machine when he didn't drop the call he was on to pick up mine. The station's system offered me the option of transferring to reception, which I accepted only to have the phone almost ring out before being picked up by somebody at an outsourced fielding service who asked me how I would like to direct my call. As the seconds ticked by, I pulled on sweatpants, a T-shirt and Asics and set my eye to the telescopic lens, panning it gently back and forth to try and zone in on what Mike had seen without disturbing any of the focus settings he had set in place.

While searching for signs of life, I asked to speak to the most senior officer on duty and, seconds later, a woman's voice, that of Sergeant Marge Newlands, asked me how she could help.

I will always know exactly what I said on that call because of the number of times I had it repeated back to me and the number of times I was asked to explain each and every word by various police officers in the ensuing hours and days.

"Hello, my name is Ariel Mignolet. I'm a friend of Officer Mike Argyll. He needs assistance right now. Back-up to assist at a scene. He told me to request two units. He's responding to an emergency here, near my house. I'm not exactly sure what it is really. Sorry. I'm trying to see what's going on. It's hard to explain, but he specifically told me to ask for back-up from Prospero. Urgently, please. I'm at The Bank, Old County Road. Next door to Caleb Freeth. Sorry, I have to go. Did you get that?"

As Marge Newlands' steady, measured voice began to respond, trying to calm me down and get more information, Mike's jeep came into view through the lens and her voice faded out as I let the hand that held the phone drift from my ear to devote all my attention to his movements. He pulled to a halt left of my field of vision so I panned a little to follow and captured him emerging from the vehicle with a flashlight in hand and kneeling down to what looked like two bodies lying side by side, face down in the sand. The night-vision was incredibly clear but had a limited spectrum of shades, rather than colors, ranging from black to luminous pale blue. Naked skin and eyes reflected light most effectively so Mike's face and hands were easiest to see and I could see that the stilled bodies were only partially clothed.

The voice on the receiver, still close enough to my ear to be audible, crept back into my consciousness as I stood to look for the lights through the window. "Are you still there? Could I please ask you to repeat Officer Argyll's exact current location? I am assembling a team to assist. Can you hear me? Please respond. Are you still there?"

"Yes, I'm still here," I whispered, having turned down all non-visual functions to keep total focus. "Why are you delaying? I'm watching him now. I'm looking through a telescope, here at The Bank, Old County Road, next door to Caleb Freeth's. He's less than a mile southeast of here out on the plateau. I think there are two ..." I dropped the receiver as I saw Mike jump up from his crouched position and raise what appeared to be his gun while backing up quickly toward his jeep. My pulse thrummed in my ears as I panned right to see what he was retreating from, all the time fearing not being able to find him again should my shaking hands inadvertently move the optic onto a new trajectory.

I looked out the window for a wider perspective, trying to see where the strange lights had moved. Now bunched together, they were moving quickly in a northwesterly direction toward where I sensed Mike was. Back to the scope, I panned left again just as the driver's window of his jeep smashed into pieces. His gun emerged through the shattered glass and a blast of light told me he had discharged a shot. Immediately after that, his pickup began to move. It veered sharply right as it accelerated so that, for a few moments, all I could see was the black well of the trailer partially obscured by a cascading spray of sand in the wake of the tires as he gathered speed through the turn.

I didn't know then what stopped his progress so abruptly, but investigations have since shown it was a second rock that hit the front windshield. I redirected the scope slightly west to see the vehicle's right headlight, now stationary, and what looked like partially clothed, torch-bearing assailants descend on it from every direction. Some climbed on the roof and into the trailer, like luminous baboons swarming on a safari truck. As Mike's driver's window was on the far side, I did not see him being taken from the vehicle but, to my horror, he was catapulted back into my field of vision, thrust onto his knees with force near the front left wheel. I watched as the horde of pale blue beings surrounded him. One brandished some type of long-handled weapon and, with little delay, delivered it violently from above his head, swinging it with both hands down on Mike's cowering form.

I grabbed a flashlight from the kitchen and ran out the open door of the house, across the road, down the embankment and into the night. Never so fast. As though possessed. Possessed with the savagery of the image I had seen. Possessed with fear of loss and a primal fear of the unknown threat. I ran with muscles strangely released, free to reach their absolute limit. I didn't draw breath in the normal sense as I covered the ground. The air stayed suspended in my lungs for too many strides to count before a heaving gasp would admit a new draft. Panic-laden words escaped between gasps during the five or so minutes it took to close in on the scene. Vain cries for help to no one. Mike's name over and over again and, maybe, "God" and "Jesus," as if they might intervene.

Some maniacal force helped me surge ever faster. I was flying across the dirt, the odd fine strand of bush grass whipping my shins in the darkness. The beam of the flashlight in my hand glanced up, down and around in the darkness with the metronomic rhythm of a sprint relay baton. I had given no forethought to how I might deal with the peril that lay ahead or what help I could possibly be to Mike given the number of assailants, which I had estimated to be at least ten.

As two headlights and one red tail light of Mike's

jeep came into view and I drew closer to the cluster of fire torches, I instinctively began to shout aloud into the blackness. "Leave him! Stop! The police are here. They're here. Get back. Mike?" I repeated myself over and over, shouting as loudly as I could through jagged breath. With only two hundred yards to go, the conical flames began moving toward me. The gap between us narrowed rapidly until I could plainly see their mostly naked torsos bathed in firelight. All male, they looked like teenagers, each one lithe and long of limb with unkempt hair and bare feet. Their trousers were dark and belted, the kind the Amish wear to work or church. Even in the terror-stricken state I was in, this part of the whole bizarre picture struck me as odd.

I was about twenty feet from the group when the first rock hit me. It struck just behind my left temple and jolted my head and neck sideways with such force that I fell to my knees after staggering on a few paces. I raised the back of my hand to stem the thin runnel of blood streaming over my eyebrow onto my cheek. I don't remember feeling any pain, just immense shock from its unexpected force. Dazed, I turned and stood to find that I was almost completely encircled by the torchbearers. One of them stepped forward and stood in front of me, holding his amber flame upwind from my face so its acrid smoke trail stung my eyes. The tallest in the group, his face had a haunting beauty, with high cheekbones, full lips, and thick coal-black hair. He was no more than seventeen or eighteen, but there was nothing childlike in the coldness of his stare. I was in no doubt that I was the prey and attack was imminent.

"What did you do to him?" I asked, looking in the direction of Mike's jeep. "The police are on their way. That man is a police officer. That man," I said, pointing. "He's a police officer. They'll be here in minutes."

Unmoved, he stepped closer and reached to lift my ponytail, rubbing the tendrils between his thumb and forefinger like loose tobacco. His other hand rose to shoulder height to reveal a double-headed stone axe glistening ghoulishly in the firelight with a smear of blood. At that moment, another of the group shouted and gestured frantically to direct his attention northwards to a beacon of light. "Look. There."

He was pointing to Caleb Freeth's house. It had passed eleven o'clock. They huddled together to stare at it. Those at the back shuffled forward, sidling between their comrades like curious penguins to get a better view.

"Is that it, Alonso?" I heard one of them say, but I didn't wait to hear a reply. Their cordon was broken and I bolted through the gap, already at full tilt when I passed them, running for my life toward Caleb's light show.

Two sequences from the whole macabre episode stand out now to haunt me in sleep and during random waking moments when I am ambushed by a wave of fear. There is the axe being delivered violently down. Mike flopping lifelessly forward like something deflating.

And the chase. That mile across the plain in total darkness. My flashlight dropped at some earlier point of peril. Through the blackness like a hunted animal. Lungs bursting and adrenalin pumping so hard that breathing itself was a violent, sucking struggle. All the time I was sure I could feel them closing, so every sound produced electrifying terror. I only glanced behind once for fear of slowing down and that is when the second rock hit me between my shoulder blades. Its force sent me shuddering forward. The tips of my fingers scrabbled in the dirt for purchase.

Months of running the trails counted for me then.

Hundreds of miles across so many gradients and unpredictable terrains, asking my feet to make the subtlest of compensating adjustments, building muscle memory for stability. This is what kept me from keeling over on my front and allowed me to maintain enough forward momentum to stay ahead of my pursuers.

Accelerating again, I heard scratchy footfalls drawing closer. Their fastest pacer must have dropped his torch at some point in the chase so he could gain speed. Nearly spent, I waited to be tackled or hit when a subtle change in the gradient underfoot told me I had reached the lower slope of the embankment. It would soon steepen sharply and turn to scree and I braced myself for the climb. The glow of Caleb's house, so long a thorn in my side, radiated over the rise like a reassuring lighthouse. Then, without warning, I knew my chaser was gone. I scrambled up the bank and stole another glance behind. The distant cluster of torches was now reduced to three faintly glowing orbs moving swiftly and silently south.

On hands and knees, I ascended the final few yards, clawing to gain a grip and, in the process, dislodging shards of shale and pebbles that slid down the slope like a series of small avalanches. When I reached the road and entered the wall of light that was Caleb's front garden, I could hear distant sirens and a burning sensation began to spread from the base of my neck to the area above my eye. Reeling with waves of dizziness, I stumbled through my neighbor's front gate.

The last thing I remember before losing consciousness was the shadowy outline of Caleb Freeth's frame in his doorway. "Did they say anything?" I'm sure I heard him say, but the words melted with me into oblivion.

Chapter Eight

MIKE

I met Mike in the Pork and Fiddle Saloon on Camelback Road in Phoenix, Arizona, on the seventh of June 2016. My high-school friend, Natalie Picardo, and I had met in the city for an annual catch-up and happened upon the place after wandering through the center of town with no particular plan for our evening. We settled on meeting in Phoenix as it is approximately halfway between her home in Pasadena and my New Mexican base, but coming to the decision had, as always was the case with Natalie, involved a long and drawn-out tug of wills and lots of needling on my part about the fact that the trip would double the number of times she had ventured outside the State of California. The tipping point in the argument came with my offer to put her up in a boutique hotel in the center of town called the Palomar, which she googled while we spoke on the phone, indicating her approval with a string of high-pitched shrieks and giggles.

The Pork and Fiddle was a sprawling, dimly-lit, barn-like structure with giant wooden propeller fans twirling above a forty-foot mahogany bar counter. Across from the bar, three blazing hearths fired up atmosphere in the restaurant area and a wooden dance floor, strewn with fake straw, filled the no-man's-land in between. The bang of barbeque sauce hit you when you entered and the eclectic mix of nineties, noughties, and country rock music was slightly too loud for intimate conversation. What it lacked in visual delights, it made up for with a vibrant atmosphere and its appeal grew steadily as the effect of their in-house craft ale, aptly named Trotter's Kick, took hold. The front doors swung on brass hinges like a Western emporium from the eighteen-hundreds and the small print on the eye-level signage on each read: IF Y'ALL CAN'T FIND IT HERE THEN FIDDLE OFF.

Natalie and I were offered the last remaining table for two, positioned at a three-way junction point near the center of the establishment. It had the disadvantage of being the farthest table from the service area, so we had to wait for what seemed like an eternity for the waiter to get to us, but this was more than compensated for by the fact that we were in pole position to people-watch between bouts of gossip. As the night wore on, the place filled to capacity. Drinkers and diners turning to dancers and daters and Natalie and I were in for the long haul, buoyed up by the fact that we were mostly surrounded by people of our own age rather than grungy students.

We had just ordered our third pitcher of Trotter's Kick and moved out of the restaurant area to stand at a round table in the thick of the throng between the bar and dance floor when the energy-filled beat of "Mr. Brightside" by The Killers came on and Natalie grabbed my arm and dragged me into the heaving crowd.

By that hour of the evening, the atmosphere on the floor had become slightly frenzied, with people lost in their own hazy world of rhythm. The air was thick with scented body odor mingled with hickory and hops and if it were not for the height of the ceiling, the heat from the mass of gyrating bodies would have been overpowering. Self-conscious at first, we soon moved with abandon, striking poses, laughing. A waterfall of blue fluorescent beams alternated with broad bands of blood-red strobes pulsing slowly like the visual equivalent of low E on a base guitar, adding to the hypnotic energy of the beat. Looking down, a forest of jeans and sports shoes in constant motion, jumping and shifting with the music. Looking up, sweat-streaked cheeks, waving hands and glimpses of dark, wooden crossbeams through the deluge of swirling lights.

A few songs into the deejay's ultra-high tempo set of Kings of Leon, Kasabian and a home brew mix of New York R&B, the crowd began to thin out and he kicked off his final act of the evening with "Atomic" by Blondie. Just as the song started, he paused the track to explain his trademark matchmaking game.

We were asked to group ourselves according to our home state with all the *A* states nearest the deejay's podium and then rows consecutively from there all the way to the start of the bar area. The dance floor was about the size of a six-car garage and, after initial confusion, we organized ourselves remarkably quickly into groups varying in size from the thirty- or forty-strong home team of Arizona to lone stragglers from Oregon and Idaho and the two Swedish wanderers who eventually decided to align themselves with New York.

At a guess, there were about twenty unrepresented states, which I thought a surprisingly low number given that this was a random Saturday night in June. The Pork and Fiddle Saloon in Phoenix must be very well advertised on the tourist trail.

I decided to pin my allegiances to my recently adopted

New Mexico, much to the hilarity of Natalie four rows away, who said I looked as Californian as a surf board. As the groups finally took shape, we were given two minutes to chat to those around us and had to commit to staying in our states for the next three songs. Our New Mexican skin palette ranged from creamy fair to deepest ebony, with the beautiful honeyed hue of Hispanic and American Indian the best represented. I was laughing with a guy about ten years my junior about how utterly sweat sodden his tee shirt was when I heard a voice behind me.

"Hey, ponytail. What train did you roll in on?"

I turned to see Mike. Tall, broad shoulders, checked shirt, cropped dusty-blond hair and a gentle all-American smile. The strongest sense I have of our first meeting is one of genuine surprise. Firework moments were outside my field of experience. For many years, everything in my life had happened by prior appointment. In the instant before I replied, an image crossed my mind of a love-struck teen at a dance meeting the person who would become an obsession.

"Amtrak Texas Eagle, Deming," I replied with a smile, leaning in close to be heard as Debbie Harry's dulcet tones sparked back to life.

"Don't believe it. I'm based just off the I-ten!" he exclaimed with exaggerated joy as though we had won the state lottery. After dancing together for three songs, we joined Natalie and some new bar-stool friends until, hours later, we were all press-ganged into departure by a rapidly encircling cleaning staff wiping down tables and upending stools.

I never got around to asking him who, if anyone, he had arrived with that night, but if there was such a person, they were long since gone by the time Natalie, Mike and I walked the short distance to our hotel. At one point along the way, Natalie sneaked a swig from a bottle of beer she had secreted out of the bar under her jacket. She asked whether anyone knew how strict they were in Arizona about drinking beer on the sidewalk, to which Mike replied that he was a cop himself and if we were on his beat he would lock us up.

"A police officer. Of course!" I exclaimed jubilantly.

He reminded me of this reaction later, wanting to understand if he was emitting some "police vibe." I reassured him he didn't, but in fact I had said it not because I had somehow had a sixth sense about what he did but because I had felt, at that moment, that some class of a hero sat so perfectly with what was missing in my life.

By the time we reached Cityscape, Phoenix's normally bustling downtown area near the hotel, it was two o'clock in the morning and there were few signs of life. At the base of the imposing flight of steps to the front door of the hotel, Natalie said a discreet goodnight and went ahead to bed, leaving me and Mike to say our goodbyes. He wrote his phone number on the back of my hand with a souvenir Pork and Fiddle pen and we laughed when downward pressure on the nib illuminated a little lava bubble of pink liquid containing two kissing piglets. The remaining moments filled up with those interesting intangible signals that can only permeate silence. Our kiss was brief and cool, a perfect punctuation to what we had somehow quietly accepted was an opening chapter.

Late afternoon the next day, I was running along the edge of the Old County Road when my phone buzzed in its armband and I knew it was him.

"Hi there."

Unable to suppress a smile, I scoped around for a pebble

mound on which to perch my Lycra-clad rear end to savor every word.

"It's Mike here."

"Yes, I know," I replied. "In fact your name came up on my phone under Mr. Ork and Diddle. Must've still been half asleep this morning typing it in."

Mike's muffled laugh had the sexy hoarseness of an up-all-night cigarette smoker.

"How did you sleep? Can't have been too many quality hours. It was, what, three going to bed? I was going to call you later myself to say what a fantastic night I had. I'm just out for a run here trying to clear the head fog. You working?"

"Yep. Back to the grindstone," replied Mike. "Just started the first of four thirteen-hour shifts this week and most of it will be indoors, which I hate. Listen, I have to jump here, but I was wondering whether you'd like to hook up next weekend? Maybe take a drive west and go hiking or something?"

I remember thinking he sounded so relaxed and unselfconscious. "Sounds great. I'd love to," I replied, enjoying the warm creep of anticipation. "My schedule's fairly free, so anytime Friday or Saturday works if that suits?"

"Friday's my day off. Let's shoot for Friday and I'll swing by and collect you. You're in that architect-designed house, right? Beside Caleb Freeth's place?"

"Yeah. Lucky me, eh?"

The same throaty chuckle.

"Let's say ten o'clock? And don't forget to bring good hiking shoes, the Chiricahua has lots of scree, but it's so worth it. It's stunning over there. You been before?"

"Nope. Only via a documentary on TV," I replied. "'The Wonderland of Rocks,' right?"

"You're gonna love it, Ariel. I'll see you Friday then. Bye."

I lingered on the stony stump seat for several minutes, pressing the phone to the side of my face.

Cochise County is untamed and spectacular. Two hours up the I-10, we arrived at the Chiricahua National Monument, having passed up a succession of tempting options to change tack and explore what towns with names as evocative as Tombstone, Miracle Valley and El Dorado might look like. Much to my annoyance, Mike liked to drive with his window down and the rapid inflow of air made it difficult to engage in serious conversation.

"Air conditioning's for townies," he quipped. "You miss out on so much of nature's perfume."

"You mean fumes," I shouted over the road noise as we barreled along at eighty, my eyes streaming behind my sunglasses. But somehow there was restfulness to be found in the lack of chatter and pleasure in simply sharing the journey.

We hiked an eight-mile loop, taking in a series of trails. Echo Canyon, Mushroom Rock and Big Balanced Rock all delivered on their promise of peculiar patterns of volcanic formations weathered into a maze of pinnacles and mini-canyons that, for centuries, provided an impenetrable stronghold for the Apache Indians.

Clusters of rust-colored columns and vertical rhyolitic statues known as "hoodoos" stand to attention across wide undulating expanses like legions of petrified giants poised for some other-worldly battle. In other areas, gigantic pale-gray boulders sheathed in a soft coat of lime lichen balance unfeasibly atop cracked and battered spires, left to teeter for eternity by the effortlessly precise silent forces of erosion. In the swooning heat, we sought out the shadows of densely packed stone columns towering above stands of acacia and juniper trees.

In general, Mike was a man of few words, only speaking when absolutely necessary, like a senior physician requesting and responding during major surgery. So I was surprised at his expansive descriptions and explanations in his adopted role of park guide, casually throwing out terms like Cenozoic, tuffs, and spherulites like a bona fide geological expert, which added hugely to my enjoyment of the afternoon's excursion.

We stopped for lunch at a small creek in the shade of a sycamore to eat takeaway tacos purchased in Willcox, Arizona, and took our time before resuming our trek.

"A penny for them," I said, casting a few fronds of grass in his direction to snap him out of a trance. He sat a few feet away, cross-legged like an Indian chief, staring upstream as though waiting for someone in particular to round the bend in the canyon.

"Is it okay if … can *we* be a secret for now?" he asked, without looking around, but it was really only the *we* I heard and remember a sense of surprise at how comfortable I was having such a discussion on what was only our second meeting. In the jaws of that ancient canyon, it occurred to me that *we* hadn't come about as the result of the gradual forces of erosion or the banality of time and familiarity. *We* were the product of something much more explosive.

I kissed his neck and cheek until he turned enough so our lips met.

"Sure," I said, not asking or caring from whom it was he wanted the secret to be kept. Someone else was setting the romantic pace for a change and it felt good.

On the journey home that evening, I switched on his car stereo to hear the voice of a preacher waxing lyrical about the evils of rock music. Baptist Radio South. Mike hastily flicked to his iPhone and Bruce Springsteen's "Born to Run" blared through the speakers.

We didn't see each other again for five nights and, from then on, fell into a pattern of meeting once or twice a week at various times, with Friday afternoons our firmest fixture. We shared a love of the outdoors and I was more than happy to fall into the role of tourist, taking in the sights in a one-hundred-mile radius around Prospero. We walked trails in Elephant Butte, the Gila mountains and stayed overnight in a rustic hotel near Truth or Consequences and stopped in small towns to seek out the best examples of Native American arts and crafts. Some days I would drive and then we usually wound up hanging out for hours in quirky Trip Advisor-recommended rustic Mexican restaurants or picnicking at scenic spots. I love to cook, rustic Italian mostly, but because Mike was reluctant to eat at my house, I would prepare antipasti in advance of our trip and extract surprise offerings one by one from the cooler with the flourish of a magician pulling rabbits from a hat.

About a month after Phoenix, in the teeth of a monsoon downpour, Mike brought me to an outdoor shooting range about ten miles south of Deming. We had to wait in the car for over an hour for the deluge to pass and then, after fees were paid, we settled into our individual bays where he handed me a .22-caliber pistol and gave me a five-minute lesson in how to shoot it.

"Let's see your form, Ariel. That's it. Line her up. Good. Right here, underneath. Now hold steady with nice strong arms. That's a really good position. Now squeeze the trigger.

It's all in the brace and the squeeze."

The kickback felt like a high-voltage shock ascending through my hands up to my shoulder, but adrenalin surged when I hit the outer edge of the circular black-and-white target forty feet away.

"Hey, that's pretty darn good for a soft-hander, Ariel," Mike said. "Thought you said you never shot a gun before."

"My powers of concentration must be coming back. I just pictured a few of the dicks I've crossed paths with on Wall Street pasted up on that board there and willed the bullet in their direction. How many shots do we get? This is as much fun as I've had in years. Could be warming to the NRA's version of the world. Might have to sign up when I get back to San Francisco."

"When do you think that will be?" Mike asked solemnly while showing me how to reload.

"The race in the Mojave is in December, but the rental runs to February so you're stuck with me for a while yet."

"I'd really like to visit there sometime," Mike said, lining up his next shot. "I nearly got the chance four years ago with the Lobos, but a thigh injury ended my plans. What's it like there?"

"The Lobos? That was your college football team, right?"

"Yeah, the University of New Mexico in Albuquerque. I studied psychology there."

"Well, that makes us perfectly compatible. You're aware I'm part basket case, right? Why didn't you end up working in that area? I mean like a therapist or whatever?"

"It's kind of complicated. No one specific reason but, essentially, I love the outdoors and didn't fancy a life of listening to big problems in small offices. My pastor in Silver City advised me toward law enforcement, as did a neighbor who was already pretty senior in the police department. They felt strongly that my calling might be in peacekeeping and, so far, they have been proven right. I love it. The curtain goes up every day and it's a new set of characters with a new set of dramas. Pay's fairly shit, but what's there to spend money on round here anyway?"

"But did you have to move to Prospero or were you posted there?" I asked. "Silver City would be a reasonable commute, right? And there's Deming? Or Lordsburg? It's just, I mean, I get the impression that Prospero is fairly hard core in terms of the influence of the church. Like, I definitely wouldn't see it as the ideal place to enjoy your twenties and thirties."

Mike took his time before replying, wiping and re-wiping the barrel of his gun while he found the words. "It's certainly fair to say that Silver City is much more liberal. I only moved to Prospero permanently twelve months ago and it sure is, well, different, you might say. Easier for work, of course. No commute was a big draw. And it's … I guess the church there has some appeal for me, Ariel. Jesus is a really big part of my life and you could say I have fallen in with the pastor's plan. He had my whole future path mapped out."

He offered this last, rather alarming statement up to me with a smile, a knowing one that suggested he understood exactly how strange this might all sound.

"Had? Until?" I prompt. "I suspect *you and I* are a fairly long ways off that particular path, Mike. Would I be right?"

In our sectioned-off bays, loaded guns pointed down at the black rubber mats and outsized reinforced-plastic welder's goggles for eyes, we had to slightly raise our heads to talk, on account of the headphones wedged under our chins.

"We're certainly well off that track, all right," he said, before replacing his earphones, indicating for me to replace mine, and firing six shots in rapid succession into the central white circle.

I found out more about him in that brief exchange than from all our other meetings. Most of the time I answered his questions about my life, my friends, my interests. The world of high finance, San Francisco's social life, the art world, my family history, my brush with depression. He covered it all forensically and I was predictably flattered by his interest.

All these elements, this accumulation of shared experiences, eventually added up to something called a love affair that led me and Mike, step by step, to that fateful night in the house.

Chapter Nine

DREAMS

The fork stands to attention like a miniature flagstaff, abandoned bolt upright in a congealing clump of half-eaten carbonara. I peer over the rim of my empty glass at Letterhead, who has been trying in vain to engage me in conversation since my return from the police station. Alphabetic conundrums suggest themselves from the far wall, begging to be deciphered, but I cannot think beyond that sketch.

I pour a second glass of Merlot and extinguish all lights with the required ritual. Off, on, off, on, off, before commencing my vigil a little later than usual. Twenty minutes in, car headlights appear in my peripheral vision and come to a halt at the roadside almost exactly at the spot where Mike's jeep disappeared from view ten nights earlier.

Not many cars pass here, day or night. Having started life as little more than a farmland track, the Old County Road was partially upgraded nearly forty years ago to service a second copper mine that failed to get off the ground. Its reincarnation as a secondary highway was completed ten years later with the purpose of connecting the newly resurrected town of Prospero to the main interstate, now the I-10.

But another twelve miles of road was constructed at a later date, connecting the town with the NM146, which meets the I-10 at Exit 49. This convenient spur is used by all the town's residents as it reaches the main highway in less than twenty minutes. The other, ill-conceived stretch on which I live heads southeast at first before looping in a wide 60-mile semicircle to intersect with the I-10 at Exit 67, nine miles west of Deming. Along its entire length, it meets only one other road, the equally isolated State Road 81, which serves a few other recently resurrected towns in the foothills of the Little Hatchet mountain range. Now poorly maintained, the two-way ribbon of asphalt on the border of which Caleb Freeth and I live is like a forgotten tributary, one of the loneliest stretches of road in America.

From time spent watching from my wooden window chair, I have identified the few traffic types. Stray holidaymakers glide westward to take in the last of the wilds of New Mexico before they reach Arizona. Ancient pickups occasionally pass, driven by shifty, bandana-covered heads probably bent on avoiding the eyes of the law. Elephantine agricultural machines trundle up every few days, bouncing and shaking before making a spectacularly sharp left turn, like the swoosh of a fat lady's petticoat, into Caleb Freeth's plant repair yard. Border Patrol SUVs are the most frequent, cruising with a passenger window lowered so outsize binoculars can scan the southern horizon for undocumented immigrants making a final desert dash into the arms of Uncle Sam.

Vehicles at night are extremely rare and this car across the road does not fit into any of the usual categories. I suspect it is either undercover police or a journalist sniffing around, and I tune the lens to get a close-up of my visitor. With the settings fixed on a distant point, it takes a minute to recalibrate and I catch only a fleeting image of a man with dark hair and large, black-rimmed glasses as he completes a three-point turn and drives back toward Prospero. The car is an ancient, pale-colored VW Passat, not exactly standard transport for peacekeepers or journalists.

I retreat to the couch to dodge the rest of the bottle of wine and check my e-mail. The screensaver on my Mac is a bouncing bubble containing the cutest image of my pug, Baxter, who died last year. Its perpetual progress around the screen is there to make me smile but, at this moment, is a reminder of something else I have lost, and it also has a hypnotic effect on my already-tired eyes.

I click on the Gmail icon and 3,026 primary message subject lines, a ten-day backlog, flood the screen in a digital storm. The first is a "sneak-in" from my social network scroll and strikes a note of spectacular irony: *A lot has happened since you last logged in to Facebook.* The bulk of the messages are work-related with a few updates and special offers from clubs and health clinics in San Francisco and renewal notices from Bloomberg News and Deutsche Bank trading.

The first heading to attract my attention is titled *Time Out* and is from my best friend, Sunil. It's dated 11:04 a.m., Saturday, Sept. 17, 2016:

> *A,*
>
> *I know you couldn't talk through the details when we spoke last week but I sensed your shock and devastation and I want you to know that I am here whenever you want to talk. You sounded so hopeless. Why don't you come home for a while? If that's not possible, I would like to come out there to see you, even if only for a day or two.*
>
> *From what I can gather through police channels, it sounds to*

me like you two were simply caught in the wrong place at the wrong time and that the authorities have a good take on the likely suspects. The Mexican angle is particularly unnerving given the kind of drug-related violence over the border.

As I said to you last week I think you are wrong to stay in that house. It could be dangerous and it can't be good for your emotional state. Would you look to at least rent in a town nearby until you can wrap up and come home to grieve among those who love you? If it's about the training you can still go to your Plan B to train near Los Angeles. Lots of desert there too, you know!

Finally, I have spoken to Emer and we are ad idem about this. You need to have someone in your corner if you are acting as a witness. I've heard through legal channels here at the office that Jules Mason (you might remember her from Psych in Stanford) has been working in criminal defense over in Phoenix for eight years and has a huge reputation. I attach her e-card. If you like, I can send her a flagging message before you call her.

I can only imagine what you are going through. The guy I saw laughing and joking with you when we FaceTimed last month was so full of life. It's just incredible to think that he is gone and we could have lost you too. His family must be devastated. Are you in contact with them or is that not possible?

Stay in touch.

Much love,

Sunil

P.S. Flying twenty-four hour visit possible Wed or Thurs. Let me know what works best?

Sunil is a very unconventional human being and the most self-possessed person I have ever known. I first encountered him in Stanford Business School at Prof. Bob Lynsky's monetary economics lecture in the vast amphitheater that is Hall 23B. A ripple of murmurs rolled through the rows behind me and I turned to see hundreds of students craning their necks to look back. There was Sunil, in the last row, farthest from the professor, peering at the projector screen through giant yellow binoculars.

On another occasion, he dressed his six-foot-five frame in a magnificent salmon-pink, brushed-silk dhoti and handed out tiny plastic shot glasses of Indian Old Monk dark rum from a silver tray to passersby in the Main Quad. When people asked what it was all about, he just smiled and asked them to simply *enjoy*. I learned later that evening from my roommate that his nickname around campus was The Lanky Buddha. She heard he was a mathematical genius and a man of few words, a combination that made him seem wiser and more mature than the resident swarm of buttoned-down, thrusting capitalists.

We didn't actually exchange words for another three months after the binoculars incident although we shared the same company at a few art-society parties and made eye contact in the corridors on the way to lectures. It was close to Christmas and I was kicking back in the tiniest of the twelve Starbucks on campus, sipping a three-shot and trying in vain to soak up the facts of a mind-numbing case study about Milton Friedman's dated theories, when Sunil arrived and ordered English breakfast tea and a muffin.

I sat nonplussed as he embarked on a complete rearrangement of the cramped café in order to tuck another chair and himself in at my table. He hadn't asked if that was okay, but that wasn't what struck me as odd. It was the sheer effort he was going to, politely asking several other customers to shift a few inches and sliding a heavy zinc-plated plant stand up against the wall, to the raised eyebrows of staff. Then he pulled the only free chair down the narrow serving runway and folded his long legs neatly under the table before sipping his tea and smiling contentedly at me as though he had arrived home after a long day.

We sat in silence for a while. Not elevator-style silence laden with awkwardness or the heavy-air kind you experience in a library or waiting room. This quietude was like those moments pregnant with anticipation that occur in the dark of a picture theater when the advertisements end and the movie you've come to see is about to begin. I can't explain it, but I knew for all the time we sat at that tiny table that I was on the threshold of something life changing.

"Idiot screwed up the econometrics lecture yesterday. He doesn't understand the stuff," Sunil threw out eventually, as though carrying on from an earlier conversation.

"I'm Ariel," I replied, with an outstretched hand and a nod of agreement.

After a passionate few weeks of missing lectures and sneaking around campus, we moved in together and remained lovers for four years until our affair melted a year out of college in the heat of career-building and self-discovery. But we have been soul mates now for fourteen years and I cannot see how this will ever change.

Another subject line from Saturday morning reads: *Please call me … No. 6!!!* It is from my mother and was sent before I picked up her call yesterday evening.

11:46 a.m. Saturday, Sept. 17, 2016

Ariel,

Just watched another news bulletin about the investigation there. Have you met with the FBI?

Are you still on those painkillers I gave you? (I meant to tell you they have a detrimental effect on the intestinal lining if you don't have a regular eating pattern, so I have posted you an alternative Rx to substitute if the pain is still bothering you).

Níl aon tinteán mar do thinteán féin. (Look it up.)

Love you,

Emer xx

P.S. Alcohol is contraindicated with those sleeping tabs!

My fondness for the grape began in my mid-twenties, right before I made the move to New York and around the time I dated Joseph Peel, the only child of a vineyard owner from Sonoma County. Up to that point, I had been a teetotaler, scared off alcohol by years of dire warnings from my mother, who always seemed more Scottish Puritan to me than Irish Catholic. I was never one hundred percent sure why she was so trenchantly opposed to it as she never used emotive stories of personal experience to underpin her arguments. As a nurse, she liked to anchor her case on health implications and case histories of lives sundered on the rocks of booze.

However, I did hear one story from her sister, Mary, over on a visit to San Francisco to mark the occasion of my eighteenth birthday, which hinted at the possibility that there might be other reasons for her depth of antipathy toward the demon drink. It related to my estranged father, Nicolas Mignolet, with whom I have had no contact since I was twenty months old, when my mother took me to America's East Coast, leaving Australia and my father behind, never to return. He is of Franco-Belgian heritage and was then an officer in the Royal Australian Air Force, based near Brisbane. Apart from a few slightly-out-of-focus photographs of him posing in full uniform, that is the sum of all my knowledge, except that he possessed, as my mother put it, a dark side.

I have never been that curious about my father, having

always felt that my mother was more than enough in terms of parental input and that seeking him out might be somehow disloyal to her. However, based on my dismal track record in relationships, Sunil has constructed a theory that his absence has left me, subconsciously at least, in search of a secure, paternalistic figure in all my relationships. His pop-psychology logic further posits that my lack of knowledge or interest either in my father or in trying to understand what it means to be a good father leaves me in the hopeless position of seeking something I can never hope to find.

In any case, it is unlikely to have been in response to a question from me that my Aunt Mary divulged that my mother had returned from work one evening to find Nicolas passed out drunk on the living room floor and no sign of me in the house. Apparently I had toddled my way out the porch door, down and then across Brisbane's main highway, only to be found sitting in a roadside field with a mouthful of dirt and a fistful of dandelions by a concerned passerby. Mary told me how my mother had always felt it was utterly ironic that the motto of the Australian RAF is *Vigilance*.

It was three months later that we flew to America. I chose never to discuss my knowledge of the incident with my mother although I came close on several occasions. She is a woman of great emotional intelligence, fun and kindness, but she is also the most intensely private person I have ever known. She must have had very good reasons to leave, and perhaps the story I heard was the least of them.

Bouncing Baxter is back on the laptop screen and my eyes yield to his mesmerizing movement. Because I am sitting upright, sleep doesn't swallow me whole and I drift deliciously in and out of wakefulness like a groggy sailor on watch. There are dreams here rather than nightmares.

Temporary respite. A kaleidoscope of images waft like visual perfume between intermittent snore snorts that jolt me awake again.

As I have been taking sleeping pills since the night before Mike's funeral, all sleep since then has been dreamless. For many months, I had been using my dreams to gauge how well I was doing. Some mornings I would wallow in their wake, delay getting out of bed to recall as much as I could of their twists and turns and delight in any identifiable connections to the happenings of the previous few days. After the protracted torture of the inferno, their sheer banality acted as a reminder of how far I had progressed from the interminable pit that the great-fire nightmare cast me into.

Ms. Paloma Weiss rescued me from that pit after a succession of fruitless conventional treatments led me to the point of extreme disillusionment. After the skiing incident, I looked for a fresh approach to the problem with renewed urgency and a somewhat broader mind.

It wouldn't be correct to describe Ms. Weiss in terms such as medical practitioner. In the referral I received from an old college friend, she was hailed as a dream expert—an occupation, I suspect, that has scant grounding in evidence-based science.

A flashing red dot on Google Maps led me through a warren of back streets to her offices in the corner of a converted warehouse near the pier district. As I rang the bell, I shivered slightly with the unsettling thought that this unorthodox sidecar hanging off the great American medical juggernaut might be my last chance to arrest the decline in my mental wellbeing.

Ben had put it more bluntly. He told me flat out I must

actually already be fully blown crazy to be seeking help from, as he put it in his inimitably unvarnished way, "a monster fucking loony quack." But at this point, I had already been through the hands of two eminent psychiatrists, one sleep consultant and a fistful of psychotherapeutic snake-oil salesmen, and their pronouncements about needing to resolve deep-seated childhood issues before each, in turn, prescribed courses of thirty sessions or thirty pills to resolve them. I had seen almost no improvement up to that point apart from moderately better pre-dream sleep quality, having taken advice to cut down drastically on my caffeine and alcohol intake. But all the while, the nightmare persisted and the exhaustion, the "lowness," the panic attacks and the compulsive behaviors continued. If I could just put out the flames, I thought.

The small square nameplate next to the bell read: PALOMA V. WEISS, DREAM EXPERT AND LI E COACH. Some joker had erased the *f* and the fact that Ms. Weiss hadn't felt the need to replace it reinforced my somewhat jaundiced view about the quality of the service. I didn't have long to wait before the door swung open to reveal a skinny middle-aged man covered head to toe in wet blue paint. He was naked apart from a skimpy swimsuit that was primarily blue with the odd fleck of orange and yellow, suggesting it had experienced many a previous dousing on their colorful host. His lower half was slightly darker where gravity had taken the drips. Both feet were covered in plastic bags tied at the ankle with elastic, I assumed to protect the floor.

"That eez my ten o'clock, Daniel," came a heavily accented Eastern European woman's voice from down the narrow corridor. "You better be wearing bags or I keel you."

I felt the urge to turn and run.

"Hi there," said Blue Daniel with a warm smile. "I'd shake your hand but, well, as you can see." He held his two azure palms aloft like a magician might before a trick. "She's just down there at the end." He nodded rather than pointed, to reduce drip damage. "Straight ahead past the plastic flowers. Don't worry. Her bark is much worse than her bite," he whispered with a conspiratorial smile.

I edged past him down the dark walkway and found Ms. Weiss standing near her desk with outstretched hand in a large room dotted with filing cabinets and book shelves and all the other accoutrements of an office on one side but a pile of what appeared to be old theatrical props resting on the other. Two frosted windows, so opaque and covered in dust they filtered all the yellow out of the sunlight, gave the room a bluish Dickensian haze. An architrave to the right of her desk was missing its door, but the space was filled with a makeshift, red-velvet curtain that was not fully drawn, and I could see that the adjoining warehouse space was an airy artist's studio where Blue Daniel was writhing around on a giant white canvas.

"You are Ariel Mignolet?" she asked to confirm, briefly shaking my hand before moving to pull the curtain fully across, taking her seat and gesturing for me to sit opposite her.

"Now, my friend, what have you heard about me?" Her tone was no-nonsense authoritative like a Jewish grandmother handing down cast-iron nuggets of wisdom. Her accent was caricature Russian, like a James Bond villain.

"I understand you are an expert on dreams," I replied, trying hard to erase any trace of cynicism from my voice. "I have a seemingly intractable problem with an unwanted nightmare and it's literally driving me insane. Every night I dream that my apartment is being consumed by fire; I wake and can't return to sleep. The lack of sleep and the sense of unease have brought on panic attacks, suicidal ideation and obsessive-compulsive ..."

"Okay, okay, yes, okay. I understand, I understand," she interjected, quieting me with a casual flick of her hand, before leaning all the way back in her voluminous beige pleather La-Z-Boy and gazing at the ceiling with her fingers arched and pressed to pursed lips as though in prayer. Silence followed and as it grew, Ben's "monster fucking loony quack" description floated ominously into my mind. What felt like minutes later and from an almost horizontal position, she began her diagnosis.

"You have heard of the Renaissance, yes? Late Middle Ages? Europe?" Her prompts were accompanied by an impatient clicking of her fingers.

"Sure. Sixteenth century," I replied, my skepticism growing with each passing second.

"Yes. It means rebirth, my friend." She fell silent again for a few moments before clearing her throat for the next installment. "Of course, I can tell that you have no significant other in your life." It was a statement rather than a question, but I gave it an answer anyway.

"You're correct," I said and wondered now how much my college friend had told Paloma Weiss.

"Essentially, you must have been so focused on one area of your life for so long to the detriment of your physical and spiritual wellbeing that your psyche is in meltdown. You need to be reborn, to self-actualize in some other area apart from work. Only then will the right-hand side of your brain be healed." With that, Ms. Weiss catapulted her chair back to the upright position and leaned across the desk, giving me a close-up of her heavily bronzed face, vermillion lipstick and wild black hair streaked badger-like with a shock of gray at each temple. "What I mean to tell you, my friend, is that you are in desperate need of a hobby, a passion." She imbued the word *passion* with the tone of a sophisticated Italian lover.

Her conclusion was so unexpected that a second silence followed between us as I tried on a few responses for size, several laced with sarcasm. "I have a hobby," I told her. "I collect art. My home is full of inspirational pieces, sculpture mostly."

Paloma leaned back in her chair and digested my response slowly like a chef tasting a new batch of stock. "Art. Ah, yes. Art is the great elixir. It is the ultimate food for the soul because it lets us tune in to our inner emotional selves. Take Daniel in there," she said, nodding toward the curtain. "Happy as a pig in sheet, that man is."

Her words were so accented and movements so dramatic, I felt at times I was watching a performance from the front row of an intimate theater in Moscow.

"Always rolling around in there. Sometimes in spasms like a man possessed, rolling around, twisting and writhing day and night on the floor and he ...," she paused for effect, "... he is the happiest son of a beetch you or I will ever meet. Yes, of course, yes, you could indeed do with some of art's healing powers, my friend. So tell me now, quickly, how you find it. This art. This wonderful art that sings to your soul?"

By now I had abandoned any notion that Paloma Weiss was going to be of help to me but I was inquisitive enough to want to know where this strand of the discussion was going.

"Well, I get catalogs sent to my workplace, by gallery owners mostly, along with invites to openings of exhibitions that they think I might like. These folks are my eyes and ears because they know what I have purchased in the past and when they come across more of the same, they call me. It's, well, it works for me because I don't have the time to browse the length and breadth of the country."

Across the desk, the dream expert and li e coach shot me a knowing look. Her body language: shoulders shrugged, palms up and a frown like a Mafia boss pleading innocence, screamed, *There you are. I told you so!*

"But surely you can see it!" she exclaimed. "You must see that you do not collect art at all, my friend. No, it is *you* who has been collected."

In case I had any doubts about who *you* was, a shiny half-inch nail coated in red lacquer attached to an arthritic-looking index finger was pointed directly at me.

"Those people have taken you into their collection, Ariel. So no, no, no, that's not what I am talking about at all. You must take this seriously. You must take the time to find something, preferably involving taxing physical or creative exertion, that can act as real ballast. Right now, the left side of your brain is so overactive, it is exhausted and the right side of your brain is like a wasteland, a drowning sailor screaming for help. Some people can coast through their entire lives like this and it is no problem for them. Others …" she flicks the word at me like a cigarette butt, "others are eventually tortured by their own mind until they change. They may have ignored many smaller signals along the way as they forge one path for years, but inevitably they reach the point where they must be reborn just to survive."

Prescription delivered, her demeanor softened and she deigned a smile.

"Ariel Mignolet. Ariel Mignolet. I must say, I do like your name. How do you pronounce it?"

"Min-yo-lay," I replied.

"I like it. It's lyrical. Like a name for a Christmas doll or a little piano concerto or something like this. Anyway that is all the help I can give you, my friend. My advice is simple. Go and find a new challenge. See it as an opportunity, if you like, but I tell you that if you do not do this, you will struggle and the fears and anxieties will grow. I have seen this case many times before and there is no magic cure."

"I'm thirty-four," I blurted out, my tone loitering precariously between a statement and a plea. "Not exactly mid-life. Why is this happening at such a young age?"

She didn't skip a beat furnishing me with an answer. "It is not the distance you have come, my friend, but the speed at which you have traveled. An alarm is ringing within the deepest part of your subconscious and no amount of talking or medication or even time itself will quell it. Here's my card. Call me any time if you need more help, but whatever else you do, Ariel Mignolet, make sure you change things. Soon."

The following week, I attended a charity luncheon in the Mandarin Oriental on Sansome. The guest speaker was Rachel Chamberlain, one of America's greatest female ultra-marathon runners. Her topic was Training for Mental Toughness with the idea being that a room of financial types could draw on some of the tricks used in sports psychology to think clearly under extreme and protracted stress.

Rachel Chamberlain was diagnosed with multiple sclerosis at age twenty-eight, and her running career began two years later with a spectacular time of 3:35 in her debut fifty-kilometer race, an astonishing average per mile of less than seven minutes, which almost matched the 1979 world record set by one of the sport's legends, Sandra Kiddy.

Radiating charm and basking in the glow of a very well-received podium speech, Rachel joined my table as part of a choreographed whistle-stop tour of the banquet hall. She chatted modestly, mostly responding to quick-fire, fact-finding questions typical of hedge fund types. I asked her what she used to get over the mythical "runner's wall" and she told us about a few key cerebral mantras to reboot resolve when the going got grueling on some of the super-long distances. She also spoke at length about the semi-spiritual "runner's high" and the peace her hobby, and then career, had brought about in her own life.

The day after the fundraiser, I bought the autobiography of Scott Jurek, the legendary ultra-runner and seven-times winner of the famous Western States hundred-miler. Jurek tells how those who get bitten by the ultra bug fully understand the feelings of that high, how rarely it occurs, and the pain they will have to endure to grab it back again. When I finished the chapter about chasing *the zone*, in which he describes the instant when we think we can't go on but do and then reap the rewards with pain-free, exhilarating mileage, I was hooked.

That night, the dream came as usual, but the ending had changed. Instead of the inferno engulfing the walls of my bedroom, preventing all avenues of escape, the point in the nightmare at which I usually woke in a state of terror, a gap materialized in the heart of the raging flames and I ran, escaping unscathed onto the hill. My own subconscious seemed to be signposting a path back to sanity. I allowed myself to imagine an alternative life, a chunk of time filled with new purpose, free of the demands of work that had essentially consumed every waking hour for over thirteen years.

Up to that point, I had never run farther than three miles on a treadmill and once around Union Square in a fundraiser. But I have always been attracted to extremes. So the notion of extreme distances in extreme isolation presented a heady cocktail. I resolved to reach the spiritual place Ms. Chamberlain and Mr. Jurek had spoken of and spent the next few weeks researching my options.

Engaging a rather arbitrary process of selection based on a generous allowance of ten months to train, I resolved to attempt the Over the Hill Track Club High Desert Ultra fifty-kilometer race in Ridgecrest, California, in early December, meaning my preparation needed to begin in February. I had also done some follow-up research about the need for balance between the left side and right side of the brain and, although I remained a skeptic, I decided to make some effort to flex my deep-sleeping inner creative by practicing sketching with my left hand. I took a night class to improve my abilities beyond doodles and stick people, invested in an industrial pallet of velum art sheets and devised a plan to sketch a chosen scene with my left hand every day of my exile.

That week I spent an hour each morning researching my base. It would have to be scenic and have weather comparable with that I would encounter in the Mojave Desert. Remote was preferable and certainly as physically removed as possible from the ever-present nightmare.

Almost by accident, I settled on New Mexico when the first page of a broad search for properties in the Southern states of the US threw up a picture of an ultra-modern, architecturally interesting glass-and-concrete house that came very close to the ideal picture of stylish seclusion in the bosom of nature. When I delved deeper into its remote location and the description of the Chihuahuan Desert, the southern monsoons and the vast lonely expanses, I was sold.

Late September, two months after my encounters with Ms. Chamberlain and Ms. Weiss and five months after the fire dream first ignited, I announced my plan to take a ten-month career break to a hailstorm of protest from my business partner, which eventually softened to reluctant resignation and a hundred-dollar bet that my February departure date would be bookended with a March return.

Thirteen years surrounded by six screens of tiny flashing numbers and blinking graphs. Thirteen years of serious shit going down, raucous laughter rising punctuated with sewer-mouth outbursts. Thirteen years of five a.m. starts and sweaty palms leading to panicky cliffhangers, huge emotional upswells and low tides. Thirteen years, twenty million dollars and a string of failed relationships. Thirteen years and one newly minted plan for temporary release.

The front-door buzzer reverberates impolitely through the silent house, bringing an alarming end to my doze. Press attention has mercifully waned in recent days, so what was, in the middle of last week, a pack stationed semi-permanently outside has now dwindled to the odd stray hound sniffing for scraps. After no callers yesterday, I had begun to hope that I might be delivered back to the glorious solitude I had enjoyed on the Old County Road.

Down the stairs, I open the front door to find a lone female journalist, whose face I recognize as one of the regulars from last week, standing in the teeth of a steady southerly breeze under the glow of my security lantern. A copy of her mother ship's latest *Gazette* shields her eyes from wind-borne sand. Flashing the briefest of brief smiles, she skips over the other pleasantries you might normally employ when springing a surprise visit on a near stranger in the dark of night.

"Hi there, sorry to disturb you, but can I, like, pick up on something you said last week in response to questions?" Her recording device magically appears inches from my face and the sense of being a living mine to be hollowed out resurfaces.

"I'm sorry. Didn't catch your name," I say pointedly, peering over her shoulder to see if her car is the one I saw earlier, but the vehicle parked in the gateway is small, dark and sleek.

"Oh yeah. Apologies. Maria Stenson from the *Tucson Gazette*. We spoke ... or ... you answered some of my questions last week out at your front gate there? After your statement?"

The subtlest rise in her voice and a momentary pause to see any flicker of recognition lets me know this is a question, but she quickly draws from my expression that I am not in any way interested in reconnecting. Her words gush forth like a teenager recounting a story to friends. "So, like, I was trying to get to the bottom of why it took so long for the police to drop their investigation into you and start searching for the real perpetrators? I'm sure you've heard the rumors? Theories about some cult and so on? Anyway, I think it's strange that it, like, took them nearly forty-eight hours to switch their focus. That seems incredible to me, given all the evidence at the scene. Sorry ... that's ... that's also from a good source. So I just wanted to, like, come back to that point with one or two follow-ups if it's okay? Think you can help me?"

She affords me another meatless-bone smile and edges closer, her right hand still shielding her face. She is clearly angling for an invitation to stand in out of the breeze, but I don't retreat one fraction of an inch and the gap between us closes to much less than standard personal space. So close I can see the riot of pale brown freckles on her cheeks beneath a light dusting of makeup. She is a petite, rather dainty young woman, more like a museum guide than a hard-nosed reporter, and doesn't at any stage of our conversation appear anything other than nervous and out of her comfort zone.

"Surely, you should be talking to the police about why it took them so long?" I reply, every fiber of my being straining to disguise my nerves. "I wouldn't mind having a better idea myself. Look, I don't want to be rude here. I said it last week to everyone and if you were there, as you say, you will have heard it, too. I am no longer a suspect and am not going to speak to anyone in the media again, either formally or informally, about Officer Argyll's murder. I have been so advised by lawyers and police. Now if you would excuse me, I am really busy right now."

"Okay, sure," she responds, but I can tell she's not finished. "I hear you. It's just that I heard from another source that you might have had a closer personal relationship with Mike Argyll than people have been led to believe and I was thinking that made sense. Like, it might explain why they were so convinced, in the immediate aftermath, that you had a role in his killing. Could you confirm the status of your relationship with the officer?"

"I'm sorry," I tell her, and hope the burning sensation I feel in my head is not the rise of a blush. "I have nothing further to add to what I said in my statement last week, so please don't call here again. You're wasting time. You should be talking to those investigating the case."

As I close the door against her nose, I hear her through the door, clinging on hopelessly to our conversation.

"So are you denying you had a close personal relationship with the officer?"

Back upstairs, I drink the rest of the Merlot and type

my reply to Sunil, slowly, on account of the tremor in my hands.

Re: *Proposed visit*

Sunil,

Please come Wednesday. Wednesday would be really good.

Love, Ariel

Chapter Ten

DICK'S HATBAND

I wake just after dawn, dehydrated and with spasms of pain needling behind my right eye. Pinching the top of my nose between thumb and forefinger, I drain what's left of my glass of water on the bedside table and brace myself for the dazzling belt of sunlight before pulling the cord to open the blinds and bringing to life the floating fractions of dust and fibers swirling around the bedroom. As I fish around in the kitchen drawers for a bottle of Advil, my phone alarm sounds from the en suite. The shocking blare of an air raid ringtone tells me I have thirty-five minutes to get to Prospero for this morning's meeting with FBI agent Paul Pitcavage.

At the station, I am directed to Meeting Room Three, a small featureless office at the end of the first-floor corridor, sparsely furnished and lit with six three-foot fluorescent bulbs lying in parallel pairs overhead. The atmosphere is oppressive, like a bunker or prison cell, with the only natural source of light struggling to reach us under half-drawn blinds in a narrow window near the ceiling.

When I enter, Marge Newlands is already seated and she gestures silently for me to take a seat at the oval table in the center of the room, as far away from her as the ten feet of polished resin will allow. After our emotionally charged previous day's encounter, a few minutes of awkward silence follow before the triangular conference phone in the center of the table rings and the sergeant picks up the handset.

"He's here. Yes. Later? Okay. Yes, what time? Yes, that would be perfect."

She hangs up, returns the receiver to its cradle and we revert to weighty silence.

My mind wanders to the comfort of the familiar. It would have been around this time last year that I sat alongside Ben in our conference room to meet with the CEO of a French building materials company whose progress we were tracking closely. One year post-startup Ben and I had contracted a master cabinet maker to craft an enormous boardroom table out of American oak in the shape of an aircraft wing, a design we felt suitably represented our plans to soar to success. As I mull over the contrasts of my life then and now, Agent Pitcavage enters the room in an awkward sideways shuffle, struggling to keep the contents of a Styrofoam cup from spilling while maintaining his underarm grip on an iPad and a batch of files. He closes the door behind him with his foot.

"Bit gloomy in here," Pitcavage remarks and uses his elbow to hit the only switch on the panel still in the off position.

Fluorescent lights five and six flicker to life overhead, a faint hum accompanying their effort. The sound of the switch—that sharp click to *on*—sends a sting of perspiration coursing down my brow and a hollow opens somewhere in the pit of my stomach to accommodate the churn of anxiety. Agent Pitcavage sets everything down across from me, nods to Marge Newlands and stretches his hand across the table.

"Mr. Ariel R. Mignolet, I am real pleased to make your acquaintance, sir," he says affably and his eyes hold my gaze while he shakes my hand firmly like an old friend. "I want you to know that we really appreciate you coming in to help us all out and to give you my sincerest apologies for missing yesterday's meeting. Just couldn't be helped, I'm afraid. Turns out I had to meet with some senior folks in El Paso. A load of bureaucratic nonsense, really. New guidelines from the experts at the Department of Homeland Security or something. Anyway, I'll fill you in on all that later." He maintains his hearty grip as he talks, like a priest comforting a bereaved widow. "It's unfortunate to be meeting you under such terrible circumstances. I believe you had become good friends with young Officer Argyll and I can tell you, surely, he will be badly missed all round. Wonderful young man. Really bright future ahead of him from what I can gather. How's your head healing, by the way?"

He leans forward to look at the side of my head, squinting slightly like a surgeon inspecting his handiwork. "I'm sure this whole experience has been very traumatic. A shocking case, right enough."

His accent is cast-iron Southern, possibly Georgia, his voice deep with the resonance of a Hollywood voiceover artist. Whether his introduction, richly laced with Southern molasses charm, is sincere or "just blarney," as my mother might say, I am not sure, but it is certainly welcome after all the brusqueness I have met with to date in this building.

On first take, dark-suited Agent Pitcavage is the personification of every clichéd depiction of a federal agent, apart from the quality of his accessories—a silk Hermès tie, a Swiss chronometer, and subtly beveled gold cuff links, all of which, I suspect, are leagues above standard issue. He is tall and broad with a tanned, close-shaven head and serious, steel-rimmed glasses, and when he takes off his jacket, the ironed-in creases along the sleeves of his freshly starched white shirt protrude stiffly either side of him like skiff sails in a strong breeze.

My eyes drift nervously over and back from the switch on the wall. "Thanks," I say distractedly while he takes a seat, sets out his notes in front of him and perches an iPad on a roll-up stand.

"Is it possible for us all to get a jug of water in here?" he asks no one in particular. "Air conditioning's not up to scratch in this heat and, if you don't mind me saying so, Mr. Mignolet, you look like you could do with some water right now. You feelin' okay?" He turns to Marge Newlands to let her know the request for refreshments is aimed squarely at her. "Should we all call down or something, Sergeant?" he inquires vaguely. I suspect it is only out of politeness as I would be surprised if there were such a thing as tea ladies you can "call down to" in Prospero Police Station.

The sergeant, who has been feigning interest in a file on the table in front of her, looks incredulously at the agent for enough time to let him know she isn't impressed and then slinks quietly out the door.

"I'm fine. Really. I'm okay," I say, but my clammy pallor and labored breathing, a struggle now to control, suggest otherwise. "I might use the restroom," I say, retreating unsteadily as though reeling from some invisible blow. "It's this whole situation. It's ... well ... alien ... I need a minute. Gimme the Chicago pits in a pork belly shortage any day." I force a smile in the hope humor might disguise my distress.

I grip the door handle in my hand while, inches away, the wall switch taunts me like a cruel jester. The torment is all-consuming. It chews on something internal and my bowel signals a sudden and barely controllable urge to void. The importance of the ritual is again superseding the importance of secrecy. Oh, the weakness of being its slave. I stand motionless with the fingers of my left hand poised.

"Is everything okay, Mr. Mignolet?" Pitcavage asks, looking perturbed.

Still in the doorway, I summon Dr. Carter's words, offered up thirteen months ago during an intensive cognitive therapy "top-up" program. "The only way to deal with fear is to go with it, Ariel. Treat the storm of thoughts as unwelcome visitors. Recognize them, but feel no obligation to give them the time of day. Separate them from yourself." Nope. That is no defense for me here, at this moment. I reach the last few inches and flick the switch off. Then on. Off, on, off and, finally, on. With all potential consequences averted, the relief is like removing a pair of tight and unbearably painful new shoes. After the initial *off* command, the lights couldn't keep up with the flurry of signals and only buzz noisily back to full illumination as I depart the room, leaving a perplexed Agent Pitcavage staring in my wake.

Back from her water mission, Sergeant Newlands looks pointedly at her watch when I retake my seat. "We will run over our allocated time for this section of the meeting if we don't start covering ground quickly," she says with a distinctly clipped edge to her voice.

"You're exactly right, Sergeant, exactly right," the agent replies. "Are you all set now, Mr. Mignolet? Manage to catch your breath out there?"

"I'm fine now, thanks. Ready to go," I say, thankful he has made the decision not to ask about my strange behavior.

"Before we begin, may I inquire about your middle name? Rónán. A most unusual name. At least, I can tell you surely, it's not common back in Atlanta—or Quantico, for that matter. Never come across it. Pardon me, shall I pour you a glass?" He holds the water jug aloft over a paper cup in the middle of the table.

"Sorry. Yes. Yes, please. It's an Irish name. It means *little seal*. Came out of a Celtic legend."

"Rónán. Indeed. Why, I'd be most obliged if you would tell us the story, sir?" He pours now for the sergeant and relaxes back into his chair. "Can you recall it?"

"Sure, I think so anyway," I say as Marge Newlands sighs loudly and taps the table with a rigid index finger.

"Legend has it that a mother seal, curious about life on land, swam perilously close to the beach until a giant wave washed her ashore where she took human form and married. She bore a fisherman children, 'little seals,' which translates in the Irish language as rónán, but eventually the call of the sea became too much and she found a seal skin and slipped back into the ocean. She never forgot her children and legend has it she swims close to the shores of the west coast of Ireland to keep an eye on them."

The sergeant's tapping stops midway through the story I have used as chat-up fodder in some of San Francisco's finest gay establishments.

"Irish names are so lyrical," says the agent. "My next-door neighbor is second-generation Irish. Galway City, I believe. Has a daughter named *S A D H B H*." He spells it out letter by letter.

"Sergeant Newlands. Would you believe me now if I told

you that that name, as I just spelled it, is pronounced as *S I V E*, with the *I* like *eye*. Sive. Ha! It took me a year to remember how to spell it correctly. Just not natural, Sergeant, is it?" he chortles. "Well, with all this preamble, I haven't formally introduced *myself* to you yet, sir. I am Agent Paul Pitcavage and the story behind my first name is very straightforward in comparison to yours. I believe Paul is derived from the Latin word for small or humble and, while I know I'm not the former, I hope you will find that I am definitely the latter. I work for the Federal Bureau of Investigation and we, that is myself and three of my colleagues from the Bureau, are here in Prospero to help the fine local force here bring the perpetrators of these murders to justice.

"Now, for the purposes of this meeting, I want you to set aside all the macho stuff you've seen on TV about FBI agents. Put that right out of your mind because that's not what I am about, sir. As I see it, I am here to do a job for Mike's family, his colleagues, for the local community and the federal government, and I will be nothing but professional in that endeavor. I will give respect wherever I am shown it and I don't see any need for unnecessary unpleasantness. So, on that basis, let us all get down to business here, shall we?

"Oh yes, almost forgot. I am obliged to tell you that all information revealed during the course of this meeting is highly confidential and may not be discussed with any third party aside from your personal legal representative. Our conversation will be recorded for all the time that I remain in the room. This is all standard practice, really, for official FBI investigative interviews. Hope you don't mind?"

"No problem," I reply with a Gallic shrug.

"Great. Now the sergeant here has furnished me with

all your statements since your first interview with Prospero police officers the morning Mike's body was recovered and she kindly spent the time yesterday filling in some of the gaps that jumped out on first reading. I just want to zone in on a few particular items in this discussion and then, once that's completed, we will be joined by others to help us fill in the picture further. You see, Mr. Mignolet, all this is now preparatory work. Groundwork, if you like, before we take the suspects on head to head and I can assure you that our plan is for that to happen real soon."

With these words, the agent has my full attention.

"First of all," Agent Pitcavage continues, "I'd like to hear a bit more about the sequence of events around seeing the lights on the evening Mike was murdered. In addition, I would be most obliged if you could tell me all you can remember about things that stood out about the group's appearance and anything you might have heard them say from the moment you first encountered … ehm … how many did you say there were?" He flicks quickly through his notes looking for the datapoint. "Ah, yes. Here. At least ten, you said. Anyway, that was your best guess. Now, I know you gave most of this evidence already and I am sure you must be tired of repeatedly going over the same territory. I do also fully appreciate that this whole experience will have been hugely traumatic for you. But, for me, there is nothing quite like hearing certain facts directly from the horse's mouth, so to speak, so I just need a last bit of forbearance on your part, if possible. So could we perhaps kick off with your first sighting of the fire torches the evening of September ninth?" The agent nods to me and he and the sergeant settle back into their seats.

Over to me. It's finally my turn. To speak to someone.

Someone who might really listen. Someone who will act. "It's, well, you are right in saying it has all been unbelievable, sir. Truly unbelievable. That night, they were … primitive, you know? And, I guess, so young, for one thing. That's one fact I haven't heard much discussion about, actually. These people were no more than teenagers. Yet the violence? It was savage. Like ISIS executioners or something, only a mile from my house. And I don't mind telling you I *am* finding it hard, sir. Hard to take in. Hard to … to recover ground, if that makes sense?"

A reminder alarm sounds on the agent's iPad and he scrambles to turn it off and switch the setting to mute. "Sincere apologies, Mr. Mignolet. Please do go on. Take your time."

"As I said to Sergeant Newlands yesterday, my plan is to stick around until I see these psychopaths taken into custody. All help I can give to that end, I am really glad to give and I'm more than happy to run through any details with you here today but, before I do, I have to be honest with you in saying that, based on what I have seen and experienced of this investigation to date here in Prospero, I have truly lost faith in its … I mean I have lost faith in the ability of the people I have come across here to manage this case. I'm no expert, but it doesn't take Sherlock Holmes to conclude that there has been a distinct lack of urgency and professionalism by the sergeant and her team since the morning of the tenth. I sincerely hope that this hasn't damaged your prospects of bringing the guilty parties to justice.

"For instance, you'll know from my file there, sir, that three of the four most senior investigating officers, including the sergeant here, detained me, under arrest, in this very building for over a day and a half. Forty hours of questions while the trail of the perpetrators cooled in the sand. A monumental waste of time. Precious time. I told them over and over they should have been out tracking those responsible. They were traveling on foot, for Christ's sake, they …"

After several indignant harrumphs, the sergeant interjects. "Mr. Mignolet, you are being incredibly disingenuous and, frankly, it is you who are now wasting the good agent's time with this tirade. I am under no obligation to explain our *modus operandi* to you. But I can say, with the utmost confidence, that the file will show we acted professionally at every stage in this investigation and, as I know you are aware, no other person acting in an official capacity in this matter has a greater incentive than I to see Mike's murderers brought to justice. How dare you suggest we have been dragging our feet. May I remind you that you were the last person to see Mike alive and, given the remoteness of the area and the highly unusual circumstances of his death, you can understand why we would have had initial suspicions surrounding your culpability."

"My culpability?" I reply, now directing my comments solely at Agent Pitcavage, who has adopted the demeanor of a benevolent referee torn between red carding one or other of his two favorite players. "A six-year-old child could have joined the dots. I mean how was I, a fucking number cruncher from California, supposed to have murdered three people with my bare hands, smashed up a jeep while taking the trouble to run around in the pitch dark making thousands of footprints? No. Sorry. No, it doesn't wash, Sergeant. Fine, detain me for questioning to aid your investigation but … did you know that these morons escorted me out of a hospital and dragged me into this building? Like a common criminal? And all in the full glare of the media? This was despite the fact that, as we now know, they had already identified weapons and one fire torch at the scene with prints other than mine. Forty fucking hours, sir.

"Pardon my language, but I had to sit there with fresh staples in my head, fielding questions from four goons while operating on no sleep and having just survived a vicious attack on my life. Forty goddamn hours despite there being a perfectly preserved crime scene out there that exactly matched my version of events. I was the public's prime suspect, Agent Pitcavage. I was treated as the triple murderer while the dozen crazies loped off at their leisure back to where the fuck knows.

"And then," I continue, drawing on a deep well of anger, "when they were finished with me, I was cast off to the wolves without help or apology. You know the pack, Sergeant?"

I turn toward the sergeant, whose eyes burn with disdain. "By first name in most cases, I'd say. Those guys who camped outside my door? That same crowd who have been feting and photographing you during all your big moments this past week?

"Are you aware that they are still pestering me? Someone here keeps throwing them meaty morsels, Agent Pitcavage. Details from the case file seem to keep seeping out into the ether and then they come to me for comments, flying their cheap little kites on my doorstep. If it hadn't been for the fact that my work colleagues hired a PR firm to help me weather this shit storm, I would have lost my good name here in Prospero as well as nearly losing my life. And then, to add to all that, I read that some TV station sent a helicopter out over the desert yesterday looking for the culprits. Mexicans, Islamic terrorists, cult crazies, whoever's scent they pick up first. Shouldn't there be a lockdown on that kind of thing or something? Have any of you considered that they might scare them off, make them harder to find?

"So you see, before we begin here, I need a commitment that you will become my only point person on this case and that all influence will be brought to bear to call off the press. A directive or something, I dunno. Call them all up. Whatever it takes. All my requests to the folks here in the station have fallen on deaf ears." I know my complaint has long since become a rambling rant, a barrage of words across the table where the two officers sit with their hands, metaphorically speaking, firmly in the air.

"Sorry," I say, my voice receding now, having got so much off my chest. "I have a lot of … *yes,* of course I want to help, but I need you to appreciate where I am coming from here. The past eleven days have been a journey to hell and back, made worse by the clear incompetence of this policing farce."

Agent Pitcavage physically collects himself up, as much as the cheap galvanized steel and padded-felt chair will allow, and attempts to draw the sting from the conversation, speaking with the confident voice of experience and authority. "Look, I totally understand where you are coming from, sir. Your suffering is clear. But as I have made clear, from this moment on, you can rest assured that all the agencies of this state and, indeed, the federal government are bringing their collective assets and expertise to bear on this case and I am hopeful, confident in fact, that within a matter of days, we will corral the guilty parties and bring them to justice." He leans forward and taps the table with his index finger in a gesture of sincerity. The gold-and-ruby signet ring cinching his small finger like a tiny corset glints in the stray beams of light filtering through the blinds, quivering on the far wall of the room like the eye of a laser pen.

"It may not be apparent to you so far, Mr. Mignolet, but I can assure you there is a team of highly trained individuals working on these murders since the moment Mike Argyll and the other two victims were found. In fact, sir, I am now in a position to reveal to you, in a highly confidential capacity, of course, that this case actually stretches a good deal further back in time than the ninth of September. We have had a file on this group for almost a year under the code name *Operation Granite*. That file officially opened December 2015 when the badly beaten bodies of three well-known Mexican drug mules were found by members of the tiny Border Patrol office down there in the Animas Valley.

"Piled on top of each other they were, like sacks of barley, in a remote dust bowl south of the Animas Mountains, a few miles from the Mexican border. Now as you might be aware, in general terms I mean, murders of non-US nationals are, unfortunately, not all that unusual in the border area these days. However, the circumstances of this one really stood out versus the prior experience of our own people investigating and that of the Mexican officers on the other side.

"For one thing, the area was incredibly remote and it was fairly easy to pick up tracks, yet there were absolutely no signs that they had any company on their journey north or that they had been followed by anyone from the Mexican side. All evidence led to and from the heart of the Chihuahua, not exactly a hotbed of criminal behavior.

The three pounds of pure coke they were carrying was still there, plumped up proud like packs of cream soda in six cellophane bags on a pocket of scrub. No gunshot wounds on their bodies, although one was found to have discharged his weapon before being overpowered. Whoever did it left the men's firearms lying at the scene, including one fully automatic that any cartel member would covet. Their remains were already in an advanced state of decomposition when discovered by Border Patrol, but forensic evidence confirmed without doubt that they died from blunt force trauma inflicted at close range. Basically none of it pointed toward a gang crime or opportunistic robbery, the motives that explain ninety-nine percent of deaths of Mexican nationals in the US border region.

"Forensics identified blood samples from a Caucasian in the vicinity and, apart from multiple tracks of persons traveling barefoot to and from the area, there were also unusual continuous twin tracks like the trail of an Indian travois so we figure this must be how they transported away their injured. The whole scene just stood out like a Yankee on Confederate Day, Mr. Mignolet, and I don't mind telling you that the investigating police officers and their Mexican counterparts in Juàrez were all left scratching their heads."

He pauses to refill his water glass. "Need a top-up?" He proffers the jug to both of us.

"No thanks," the sergeant and I chime in unison.

"A few weeks in," Pitcavage continues, "and the investigation into the case drew a complete blank in terms of forensic matches and trawls of the area by air and land. Essentially the file was put on ice, resting in a pile on my boss's desk at the FBI's El Paso field office. Then, a little over two months later, a freshly minted Quantico graduate trainee working under me made the first link between the Mexican three and another murder whose file was sent on to us by the folks at Deming Police Department on the last day of February. That was just before you moved to this neck of the woods yourself. Am I right in my dates?"

"Yes, sir. I think it was the twenty-sixth I arrived."

"Anyway, where was I? Yes, it was the case of an experienced Border Patrol officer who was reported missing while on duty patrolling inaccessible terrain on horseback along the outer perimeter of the Whitmire Canyon Wilderness Study Area. His half-buried body was discovered in a dry river bed a week later by trail walkers. The man had been beaten to death and, let me tell you, it was brutal. I ... let's just say it was even hard to look at in black and white.

"Forensics indicated he had been pelted with stones before he died. The stones, every one of them stained with that poor man's blood, were left lying there, scattered around him like a mini, macabre Stonehenge. Again, there was evidence of medieval-type fire torches at the scene. Investigators found burnt rags, with kerosene, pitch and animal fat used as accelerants. They identified the head of a flint axe like you might find in an archeological site, except it had clearly been fashioned only a few weeks before. Officer Alvarez left three young children and a widow behind him. His wife calls me every other day since she found out I was looking at the case. Lovely woman. Broken."

The agent touches the screen on the iPad in front of him a few times before turning it around and sliding it across the table toward me so we can both examine the map of the New Mexican boot heel.

"I just want to give you a better perspective on the locations and distances involved here, sir. My apologies,

Ariel. Do you mind if I call you by your first name?"

By now I have warmed to Agent Pitcavage to such an extent I'm looking for the catch, wondering whether I am being gently ambushed in some way.

"No, of course. Please do. May I call you Paul? Or is that against the law or something?"

"I'd be only too delighted for you to call me by my first name, Ariel. We have a lot of ground to cover, so formalities will grate after a while. As I said to you earlier, cast aside all your preconceived notions about the FBI when you're in my company. I'm all about politeness and professionalism but not protocol. Caused a few problems for me with the stiffs during the early days at Quantico, but they liked my work, so, well, you know, they're willing to overlook my dangerously personable nature."

It's the first time I see him break into an unrestrained smile, his whole face involved and so open it's hard to imagine anything sinister lurking behind it. At the far end of the table, Marge Newlands clears her throat to stifle another scoff.

"Here *we* are, at the top left of the boot heel. Down *here* is the location of the first murder, the Mexican three, at the Animas, on the edge of the massive Diamond Ranch, see? There's about forty miles of dust, scrub, desert vales, one-horse towns and mini-mountain ranges between here and there. Now, hold on, just let me hit the arrow ... *Here* is where Officer Alvarez was found, no more than twenty-five miles between the two sites. Then Mike and the other two Mexican nationals were murdered here, off the Old County Road, ten miles southeast of where we are sitting. Over *here* then is the other case that fits the mold. You see? Just *here*." He uses the butt of his pen to trace across the screen to an area about twenty miles due east of the Animas site, between a small range called Gilo Peak and the remote secondary route, State Road 81.

"On the sixteenth of July, the body of a middle-aged trail walker was discovered. Poor gentleman had to be identified by dental records. Forensics think he was murdered three weeks before that and the MO and crime scene matched that of the others I have described to you. A group of campers were looking for brush wood and came across his corpse. Unfortunately, the coyotes had got there first. Man's name was Eddie Romero. You might have heard mention of it in the local news at the time?"

His question dredges up the faintest memory of a news headline, and I nod in acknowledgment.

"BORTAC—sorry, that's the tactical operations side of Border Patrol—and our guys in the El Paso office were on the scene within hours once the details were disseminated by the police over there in Deming. Didn't take long for us to confirm it as another murder that matched the unusual circumstances of the other three and at that point, late July, Bureau experts on terrorists and Kool-Aiders were officially drafted into the investigation. Hell, I even called in our serial-killer people to review all three cases although we knew at all stages we were dealing with a group rather than an individual. Just thought they might be good at joining up the dots, you know, finding all the common denominators."

A cluster of questions clamor in my mind like unruly children.

"Excuse me, Paul. Can I stop you there for a second? Why ... can you tell me why it took so long for you guys to arrive on the scene? The scene of Mike's murder? Your investigation was alive, right? So even the news bulletins must have piqued your interest. I described everything to the police that morning and every detail would have pointed in the same direction as these others. Every single—"

"We weren't aware of the broader investigation here, Mr. Mignolet," interrupts the sergeant. "What you fail to grasp is that on the morning of the tenth of September we knew nothing of the connectedness between the other cases in Hidalgo and the three murders off Old County. As I have since come to understand, several senior officers in Deming and Lordsburg, along with case teams in both Hidalgo and Grant Border Patrol and even a few top brass in Las Cruces, were privy to the details of Operation Granite at that stage. But us? Here? Well, I guess we're not high enough up the totem pole to have merited a heads-up." Her tone suggests this whole issue is a serious sore point and she is only betraying a fraction of the depth of her feelings on the matter.

Pitcavage appeals for calm like a conductor cuing the end of a movement. "Okay, folks, let's take a step back here," he says diplomatically.

But I am not letting this go so easily. "No, sorry, Paul. I have to stop you there again. This is my life, my reputation we are talking about here and I need to understand. You are telling me that I was left to stew in the bowels of Rapunzel's castle here for almost two days as prime suspect because of interagency secrecy? Is it now the case that the FBI no longer trusts local law enforcement? Maybe I should call up a few of the media friends I made during the feeding frenzy last week and tell them they're missing the real story here."

"Calm down, Ariel. Like I said already, we are real, real sorry that you were put through that experience. It's mighty unfortunate and I can promise you that when I leave this meeting today, I am going to do whatever I can to ameliorate the situation you find yourself in with the press. You need to understand, though, that everything we have done, and indeed everything we have not done—like the decision not to inform all the local police forces along the border area—was to maintain the confidentiality of our investigation.

"We want to do things differently, this time. Y'all must remember Waco? You know, the shit explosion with the Branch Davidians in ninety-three? Seventy-six people died in that fire, Ariel. I would say needlessly. Set the Bureau back years. Greatest administrative fuck-up of all our times at the FBI and mostly it was just down to loose tongues and poor planning. That's not gonna happen on my watch. We will not be caught out like that again. Not while I'm in charge, at any rate. Hell, we were even willing to sacrifice early access to the crime scene here so that we could quietly establish through back channels that the MO was a match. And that is because we are *already* close, very close, to closing the net around these people. But, and it's a big but, were the press to get wind of the operation's details, those vultures would be looking for a ringside seat at another Texas massacre. In my view, their presence alone could jeopardize everything so we needed to keep this operation as tight as Dick's hatband."

I lean back in my chair, shaking my head slowly with disbelief as a large bank of the information fog I had been suspended in for days suddenly clears. "So I was merely a bone? Conveniently distracting the pack?"

"Well, now that really is a very negative kind of spin to put on all this." Pitcavage says in a conciliatory tone. "No, I'm more inclined to describe your terribly unfortunate experience as collateral damage, but damage that will seem justified when we reach the goal we are all aiming for."

With the air conditioning on the blink and the strong midday sun now firmly elbowing its way under the blind and spotlighting on the surface of the table, the heat in the room is stifling and I take off my hoodie and pour another glass of water. A combination of a maturing hangover and the seriousness of what I am hearing has given me a sudden craving for salt.

"My apologies for interrupting, but is anyone else here hungry?" Blank faces across the table give me my answer. It is only twelve fifteen. "I don't really want to stop, but is there any possibility of a snack right now, a pack of potato chips or something? Anything?"

Once again, the refreshment request is aimed at the sergeant as both Paul Pitcavage and I look pleadingly in her direction. We are met with a glare and, through pursed lips, she resignedly asks, "Ready salted or flavored?" She takes my "anything" response as her cue to head off on a foraging expedition.

"So you see, Ariel," the agent says, picking up where he left off, "the reason none of this has entered the public domain is that we have kept the investigation exceptionally tight up until now. But the hour for action is very close and we must stay vigilant in protecting all details of our plans. It falls to me to shut the file on this case, here in Prospero, and I see you as a vital part of this effort. We will be relying heavily on your help as the only person who can give first-hand testimony of these terrible events, the only witness who has seen the perpetrators up close."

His words, his sentiment, are like a salve, and for the first time since the moment I heard through the young police officer's radio that Mike's body had been found, I feel the sting of tears. I look up at the ceiling and take sharp breaths through my nose to stem their flow while, without comment, Agent Pitcavage quietly hands me a handkerchief from his trouser pocket and I am glad Sergeant Newlands is not in the room.

"Let's all take a few minutes," Pitcavage whispers. "I have some e-mails to read. You take your time. There's a lot to take on board."

Chapter Eleven

FIRE AND BRIMSTONE

"But the fearful, and unbelieving, and the abominable, and murderers, and whoremongers, and sorcerers, and idolaters, and all liars, shall have their part in the lake which burneth with fire and brimstone: which is the second death."

— REVELATION 21:8

It's six days since my mother and I ran the gauntlet of accusatory stares as we took our seats at Mike's funeral service in the Resurrection Baptist Church on Prospero's Main Street. Six days since we were snubbed as we attempted to commiserate with his close friends and family beside the church door. Mike's father seemed ignorant of who I was at first, despite all the headlines, and gracefully accepted my hand like any of the other mourners before a dark-suited interloper swooped in from left field to rudely break our connection and whisper in the confused man's ear.

Furtive glances and curious stares were cast in our direction throughout the sermon, many from behind fluttering paper booklets. Ill will surrounded us as palpably as the noon's sticky heat and the few feet of room either side of us in the pew was the only spare space in the otherwise crammed church.

Apart from these cross-currents of opprobrium, the funeral began like any other. Somber organ music droned broodingly in the background, as people made their way to their seats up the aisle, at the top of which Mike lay in an open casket adorned with a mountain of white lilies. Seconds before noon, two saturnine attendants fussed on the altar with microphones, electric fans and flowers, like roadies preparing the stage for a rock star.

"Yea, though I walk through the valley of the shadow of death, I will fear no evil." The amplified base tenor boomed into the crowded chapel from everywhere and nowhere. "Yea, though I walk through the valley of the shadow of death, I will fear no evil."

Pastor Funchess appeared from a side entrance, a small microphone on his lapel projecting his words to all assembled. "But a coffin is really a hope chest, my dear people," he began, his gravelly, emotion-laden voice now thundering from behind a V-shaped wooden lectern anchored to an elevated altar. "A coffin is really a hope chest for those of us who follow the Lord and I'm going to tell you about that now, so listen carefully to my words, please. Listen, everybody here who is broken-hearted. Listen up now, all you gathered here with broken hearts."

A minute of silence followed during which the congregation seemed to grow taller in their seats. All background mutterings and low-level chatter extinguished, leaving total hush apart from the odd tissue-bound sniffle or shuffle of shoe leather from stragglers squeezing in the back. He would have us wait.

"Did you know that the word coffin is used only once in the sixty-six books within God's Bible? Did you know that?" He scanned the room thoroughly, scouring the sea of faces as though it were conceivable that someone might have the temerity to respond. "All those deaths, all those burials, murders, graveside orations and resurrections, but it is only mentioned one single time. If you ask me, I believe that God was very careful to allow it to be used only once, only in that verse in Genesis which talks about Joseph. Joseph the Israelite; Joseph the slave; Joseph, once king of Egypt, who died age one hundred and ten years.

"We humans don't like thinking about death at all, do we? That fear which rises above all others. It must be suppressed in the back of our minds. Tethered, like a savage beast, outside our everyday thoughts. But when we have to come to funeral services of those we love? That is when we have to brace ourselves. That is when we must face up to that fear for a little while.

"Now I, as a church pastor, have a privileged perspective up here on the altar, my friends. I get to look right into people's eyes as they file past at the end of the funeral service." Elbows raised high, he pointed to his eyes, which were opened as wide as possible. "I watch people file past up here and I can tell you all that I surely know the ones who are not saved. I can see those who do not live for God. I know them, my dear people." He crossed his arms over his chest and geared down to a hushed, solemn voice. "Because I see how they only allow themselves the briefest little glance at the coffin before having to look quickly away." Then he pounded the lectern with a closed fist and shouted, "Because, you see, they know, my friends. They know they have only served the needs of their flesh throughout their earthly lives and not the needs of their soul. Yes, I can see it in their eyes as plain as day, my dear people. The fear in them that they shall reap, that they shall reap my friends, that they shall reap the corruption they have sown—" Demons seemingly expunged, his voice quieted again to a calm conspiratorial whisper, his words descending on the crowd like a silk sheet "—and not eternal life."

Few could resist his spell. Rows of heads nodded. Now and then, the pastor took a little time to acknowledge individuals in the crowd with brief eye contact or a fleeting salute, like presidential candidates do at convention rallies.

"When my wife was sweet seventeen, she had what she described to me as a hope chest, a cedar chest, her *bottom drawer,* as they say in England. She put a lot of things in this special place in preparation for the marriage she looked forward to one day. She had put aside things that had meaning and importance to her, like pretty lace or crafted household items. She stored them in that hope chest in the knowledge that investing in these things in the present would give her a good start in the married life she hoped for.

"If you are a born-again believer in Jesus Christ, my good people, then you will never be in a coffin. You will wait in a hope chest for the ultimate day of reckoning. When that day of reckoning comes, your soul will contain all you need for your new life at the right hand of our Lord God while those who have chosen in this life to shun Jesus and embrace the devil will sink from their caskets and wither in Hell for all eternity." Gripping the lectern, his knuckles gleamed white against the sleeves of his charcoal suit and his voice rose once again, building steadily to a crescendo. "Faithful members are not buried in a coffin but a hope chest. The only way to make yours a hope chest is Jesus. Jesus is your only hope because the same power that raised Jesus from the dead lives within you, and with it we all can have victory over death. I can tell you with one hundred percent cast-iron certainty, friends, that Mike Argyll is buried today in a hope chest and he will be ready when the day of reckoning is upon us. I can tell you with one hundred percent cast-iron certainty that Mike will enjoy the power of resurrection when the day of reckoning is upon us. How am I so sure? How do I know? I am one hundred percent cast-iron certain because when Mike offered up his life to Jesus, here on this very altar last year, he was saved for Jesus. He booked his place in Heaven."

Heads nodded, fans flapped.

"So when you look up here and file past to say your goodbyes, when you walk past your loved one's physical body for the last time, I want you to look upon this casket up front here as Mike's hope chest and do not be afraid. Do not fear for him and do not fear for yourselves."

The rhythm and resonance of Funchess's voice was mesmerizing, like the chant of monks or the sound of a heartbeat. It spoke to primal fears, and like all those gathered, my pulse raced with the rapid emotional gear changes and passionate rhetoric. Where he couldn't command attention, he demanded it.

"Sit up straight, there, in the third last row," he yelled at a young boy sitting across the aisle who had leaned to whisper something in his neighbor's ear. No one in front bothered to look around to identify the culprit, suggesting such admonishment was standard practice for the pastor. "Sit up straight now. Have some respect."

"In the Resurrection Baptist Church, we know that Christ died on the cross to save us from our sins. We know he was buried and then on the third day he rose again in accordance with the Scriptures. Resurrection. The power of resurrection. One key word that separates our religion from others. Our savior, Jesus, is not in a tomb. Jesus is risen and the reason we come here to pray is the fact that he rose again. The reason we can even begin to tolerate, begin to absorb, begin to take in the heart-wrenching, gut-churning pain of losing Mike at the hands of evil is the fact that Jesus rose again.

"Take that crying baby out right now, please, that lady there in the red bonnet."

A row of people sprang to their feet midway up the aisle to allow an embarrassed woman with crying babe-in-arms to squeeze by. The rattle of previously suspended coughs and clearings of throat punctuated the short hiatus as she departed. It felt like school.

"God has told us that there is a way to live on Earth that will be almost exactly the same as the life we will enjoy in Heaven. There is a spirit-filled life that you can live so that moving into the afterlife will be like taking one single step, or maybe just one of those leaps Mike was famous for when crossing that line to score a touchdown. God has given us the map. He has pointed us in the direction of the heavenly life to lead so we can lose the fear of the afterlife. The map is here in this book. God's Bible. His holy word. Mike followed that map. Mike and Eliza would have followed that map together had he not been snatched from her by those who do the Devil's work."

My mother gently nudged my side for me to raise my head, momentarily lowered in contemplation. Pastor Funchess was walking a circuit of the church, proudly holding aloft a large leather-bound Bible like a boxing-ring girl with her round number. Then back to the altar for another bout.

"Of course, I know we will all miss Mike physically. His beautiful broken-hearted fiancée, Eliza, up here, daughter of one of our church's founders, has lost the physical manifestation of her future. His parents and sister will miss his physical being desperately as will his friends from college, his teammates from football and his peacekeeping colleagues. All who knew the man will miss him in the physical sense. But I want to comfort you with the knowledge that our beloved Mike did not feel the sting of death. In the moments before he died, he did not feel that sting because Jesus conquered death, and those who live in Jesus will enjoy that victory for eternity. Mike was in Christ's family on Earth and he lived a heavenly life, so he moved quietly over the threshold into the Father's kingdom.

"Yea, though I walk through the valley of the shadow of death, I will fear no evil. Mike has moved on to the promised land and each one of us, each one of us who have been saved and have made it right with God on this Earth should not be afraid of death because one day we will follow him in stepping over the threshold.

"Rest assured that our brother Mike is now enjoying the warmth of the divine and supernatural light in our Lord's kingdom. If you truly believe that, then your tears will be dried, your heart will heal. God will give you that grace if you ask Him.

"And when the day of the final reckoning comes and the Lord reaches down to re-gather his faithful flock, will we be among that flock? Yes, we will. Will we bask in the rapturous, joyful, endless glow of our Father's light? Yes, we will. Will those who have turned their back be smote? Yes, they will. Shall they perish for their sinful, godless existence? Yes, they will. Oh yes, they will. Oh yes, they will. Oh yes, the crawling vermin will pay and they will see the error of their ways too late for redemption.

"At that moment of deliverance—and it is not too far away, my good people, no it is nearer than you think—we will be reunited with our fallen son, Mike. And as for those who murdered Mike? God will judge them from His great throne of judgment along with the whores in Hollywood, along with the homosexual deviants who prey on our children, along with the foul-mouthed screeching harpies pouring their poisonous lyrics into young ears and the beastly purveyors of drugs and liquor. God is watching very closely and he will judge the usurer bankers and the crooked politicians that take your money to support lay-abouts and criminals while spreading their liberalist bile on the Internet. They will all be judged, my dear people. They will all face the wrath of the Lord for turning their backs on His word when they had the chance in this earthly life."

Later, as they lowered Mike's remains into the red earth, the casket jolted unceremoniously to a halt, dangling precariously for a few moments with the head end lower than the foot end when a young gravedigger at the helm struggled to release the blue nylon tie ropes in tandem with his henchman. For some reason the unexpected interruption broke through the defenses I had erected to keep my emotions in check during the day's ceremonies and a deluge of loss filled the pit of my stomach, churning like the gut-wrenching fear a young child feels when lost or left behind. I searched the faces around me as though an unexpected hero might emerge to call the whole thing off, say there had been some kind of mistake. My mother gently squeezed the tips of my fingers, sensing I was coming undone. I swallowed hard and took short, sharp breaths to stem the flow, fearing that even one tear could tell too much of our story.

The crowd was thirty deep in places. The stiff uniformity of the police guard of honor at the northern end of the grave added to the air of solemnity. Evening shadows had begun to grow as the warmth of the fall afternoon faded. We stood in the shadow of a majestic line of yucca trees, their green spiky crowns adorning lithe trunks, some straight and proud, others bowed gracefully like a band of grazing giraffes.

Eliza Marron stood alongside Mike's parents, his sister and her own father in a roped-off area at the graveside, their arms around one another's shoulders like huddled troops facing into combat. When the burial men had repositioned themselves, bare forearms straining, their entire bulk leaning back onto their heels as they braced for the dead weight, Mike's remains were lowered quietly to their final resting place. The voice of Pastor Funchess, who held aloft a highly polished, two-foot wooden crucifix with all the drama of a Shakespearian actor, carried solemnly to all present: "Jesus said unto her, I am the resurrection, and the life: he that believeth in me, though he were dead, yet shall he live. And whosoever liveth and believeth in me shall never die. We say goodbye to Mike in the full knowledge that we will meet again by our Lord's great throne. Pray with me now, all present."

The majority of assembled mourners repeated the prayer three times, in perfect unison with the preacher, their plangent voices a soothing wall of sound. Their solemn chant struck a chord in me and, for the first time since I was a young boy, I tuned in to the strength and power of collective faith.

"Father, we commit his body to the earth, from which our bodies were originally created and we rejoice in the fact that his spirit is now with You, the Father of spirits. We anticipate the day when spirit and body shall be united again at the coming of the Lord, and we find great comfort in knowing that we shall forever be together with the Lord. Amen."

Recitation over, the sounds of muffled crying around the grave intensified again, accompanying him down the last few feet. It was not a hope chest I saw there, being swallowed up by the red earth, but something stolen being stashed beyond reach. For his sake, I cried on the inside.

Chapter Twelve

The Rapture

"And he shall send his angels with a great sound of a trumpet, and they shall gather together his elect from the four winds, from one end of heaven to the other."
— MATTHEW 24:31

"Your sketch here, Ariel, how accurate would you say it is?" Pitcavage's words edge slowly back into my consciousness like a stewardess wakening you on the red eye. In front of me on the table sits a laminated copy of Ms. Gregan's production alongside a bowl of peanuts and salted chips, the paltry product of Sergeant Newlands' ten-minute foraging expedition.

"Sorry. Yes, all I can say to you is that it is an uncanny match of the image I had in my memory. Freakily so."

"What about the other faces? The others who surrounded you before you escaped? Do you think you could identify any of those individuals?"

"The others … all the others were also teenagers, some possibly a little older. It was so dark. I *can* tell you that, unlike the leader, they were mostly fair haired, but would I be able to pick one out? I'm really not sure. Maybe one or two. The one who spoke, perhaps. It's hard to say, really. In my mind's eye, the rest of them were fairly nondescript because the leader stood out in every way. His face was more … ethnic, if that makes sense? He seemed bigger, certainly more striking. You can see it in the identikit. He looks like a Greek god or Jim Morrison or something. But when he looked straight at me? It was with unvarnished savagery. No words necessary. I simply knew I was next to die."

"Tell me the story again of how you managed to escape," Pitcavage continues, all the while tap-tapping notes into the iPad in front of him.

"There was a delay. I'm still not exactly sure how it came about. Why they delayed, I mean. It was only a few seconds but … they were preoccupied looking at the lights on Caleb Freeth's house and it distracted them for long enough so a gap opened up and I ran. They were very interested in those lights."

Pitcavage replaces the image in his file and slides his glasses a bit further down his nose as he flicks through the other pages to another segment he wants to go over.

"When you mentioned Waco before. Is this the same kind of situation?" I ask while he searches. "I mean have you found a compound of some kind?"

"Yes, it's similar. Or at least it could be," says Pitcavage. "I will come on to all that in a moment. Let me get these last few clarifications and we will get straight on to what we know and what final gaps we need to fill in. I am interested in hearing a first-hand account of the timeline of events. The chronology leading up to Officer Argyll driving his jeep to the murder scene of Señors Luiz and Hernandez. The records show that you had a short phone call with Officer Argyll at six-fifty-six p.m. earlier that evening, Friday, the ninth of September."

It takes me a few seconds to realize that there is no specific question coming. He is simply stating the fact to provide me with a jumping-off point, an invitation to take it from there. Sergeant Newlands pierces the pregnant pause with a sharp clearing of her throat and Agent Pitcavage responds by topping up her cup of water, but I am acutely aware that her unscripted cue is aimed squarely at me, in case I need reminding.

"Sure, Paul," I begin nonchalantly. "I called him for two reasons. First to tell him that my neighbor had so far adhered to the request Mike had put to him three days earlier. You know, to keep his security lights off until eleven p.m.? And then I asked if he would mind stopping by to check out the strange lights. I had seen them again on the plateau in front of my house the previous evening—that is, the night of September eighth. As you no doubt learned from his files, we had discussed the lights on other occasions and he was very curious. I … I understand from the sergeant that he even made notes.

"Anyway I hadn't seen the lights for a while, at least several days, until they reappeared that Thursday night. Our conversation was cut short because Mike was in the middle of something. I can't remember exactly what, but he said he'd pay a visit later that evening, after his shift, to have a look. As you are aware, we had become friends, good acquaintances anyway, through the whole Caleb Freeth problem and our various discussions about those lights."

My heart races ahead of the lie and it's hard to maintain good eye contact with the agent. Lying was never a strong point of mine although I have often had the point made to me that selling financial products requires the ability to finesse the truth somewhat.

"He got to my place around ten or thereabouts," I continue. "Can't be sure exactly, but it happened that when he arrived, the lights were there again, in a different area to the previous night but … and, well, you have my account of what happened next. I know it's futile but I keep dwelling on the fact that Mike would still be alive if the people who rented the house to me hadn't left that goddamn telescope behind. Or even if he hadn't had training in that kind of equipment. I can't help obsessing like that."

For what seems like minutes but is really a matter of seconds after I stop talking, Paul Pitcavage is still eyeballing me with intent, tuning in like a hypnotist might to identify any weaknesses or susceptibilities to make use of later in his act. His chocolate-colored eyes are slightly enlarged and blurred by his varifocals, and somewhere in their midst I'm sure I see disbelief or, at the very least, doubt. "Packed a lot into a thirteen-second phone call," he remarks pointedly but, mercifully, decides to push ahead.

"In your statements, you say that the leader of the group, this individual called Alonso, never spoke during the entire encounter. Just give me one second. Yes, here are your words: *They were surrounding me. A complete circle. One of them pointed at the powerful lights at the house and said, 'Look. There.' Then another one of the group asked of the leader, 'Is that it, Alonso?' They all turned at that point, sort of moving together to look at the lights, leaving me to the side.* Are you one hundred percent certain these are the only words you heard, Ariel? For instance, did any of them call out any other names at any point?" Pitcavage asks.

"Absolutely sure. Absolutely nothing else. Even when they chased me, there were no words. No shouting to one another to go right or left, no urging each other on or attempts to spook me. They chased in silence. No names, no words. By the way, you're not the only person to show particular interest in what they said that night. I didn't mention this before as it didn't seem important or crop up in any of those ... those *interrogations* you put me through," I say, ladling sarcasm for the sergeant's benefit.

"When I met, or rather fell upon, my neighbor, Caleb Freeth, that night, he didn't ask how I got injured or why I was running out of the desert so late. Nothing you might expect him to ask. I thought I might have dreamt this initially because I fell unconscious for a short time after I arrived at his house. But I have run the reel over and over in my mind and I'm fairly certain now of what I heard. Caleb asked me if *they* had said anything."

Sergeant Newlands and Agent Pitcavage look at each other knowingly as though I have confirmed a theory and then both begin to speak at exactly the same moment before Pitcavage gallantly excuses himself for the sergeant to take the floor.

"We were just about to come on to the topic of Caleb Freeth, Mr. Mignolet. What you've just told us here is very interesting and we won't be slow in asking Mr. Freeth exactly what lay behind his question. In fact, you can hear his answer first hand if you like because he's scheduled to join this meeting in—" she steals a glance at her watch "—about six minutes or so. He's waiting out in the corridor right now."

Blindsided, I struggle for a response. "Caleb Freeth. Here? Have you people any understanding of the relationship between him and me? What could possibly be gained by having him here? In fact, no. You know what? Don't bother answering that. I'm not having it. No way I'm going to sit here with that scumbag. We're all done here for now." I push my chair back from the table and snatch up my phone and keys.

"Hold on now. Hold on one minute, Ariel. Give us a chance to explain, will you?" pleads Pitcavage while Marge Newlands sits back with crossed arms and a distinct look of *I told you so* on her face. "Please, take your seat and just listen for a second before deciding whether you want to stay or leave."

"Go on," I reply doubtfully from the door.

"Look, I am familiar with *all* of the man's shortcomings. I've read the Army's medical reports on him and I can tell you that, all on his lonesome, he would make a challenging subject for a psych Ph.D. student. But it is also true to say that your neighbor out there is as important to this investigation as you are. You see, Caleb Freeth is one of *them*. He spent most of his early life and a good chunk of adulthood living with the group we have zoned in on. I'm talking religious extremists here. A totally isolated fundamentalist Baptist cult who have lived for over twenty-five years in a compound about thirty-five miles south of here in the Chihuahuan Desert. We have identified this group, or at least a group from within their ranks, as the main suspects in the trail of violent deaths I have outlined for you and that man knows these people, Ariel. From the inside. Their encampment, the main players, their capabilities, their mindset. He is a key source in helping to bring Mike's murderers to justice. You think you might wanna hold your nose for a while in here now and listen? If nothing else, purely out of interest?"

I retake my seat hesitantly, turning over what I have heard, rotisserie-like, in my mind while maintaining eye contact with Pitcavage, the sorcerer who keeps altering things I was sure of. "When? How long ago did he leave?" I ask.

"He left them for good about fourteen or fifteen years ago. We are not one hundred percent sure of the circumstances, but it had something to do with his wife and children. Apparently, he swore never to return so there must have been a lot of acrimony involved," he adds.

"How do you know so much about him?" I ask.

"Well, obviously, I've accessed all his military files and there's no question but he suffered a few traumas during his two tours. Wasn't too sociable, you won't be surprised to hear. Cited for inciting racism. Twice arrested by MPs for conduct unbecoming and fighting. That sort of thing. Then there's the pastor here in Prospero. Pastor Funchess. He's been a very significant source of information on Caleb's background and on the target group's compound. Turns out he has traveled there by helicopter on more than ten occasions over the years to deliver medical supplies and other essentials. Do you know Pastor Funchess?"

I nod.

"He is another key source for us in this investigation and he's airtight. You know? The seal of the confessional and all that stuff?"

"I think you are mixing up your churches there, Paul," I say drily.

"Sorry. Not really my area, I'm afraid. Anyway, to summarize the background for you, it turns out that the pastor here in Prospero graduated from Galen Johnson College, in Indiana, in nineteen-seventy-nine, the same year as the head of the cult, man by the name of Anthony Blount." Pitcavage thrusts a black-and-white newspaper photograph from 1967 under my nose of a strapping athlete shaking hands with then-Governor Ronald Reagan in Los

Angeles. "In fact, when I looked into it," he continues, "turns out they were classmates with Jack Brady, son of the infamous Pastor Brady, who was jailed in two-thousand-ten for having sex with a minor. Off the point, I know, but it's just one controversy in a long series for Galen Johnson College over the years. Strange place. Anyway, they were commissioned, if that's the right word, as a hotshot pastoral duo, nearly thirty years ago, by the big-business cheese here in Prospero to promote the spiritual development of the town in the fundamentalist Baptist tradition. Now, you'll have to keep up with me here, Ariel. Millenarianism or as I've been calling it, Rapturism, for want of a better description, is *not* in keeping with Pastor Galen's original Baptist teachings but, for whatever reasons, Blount switched horses after graduation and was fixed on establishing his own independent church in line with the Rapturist beliefs. I myself wasn't all that familiar with this strand of the Baptist tradition until a week ago. You know much of it?"

"I'm somewhat familiar, yes," I reply, glancing pointedly at Marge Newlands, who I notice has acquired a nervous tic, repeatedly and meticulously sorting the pile of papers in front of her that are already stacked with regimental precision.

"So, basically, it all seems to revolve around the second coming of Christ and a period of great wrath called the Tribulation," Pitcavage says. "Either at the start or at the end of this period of Tribulation, there will be a gathering up of the faithful to heaven and then, when all that's over, there will be a thousand years of peace and tranquility on Earth.

"Now you would not believe how much infighting there is between these folks concerning whether the gathering up, as it were, will happen pre- or post- this day of the apocalypse but, believe you me, groups out there are fairly entrenched on one side or the other, *and*, I might add, the mud-slinging back and forth is spectacularly unchristian. Cursing, death threats, the lot. Seriously, you should check it out on line. It's the spiritual equivalent of pit bull fighting."

If I had been in doubt up until this point, Pitcavage's generally disparaging tone confirms he is oblivious to the fact that the sergeant adheres to a fairly puritanical strand of the Baptist tradition through her membership in the local church.

"Which side of the pre/post Tribulation argument are you on, Sergeant?" I ask, launching myself into the conversation to the surprise and slight embarrassment of Agent Pitcavage. "It never occurred to me before to ask if your Fundie buddies here in Prospero have a strong view on this. Tell me, will you guys have to endure the apocalyptic wrath of Christ for a few years along with the rest of us? Or will you all be watching smugly from the right hand of God while us heathens are swept aside?" It feels good to be asking the sergeant a question for a change.

"My apologies, Sergeant," Pitcavage says before she gets a word out. "You'll have to excuse my ignorance on this whole area, I'm afraid. Parents both agnostic and I have never settled on words to describe my own spiritual disposition, although eternal skeptic might do it, I'm ashamed to say. Sorry, but I am a live-and-let-live person, really."

He isn't finished smoothing the terrain when the sergeant responds. "I am not in the habit of explaining or accounting for my personal beliefs, Mr. Mignolet, in the same way I have never asked you about yours. It's not of any relevance here and really we are just wasting time, but I can tell you that our church here in Prospero does not subscribe to the End Times philosophy. Now we are under time pressure at this stage, Paul," she says with annoyance. "The others will be wondering."

"Of course, yes, I know. Look, Ariel, I'm gonna summarize things as they stand real quickly for you so we can invite Mr. Freeth and Mr. Branson to join us. Basically, I was describing to you just now how the two preachers began building the church here as a team. Well, as is often the case when it comes to religion, there was a parting of the ways about twenty-five years ago and Blount headed for the proverbial hills with a raggle-taggle band of his own hard-core followers, leaving Funchess behind in Prospero to cultivate his own patch in the desert, so to speak. The parting of the ways ultimately came about because Anthony Blount wanted to marry a divorcée, one Cora Freeth, mother of your then-teenage neighbor.

"Turns out her first husband, Saul, was a philandering alcoholic who physically abused her so badly, she lost her sight in one eye. Anyway, all her suffering and religious devotion didn't grant her any exemptions from the rules here in town. Divorce is such a no-no in the Resurrection Baptist Church, Blount was told that if he married her, he was out and, so it goes, he took the exit. Now, like I said, I *am* summarizing, but apparently there were fairly major differences in terms of their beliefs with the gist of it being that Blount was more hard-core in every sense, apart from his self-derogation on the issue of remarriage. Blount, his new wife, her son Caleb and fifty or so believers with a pioneering spirit headed out into the desert to separate themselves from the rest of the world and start a new religion. I saw some photographs yesterday of the day they moved out. Looked like a Western wagon train, only with shiny nineteen-sixties and -seventies Airstream RVs.

"Folks here tell me their numbers grew early on, but as the years rolled by, they had less and less contact with the outside world and it appears they developed a highly regimented, survival kind of lifestyle to cope with the isolation. Think puritanical, or Amish if you like, but without equality because, by all accounts, Anthony Blount is an exceptionally domineering character who believes strongly in military-style training going hand in hand with spiritual formation.

"Maybe Caleb Freeth will have something to add to this description, but one elderly local person suggested to me that Seb Funchess is like a benevolent uncle compared to Blount. Our investigation team now strongly suspects that something drastic has gone wrong within the compound or some new radical force is exerting an influence on this group and that the actions of the murderers you encountered eleven days ago are a byproduct of this.

"I interviewed Seb Funchess the day before yesterday and his most recent visit to the compound was over a year ago. He says Blount's health is failing and he detected some evidence of infighting, but he is still adamant they are not capable of this extreme brutality. Funchess's information, combined with satellite imagery, has helped us locate the compound and plan our approach. The pastor will be accompanying us during Operation Granite and I wanted to ask you whether you are willing to come, too? The mission has been categorized as relatively low risk and we are hopeful of being able to achieve a suspect line-up situation or, well, who knows exactly how that aspect will pan out, but we think it will expedite matters if we were to have our key witness *in situ* during the mission. The Bureau tends to be reluctant to involve civilians in raid operations, but this case is coming hot on the heels of a farce in Texas where six suspects were airlifted out of a border town and flown to El Paso for questioning. Despite all their photographic and background intel, it turned out that not one had the remotest involvement with the target group. One man was a local school principal, if you can believe that. Anyway, as you can imagine I'm sure, the powers that be are a little more inclined to ensure accurate IDs now before they commit resources. How do you feel about the prospect of accompanying us, Ariel? I'm talking about three or four days' time, and of course it won't be without risks. We are currently finalizing plans."

My head reels under the barrage of sensational facts. Newly mined nuggets of information instantaneously resolving questions that have tormented me for days.

"I will go. I really want to go," I say without hesitation.

"Thought you might say that," replies the agent. "Just make sure to be at the other end of your phone for the next three or four days and you will hear from me about the details."

"Let's get the others in here," says the sergeant, moving to the door. "And remember, Mr. Mignolet, you may not discuss anything we have spoken about with anyone outside of myself and Agent Pitcavage. *Anyone,* of course, includes Mr. Freeth, who may touch on or ask about some of the topics we have covered. Do you fully understand this point? We have made you an insider to Operation Granite and we expect you to maintain total secrecy."

Fate keeps intervening to force myself and the sergeant onto the same team. "Sure, I get that," I reply. "I've spent all my working life keeping important secrets."

Marge Newlands raises her eyes scornfully before summoning the waiting pair in from the corridor.

I don't think about where they might sit until it is too late to intervene. Officer Branson, who I quickly ascertain is junior to Pitcavage, enters first and takes the seat directly in front of him, leaving Caleb with a choice of sitting beside me or walking around the room and taking the free seat between Pitcavage and the sergeant. To my dismay, he takes the first option and, as he pulls his chair up to the table, a current of negative energy charges into the small gap between us.

Officer Branson is a squat, flat-faced man with big round eyes. His white shirt and diamond-patterned top complete the impression of a ventriloquist's dummy, which is further enhanced when he speaks, revealing two rows of white picket-fence teeth crammed into his mouth. He introduces himself as a senior BORTAC officer with five years' operational experience and specialist knowledge of the Texan and New Mexican border areas. His introduction has a ring of over-rehearsed nervousness as though he were interviewing for a job and eager to impress, perhaps demonstrating the inflated status FBI agents enjoy when among their state-based brethren.

"Thanks for that, Steve," Pitcavage says before switching his attention to Caleb, who sits rigidly, glowering like a gloomy Puritan.

"Mr. Freeth, thank you for joining us. I believe you know Ariel Mignolet here? We have a few questions for you regarding the religious grouping you once belonged to out there in the Chihuahua Desert. I understand their correct name is the First Truth Church, is that correct?"

"Yes, sir," shoots back Caleb, like a cadet to a drill sergeant.

"Relax there, Mr. Freeth," says Pitcavage. "There's no chain of command here. Just two people talking. Now before we go any further, I want to reiterate what Officer Branson no doubt explained to you earlier, that everything we are about to discuss is absolutely confidential and, while I have just discouraged you from lapsing into military mode, I do want you to fully understand that I will view any breach of secrecy surrounding our discussions as a direct attempt to undermine state security. This interview, for want of a better word, is being recorded and should you at any stage require the presence of a lawyer or feel you cannot answer without consulting a lawyer, then please just say so and we will postpone until you can be facilitated. Are you good with all that, sir?"

"I understand," says Caleb in a surprisingly subdued voice while I munch on a handful of peanuts as quietly as humanly possible.

"Mr. Freeth," Pitcavage resumes, "we have spoken to Pastor Funchess about the core beliefs of the First Truth Church and, as he understands it, the date they had expected the end of the Rapture or Tribulation period to occur has come and gone. He told us that date was September twenty-ninth, two-thousand-thirteen. Does that tally with your own understanding?"

"That is correct, sir. Came and went like a summer breeze," Caleb replies sarcastically.

"So, I'm interested in what effect you think this might have had on the group, Mr. Freeth. In psychological terms, I mean. Their frame of mind? Also, to your knowledge, were there any—how shall I put it?—were there any what you might call contingency plans within the group? A plan of what to do in the event that this great Rapturing event failed to materialize as hoped for all those years?"

I push my chair back from the table to create a bit more space between us so I can adopt the roll of observer, fascinated with every new detail about a community that could produce both Caleb Freeth and the band of savages who murdered Mike.

"Hanged if I know," he replies. "Pastor might be able to help you better there, sir. I haven't clapped eyes on those vermin for fourteen years. Wouldn't bother me were they all burning in hell." His voice is laden with revulsion.

"But your mother and stepfather still live there, Mr. Freeth. Am I right in saying that? And your wife and children? Where are they to your knowledge?" Pitcavage asks.

Caleb's demeanor darkens at the mention of his family. "My mother is dead to me, sir, and as for Blount? That man is evil, pure and simple. May even be the devil himself reincarnated."

"And your family? Are they still in the camp?"

The unventilated atmosphere has deteriorated to stifling airlessness as though the room itself is holding its breath. Caleb wipes his sweaty calloused palms on his tattered jeans as though gearing up for action and directs his reply to Agent Pitcavage in a low emotionless voice. "My wife took my kids and left the group over fourteen years ago," replies Caleb. "All's I got from her—I'm talkin' about the last I heard—was a letter that came through in Afghanistan. My first tour. There I was, answering my country's call to stem the Muslim cancer, and that bitch squaw wrote me two paragraphs to say she couldn't bear the life there anymore and was set to move back to the Tohono O'odham tribe I plucked her out of in Arizona. Told me not to look for her or the kids. Twins. Boy and girl—Ces and Cehia. Sometimes I think maybe I should have listened to old Blount for once. He always said never trust a red."

"I'd advise you to curb your language, Mr. Freeth. I won't accept that kind of racist bile in a public office and if you utter one more slur, I'll cite you for hate speech and make it stick. You understanding me clearly, *sir*?" Pitcavage is back to tapping his index finger on the table but with palpable aggression this time, like a headmaster delivering a final warning.

"Can you give us dates around those facts, Caleb? Sorry to interrupt, Paul. I'm just taking notes here," pipes up Sergeant Newlands, who hasn't uttered a word since she ushered the two men in. "I'm referring to the date you received the letter, Caleb, and the date you last visited the group. I presume you went out there after you came back? You know … to try and find out more? Can you remember those dates? Even an approximate timeline?"

"Well, maybe I won't nail it right to the month, Sergeant, but I'd put my getting the letter around April aught-two, not long after deployment, and then I took leave a few months later and headed back out there to inquire after my kids and pick up my belongings. That would have been in August, I think."

Sergeant Newlands jots down the dates and circles them a couple of times on the page in front of her. "April 2002," she repeats. "How sure about that are you, Caleb?"

"Pretty certain. It can't be much earlier anyway seeing as how I was part of Operation Anaconda, which I know for sure kicked off in March."

"What age were the children then, Caleb?"

"More than two years when she left. But I hadn't seen them since they were twenty months. When I left for military training in two-thousand-one."

"And, tell us, what did you find of them when you went back?" the sergeant continues, her note-taking suspended for now.

"She'd taken pretty much everything from our home. Didn't even leave me the only photographs. We got 'em in a booth in Las Cruces Hospital when they were eighteen months. Believe me, I tried. For nearly a year. Even from over there at the start of my second tour. Tried everything to trace them. I hired a private investigator to pick up their trail out in the camp and track them down in Arizona, a retired marine I knew from Pendleton, but it turns out those Indian reservations are like the godforsaken Bermuda Triangle. Eventually, some Chief Antone of the Tohono did write me in 2003. Maybe he read the fliers I left on the res and felt sorry for me. Anyway, he said my wife was happy and settled in a new relationship with another child to take care of and that she wanted no more to do with her white husband. He wrote she wanted me to just leave them alone." Mid-sentence, the steel in his voice melts and a short sympathetic silence descends on the room.

On many occasions amid the social swirl of San Francisco's moneyed classes, I have witnessed moments where carefully constructed masks slip from highly polished faces. The ranks of the rich are swollen with fakers parading as all kinds of perfect, but their dirty underbelly is often betrayed with a single stray word or sentence. Sometimes a fleeting look. It's usually after one-too-many alcoholic beverages and always in the company of folk who they suspect are like-minded. Bigots, racists, prigs, homophobes and misogynists revealed. Iced-over rotten cores laid bare with one loose disparaging comment about someone they view as a lesser being.

Here, in the oppressive atmosphere of Meeting Room Three, I see Caleb Freeth's mask slip and a soft center exposed. A glimpse into the human suffering behind the coarse facade. I can suddenly somehow imagine this man loving and being loved or gently holding a treasured child in his arms.

"Thank you for those questions, Sergeant," says Pitcavage. "Was your family's departure the only reason you left, Mr. Freeth, or was there also a disagreement with Blount?"

"Not really any specific disagreement as such, sir, more like layer upon layer of loathing. Simple fact is, that man lusted after my whore mother, but I was an inconvenience and he detested me from the moment he laid eyes on me. Cora, that's my mother's name, asked me to meet her at the church here in Prospero after school one Monday. I had no clue what it was about. No idea that bastard I bowed and scraped to every afternoon from the pews had already laid his filthy hands on her.

"While I waited for her to arrive that day, I remember thinking that I was going to stand up for myself. Tell her that six afternoons praying a week was enough and I wanted to keep Mondays free. Then Blount appeared out of nowhere and sat next to me. I was just a scrawny teenager and knew little of the world of men apart from drunkards, but I could tell straight off that his smile was as fake as a three-dollar bill. He told me right up he was going to make an honest woman of my mother and make a man out of me. Said he'd stand in where my no-good father never could.

"Way it worked out, he treated me like a slave and damn

near killed me. I was chief laborer for the setting up of the camp, building the fences, raising the church and all in the baking heat. If I wasn't building, I was training the younger children, foraging, hunting or traveling far and wide to trade with Indians, Mexicans and any other off-the-beaten track sorry-ass sons of bitches I happened upon on my trips into that desert and beyond.

"You name it in the way of hard labor, sir, and he had me working at it. Dusk 'til dawn. He was obsessed with the notion that the devil loves idle hands, so I worked, prayed and slept, day in, day out, and if I didn't do something exactly to his satisfaction, he beat me until I begged for mercy.

"You see, Blount was fully signed up to the belief that the will of a child must be broken before it ever has a chance to develop. He used to tell the mothers in church that a fussing or crying baby is exerting its selfish will and that will needs to be eliminated since wherever human will is, God's will cannot be. *Thou shalt beat him with the rod, and shalt deliver his soul from hell.* He quoted as he whipped. Thing is, he was always telling my mother that he was worried I had missed out on the right kind of training when I was very young and he thought he'd go about helping me catch up.

"Not much came my way in terms of food, either, but I got so good at hunting I would gorge myself when I trapped a few extra and that's what kept me alive. He only let me marry to help boost numbers, and when he met my Indian fiancée? Well, that was something to behold. Have you heard of the Bible reference to the mark of Cain, sir? The blackness that came upon the children on Canaan?"

We all stare at him, captivated with his story, but all his communications are directed solely at the FBI agent, who nods from time to time to keep the flow going.

"Well, old Blount despised all people of color and his racist views were poured onto us at every sermon, every day, like being baptized over and over with an unholy water of hate. Nope, there was nothing that goat hated more than off-white. 'Dirt on the skin means dirt on the soul,' he used to say."

"So he never accepted your wife, sorry, did you say her name?" asks the agent, searching down through his notes on the iPad.

"Her name was Anegam. Anegam Cesar. We met while I was on a trade mission in southern Arizona. Best twenty-eight days of my life, up to that point. But, boy, did she turn his stomach. Not only was she as red as a turkey's wattle, but she was Roman Catholic, too, and there was damn near nothing on this wide Earth that old bastard hated more than the pope's children. Actually, I remember thinking he'd had a heart attack the moment he clapped eyes on me arriving back to camp with her. He turned bright blue when we walked in the door of the communal hall. Bent over double he was, like he was about to croak right there and then. Turned out it was just a tepary bean gone down the wrong way and he coughed it up after my mother hit him on the back with a rug duster. Shot that sucker out like a lead pellet from a two-bore. I'm sure he would have marched her straight out the gate again if she wasn't so young and pretty and able for hard work."

"Course, I'm damn sure he must have made her life difficult when I was away," he adds somberly, "and no doubt my mother went along with it, or at least didn't object. Cora was … she's that pathetic bitch that exists in every dog pack. You know. The one that spends all its time rolled over in submission, four paws up, when an alpha comes sniffing around.

"So I guess I can't really say it was a huge surprise to hear that Anegam couldn't hack it anymore with me overseas. Might even have left sooner if it weren't for having the kids to occupy her. Neighbors told me as much when I went back that last time in the summer of aught-two. It's just a pity she couldn't have waited that bit longer, coz I s'pose … I had plans."

"You mentioned training of the younger children," says Pitcavage, doubling back to an earlier comment and perhaps eager to change the subject. "What kind of training are you talking about?"

"We trained them from knee-high in wood-crafting, hunting and survival skills like settin' fires and all manner of traps as well as fashioning weapons and shooting slingshot. By the time I left, every sister and brother over the age of ten could hit a black tail from thirty feet. If you aren't doing much else with your days apart from kneelin' and readin' the Bible, you can get very good at that stuff. Then there was practice in hand-to-hand combat like wrestling and martial arts and using basic weaponry," Caleb says.

"Blount's file has a whole section on his martial arts prowess," Pitcavage interjects. "Apparently, he qualified for the US Olympic judo squad in '64 but didn't participate due to injury."

"I have never heard that before, sir," says Caleb, nodding with interest, "but I have been on the receiving end of his talents on many occasions. He once flung me onto a crusted river bed so hard he fractured my skull. Went blind for two weeks." He bends his head forward, tilts it to the right and uses the palm of his hand to flatten a section of his short snowy hair to reveal a crescent-shaped, five-inch ridge in his scalp.

"Blount organized knockout tournaments every month to, as he put it, separate the wheat from the chaff. Could get the shit kicked out of you twelve times a year if you were lacking in some way, but that never bothered him. Preparation, he called it. Young and old, we were all preparing for the last three years of End Times when every flavor of shit was going to rain down on Mother Earth. Wars, disasters, plagues. All manner of hellfire and damnation. He told us that, as some of God's chosen few, we might have to fend off hordes of heretics wandering into the desert looking for a fast pass to eternity. I mean of course it was fairy tales. Like, I mean to say, you and me ..." he addresses Marge Newlands, who looks a bit taken aback at being included in his gang, "... we have a strong faith in Jesus, right, Sergeant? But we know these kind of beliefs don't make any sense. Ain't no way folks are gonna be lifted up to the sky out of their Ford pickups and office chairs one fine day, leaving everyone else behind. It's just that Blount was real good at peddling fairy tales, sir. Real, real good. He has—"

"How did he or the group ultimately fix on a specific date for the start of the Tribulation period, Mr. Freeth?" Pitcavage interrupts, posing the question that has nagged me since Caleb began his story. "In the past week, we have trawled the Pre- and Post-Tribulationist websites looking for a generally accepted start date of the so-called Abomination of Desolation, the starting gun of Daniel's fabled seventieth week. We couldn't find a single date that everyone agreed on, just debates and arguments, a list of possible years and a succession of unfulfilled prophecies from previous decades.

How did Blount settle on that day in particular, the twenty-ninth of September of two-thousand-thirteen?"

"He had it all worked out," Caleb replies. "And I swear to you that man could convince the wind to turn. If his passion before I left there was anything to go by, I'm certain he must have had everyone whipped into a fever by the time the start date in two-thousand-six actually came to pass.

"Basically, each week of Daniel corresponds to seven years and he maintained that the seventieth week would commence on the twenty-ninth of September of aught-six and end seven years later, with the second coming of Christ, on the ultimate day of atonement. On that last day of reckoning in two-thousand-thirteen, the heavens were supposed to open and we, along with all the born-again faithful who had gone before us, would be drawn up to the Lord for eternity. The prophecy holds that once all the heretics and non-believers were obliterated, the Earth would enjoy a thousand years of Christ's peaceful reign.

"His calculations were based on a set of complex signals embedded in the timing of the Jewish New Year and a succession of three special feast days that fell on specific dates in aught-six. He predicted the appearance of an antichrist three-and-a-half years into the Tribulation period who would make a new covenant with Israel and then break it to unleash the war of all wars, wiping out half the population of earth and leaving only the faithful behind, who would then be swept up to God's everlasting kingdom.

"I've often wished I could have been a fly on the wall when the old bastard first got wind of there being a black president sworn in in January aught-nine. Must've run around knocking on all the homes shouting, 'I told you so.' I figure the patrols must have been sent out there to guard the whole circus morning, noon and night, waiting to be attacked from sand or sky.

"I can assure you, it's no joke sitting out in the freezing-cold, black desert nights with the coyotes and the rattlers, but to do it night after night for over twelve hundred days with no enemy to speak of showing himself? Well, that's a slow death right there. Poor undernourished sons of bitches must have been getting themselves all prettied up inside and out in preparation for their big day and then when it came and went without so much as a stray firework, I can only imagine the scene around that central fire. One and all stuck there. Hopeless. Sheltering from the cold night winds and still looking at the same ugly faces like kiddies with empty stockings on Christmas morning."

"Funchess might have mentioned to you that he thinks Blount is sick," Pitcavage says. "Of course, he is seventy-one and it sounds like living conditions are fairly harsh out there, but would you say the false dawn you describe might have had a big impact on him, too? In terms of his mentality?"

"Hard to say really, sir. Don't forget you're talking about one of the most self-important people on this here Earth. One of them fancy shrinks in the Army would describe him as a psychopath or egotistical maniac and, by my reckoning, those types don't do disappointment, sir, do they?"

Pitcavage presses on. "The pastor has guesstimated there to be between seventy and a hundred people in the camp in total. Would you agree with that tally, Mr. Freeth?"

"I'd say he's right enough with those kind of numbers. There was a lot of breeding taking place around the time I left. At that stage, there would have been about seventy adults so that sounds like a good range, although I wouldn't be surprised if some left after the disappointment in 'thirteen."

Caleb's casual use of the word *breeding* sends a flicker of disgust around the table.

"What about arms and other weaponry in the compound? What would be your expectations along those lines?" asks the agent.

"Well, that's harder for me to say as I been gone so long, but I can tell you that when I was there, the stone barn alongside the main building housed a stockpile of slingshots, flint-headed axes, cudgels, bows and other very basic weapons. You'll never find swords or knives or firearms in First Truth. No electric goods, neither. Old Anthony told us those were false gods that had led men down the path of evil. *Put up again thy sword into his place: for all they that take the sword shall perish with the sword.* That's what Anthony quoted to me over and over when I told him I was going to fight Muslims in Afghanistan."

"What about the camp perimeter? How robust would the defenses have been when you were there?"

"Why? You planning Desert Storm or something?" Caleb replies sarcastically to a withering stare from Pitcavage suggesting that he just answer the question.

"There is a natural stone edifice that runs almost the whole way around the camp, but the first thing we did was build an inner fence to encircle the homes and the water well at the center. We added to it over the years, but it was still fairly flimsy. No doubt they would have secured it more in the run-up to aught-six End Times, though I can't say how much."

"Pastor Funchess has told us he noticed a significant shoring up of their perimeter defenses during his last two visits there in 'fifteen versus previous visits the year before," Pitcavage says. "Can you think of any reason for that? For instance, when you lived there, were there ever any problems of coming under attack from Mexican gangs, border jumpers, smugglers or other groups of that nature?"

"We had a few Mexican strays wander in over the years looking for sustenance, all right. Dumb sods never got anything but a shower of stones. But there was never any concerns along those lines in the camp, as I recall. Of course, these times are different, ain't that so? It's like a proper war zone down there nowadays in some of those border towns. All manner of savagery. Seeing as they are only ten miles from Mexico, maybe they have come under attack in recent years."

Pitcavage lays the iPad he has been note-taking with throughout the meeting down flat and leans back. "That's all of great help, Mr. Freeth. Thanks again for your time. We're nearly done here. I understand you are familiar with your neighbor on your right there, Mr. Mignolet, and we had a question-and-answer session with him earlier. His recollection is that on the night of the murder, you asked him whether *they* had said anything to him. In his mind the way the question was asked, it sounded like you might have had a pretty good idea who *they* were. What's your reaction to that assertion?"

Caleb hesitates and, for the first time in the hour or so since he arrived, turns and looks straight at me. Up close, his palest of pale blue eyes are mesmerizing, the color of glacial ice and just as menacing. "So the little bird has been chirping again. Tweet, tweet." He blares the last two words inches from my face, to shock, in the way that a "boo" might startle a child. I cast a see-what-I-have-to-deal-with look across the table to Pitcavage, who throws his eyes to heaven.

"Twelve years ago," Caleb continues, "when I had pretty

well given up trying to trace Anegam, I asked Clayton Marron to deliver a letter to my mother asking that she direct my family to where I live should they ever show up back at camp looking for me. She knows the Old County Road and I told her in the letter about the cross and the lights to reassure them that they would always be able to locate the house by day or night. When I saw fire trails on one of the nights leading up to the incident with Mike and the others, I held out some hope. Damnedest thing is, they may have been out there for months, but I missed 'em because of my high watts. Anyway, my security lights were switched off until eleven for a few evenings so I had seen torches on the—"

"You have me to thank for that," I interject.

Caleb, now bristling with annoyance, continues, "As I was saying, I saw the fire trails again on the night of the attacks and knew it was them. All First Truthers can make torches. The very best. Flame heads that can burn through the night. Pitch and fat, if they can't get kerosene. I had saddled up to head out there when *he*," the faintest nod of his head to the right indicates he is talking about me, "appeared out of the darkness and I heard the police sirens approaching."

"Do you think some of your family members could be among the troop we are after, Mr. Freeth?" Pitcavage asks.

"Not likely, sir. More's likely you'll find them waiting tables in the Desert Diamond Casino over there on the res in Arizona. Dumb-ass Indians auctioned off their culture for poker dollars. You know they barely have any of their hunting and fighting skills left, just breeding up their young to spin wheels, deal cards and ferry cocktails to addict trailer trash. I've no respect for that life and it makes me sick to think of my kids coming up there."

"But, Mr. Freeth," Pitcavage says his name as though rousing him from a deep sleep. "Mr. Mignolet tells us that they referred to your house. One of them pointed at your house and asked another, 'Is that it, Alonso?' Doesn't that suggest to you that at least one of them had read your letter or at least heard about it from your mother? Look here … this is one of them … the leader, Alonso, as witnessed and described by Ariel here."

The agent rustles momentarily through the papers in front of him and pulls out the identikit, turning it around for Caleb to examine. "Recognize anything in this face? Kind of distinctive, wouldn't you say? Maybe a likeness to one of your peers? Bear in mind the passage of time so this could be the son of someone of similar age to you."

Caleb takes the picture in both hands and looks fixedly at the face for a few moments. He inhales sharply through his nose and I notice the muscles in his jaw clench tight and tense repeatedly as though in spasm. "Alonso," he says quietly, as though trying to trigger some memory and I feel certain he is about to make a useful suggestion. Instead he shoves it unceremoniously back across the table. "Nothing familiar there, sir. I've always thought those black-and-white sketches all look the same. Tainted, you see. Tainted by the artist's reckoning of what a criminal should look like. And now that I think about it, I'm sure it is very likely that Cora would blabbermouth my business around the camp. You could never rely on that woman to keep a secret. She always shopped me to Blount when I stepped the tiniest bit out of line."

The phone in the center of the table trrr-rings as Pitcavage replaces the sketch in its sleeve. Sergeant Newlands hands the receiver to Officer Branson after speaking to the caller.

Standing up to take the call, the Border Patrol officer paces up and down at one end of the table and, as he talks, his battery of shiny teeth brush the butt end of the receiver every so often as though preparing to take a bite.

"We need to go to reception for a few minutes, Paul," he says, returning the phone to its cradle. "Our four o'clock's a bit early. We just need to meet and greet, really, so you'll have time to come back and wrap up here. Is that okay, sir?"

"Folks, my apologies, but these guys are from out of town. I'll be back to sum up. Won't take long. Maybe five minutes."

Awkward silence descends on Meeting Room Three once again when Pitcavage and Branson depart and I am about to remove myself and head for the temporary sanctuary of the restroom when Caleb addresses the sergeant. "I'll be wanting to be on that trip, Sergeant. I know full sure there's something planned and I'm coming, so you better line that up with Mr. Pitcavage there after I leave. Tell him about my knowledge of the area and tracking skills or such like, but whatever it takes, you need to make sure I'm in the posse." His words spill out like an addict trying to score a fix.

"Caleb, I'd advise you to stop your talk and sit quietly now," replies Marge Newlands in a matronly tone. "You don't know what you're talking about. This is police business and you are here to help in whatever way we ask you to. It is not for you to ask any favors and if you speak to me again in that tone, I will talk to the pastor about your behavior and you will undo all the hard work you've put in with him to rejoin the church. Am I making myself—"

"I'll tell them, Sergeant," Caleb shouts with such venom that spit spatters his chin. "All the dirty filthy details about your precious Mike's homosexual lover here. Do you want to hear? I swear I will tell all of them if you don't arrange for me to be in that posse. I'll tell them about that big wet kiss this lady-boy here had with him on the doorstep the night he was murdered. Nearly turned my stomach, it did, coz I never seen two grown men writhing and licking each other like that. Like Hollywood movie stars they were, only acting out their pornographic shoot fifty feet from my front gate. Up the stairs then with them, too busy hanging off each other to even pull the door closed behind them. What do you think Mike's pretty little fiancée would say, Marge? What about his family or his police family? Pastor would have to take back everything he said last week at the funeral and, well, you were there, too. He sure said a lot of stuff about Mike, Marge. A lot of stuff. Now I want to be on that trip and I need you to make it happen or I'm gonna lift the lid on the two golden boys."

It is clear from the change in Marge Newlands' normally cool exterior that Caleb's outburst has landed the emotional equivalent of a low counterpunch, knocking all the wind out of her at a time when she was reaching out to land a shot herself. It is hard to tell whether the revulsion evident in her features is a reaction to Caleb's blackmailing tactic or to what she was hearing about the secret private life of her beloved godchild. Yes, she already knew that Mike and I were lovers, but to have the picture painted for her in Technicolor is undoubtedly harder to take on board.

"You're one sick and twisted son of a bitch," I fume as some internal pressure valve bursts open. "Mike, who by the way, for some unknown reason, always stood up for your racist, homophobic ass, is not here to defend himself, but if he was, I'm fairly sure he would remind you how obsessed you have always been about keeping your own private business private and ask why you wouldn't afford him the same courtesy. He's not even two weeks dead, for Christ's sake. Have some respect. This is the guy who bailed you out of jail, you worthless piece of shit. I mean what's wrong with you people?" I'm really addressing both of them now. "It's screwed-up thinking. Your version of God is as twisted as the Jihadis'. It's so narrow and austere that it forced an incredible human being like Mike to live a lie. What loving creator? Look, I promise you one thing, Caleb, if I hear back that you have whispered so much as one word about Mike and me, to anyone, I promise you here and now that I will devote every resource at my disposal for the rest of my life to making you pay. That will be pure, unchristian vengeance, Caleb, served hot and cold and for years to come."

My adrenalin courses faster when a self-satisfied smirk creeps across Caleb's face and, without forethought, I grab him by the throat and momentum carries us and our chairs to the floor with a clatter of chrome and plastic. The element of surprise lasts long enough for me to land two punches on his face, my left hand braced on his chest, propping me up to deliver blows to his cheek and nose.

I was not that boy in school who got into scrapes. Fighting in general just wasn't part of my fairly sheltered youth, but punching Caleb Freeth feels surprisingly satisfying and I'm not sure when I'll stop until he takes a vice-like grip first of my flailing right arm and then, with his other hand, my throat. His body beneath me, now twisting and easily gaining the upper hand, has the feel of a giant ship's rope. Taut, dense sinews primed for power by a life of hard physical work. Before Sergeant Newlands comes around the table, he pins me down and my hands are frantically trying to dislodge his grip on my throat. He smiles calmly like a cat toying with a mouse.

"Idiots. Pathetic idiots. Get up!" I think I hear the sergeant shout.

"Nothing you have in your little fanny pack you call a life can hurt me, you filthy queer," Caleb says, releasing his grip and shoving my head back down to the floor.

"Are you all right, Mr. Mignolet?" Newlands asks as I gasp for air like a landed trout.

Caleb rises to his feet and looks down at me, his nostrils flaring with aggression.

"Nothing you have or can buy holds fear for me, you hear me? Nothing. Don't threaten me again if you want to stay alive. Don't talk to me again. Don't even look at me again. You understand? And Sergeant, you know where I stand on this now and I know you folks have my number, so you can take it that I'm gonna be waiting by the phone tonight and tomorrow for the call up and you know full sure what I will do if that call doesn't come."

He slams the door on its hinges with such force as he departs, one of the pair of strip lights that caused me so much distress hours before fizzles and dies.

Chapter Thirteen

Love Thy Neighbor

Before heading home, I drop in at the Cuppa Jo to forage for anything that might qualify as dinner. Miranda is busy serving a group of customers. "No graphs for analysis today, then?" she chirps from behind the counter when she sees me come in. "Made enough money outta me already?" She throws the words in short bursts over her shoulder as her attention is fixed on carefully controlling the coffee machine's steam output. Submerged, the spout works its bubbly magic to produce a tray of frothy cappuccinos for a band of bricklayers waiting expectantly by the door. The guttural groan of the jets builds to a hissing crescendo as she turns the dial until milky foam erupts over the edge of the jug.

"Chocolate today, or are you sweet enough already?" she asks the men before fixing the plastic takeaway lids in place and sending them on their way with a smile.

The nutty aromas of freshly ground coffee permeate the space along with a background hint of cinnamon from the mound of sticky buns to one side of the checkout. I am momentarily transported to ritualistic 5:45 a.m. pit stops in the Billy Can Coffee House off California Street in San

Francisco and am taken by surprise when a pang of longing for my real life nudges the pit of my stomach.

"Cheer up," Miranda says, snapping me out of my trance. "Mike would want us all to cheer up a bit."

"I agree. He would. Large Americano, please," I croak. "Intravenously, if it's an option. And these too, please." I hold up a half-eaten, super-size pack of barbecue-flavored Lays and a tuna wrap, the only soggy leftover from the lunchtime trade. "An athlete needs sustenance."

She looks at me as a mother might glare at an errant child. "Did you pull another all-nighter in the casino last night, Ariel? Thought I warned you before about Prospero's social scene. It will chew you up and spit you out." She proffers a pink cardboard cup, snug in a corrugated cardboard sleeve, and waits a few seconds for me to take it while I drain a Gatorade.

"You finished at the station for today? Mom told me they are making good progress, but the whole town is on edge. There are border officers in from Lordsburg and Deming and even the FBI has been spotted. Haven't been as busy here since I started. An actual army of vehicles passed out front only ten minutes ago. Seriously. A presidential parade. I guess at least we know they are serious."

"Permission to shoot from left field?" I ask, to herald an abrupt change of subject.

"Shoot," she says.

"What can you tell me about the practice of foot-washing in the church here? I mean, what it signifies. Who does it?" I'm not entirely sure why, but I feel a little embarrassed asking the question and wonder if she might be taken aback, but her response is nonchalant.

"Well, I've never had to do it myself, but I have seen it

done a few times in the town hall. It's called Maundy. An ordinance. A kind of ritual like baptism. It's seen as a sign of humility or someone reconciling with the sins of their past before being born again through baptism. The people washing are mostly outsiders or non-believers who want to join our church and have proven they are ready. Sometimes batches of them wash Pastor's feet at a small ceremony ahead of their baptism. It's fairly standard, really. Why? You thinking of joining up? I'll vouch for you, if you like," she teases.

I force a smile to maintain the air of frivolity, but my mind has strayed to an uncomfortable image of Mike kneeling before the pastor. "Miranda, as a friend and as someone who is frankly in awe of your potential, please make sure you get the hell out of this place as soon as possible. Before it suffocates you."

"It's not that bad. Is it?" She looks genuinely taken aback.

"Okay, I am speaking as an outsider, but none of my experiences in this town over the past seven months have lived up to the Bible's basic tenet of *Love thy neighbor as thyself.* All the evidence out there tells us that extreme religious practice dehumanizes, Miranda, and I can tell you for sure that extremism is alive and well here in Prospero. The Southern Baptists I know in San Francisco generally couldn't be more accepting or fair-minded and none are consumed with the prejudice that came across loud and clear at the funeral. My advice is to leave as soon as you can. Gain your own perspective, if nothing else. You want to be a vet? Please, please go and do it. Seize the day. As I said before, if I can help you with that then all the better. It would be my honor to do that given how much I feel you would thrive. I think that once you get out, your own view of this place will change."

"I hear what you're saying, Ariel. Unlike most of the kids in town, I have access to the Internet because my dad turns a blind eye, so I know that the big world out there is brimming with pleasures. But you need to understand that most of the people living here have chosen to take a different path. It's not easy, but many take it just so they can bypass the pitfalls of mainstream life. You know? The mindless mall trawl? The greasy pole? That corporate hamster wheel? This town offers people an alternative. And, okay, Pastor can be a bit of a bully, I'll certainly give you that. But if you accept that the Bible is God's divine and untainted truth, then it's easier to accept his leadership because, faults and all, he is a man totally devoted to the Lord's word. He's only human, so he makes mistakes, but he's basically a good shepherd, Ariel."

I suddenly realize the depth of Miranda's faith. "But where is Jesus in the language we heard at Mike's funeral, Miranda? Didn't John give us God's commandment to *Love one another as I have loved you*? How can you reconcile that with the language in Funchess's sermon? The dress code, the hell-and-damnation preaching, the ban on rock music? I mean, I ordered a glass of wine in the restaurant off Main last week and the lady looked at me as though I were warming up a spoon of heroin. And my mother and I? We were treated like the lepers. With outright contempt. By pretty well everyone in this town, apart from you."

"In fairness, there is no justification for that," she concedes. "Maybe folks are still suspicious about you. Mike was really loved, Ariel. He was about as close to a local hero as we've ever had. People are hurting and maybe they just want someone to blame."

I shake my head. "The Resurrection Baptist Church is something apart, Miranda."

She is starting the pre-close clean-up when I bid farewell and, as I walk to the car, I begin to regret my unprompted tirade. The drive home takes longer than usual as the day's tumult makes concentrating difficult and I keep drifting to the highway's edge.

On returning home, I decide to take a full sleeping pill and pass out on the couch, awakening ten hours later with pristine dawn sunshine licking the side of my face. Even Caleb's lights had failed to disturb me. Still groggy and shielding my eyes from the sun's rays, I stumble in the direction of the kitchen but trip over my laptop, which sits open-mouthed beside the couch where I set it down on Monday night. On all fours and cursing, I glimpse the battery light flashing red and open it wider to turn it off.

Time to Come Back is the subject line of an e-mail that catches my eye. Sent at lunchtime the day before, it is addressed to my work nickname, PT (short for ponytail), and is from my business partner, Ben.

12:45 p.m., Tuesday, Sept. 20, 2016

PT

I told you the desert was full of weirdos. Run your ass back to the magic black chair. It will help take your mind off things and you'd fucking die for the pairs right now. Check out SPY/DIA and USO/OIL attached. Come on, let's make more Monnnnnneeyyy!!!

Heading out to pick up some of Sammy's dim sum this lunch—can't get those babies in New Mexico!

BEN

P.S. The guys at Everest and Coyle are doing a great block-and-tackle job here since last week's news item. Clients hopefully all set straight by now. Will keep you posted on feedback as it comes. Still need you back for performance though. Slipped

110 bp v peers last quarter (better this month).

Ben Talbot
Managing Partner
Cardinal Nine Capital
Suite 68
Embarcadero Center
San Francisco CA 94111

Typical of Ben to put the funnies first and sneak in the serious stuff in the postscript. The faintest smile flickers across my face as I imagine him having the chat with Sammy on Kearny. Ben is an uncomplicated, fast-talking, slightly overweight, non-practicing Jewish New Yorker who finished top of his class in applied mathematics, part funding his college fees by doing stand-up in late-night bars in Soho. In the eight years since he moved to San Francisco, his New Yorkese has intensified rather than waned, to the point where he now speaks only in heavily accented, rapid-fire witticisms that make him the dream colleague in an intense working environment.

If he's headed out early for dim sum, it means he must have had a good day's trading and probably told Sammy Sung, proprietor of the best Chinese kitchen in San Francisco, a little bit too much about how much money he made with all the excitement of a soccer-crazy seven-year-old turning post-goal celebratory tumbles. Sammy, no doubt, tut-tutted ruefully about not having a college education but reminded Ben that the Descendants of the Dragon are coming over the Pacific to kick the Americans up their ass. Then, with that cheerful, wrinkly smile that makes the whites of his eyes disappear, he would have asked in his strongest Chinese twang, which we all suspect he hams up for effect, "Extra fine soy or sachet for you?" before beckoning, "Next-best customer, please now."

The last time I spoke to Ben was three weeks ago when I called to ask him to stop copying me on so many work e-mails. I got through to Bess who told me that Ben was under his desk and too busy to talk but would get back to me shortly.

His tendency to take cover in the office was a habit he brought with him from the vast football field that is Morton Gannon's equity trading floor in New York. He had worked there as an institutional equity broker in the late nineties before joining me on the buy side of the house in 2006, managing money for ultra-high-net-worth clients.

The noise levels in the equity dealing room in those days were not far off the decibel count of an aircraft engine at full tilt. His solution, when trying to concentrate on brokering a deal, was to take the conversation under his desk, tucked in beside the computer tower, the shredder, his briefcase and a spaghetti junction of cabling. A small red flag on top of his Bloomberg screen alerted colleagues to his presence.

At first, Ben's behavior was a source of great hilarity, but this peculiar practice began to catch on as his commission statistics skyrocketed from just above average to top of the pile, despite having an institutional client list considered to be of moderate potential.

Word of his success spread month after month as the brokers' score card was distributed by the head of the desk to be passed along for each to peruse briefly. Held together with industrial-strength staples, the top-secret document had one sheet per broker with their name, list of clients and commission vital statistics. Of huge value to rival firms, its progress around the room was supervised by an intern or compliance specialist who stood uncomfortably close behind your seat to avert the threat of espionage using phone cameras.

The score card told you, in terms of commission dollars earned per client, how you were tracking year-to-date versus the year before. As you could also see at a glance how others around you were doing, it had the express purpose of fanning the flames of competition among a cohort of the world's population whose natural dog-eat-dog disposition was already close to problem levels. It was a thin document with the metaphoric weight of a nuclear warhead. It was never enough to just do as well as last year with the same clients, even if last year was a bonanza year. The target was always moving ahead—and staying ahead of a rising target was how to earn a huge bonus.

As Ben's numbers crept ever higher and his list of new clients grew, sub-desk self-entombment began to catch on, and the heads of the previously scornful began to disappear until, at times, you might wander through the room at peak mid-morning call time and think the majority of Morton Gannon's institutional equity brokers had taken an early lunch.

Our own office environment at Cardinal Nine is, relatively speaking, calm and geared toward research and contemplation as opposed to energy and high intensity, but the main trading room is open plan and prone to the odd bout of noisy haggling, and when Ben wants to clear his mind of all outside stimuli, he still takes refuge under his desk.

As Bess had promised, Ben did FaceTime me shortly after, although it was not his round sallow face that greeted me but a Bloomberg screen showing the five-year graphs of both FTL (Festival Plc) and RMT (Royal Maritime), two Holiday Cruise companies with a historical correlation of over ninety percent. A ticker-tape news scroll described a ship delivery delay at Festival. The quiver in the graphic from the shake in Ben's hand as he held the iPad did not disguise the attractive potential of the sudden divergence from trend. His voice in the background crooned a mantra, "Screw New Mexico. This is the most beautiful scenery," before he turned the camera on himself and hung up mid-belly laugh.

As I read, a new e-mail jumps into the top of the scroll. It is a follow-up from Ben and, reading the heading, I immediately understand its import. To give it my complete attention, I ferry my laptop to a power source in the office.

7:05 a.m., Wednesday, Sept. 21, 2016

PT

Spoke to key folks at Garton this afternoon on advice from Everest. Am now worried they are going to need serious hand-holding from both of us to keep them on board. Jim Bretworth (remember that dickhead at the Kaua'i barbecue?) has been looking for an excuse to persuade his board to cut us but performance has always stood in his way. Your shit storm there in Nowheresville has given him his reason. Can you come home to meet them?

Ahead of you meeting with them in person (is next Wednesday a possibility?), I have arranged a conference call with the Garton Board this Thursday 2pm and have advised them that you will participate in order to answer any urgent questions they have. Up to twenty others including our core investment partners will dial in. Please call Bess at noon tomorrow for a pre-meet download re performance, sample incoming queries and dial-in details. We need to nail this one.

Ben

Garton is a massive fund-of-funds investor. Registered in the Bahamas, managed out of London, with $30 billion under management, they have had $2 billion invested with Cardinal Nine Capital for the past four years—a long time in the fickle world of hedge funds. I can only imagine the slither of compliance personnel from meeting to meeting since my name hit the headlines eleven days ago. Conference calls between partners to discuss the "whiff of sulfur" surrounding Cardinal Nine. Discreet lunches with wringing of hands and mutterings over knuckles concerning collateral risk, indefinable risk, unnecessary risk, all manner of risk associated with being associated with someone with even the whiff of a whiff of sulfur.

Out of respect for Ben, I reply immediately.

Hi Ben

Not surprising from Bretworth but other key folks at Garton must be made to understand that I am both a victim and a key witness here. There is absolutely no suggestion whatsoever now, from any quarter, that I am, in any respect, a suspect. All records relating to my arrest have been expunged. I am the chief witness assisting investigations here and the FBI is now on the scene. Send me an e-mail letting me know exactly what you think needs to be said on Thursday. Whatever personal reassurances I can give, I will give. If they need to speak to senior investigators on the ground, I think I can arrange that too. I will call Bess at 1pm Wednesday and we will hit Bretworth et al with everything on performance metrics.

PT

P.S. Prep some slides on latest successful trading positions and new ideas ahead of the call. We will drop these into the discussion. Nothing will turn neutral heads better than tangible, new money-makers.

For the first time in seven months, I log on to Cardinal Nine's website to update myself on our current positions and performance metrics and quickly lose myself in a sea of spreadsheets, price ratio charts and research analysis. Far from reigniting stress, this exercise surprisingly offers relief as I find that my eye has sharpened and I trawl the data with ease. Head down, time accelerates to the point where I am in danger of being late to meet Sunil's flight, due to land in Las Cruces at eleven a.m.

Chapter Fourteen

Visitations and Encounters

Hugs are a part of Sunil, as natural as breathing. I have often thought that what he lacks in verbal expression he more than compensates for with physical display, such that it might make most people feel slightly uncomfortable. I am very *most people* but have grown used to this tactile aspect of our relationship and, over the years, have come to appreciate it more and more. When we meet amidst the throng of the arrivals hall in Las Cruces, he doesn't hold back, drawing me into the folds of his skull-print chiffon scarf, despite disapproving glances from a nearby group of God-fearing pensioners standing protectively around their luggage.

"You look awful, Ariel," Sunil tells me as we exit the airport parking lot. "Sorry man, I don't want to make you feel worse, but I have never seen you so thin, even during the finals. Before I go tomorrow, we're going shopping for some basics and I'll be sending you hourly e-mail reminders to eat until we get you home. You need to build yourself up. To absorb the shock, you know? How many miles have you been covering these past few days?"

"Don't really add them up," I say, lowering the driver's window and enjoying the rush of air as we hit the freeway.

"Hundreds, I guess. It's the rock I'm clinging to." I have to raise my voice so he can hear me over the road noise and the screech and flap of the wind wrestling the window frame as we reach cruising speed in the fast lane. "If I don't run, I find it hard to get going at all the next day. And I mean get-out-of-bed going. It's only been a week, but that's my routine and it's really helping."

"Shut the window, man. This thing has air conditioning, and the noise …"

"If you open your side as well, it's not as bad. Really. Try it. It feels good if you don't talk."

"The reason I came here was to talk with you, Ariel. Now would you please shut the goddamn window?"

Unlike me, it takes a lot to make Sunil curse. It's just not his style. The last clear memory I have of hearing him utter an expletive of any hue was over a year ago at a charity ball in Oakland where the mayor, a Democrat to whom Sunil had acted as adviser during his 2010 election campaign, was repeatedly heckled by a Tea Party supporter while he made his after-dinner speech. Sunil kept a poker face throughout, but we left before the end to lie in ambush. As the offender hastily exited through the building's giant electronic glass doors, Sunil shadowed him all the way down each of the twenty or so marble steps to his waiting car, taking him so aggressively to task over his rude behavior that the man unceremoniously jettisoned the valet and accelerated away like a Formula One driver out of the pits with Sunil roaring "dickhead" in his wake.

Arguing, on the other hand, has been part and parcel of our friendship since the very beginning with each and every difference of opinion getting a free and frank airing only to be lightly shrugged off later. Sunil is the only person in my life with whom I have this dynamic and I value it more than any of the benign listening ears that characterize the majority of my friendships.

"Do you want to go to the house first?" I ask quietly, having raised the window.

"Look, I'm sorry. I shouldn't have reacted like that. I just … I want to fix this mess. At least to help *you* fix it, if I can, and we don't have a lot of time. Let's go to the house, drop my bag off and then head to Prospero. I really have to see this place for myself."

We pull into the driveway and as we wait for the automatic garage door to rise, a smiling face appears at my window, as though conjured out of thin air.

"Hi there, Mr. Mignolet," Maria Stenson pipes cheerfully as though we are old friends. "May I, like, ask you a couple of questions if possible? It won't take long. Five minutes max." She sounds a lot more confident than last time.

"Sorry, I have a meeting with my lawyer," I reply through the glass and point to Sunil. I don't want to encourage her in the slightest by rolling down the window. "I'm tired of telling you I have nothing more to say to the press. Period. You're wasting your time driving all the way out here. Where's your car, by the way?" I ask as I inch toward the open garage. "Didn't notice it as we came in."

"Your neighbor let me park it in off the road. He couldn't have been more obliging."

The subtlest enigmatic nuance in her delivery and smile sparks a sinking feeling as I wave goodbye and, once inside, I sit trance-like in the Jeep waiting for the clunk of the garage door behind us.

"Fuck. He's told her everything, Sunil. I know it. The way she said that back there? Yesterday at the meeting, my neighbor threatened to reveal my affair with Mike and that woman is the journalist I told you about the other day, the one sniffing around asking about Mike and me. Christ. I won't survive this, Sunil," I say breathlessly, my knuckles taut on the steering wheel, which at this moment is all that is keeping me from physically curling up in the seat. "I haven't got the reserves. And his family—they will be crushed. That prick."

"Calm down and breathe," Sunil says in the dependable, soothing tone I recognize from years ago. "Let's get you upstairs, get some sugar into you, and when the lady is gone, we'll head into town and talk everything through. Try and think positively for a second here, man. She might simply be flying a kite."

Upstairs, Sunil drops his overnight gear in the guest room and tries to free me from the grip of an acute anxiety attack with two co-codamol washed down with a tall glass of out-of-date orange juice.

"You'll have to get up to use the john at some point soon if nothing else," he jokes as I swallow the last of it.

"This space is off-the-charts stunning," he says, admiring the view from the center of the glass surround. "Truly awesome. I've tried to imagine it these past few months from the FaceTime glimpses, but this is way beyond what I visualized. What mountains are those?" His pointing finger sweeps in an arc across the distant indigo-and-maroon ranges on the eastern and western horizons.

"Small Hatchet and Big Hatchet ranges on your left and the Animas Mountains to the west," I reply from the couch. "You can see exactly twenty-seven peaks in all from here. Seven tall and pointy in Little Hatchet, including Playas Peak and Wave Mountain, and the rest small- to medium-size smooth tops, apart from Gillespie Peak in the middle of the Animas and peak thirteen off in the distance in the center of Big Hatchet. That one's the most perfectly triangular of all the pinnacles."

Sunil stares at me in a way that suggests he thinks I may have finally gone over the edge.

"Take a look over there in the corner," I tell him, pointing lifelessly to the right of the fireplace at an easel and, next to it, a thick pile of A3 vellum sketch sheets draped unceremoniously over a three-legged footstool.

Sunil says nothing at first, just kneels down and flicks through the drawings, each one sketched with some combination of only six shades of acrylic crayon, boxes of which are stacked neatly against the wall. All the drawings are in time order, with the most recent, at the top of the pile, dated September ninth, 2016.

"There should be one hundred and ninety-seven of them," I inform him. "About half and half Hatchet and Animas. Prefer the Hatchets myself because it gets more cloud action and the purples are more intense," I add, not looking at Sunil but lying on my side in a state of paralysis, rhythmically opening and closing my eyes to take brief snapshots of Letterhead, whose messages are indecipherable today.

This is the first time anyone else has seen my drawings. I hid them during my mother's visit so she wouldn't worry that I had developed another obsessive-compulsive behavior, and I don't know why but I felt the need to stash them under my bed on the few occasions Mike was in the house. It surprises me when a tingle of nervous energy reverberates through the base of my stomach as I wait for Sunil's reaction.

"I wouldn't give up the day job yet, but some of these later ones are really good, A, especially considering that it's your left hand and what I know about the extent of, or should I say complete lack of, your artistic talent. Have you thought about hanging them up in here to fill up all this wall space? It'd be like *A Beautiful Mind* meets *My Left Foot*," he adds with a chuckle.

A meditative quiet descends on the room as Sunil spends more time going through the sketches one by one.

"Did this whole journey help at all, do you think, Ariel? Therapeutically, I mean?" he asks, coming to sit beside me on the sofa.

"Yes, it did. It was great, Sunil." I gather myself up into a seated position and am treated to a blast of early-afternoon sunshine on my face. "Those weeks leading up to the night of the murders I ... really, I can't say it was one thing or another so maybe it was a bit of everything, but however I got there, I had ... peace, I guess you could call it. And, maybe, love. They crept in together, here in the middle of nowhere. Now? I don't know what's left of all that."

"I suspect it's still in there," Sunil says. "The regained ground. You will get through this and, when you do, all this ... this self-healing will stay with you. Obviously, you can't be objective about it now, but I bet you time will show that none of it has been in vain. Come on. Let's get out of here." He hauls me to my feet. "You've spent enough time wallowing."

Prospero is unusually quiet for mid-morning and we find a parking spot easily on the main drag across from the police station. Sunil is surprised by the attention he attracts as we progress along the sidewalk and the eyes of every passing shopper rest on him for fractionally longer than a normal inquisitive glance.

"They must never get to see any Alexander McQueen around here," he jokes.

We stop in the tiny drug store to buy a toothbrush and on to The Fairfield for a newspaper. There the surly woman at the checkout is so enthralled with the sight of us she struggles to get the right change out of the cash register, fishing noisily for a dime like a clumsy toddler, unable to stop gawking at us long enough to establish its exact location.

"How far are we from the border?" Sunil asks as we leave.

"About thirty-eight miles to the nearest point."

"Then why is everyone so pasty?" he asks. "I always thought New Mexico was as much Latino and Native American as Caucasian."

Instead of answering, I point toward the end of Main Street at the church steeple and bid him follow. The freshly painted four-foot sign outside the neat, red-brick church gives the times of the five weekly services in large block letters that can be slid into place. The next one is due to start at two-thirty, in just under thirty minutes. Underneath the times, in smaller, permanent text, a paragraph describes the fellowship's creed:

> The Resurrection Baptist Church (est. 1987) believes the King James Version of the Bible to be the perfect and infallible Word of God. We believe the Word of God as presented in the King James Bible to be inspired by God in its origin and divinely preserved through the generations. We don't compromise. We live God's Scripture. We bear witness to His clear and simple truth.

"Sounds fairly benign until you actually read some excerpts from the King James Version," I tell Sunil. "I did a bit of research myself a few months ago, after I read this. The

Bible was produced by a committee of English academics in sixteen-eleven and they must have been a fairly dour bunch because there are verses in there warning against pretty much everything enjoyable. And if the warnings aren't made explicitly enough, the folks that follow its instruction today seem hell-bent on interpreting everything along ultraconservative lines. Look at this." I hold my phone up to Sunil on the first Google result page showing the KJV Bible's verse concerning homosexuality: *Leviticus 20:13: If a man also lie with mankind, as he lieth with a woman, both of them have committed an abomination: they shall surely be put to death; their blood [shall be] upon them.*

"Basically it's a Puritan's procedures manual, chockfull of advice about smacking your kids and covering up your women. The majority of folks who chose to move to this town over the past thirty years may or may not have been predisposed to this kind of extremism to begin with, but once they sign up to the club, they sit in this church week in, week out and are asked by a persuasive pastor to adhere to his personal interpretation of the book. The lack of diversity around the place seems to simply be a byproduct of this brand of Baptist teaching. It's not a requirement to be white, it just seems to pan out like that. Like subliminal negative racial marketing."

We turn to walk back to the center of town and I immediately recognize the woman walking toward us as Eliza Marron. At no stage during or after the funeral had I seen her at close quarters. When I made my attempt to commiserate with her father, she had already been ushered away by another group of mourners and I was careful at the graveside to stay well back from the inner circle of grieving friends and relatives.

Mike's fiancée would stand out at any distance. She carries

her tall, slim frame with poise and grace and her honey-blonde hair falls in soft curls around her shoulders, framing a pretty face that's more girl-next-door than femme-fatale. Up close, her pale skin accentuates the dark circles beneath her eyes where pain and sadness have made their first assault on her youth.

I would probably have kept walking, perhaps offered a polite nod as we passed, but before she reaches us, she stops, looks directly at me and waits for us to draw alongside.

"You're Ariel Mignolet," she says.

I nod and smile. "Eliza Marron?"

She extends her hand politely in turn to myself and Sunil.

"I'm so sorry for your loss, Eliza. I didn't know him very well, but from what I did know, I'm sure Mike would have made a great husband. It must be really hard for you." I have to focus extremely hard to make the words I had mentally rehearsed so often before the funeral sound spontaneous.

"I keep thinking it's strange," she muses distractedly, as though picking up the loose ends of a separate conversation. "I mean I can't stop wondering why the Glass House had to be his last port of call on this Earth. Sorry. That was the name we had for your house, Mr. Mignolet. The Glass House. I do know the *factual* why of course. I got all the whys and wherefores of his last hours from the police. But it's a different why I am interested in. More in the realm of fate, if I can put it like that. Only, answers to those kinds of questions will never emerge, Mr. Mignolet, will they?" She trails off wistfully and Sunil and I remain as silent as we are confused.

Her grief is so tangible, it is distressing to witness. Her words, clearly born out of acute loss, might have been delivered to any random passerby. We are not required to engage in conversation here but can help by simply listening. I feel a strange kinship with her. We, the human wreckage. The living breathing collateral damage left standing in the aftermath of Mike's untimely passing. I'm certain that in all his reckonings about how his future might ultimately unfold, he would never have anticipated a collision as dramatic as this between his two lives. She and I together, chatting outside the Resurrection Baptist Church. She and I and the sordid secret floating in the air between us like a noxious gas.

"I mean of *all* the places," she continues in a tone of annoyance as though a little bit demented by the whole issue. "Must have been ten times we drove out that lonely highway to look at it. Photographed it, too. From all angles … your house." She shakes her head in disbelief. "We were drawing up plans, you see, for our own place, and we loved the design. What's it like to live there?"

Sunil turns away, staring down the street, unable to look at her.

"It's a great house, Ms. Marron. It's one of the main reasons I chose to come here actually," I reply, deciding the less said the better, as my head explodes with images of drive-by photography and domestic bliss along with the gnawing sense that I didn't know Mike at all.

"Have you come across a journalist from the *Tucson Gazette*, Mr. Mignolet?" she inquires in a blind-siding change of topic.

Sunil has his poker face on, but if Eliza was looking closely enough, she would have seen me physically flinch.

"I picked up a message on my phone this morning and your name was mentioned as someone else she has spoken to," she continues. "It was a bit garbled, but basically she said she has a few questions for me for a follow-up piece. Do you know her?"

I need to grab this conversation by the scruff of the neck. "That woman's name is Maria Stenson. A tabloid hound passing herself off as a proper journalist. She's bad news, Ms. Marron, and my advice to you is avoid her calls and don't let her in if she doorsteps you. I came across her during those crazy few days after Mike's murder and since then she has been like a leech."

Early churchgoers have begun arriving, maneuvering their cars into the few parking spots along the curb but remaining in their vehicles while talking on their phones or reading newspapers to fill in the twenty or so minutes left before the service is due to start.

"Do you know if it was quick, Mr. Mignolet? You know, his final moments?" she asks, leaning closer, her doleful gray eyes studying me in great detail so as not to let a scintilla of the truth escape. "He had so many injuries. Did you know? They … they were messy killers."

"I think it was very quick, Ms. Marron. No more than seconds. From what I saw, I believe the first strike ended his life." This is a lie. I can't be sure. "I can also tell you, with some confidence, that the investigation is gathering momentum now, so you can rest assured those responsible will be brought to justice. Hopefully that will bring you some solace."

"Yes, maybe that will help," she says but looks utterly unconvinced.

Having stayed on the periphery of the conversation up to this point, Sunil moves nearer and squeezes my forearm to draw my attention to a black BMW SUV with darkened windows that has pulled to a halt almost in the middle of the road alongside us.

"That's my father," she says, raising her hand to acknowledge him just as the passenger window slowly descends and Clayton Marron's round face appears, leaning across from the driver's side.

"Stay away from us, you hear me?" Marron bellows in my direction and I notice that one or two of the early arrivals have now stepped out of their cars to get a closer look at the minor drama unfolding.

"It's okay, Pop, we're just talking," his daughter shouts over to him from the edge of the sidewalk, and I notice how dowdy her clothing is for a woman in her early twenties. Long dark-green skirt and beige cardigan, with short socks and black leather shoes.

"Come with me now, Eliza. I'm going to collect the pastor," he says, and the steel in his voice suggests there is no room for negotiation.

"I better go," she says resignedly. "I'm glad we met, Mr. Mignolet. Mike told me all about you. He said you weren't well when you arrived here, but the countryside had worked its magic on you. Told me you had an amazing life in San Francisco and I do hope it's as good to you when you go back there. Good day to you now."

"Goodbye, Ms. Marron," I say, and as she crosses the road and gets in beside her father, I have the strangest sensation that Mike has just spoken to me from beyond the grave.

At the Cuppa Jo, I introduce Sunil to Miranda and am delighted when an immediate rapport develops between them. Sunil's level of comfort with people is directly correlated with how many words come out of his mouth in their company, so when I struggle to gain a foothold on their chat at the counter, I know he is completely at ease.

For everyone in the world who admires him, there is probably an equal number who would describe Sunil as aloof or arrogant because his standard response when confronted with a person he doesn't like or has nothing in common with is to clam up. This passive-aggressive behavior didn't serve him well in the early years of his career in law and he was forced to acquire a kind of feigned diplomacy that just about gets him through but doesn't sit well with his soul. As a consequence, in his down time he relaxes back into a more reserved, taciturn demeanor that is becoming more pronounced with every passing year.

We take a table near the window and I ask Sunil to place my order while I step outside to call Marge Newlands.

"Hello. Sergeant Newlands." The sergeant always answers by saying her name very quickly.

"Hello, Sergeant. It's Ariel Mignolet here. You said to call your cell with any questions or problems."

"Yes?"

Her predictably economic use of words makes me shake my head, much to the confusion of Sunil who is watching me through the window and miming pouring gestures to ask if I want a coffee.

"I mentioned to you and Agent Pitcavage about the fact that the press continues to be a problem. That situation has escalated today because I am now certain that one individual from the *Tucson Gazette* is gathering evidence from a variety of sources to write a story about the relationship between me and—"

"Stop!" she blurts, cutting me off abruptly. "One moment, Mr. Mignolet. Sorry. I'm just in the middle of something. If you can stand by there, I'll call you back in two minutes, okay?"

Less than two minutes later, my phone rings again as Sunil points to a picture of a green salad on the one-page laminated menu, to go with the quiche I ordered, and I give him the thumbs up.

Intermittent clicks on the line tell me Marge Newlands has called me back from a phone booth. "You were talking about the journalist," she continues earnestly.

"Basically, Sergeant, I met Eliza Marron today and this one particular journalist is now knocking on her door, having already hounded me for two days. I also suspect she interviewed Caleb Freeth this morning and I think there is every likelihood he has told her about me and Mike. I'm not sure if you can help, but it … it's an appalling vista."

"Is it Maria Stenson?" she asks over another click.

"Yes."

"Okay. I'm glad you called. Leave it with me."

Miranda asks us to stay on for a coffee "lock-in" once we have finished eating and the last of the late-lunch customers have departed. We happily agree and order a fresh pot of Arabica. After officially engaging him as my sole personal legal counsel, I fill Sunil in on all the details of the meeting the previous day with Paul Pitcavage and Caleb Freeth.

His response is conclusive and unequivocal. "This is not a good situation, Ariel. It's not good and you know it's not. For one thing, if the press is sniffing around your affair with Mike, it strikes me the best thing you can do to kill it is leave town. The story is more likely to die without any live bodies around to feed off. Then there are the very real threats of the torch-wielding crazies returning in the dead of night and finishing what they started or, more likely still, a visit from your unhinged neighbor who is clearly more than a tad unpredictable, with a predilection for violence. And my primary concern, frankly, is that you were not exactly coming into this whole situation from a strong place, man. Don't tell me you want to stay to be near all the friends you've made either because it's quite clear from our little encounters this morning that the locals don't want you to linger."

He holds up his coffee with cupped hands and the steam rises between us. "You do know that you're under no obligation to stay. For example, have you given any thought to offering to make the identifications they're trying for remotely? You can be sure the FBI will have satellite technology up the ying yang with them when they head out there and you could just as easily play spot-the-terrorist online from your favorite armchair in San Francisco when they get up close to the suspects. In my view, staying here a day more than necessary is high risk from whatever angle you want to look at it and I can't think of any reason why you wouldn't fly home with me tomorrow and tie up the remaining loose ends over the next few weeks."

"I get the logic, Sunil. All of it. Ben needs me back as well to help shift shit arriving on his doorstep because of my recent notoriety. I know I should leave. I know I should leave tomorrow. Logic is screaming, but something closer to instinct is shouting louder that I should stay and take this chance to face his killers. It's not ... I mean I don't necessarily expect you to understand why ... I just feel compelled to go out there and see it all going down, for myself. The mission is set to happen in two or three days' time, Pitcavage said, and once it's done, my plan is to go home. For good. I figure I can duck the press until then and I've arranged to FaceTime with Ben and some clients tomorrow to smooth things over until I get back to the office. As for Caleb Freeth? I'm not worried about him, so you can strike that off your list of concerns. In fact, speaking of my crazy neighbor, there is one thing I was hoping you could help me with. Have you any dealings with the Native American lobby in Washington these days?"

"The odd occasion, in a once-removed kind of way," Sunil says. "They have a big stake in ... or at least they keep a close watching brief over all the civil rights cases that go through and some of the tribes are really well represented now. Which tribe in particular?"

"It's the Tohono O'odham in southern Arizona. I'm hoping you could help me track down three people. A woman named Anegam Cesar and her twin children, whose names escape me now, but I can get those details to you later."

"Who are they?" Sunil asks, taking out his phone to enter the details.

"She's the long-estranged wife of my neighbor, Caleb Freeth. I think the best starting point to track them down would be to locate the guy who was chief of her tribe back then, if he's still alive. I'm fairly sure his name was Antone. He wrote to Caleb in oh-three to say that Anegam had returned to the tribe with the kids sometime after he signed up for the military. Caleb tried without success to trace her, but I was hoping you could use political or DA channels to find out her current whereabouts. I'm not sure why I feel the need to do this really, but Mike always felt sorry for the pathetic son of a bitch and I think if he were alive, he'd want me to help."

"I prefer Ariel the self-obsessed capitalist," Sunil says drily. "I'll give it a try anyway. A friend of mine works for the Senate Committee for Native American Affairs. She might be able to help. Is there good Wi-Fi in the house?"

"Satellite. Like my phone," I reply. "Industrial. Never glitches. Better than home."

The whirr of the front-door blind being pulled down sharply marks the start of Miranda's post-lunch break and she arrives at the table in a flurry, hurling her apron at a nearby chair and plonking down her tray ferrying a small sandwich and a large pot of tea before noisily pulling her chair in with an exasperated "whew."

"You have the most beautiful skin I have ever seen. Like *ever*," she announces unabashedly to Sunil and later, when they share a joke about some YouTube clip of a newly famous over-the-top weather reporter in Baltimore—the second in a sequence of random topics covered over an hour—I notice how, now and again, she unselfconsciously slides her hand across the table to touch his wrist in the way of old married couples or mother and child.

"She'll be too modest to tell you, Sunil, but this young lady scored an off-the-charts ACT composite of thirty-five and is mulling over her college plans for next year," I add, only to be met with a reproachful look from Miranda.

"As Ariel knows, I really haven't decided yet but, law is one of the areas I might end up in," she says demurely. "I understand you're involved in civil rights law, Sunil. Must be fascinating."

"Wow, thirty-five! Brain box," says Sunil. "I'm sure you'll have your pick of courses, but I'd recommend shooting for whatever undergraduate program you have greatest interest in. You can always get into another area after that. So many people start out studying courses because they think it will get them a good job or whatever, but they don't finish or they come to regret it later in life because their heart was never in it. Don't listen to Ariel here, whatever you do. He's an intellectual snob who sold his soul to the capitalist overlords." He leans his rangy frame across the table to whisper to his young admirer. "All cash and no substance, I'm afraid."

"Thanks, Sunil, my great friend. Just remember you said that about me the next time you come looking for a fat check to help elect one of your liberal pals."

Chuckling at our repartee, Miranda goes to reverse the "Open" sign on the café door. When the blind retracts, the face of a young man appears, eyeballing her through the glass. He must have been waiting there. His greasy forehead is pressed against the window and his face is pinched in a sneer.

"Finally found somebody to bring to the prom, Vasquez?" he shouts while prodding his finger on the glass in our direction. "Half black, half latte. Just like yourself," he adds before running down the sidewalk followed by several other youths who had secreted themselves around the corner. Laughter echoed in their wake.

"I heard you're so dumb, you'd fail a survey, Charlie Thompson," Miranda shouts up the street after them before I reach the door.

"Who the hell?"

"Don't worry about it," she says, raising a shaking hand to stop me going after them. "Local kids. Real assholes, but they don't frighten me. They're all talk."

"Has this kind of thing happened before? Have they threatened you?" I am surprised at how protective I feel.

"Naw, don't worry. They wouldn't be that brave. Anyways, I could sort them out no problem if I told Mom but I don't want to bother her about it. Still, you can see why I can't wait to get to college."

"Are you going to the prom?" I ask a little sheepishly, not wanting to seem to pry.

"I'm on the school list because I had to attend there from time to time to build up a grade point average, but I won't be there."

I want to ask why but don't.

"Why don't we swing by and pick you up here later?" Sunil chimes in. "Let us show you the house and serve *you* a beverage for a change. The view alone is worth coming out there for and we can chat more about your options. I'm guessing you could do with a change of scene. What time do you finish up here? We could drop you home in time for dinner. What do you think, Ariel?"

"Ahh, I'm not so sure about that. The problem is that Miranda's mother and I aren't exactly best buddies and whisking her away behind her back won't help that situation."

"I think she has more time for you than you think, Ariel," Miranda counters with a surprising note of assuredness. "Besides, I've always wanted to see your house. It was the talk of the town when the artist lady brought in all those builders and architects from Albuquerque. Look, if it will make you happy, I'll check with Mom and Dad first and, unless you hear otherwise from me, maybe you could swing by around five?"

Still skeptical, I reluctantly agree. "We'll be waiting outside in the car and you can let us know then if you got the okay from home. If we have time, we might even take a tourist-y detour to show my office-bound friend here some of the local sights," I say before Sunil and I head to Deming as he is determined to fill up my fridge, despite my planned weekend departure.

The temperature has risen to a pleasant eighty-five degrees

and, with little humidity, it is the kind of glorious day that gives New Mexico its Land of Enchantment nickname. We opt for the circuitous Old County Road route rather than the interstate and travel in restful silence. As a smiling Sunil drinks in the scenery, I am glad he is relaxing a little on what I know is a rare day out of the office.

I reflect on our earlier encounter with Eliza Marron and anger churns. What a pair. Me, the narcissist. Little interest in Mike outside the bubble in which our relationship existed. Mike, the cheat. Keeping his real life hidden while gorging on my story.

Pam's Fancy Food Market on East Spruce Street in the center of Deming is my regular destination for groceries. It's a proper, more authentic version of the high-end artisanal food emporiums in San Francisco. Rows of hand-woven oval baskets laden with gleaming fruit and myriad varieties of vegetables rest on wooden pallets carefully angled along the whole length of one wall. Other produce is displayed tastefully along aisles delineated with trestle tables and shelves fashioned from timber wine boxes. A sturdy loin of serrano ham, its paprika skin and ruddy pink flesh seamed with fat, sits proudly in a *jamonero* upon a giant butcher's block at the far end of the shop. It is the centerpiece of the deli counter, where cheeses and delicacies from all around the world nestle in parchment or straw in brown ceramic bowls.

At the checkout, the friendly lady hardly looks at the items as she scans them out of my basket into the brown paper bag because she is too busy making eye contact and smiling at the two of us like she's known us for years. I feel compelled to say something, almost by way of gratitude. "This place should open a branch in San Francisco. Seriously, it'd blow people away in the neighborhood where I live."

"Gee. Thanks for the feedback, sir. I'll pass on your comments to my manager," she replies sweetly. "That'll be ninety-eight dollars and fifty-four cents, please, folks. Need another bag?"

When I was researching this area of New Mexico, I had read that the early history of Deming, in the mid to late eighteen-hundreds, was marred by the violence and social ills common to many frontier towns. On the railway line and only thirty-three miles from the Mexican border, it seemed to have been a magnet for ne'er-do-wells and border jumpers from all corners of the United States. Murders, brawls and shoot-outs were a common occurrence in the town and some of the downtown buildings were home to brothels. It had such a bad reputation that many law breakers rounded up in Arizona were given one-way tickets to Deming to be with their own kind. But the ghosts of the long-dead outlaws are no burden on the town. In fact they may have left a positive legacy. Outside of a big city, the population is about as racially mixed as it gets in the US and the vibe is laid back and casual. *Have a nice day* has no hint of saccharin here and everyone I have encountered appears to be going out of their way to be friendly, as though eager to compensate in some way for the sins of their ancestors.

As we depart with four paper bags jammed full of charcuterie, vegetables, breads and an organic chicken, we discuss how well a convenience franchise like this might do in Pacific Heights or on Sansome and rehash our well-worn plans to realize a pipe dream we have shared over many years to chuck our careers and open a chain of SuRo Gourmet Delicatessens along the lines of Dean & DeLuca.

Setting the bags on the ground in the mall parking lot

to fish out my keys, I hear an indecipherable shout and look behind to see Sprite lady, Bertha Walton. Sitting on Walgreen's wall, she swings the foot of her crossed leg up and down in a manic manner as though trying to shoo away a fly. Cigarette smoke hangs in a cloud above her head with no breath of wind in the air to whisk it away. Her pale face and sparklingly white shirt accentuate the redness of her backcombed beehive and lipstick (which looks like she may have applied and reapplied it many times over in the dark).

"Wait there, sir. Stop there!" she screams before setting down the bottle of Sprite so she can travel the distance between us unencumbered, the overhead smog dispersing as she sets off.

I hastily stash the bags into the back seat, spilling a basket of apples across the floor as I do, before wedging myself into the driver's seat as fast as humanly possible.

"Hurry up, Sunil. Get in. Quickly!"

Trying to make sense of the unexpected turn of events, Sunil scrutinizes me through the passenger window while a small group of shoppers rubberneck from the walkway, attracted by the commotion of a screeching lady click-clacking across the parking lot.

"Get in, for fuck's sake. Before she gets here," I plead frantically and lean over to push open the door for him.

Sunil takes his time, getting in awkwardly as his arms are still enveloping two bulging brown bags, which rustle under his chin as he sidles over the leather. "Who the heck is that?" he asks, leaning forward to assess her progress.

"Don't ask. Hold on." I reverse aggressively out of our spot. As I cruise between the cordon of parked cars toward the exit, I have to swerve slightly to avoid Ms. Walton, who has stopped shouting and takes a reluctant step backward out of our path.

Time seems to slow down as we pass her by and, from the safe vantage point of the car, I take a moment to look directly at her. She looks crestfallen, like a child who has just missed the ice cream van. Sunil sees it, too, and I feel his eyes boring into the side of my head as I rejoin the heavy stream of traffic on the I-10.

"What in God's name was that all about, man?"

"It's a long story but, basically, that woman is completely nuts and unfortunately has developed some kind of obsession with me. That's the second time she has chased me to my car. She lives in a community care program, but I'm thinking maybe she needs to spend more time indoors, if you know what I mean?"

"Have you ever spoken to her?" Sunil asks, clearly unmoved by my explanation.

"No. But, like, you saw her back there, right? She's borderline psychotic."

He shakes his head in disbelief. "She might be mentally ill, Ariel, but she's not a terrorist assassin."

The issue hangs in the air on the journey back to Prospero, with Sunil maintaining silent possession of the high moral ground.

Miranda emerges from the café about two seconds after five o'clock sporting an electric-pink T-shirt and jeans. She waves enthusiastically at us as she locks the door before sprinting over to the Jeep. The last tendrils of hair that stayed in their clasp during the exertions of a full day's work break free from their tether as she runs and I see her for the first time with her hair loose around her face. It suits her.

"Off now for three days," she tells us excitedly, once settled in the car. "The owner's wife takes over. She's working two jobs to help pay their mortgage and I'd say it only just about makes sense for them to have me in there at all. Some Mondays are so slow we barely take in my wages. Are we going straight to the house, guys?"

"I thought we'd make a quick stop in Shakespeare first, if you're okay with that?" I say, enjoying the look of confusion on my friend's face as he processes the prospect of an unexpected trip to the theater.

"Shakespeare? Another new friend?" Sunil inquires laconically to a giggle from Miranda.

"It's a tiny ghost town up near Lordsburg," I explain and Miranda proceeds to give him the tour-guide summary.

"It was a lawless pit stop for gold miners going way back and then a mining town itself in eighteen-seventy when they found silver nearby. The last person left in nineteen-twenty-nine, but it's perfectly intact. It's a bit creepy but interesting … in a *Mary Celeste* kind of way."

"I discovered it by accident the very first full day I spent in New Mexico," I say. "Went for a five-mile jog on a well-advertised trail near Lordsburg. A dust storm blew up about two miles out of town and a walker directed me to Shakespeare to take shelter until it died down. A few of us sat it out in one of the buildings and a strange thing passed by the door. I swear to you both, on my life, it was a ghost."

"Seriously?" Miranda says and I see her intrigue when I nod into the rear-view mirror.

"Right, that's it. You've finally gone over the edge," says Sunil. "Did you see this ghost when you were reading each other's palms or sharing a whack pipe, by any chance?"

"Scoff if you like, but I know what I saw. It was a Native American in full traditional dress. Long black hair, leather tunic, small feathery head dress, necklaces, the whole shebang. I swear. Passed by the open door in the same direction as the swirling sand. We all thought it might be some kind of actor that came with the town's tourist offering or something. But all three of us in that room went straight to the entrance to see where our strange friend was going and he or she had vanished. I felt unsettled for days. Kept looking over my shoulder thinking there was someone following me. Weirdest experience of my life."

"Wow! That's cool," Miranda says.

"Like I said. Finally over the edge," mutters Sunil.

We reach Shakespeare by five-thirty and are the only tourists in town. Nestled into a small windswept valley at the foot of some arid hills coated in burro grass brush and clumps of cactus, the seven buildings and collection of rickety corrals are pleasantly under-commercialized with simple signs for spring water, a discreet gift shop and shaded seating the only evidence of modern civilization.

With the sun beginning its descent, we park outside the wooden perimeter fence and walk up the dusty main street to the largest building. Intermittent gusts make rickety shutters flap, and hidden hanging chains squeak a ghostly Morse code, suitably eerie sound effects for a place where the after-whisper of cattle rustlers, gruff marshals and cocky hired guns lingers in the atmosphere.

We haven't enough time for a comprehensive tour so we peek in the windows of the saloon, hotel and assay office before making a quick stop in the "big house" where I encountered the apparition. Sunil sits to peruse a tourist information brochure that someone left behind on the long dining table.

"Says here the only curb they had on indiscriminate shootings in this town back in the late eighteen-hundreds was the rule that if you killed someone, you had to dig the grave," Sunil says. "Maybe your friend was looking for a shovel."

"Very funny. Anyway, are you guys all set? Miranda hasn't a lot of time."

"There's always time for a quick selfie," she says and, in an instant, has her phone cocked, camera reversed, and marshals us so close together there isn't a hint of background in the photograph, which she immediately forwards to my number and insists I save under her contact details.

Having discussed every conceivable option to study law during heavier-than-usual rush-hour traffic on the stretch of interstate between Lordsburg and Prospero, we are left with half an hour of down time in my house before we have to get Miranda back home. Sunil catches up on e-mail and follows up on the Caleb Freeth query in the office while Miranda casts off all reserve on her mission to inspect every inch of the upstairs living space, opening wardrobes, looking behind every door and running her hand along countertops and soft furnishings like an over-zealous real estate agent. Feeling buoyed by the company after so long in exile, I busy myself in the kitchen assembling a platter of olives, fresh figs and cured meats served with a pitcher of iced tea. When I go to set the refreshments down, I find Miranda on the edge of the couch, head cocked, staring at Letterhead.

"I've never seen anything like it, Ariel. No matter what angle I look at it from, it always draws the attention inside, beyond the surface. Then letters keep suggesting themselves in little groups. It's so clever. And I think it really does need all this space." Her own tiny frame looks lost in the cavernous room.

"It's by a young Spanish artist," I tell her. "He produced

a whole body of work along those themes. The relationship between inside and outside, light and dark, order and chaos. This is my absolute favorite piece from my collection in San Francisco. I'd love to show it to you sometime."

"Are you kidding? I would so love that," she says, chewing on an olive and nestling so far back into the couch to take in the view that her feet lose contact with the floor. "If I looked at this view every day, it would give me itchy feet," she declares. "It's so unbelievably inviting. Like the world offering you its hand."

"And I'm sure you will take its hand and travel far, young lady," I say at the risk of sounding patronizing. "You could start by taking up my offer to sponsor your college fees and I'll kick it all off with a cultural weekend on the West Coast. You'd be doing me a favor. I really want to help out."

She doesn't take the bait but casts me a knowing smile and gazes wistfully out at the stark outline of the mountains and streaky orange clouds, all that remain of the day as the sun's golden arc disappears.

"Maybe I will get lucky," she says. "Most women in Prospero have one destiny from the moment they are born and that is to submit. First to their fathers and then to their husbands. When you have kids, they become your mission field. Suits some, I guess."

She gets up from her nest to examine the painting over the fireplace and, after a few moments of silence, asks me the question I suspect she may have wondered about since we first met. "Were *you* ever married?"

"No, it never worked out for me. Too busy working, I guess. In fact, that's the reason I came here to New Mexico in the first place. My life had become too focused on one thing to the exclusion of everything else. Never healthy."

I am not ready to tell her the truth, or not sure if she is ready to hear it.

"Would you like to marry? One day?" Her stuttered question hangs in the air like a loose thread and an unforeseen problem seems to be presenting itself.

"I don't think so. I'm not the marrying kind. In fact, I—" Before I finish, Sunil shouts in from the office.

"My friend put me in touch with a woman at the Bureau of Native American Affairs. She's heard of Chief Antone and is hopeful she'll have an answer by tomorrow. It's six-fifty, by the way. Shouldn't we get going?"

Darkness has fully descended when we pull up outside Miranda's house about three miles southwest of Prospero at the end of a long, dusty single-lane track bordered from start to finish by carefully pruned creosote bushes. It's a small, single-story, hacienda-style ranch replete with side arches, a terracotta-tiled roof and surrounded on all sides by paprika-hued earthenware pots of every conceivable shape and size housing vigorously healthy-looking desert shrubs.

The prospect of encountering Marge Newlands on her home territory is making me nervous as we pull into the driveway. Miranda seems to sense this and reassures me that her mom is still at work, having spoken on the phone with her, and everything is teenage *cool*.

"I know my dad would like to meet you, though. We don't get many visitors. Could you come in for a few minutes?"

A chorus of katydids serenades us through the Jeep's open door, their curiously hypnotic chirps inviting us to step into the night.

"Come on, guys. Just a few minutes. He won't bite. Honest. And I really want to show you my horse. I'm getting him ready for showing and selling at the racing sales up north.

Please come in, won't you?" Her appeal is tinged with that whiny pitch perfected by the teenage TV characters I flick past on weekday evenings.

"I'm going to sit this one out and catch up on some work here if that's okay with you, but I think Ariel should show you to the door. A, why don't you go and introduce yourself?" suggests Sunil, his laptop already out of its sleeve in anticipation of a yes.

In light of the incident with the teenagers at the café this afternoon, it occurs to me that I may qualify as one of a very small circle that Miranda considers friends.

"Did he actually *say* he wanted to meet me?" I ask tentatively, feeling something of the nerves a high-school student might endure on his date's doorstep the night of the prom. Whenever possible I always sidestep situations that might involve open conflict and, given the range of negative experiences I've had with the Prospero locals since I moved here, I am taking nothing for granted.

"Yes, he said it yesterday. Said he'd like to see you for himself, having heard so much about you from both the women in his life." Her note of humor puts me at ease although I am trying to imagine what words her mother might have used to describe me.

"Sure, why not?" I say. "I'll leave the engine running for you, Sunil. The temperature drops like a stone here after dark."

"Hey, Dad, I'm home," Miranda projects her voice to fill the house. "Ariel Mignolet is here with me, Da-aad!"

The succulent smell of roasted meat intensifies as we walk down a short, dimly-lit corridor from the front door to the kitchen that spans the full width of the back of the house but is a warm and welcoming space constructed almost entirely from unvarnished pale wood. Two large landscape windows and a central, glass sliding door provide views of a tastefully lit patio. Beyond the patio, I catch the odd glimpse of waving branches in the moonlight suggesting a garden. Off to the right, no more than a hundred yards away, a strong spotlight illuminates the top of what looks like a barn door.

"Will he stay for dinner?" comes a reply from the business end of the kitchen, which is separated from the rest of the room by a series of worktops, but I don't see anyone until a few moments later when a head pops up slightly over the level of the counter.

"It's roast pork," says the head. "Been in there five hours so the meat should be tender as butter and skin'll be like a razor shell."

The head rolls along at the same level until its owner appears from around the end of the cabinets in a clunky wheelchair and offers a hand up to me from a well-worn floral oven glove.

"It's nice to meet you, sir. I'm Miranda's father, Gonzalo Vasquez."

"And her teacher, I believe," I say, shaking his hand. "Ariel Mignolet, sir. It's a real pleasure to meet the man who has inspired such a love of learning in my friend here."

"Yes, well, she's a real smarty pants, all right. Lucky that way. You staying for chow?"

It's clear to me now where Miranda gets her easygoing charm.

"I won't, thanks, sir, although I really appreciate the invite. It smells delicious, but I need to get back to my friend outside. He's catching up on work out there so he's happy for now, but I told him I'd be back in five. Miranda wants me to see this horse she's been telling me about for months."

"Ah, yes, Pirate," he says, raising his eyes to heaven. "We should be thankful, really. Most teenage girls sneak out at night to meet boys. We got us the baby Jesus."

Miranda smiles sheepishly at the gentle ribbing.

"Ask her how often she has slept out there in the manger, Mr. Mignolet."

"Please call me Ariel."

"Two nights a week she's out there, Ariel. Madness. Coffee?"

He negotiates the narrow spaces between the wooden cabinets with practiced aplomb, retrieving cups, filling up pots and fishing in shoulder-height drawers. An array of different-size bowls and Tupperware containers filled with pre-prepared vegetables for dinner sit on the counter space to the right of the stove and, on the other side, the knives, pots and flavorings required for tonight's fare are laid out ready for action. All the work of a highly ordered mind.

"Thanks. Lovely. Black, no sugar, please," I say as I watch Miranda vanish into the abyss between the paved area and the barn before emerging moments later as a ghostly shadow under its gaping door and disappearing inside.

"Sorry, Ariel. Please take a seat. There at the window, maybe? You'll see them coming from there." Gonzalo carries two mugs of coffee toward me with his right hand while his left deftly propels his chair forward.

"She's probably giving him a brush down before she brings him over," he adds and dons his glasses in anticipation of the parade.

Gonzalo resembles my mental image of a noble Aztec chief. His centrally parted coal-black hair is cut in a bowl shape with a razor-sharp fringe halfway up his forehead. His face is lined and leathery with high cheekbones, a proud Roman nose and kind eyes of the deepest brown, slightly magnified now through dark, thick-rimmed bifocals.

"I saw you," I say quietly because now I am sure and I want to ask while his daughter is out of the room. "The other night? Across from my house? You pulled up in your car." I watch him closely to glean what I can from his reaction.

"I didn't think there was anyone there," replies Gonzalo hesitantly. "Your house was in darkness and I didn't see a car. I would have called in otherwise. I was there to see you. To talk."

"I … the car was in the garage. I try and keep it out of the wind as much as I can because the sand plays havoc. So I was there but had all the lights out because … I was looking … I was hoping to catch sight of the torchbearers."

A voice in my head asks why I am revealing so much to this veritable stranger who, quite possibly, knows nothing of my story. Why not say I was heading for bed when I saw his car. Easier still, say nothing.

Gonzalo's expression doesn't change one iota in reaction to my slightly bizarre explanation. He peers at me in a calm, neutral way and I can tell he won't be asking me to elaborate. He is simply waiting for me to ask him why he was there.

"May I ask the reason for your visit?"

"Of course. I wanted to ask you face to face if you were serious about the generous offer you made to Miranda the other day. As she reported it to me, you propose to give her an interest-free loan to finance her college studies. Of course, as she is still young, and very naive, I was a bit concerned that she may have misheard or misinterpreted somehow. As I'm sure you know yourself, sometimes we only hear what we want to hear."

My shoulders slump slightly with relief. "I have never been more serious about anything, Gonzalo. In fact, I would go further and tell you that I am more than happy to sponsor her first year's fees outright and then go with the loan option from there on if that sits comfortably with you. To tell you the truth, it would be hugely exciting for me to see someone as bright as your daughter fulfill her potential. I have the resources, sir, and I find myself in a place in my life where I want to give back. One of the few things I am passionate about is the power of education ... for enlightenment. To be frank, I'm just delighted that you're receptive to the idea and you certainly didn't need to go to the trouble of driving all that way either, by the way. Call me. Anytime. No doubt you're aware your wife has my number."

"Enlightenment," Gonzalo smiles and nods slowly, repeating the word as though remembering a long-dead, much-loved relative.

"Miranda and I have been busy letting the light in these past years together here in this house but, unfortunately, there are many about who want to stay in the shade. Marge, the pastor and most of her so-called friends in Prospero are all excited for her to take the road the church has laid out. One in a million is how Seb Funchess described her to us the other day and that man could talk the sun out of setting. They want her for themselves, you see," he says. "Even got the head of Galen Johnson College to call last week to tell us *in person,* mind you, that if she attends for the first year, they guarantee to finance a move for her to one of the country's top law schools. Imagine that, Mr. Mignolet. He came all that way, in person. But Galen? It's not even accredited, you know. Anyway, the way I see it, they just want to—I'm not sure of the word to use—but maybe to brainwash her into a certain way of thinking. Train her to play for their team."

He pauses momentarily to take a sip of coffee, and the harmony of the crickets' night song and the kitchen clock complement the weighty atmosphere of our little summit. "The thing is," he continues, "I'm finding it very hard to play monkey in the middle at this stage. I don't want to upset or frighten her about the Galen option in case that is where she ultimately finishes up, but I am having to draw on all my powers of persuasion to talk her mother around to what both Miranda and I would aspire to, which is a clean break from the church for the years of her education and then, if she wants to come back or serve them after that, so be it. The local school, attached to the church, has hijacked her scholarship route so your offer now at least makes our preference a possibility, although—and I hope I don't cause offence by saying this— they sure wouldn't be pleased about the source.

"I wanted to meet you for myself to see if everything Miranda has said was true. She's a big fan, but as her father, I need to be sure your interests are, well, honorable, if I can use that old-fashioned term."

"Sir, I am very glad to have the opportunity to talk to that very point. When I made the offer, it occurred to me that it could be misconstrued. But the assurance I can give you—how can I explain—I pose no threat whatsoever to your daughter. I can assure you that Miranda, or any woman for that matter, will never be of interest to me, in a romantic sense at least, if I can put it that way."

I have thrown the proverbial dice and Gonzalo's inscrutable expression doesn't reveal if my number has come up. He maintains quiet eye contact, reading me like a complicated document.

"Look, Ariel! Over here."

Engrossed in conversation, we hadn't noticed Miranda leave the barn. I step outside the patio doors to get a better look at the colt, cresting its neck, sidestepping and nudging Miranda's hand playfully with its nose as it dances along behind her on the lead rein. A gleaming, copper coil of energy.

"Whooaaa, boy. Hush now, that's it. Slow now." She soothes the horse constantly while leading him proudly over and back across the patio.

"I'm no expert, but he's a stunner," I say, just about able to appreciate a healthy coat and good confirmation from regular corporate junkets to Santa Anita with owners who could bore you for hours with the vital statistics of their equine investments. "What age is he?"

"Turning four in January," she shouts over a series of sharp snorts from Pirate's flaring nostrils. "We're hoping to get a good price for him in Ruidoso quarter horse sales next August. Mom's brother owns him. Bred him up in Silver City. But I stand to get a cut from the sale price and we have high hopes coz he comes from a fast line and so far it seems he got the sprint genes. You should see him in the paddock when the wind gets up. My job is to break him nicely and make sure we present him in peak form, give him manners on the lead rein, which is, as you can probably see, not proving that easy coz he's such an extrovert."

She smiles proudly at him and, as if on cue, Pirate emits a shrill whinny and rears up, forcing Miranda to rapidly feed out more of the long rein and step back several feet to avoid injury when his hooves return to earth. I find the notion of having a half ton of bone and muscle launching itself unpredictably around the narrow confines of the patio rather alarming, but an unperturbed Gonzalo three-point turns his chair and nonchalantly heads back in the direction of the oven while Miranda stands tall with no hint of panic and expertly guides the horse back to a steady walk behind her before resuming their last lap of the patio parade.

"He's pretty high-spirited. Borderline dangerous?" I say, knowing I sound like a nervous city slicker.

"Don't worry. He has no meanness in him at all. Just a lot of energy. Playfulness, really." Her voice is barely shy of a shout to be heard over hooves clattering on concrete. "It's all there to see in his ear movements. Did you know horses have sixteen individual muscles controlling each ear? With the two combined, they can tell you just about everything they are feeling with one twitch. It's like reading a book, once you know their code. Make sure you wait for me to get back before you leave, okay?"

With a jaunty swish of his tail, Pirate obediently trails his mistress down the path to the barn.

"You really should stay for dinner," Gonzalo hollers from his kitchen enclosure as I drain the coffee. My dice roll has paid off. "Go and tell your friend in the car that we have a huge shoulder of slow-roasted pork in here and we insist he at least come in to taste it. Let us show you folks a proper New Mexican welcome."

The first few emotionally charged bars of Elgar's Cello Concerto fill the room and snuff out my last lines of polite resistance. "I would love to stay for dinner, Gonzalo. Give me a moment to get him."

It is pitch dark at the front of the house and I see Sunil's face through the car window, a mask of concentration bathed in pale electric blue. He is so consumed with whatever he's reading that he doesn't notice my approach and jumps when I knock inches from his ear.

"God, I hate when people do that," he says, lowering the window.

"We're staying for dinner, Su," I say, but am met with a special look of incredulity perfected by Sunil over years of listening to professional-standard lies. "Seriously, her dad is an amazing guy. Wise. Come on, it'll be good."

"What will you do when Mommy comes home?"

"I'll worry about that when it happens. Anyway, she's not an ogre, just morbidly uptight. It'll be fine. Come on, it's slow-roasted pork with crackling. Your favorite."

Inside, a still slightly skeptical Sunil is at his diplomatic best with Gonzalo, giving him a hearty handshake, rolling up his sleeves and offering to help set the table. Our chef conjures up a feast of pork, French beans, carrots and mashed potatoes, and after Miranda says a brief grace, which Sunil and I mouth along to out of politeness, a convivial atmosphere descends on the table.

"How is your head healing?" Gonzalo inquires midway through the meal on the heels of a discussion about running gun battles on the streets of a Mexican border town. It is the first time in the evening that anyone has touched on the subject of the fateful night and an immediate listening silence descends apart from the clang and scrape of busy silverware.

"Not bad, all told," I say, running the three middle fingers of my left hand along the line of metal staples beneath my hair. "Supposed to get the clips off on Saturday, but I'd say they could snip them off now and it'd be fine. The headaches went after three or four days, but strangely enough, the other injury is giving me trouble now. The rock that hit me here, I mean, on my right shoulder blade. I still can't sleep on that side or raise my hand higher than this."

Knives and forks are stilled while my fellow diners watch my Third Reich salute over the fleur-de-lis china terrine and its remaining mound of mashed potatoes.

"I can only imagine how terrifying it must have been for you, Ariel," Gonzalo says, and I suspect he knows most of what I reported to the police. The expression of bewilderment on his daughter's face, on the other hand, betrays her complete ignorance of events.

"It's hard to explain, really, sir. I'm sure I will eventually have to talk it through with an expert in shock and its aftereffects because there are things, images mostly, that I can't shake off. Like the moment Mike's life was ended. It ... it was completely ... sorry I'm struggling to find the right words here ... merciless."

Sunil takes a lead on changing the subject by asking if he can help anyone to more potatoes.

"Miranda told me you and Mike had become good friends," Gonzalo says quietly. "I'm not at all surprised about that now that I've met you. The one thing that stood out about Mike for me was how much he loved people and the more different they were to him, the better. It's how he learned about the world. Through all his years at football up in Silver City or then when he'd pay us a visit from college and, most especially, after he joined the force here in town. The good, the bad, the ugly. Their life stories, their travails, their travel tales and every other kind of personal report. He was always telling us stories about folks he'd met. Am I right, Miranda? Oftentimes, in fact, from that very seat you're sitting in."

I allow myself to imagine Mike relaxing in the bosom of the Vasquez family and another time or universe where we might have been able to share such good company together.

"That was him sure enough, Dad," Miranda says, clearly happy to have the opportunity to remember him out loud. "Mike could talk for America on two subjects. Nature and people. Wasn't much for newspapers or TV, but he would listen so well to folks and ask such good questions, he always had the latest on the weather, politics, sports... Remember the time he wrote up a speeding ticket on that lady on the Interstate? Remember, Dad? That weird woman last year with the Bongo drum in the front seat and the weather vane attached to the roof rack."

"Yes. Yes, I do," replies Gonzalo, laughing with Miranda as they share the memory. "Remember he told us she had 'The Belle of Belmont' spelled out in diamante studs on a plaque above her plates and they ended up going—"

"Dad!" Miranda interrupts with a childish pout. "*I* was telling the story."

"*Sorreeee,*" Gonzalo says, smiling. "The floor is all yours, my dear."

A little abashed, Miranda soon winds back up to her excited best to deliver the tale. "He wrote her a ticket, but they got chatting and turns out she was the daughter of one of Bruce Springsteen's longest-serving roadies. She was in a hurry to get to play a lunchtime slot in a fringe music festival up in the Gila reserve and since he was about to start his break between shifts, he followed her up there to hear her play and they got along great. Ten days later, two tickets and a backstage pass arrived in the mail for him and Eliza to go see Springsteen in Albuquerque. They had to sneak behind Pastor's back, but went. All because he took a little time to chat and look past her eccentricity. He never rated face value."

The story brings a welcome distraction from the

somberness of loss, but in the midst of all the smiles, I reflect with regret that this just holds another mirror up to the shallowness of my relationship with Mike. Indeed, Gonzalo was right, he *was* forever asking me about my life. In the ten weeks we knew each other, he had comprehensively covered every detail of my work, my struggles with stress, my upbringing and, of course, *the scene* in San Francisco, all of which were endlessly fascinating to him. Had I shown no interest in *his* backstory or was he very good at avoiding questions? I cannot remember which it was. I am only certain of how little I knew.

"What in the world did the pastor have against Bruce Springsteen?" Sunil inquires, doubling back on Miranda's earlier comment. "I mean, I'm sure his political leanings wouldn't tally with those of the Baptist tradition, but he's not exactly Eminem. Most of his stuff is kind of homespun wisdom, the voice of the common man and all that. He might be a bit of a smoked salmon socialist, but I would have put him firmly on the same side as small-town America. What am I missing?"

"Well, I'll confess first of all that I'm no expert on The Boss," replies Gonzalo with a wry smile. "I'm more of a classical man myself and luckily that makes it in under Pastor Funchess's radar. But the church here in Prospero is a fairly strict strand of the faith, and there are rules. Oh, there are rules upon rules—all aimed at helping us adhere to the teachings of the Bible. Some relate to the bad influence of rock music and the evils of Hollywood, and the rules pertaining to the Internet are draconian. It wasn't always that strict, mind you. Most of the people who arrived over the years were not especially fundamentalist in their beliefs but, as the years pass, Pastor Funchess works hard at selling a way of life that does seem to offer hope to folks and most gradually succumb, I guess."

"Is that why Miranda is homeschooled?" I ask. "To keep with traditional Baptists' guidance on separation?"

Gonzalo looks at his daughter and back to me, deliberating how to answer. His muscular shoulders look as though they belong to a much larger person, as the lower half of his body is dramatically shrunken through muscle atrophy.

"Well, that is how her mother would see it. I used to think along those lines, too, myself ten years ago. But now? Now it's my way of saving her from them."

"Dad. Stop!" exclaims Miranda, clearly tiring of being the topic of conversation.

"I'm completely serious," he continues. "I do fear for the future of some parts of this country. There are big cutbacks in some states' schools budgets and, where the churches are stepping in, religious instruction is starting to dominate the school day. It's like whole swathes of America are lurching to the right, or, I guess you could say, regressing."

While making his case, the ever-industrious Gonzalo scrapes the remains from Miranda's plate onto his own and reaches to do the same with mine, gesturing insistently for me to retake my seat when I rise to help.

"I couldn't agree with you more," says Sunil in his polished courtroom accent. "I'm seeing it at the other end of the spectrum in Washington. In the last few years, Baptist Fundamentalism has expanded dramatically on Capitol Hill. Big money backing far-right candidates and lots of well-versed lobbyists and lawyers working the circuit for them."

"Maybe that's the end game they have in mind for Miranda," says Gonzalo. "That Clayton Marron. He's the kind of man who arrives late and then stretches his feet out under the table. I understand he has a lot of political connections through the Rotary in Silver City and those guys are about as far right as Genghis Khan. The way I see things, what happened out there in the Chihuahua is a warning to us all of the kind of outcomes you get when any society only looks inwards, even when it's slap bang in the middle of the land of the free. I knew Anthony Blount for about a year or so before he broke away. Introduced to him up in Silver City by Pastor Funchess. That time, as best I can recall, he was only a little more extreme in his views than the church here, but it looks like the years of total isolation have caused something to go terribly wrong. Let's just hope the perpetrators are caught quickly now the Feds are in town."

On that note, we hear the click of a key turning in the front door and, moments later, Marge Newlands emerges from the shadow of the narrow entrance hall to stand and survey the scene at her dining table. An uncomfortable silence descends on our little gathering before Miranda casually chirps, "Hi, Mom" and Gonzalo makes an admirable attempt to act as though everything is perfectly normal.

"Can I help you to some dinner, honey? I kept a plate warm for you in the oven although it might have dried up a little by now. Did you get delayed?"

Despite our marginally less testy exchange earlier, my view of Marge Newlands remains tarnished by twelve days of generally unpleasant interaction and I am struggling to imagine her as anyone's *honey*. The struggle isn't helped by the expression on her face that registers somewhere between hurt and distaste as she stands stiff and straight in her uniform like an uncomfortable outsider in her own home.

"Could I speak to you for a moment, Gonzalo? In private, please?" Her words are clipped as though she is making a great effort to restrain herself. "I'll be in the other room," she tells him before retreating back into the dark.

"Don't worry, Ariel. She'll come round," Miranda says confidently, but the muffled sounds of a heated exchange from wherever *the other room* is suggest otherwise.

Sunil and I hurriedly clear the table and, as Miranda opens the front door for us to leave, the argument appears to be drawing to a close and we overhear a scattergun of words including *surprise guests, lies, unfair* from Marge and *eighteen* and *promised* in Gonzalo's final salvo on the other side of the wall before he wheels himself out to the porch full of apologies, thanks and good wishes until we meet again.

"No need whatsoever to explain, Gonzalo," I say, shaking his hand. "In the context of what has taken place in the last two weeks, your wife's misgivings about my being here are completely understandable. When you boil it all down, Mike would still be alive today if I hadn't called him that evening. I am finding it hard to forgive myself for that."

"Don't do that to yourself," Gonzalo says sternly. "Everything happened exactly according to God's plan, Ariel. Hard and all as that plan is to understand. Good luck with your journey. I'll call you about Miranda's application before the weekend, but you can take it that we are good to go on our end if you are still inclined to help."

Sunil takes the driving duties, and as I wave goodbye to our hosts through the passenger window I find myself wondering which journey it is that Gonzalo is wishing me luck on.

Once on the main road, I check my phone, which has

been set on meeting mode and buried in the pocket of my windbreaker since we arrived at the Vasquez house. There are seven missed calls. One from Ben and six from Marge Newlands' cell. Her attempts were staggered at even time intervals over the last four hours with the most recent made at nine-forty-five, minutes before she arrived home. I skip voice mail and dial her number immediately in the hope that she has follow-up news regarding our earlier conversation about Caleb Freeth.

"Marge Newlands," she answers on the second ring with that by-now familiar impersonal tone.

"I see some missed calls from you, Sergeant. Sorry about that. I was busy with friends the past few hours." I know she will think I am being a smart ass.

"I thought Mr. Pitcavage made it clear to you yesterday that you needed to stay accessible at all times for these few days, Mr. Mignolet. Perhaps this investigation has already fallen off your priority list, what with all your *visiting* and … *entertaining.*"

"Sunil is an old friend, Sergeant, and now, officially, my legal counsel for the duration of my involvement in this case."

"Fine. I suggest you consult with your counsel about whether you are willing to depart tomorrow morning at oh-seven-hundred with a team of FBI and Border Patrol officers on a mission to identify and arrest those suspected of murdering Mike Argyll and the other victims referred to during our meeting yesterday."

"Tomorrow morning? That's sooner than planned, right? May I ask why?"

Sunil, who seems to be getting the drift of the conversation, flashes me a look of alarm and decelerates to crawling pace.

"Fear of leaks," she responds curtly. "Look, Mr. Mignolet,

the following are the details I was asked to relay to you. It's a seven a.m. briefing session in Meeting Room Four at Prospero Police Station and, after that, you will be transported to rendezvous with air transportation at a secret location. I can't be …"

Although intent on listening carefully, the pointless thought enters my mind that, after tomorrow, I will have achieved the dubious honor of enjoying the hospitality of all four of Prospero Police Station's Meeting Room facilities.

"… the entire group but Officer Branson has sent you an e-mail with details about what you need to wear and the likely time commitment and you need to reply to this with your size measurements. Do be aware that these specifics will all be couched in a generic mail about some planned Border Patrol maneuver or other because Paul Pitcavage is paranoid about putting any details through the Net and has asked people to avoid all explicit digital reference to Operation Granite. Any last-minute queries between now and then, you are to call me on this cell number and I will redirect to him or the relevant person on his team, but my advice now—and it would have been more useful advice four hours ago—is to get as much sleep as you can if you are planning on going because tomorrow will be a long day and possibly a long night as well. Can I take it you are still as eager as you were yesterday?"

"I am, Sergeant. Nothing has changed in terms of my commitment. However, I do have a snag. Because I understood the operation would go ahead Friday at the earliest, I agreed to an important work call tomorrow so, if it's okay, I do need to reorganize … at least to see if I can reschedule that. I will make the necessary calls and revert to you as soon as possible. Is that okay?"

She remains silent for a few moments and I feel like an unfavored pupil who has once again failed to meet the already very low expectations of his teacher.

"There is always the option for you to identify the suspects remotely," she adds stiffly. "If you take that option, you will be able to help the investigation but also make your priority call. Either way, please let us know your decision before six a.m. tomorrow so that we can put the comms technology in place if necessary. If you do decide to travel and I don't get a chance to talk to you with all the comings and goings, I wish you good luck. I hope to God you find them."

Her words puncture the pressure balloon of tension between us.

"Thanks," I reply. "And by the way, how did you get on with Ms. Tucson Gazette?"

"Don't worry about it," she says in a reassuring tone. "Pastor Funchess talked sense into Caleb. He has called the reporter and fully retracted everything he said to her this morning. I understand from Seb that he has traveled to some farm machinery convention in Albuquerque for a few days."

"Thanks again," I say a little awkwardly, unsure how far our new more friendly footing extends. I get my answer when she hangs up abruptly without responding.

Chapter Fifteen

DESERT ISLANDS

I am finding it hard to sleep without the aid of medication, which I am afraid to take in case it renders me un-rousable before six a.m. Voices of Sunil, Ben and Gonzalo join a confusing chorus of advisers and critics striking discordant notes in my head. After finally dozing off around eleven-thirty, I wake an hour later in the throes of a vivid nightmare. Replaying its outlandish sequence over and over in my head, I fish around in the messy bedside drawer for her business card. 1-415-555-0119. It is nearly midnight in San Francisco.

"Hello?" I blurt somewhat nervously.

"Hello? Eez that you, Marvin?" The groggy voice of Paloma Weiss has an accusatory ring to it and I am tempted to hang up. "I am asleep. Why are you calling now? Marvin?" she croaks crankily.

"Ms. Weiss. I am really, truly sorry for disturbing you. It's Ariel Mignolet here. Ariel Mignolet. We met in July. I—"

"Little piano concerto. Big fire," she interjects.

Her long sigh fizzles electronically in my ear. It is the sigh of someone who has been forced to suffer one idiot too many. Then follows a sharp exhale as though she is collecting herself and to my great relief, she skips the opportunity for a rant.

"How are things with you, my friend? The dream? You take my advice?"

"I did and it worked. You were right about, well, everything. That's why I need your advice again. I have run into some trouble here. Sorry, I need to fill you in. I moved to New Mexico in February to train for a long-distance race. I met a—"

"No, no. Stop there. Don't tell me anything else. I will ask you questions. Okay?"

"Sorry. Yes, of course."

"What dreams have come with theez new big problems of yours?"

"Sleeping pills killed off all my dreams for the past two weeks. It's a long story, but I couldn't sleep without them, until tonight. Tonight I dreamt I was climbing. I'm not sure what I was climbing or where, but it was in the dead of night. Then after what seemed like a long time ascending, I reached a plateau and crawled on all fours on a cold, smooth surface. Flashes came in the sky, like artillery fire. They illuminated an enormous map encased in glass beneath me. A missile of some kind struck my chest and I slid backward until I was left hanging by my fingertips over the edge of whatever precipice I had just scaled. Then, when I had managed to heave my top half up again, a small black snake slithered over the glass casing and bit my hand."

"Did you fall?" she asks in a low, serious voice.

"I must have. I woke with one of those jolts where you think you have hit something."

"That is a myoclonic jerk. You fell. Tell me more about the map."

"It was a relief map of some kind. Old. There were concentric circles. Mountains, I presume. And lots of red

248

arrows. There were lots of red dots, too. I think those marked the towns. That's all I can remember."

"What way were the arrows pointing?"

"They pointed up the mountains, like arrows for wind speed or air flow or something."

A pause and another sigh. "You have a big decision to make, my friend."

"That is exactly why I called," I say and sink further back under the bedspread, closing my eyes to concentrate on her every word.

"All right, this is what I can say. If the choice you have involves either going somewhere new or going back to somewhere familiar, then you should choose the option which involves going somewhere new. But you must be careful. The little black snake represents a threat that you have been underestimating. Stay alert for that."

I feel like Cryptic Sid chatting with Sorcerer Sue on 1-800-PSYCHIC but cling to the understanding that I know this woman has shown herself capable of spectacular insight.

"What about the tracer fire and the missile?"

"Meh. Circumstances. Only circumstances, my friend."

In my mind's eye, I see her shrugging against a plumped-up silk pillow. She says nothing for long enough for me to know our session is at an end.

"Thanks for taking my call. I know it's very late, but I am really up against it here time-wise. And for the advice, of course. What is the best way for me to make a payment?"

"When I wake in the morning, this call will be like *my* crazy dream, my friend. I know you're good for it. You can take it I am running a tab. Goodnight to you now, Ariel Mignolet, little concerto."

"Goodnight. Thank you so much again," I say, but she is already gone.

I switch on the bedside light, shave and don a business shirt and tie for the first time in almost seven months. After an hour or so of research and screen grabbing on Bloomberg, I sit on the edge of the bed, prop my iPad on the window sill and train the camera on my corporate-clean face. Recording the presentation takes twenty-five minutes after which I e-mail it to Ben and sink back into bed to try and sleep for what time is left.

I wake again at five-thirty but don't want to disturb Sunil, so I while away the time watching morning shadows evolve on the ceiling, nervously contemplating my imminent plunge into the unknown. Outside has the look of a day in waiting. Absent wind, a cool dawn mist has rendered everything from sky to sand an amorphous gray wash so it is hard to decipher mountain from cloud or asphalt road from damp earth.

Sunil wins the breakfast battle and force-feeds me bacon and eggs against the wishes of my nervous stomach. His flight from Las Cruces departs at ten and the driver I have arranged to collect him is visible from the window, sitting patiently in his town car reading a magazine. He called Sunil twice on his journey here after the desolate drive along the Old County Road caused him to lose faith in the reliability of his satnav system.

I'm glad we are leaving at the same time so I won't have to endure that particular pang that comes with being the one left behind.

"You're sure I can't change your mind?"

I shake my head.

"Then stay safe and call me the minute you get back,"

Sunil says as we hug at the top of the stairs. "See you this weekend, whatever happens. Okay?" His intonation suggests he is double-checking my planned return and I acknowledge by way of a smile.

Prospero is still asleep at ten to seven when I park around the back of the police station amid a fleet of impressive, muscular-looking Chevrolet Jeeps and minivans with blacked-out windows that are lined up with military precision as though assembled for inspection. A white armored car that looks like a windowless single-berth caravan idles in a reserved parking spot behind the row of other vehicles and I can make out two Kevlar-clad, helmeted men in the front seats. One of them looks unwaveringly at me while speaking into a handheld device.

I push the lighted bell beside the only door at the rear of the building and try to muster a suitable expression for the security camera trained at eye level. A wiry young man with an intense look on his thin face introduces himself as FBI Officer Patrick Koper and ushers me into an elevator. We emerge moments later onto the second-floor landing, which is a hive of activity with uniforms of several different law enforcement agencies in shades of green, black and navy sipping coffees, filling in forms, filing past with intent or simply loitering expectantly. Most wear what looks to me like full-combat clothing of bullet-proof vests, gun belts, heavy-duty boots and backpacks filled with various man-scout accessories including night-vision goggles. When I notice these, I am prompted to compare notes with one officer about their strength and distance capability versus my own monster lens at the house.

My chaperone guides me into Meeting Room Four, where Paul Pitcavage, sporting a dark flak jacket with FBI emblazoned on the back in bold yellow letters over a short-sleeved navy tee, stands in deep conversation with two other men. All three pore enthusiastically over an old-fashioned ordnance map like mountain climbers plotting their final ascent.

"Ariel Mignolet. Welcome, good sir," Pitcavage says, giving me another full belt of Southern charm and introducing me to the others before taking me to one side.

"We're all about to start a fifteen-minute session in here with the twenty-six members of the mission team now, Ariel, so what I want you to do is go back with Officer Koper there and get suited up in the locker room. Once I have finished the strategy element of the presentation, I will come out and get y'all because I want to introduce you to the whole operational personnel in one go. They need to know your face and you need to know some of the key players and the action timeline because I want you to have as few surprises as possible today. That all good?"

I just about get the chance to nod as Pitcavage pushes my arm gently toward Koper at the door and gets back down to business.

As we exit, we are forced to struggle through the tide of officers advancing on the room in response to a shout of "Ready, team?" from Pitcavage before we descend a flight of concrete fire stairs at the other side of the landing.

In keeping with the generally quirky design standards of Prospero Police Station, the locker area is a childlike riot of primary colors with fire-engine-red lockers, a blue resin floor and bottle-green plastic seating. Officer Koper's skinny, alien-like fingers untie the laces on the stout pair of brand-new military boots that await my feet beneath locker 27 and I find myself wondering if it's possible that the man can't join the mission because he is actually ill.

He helps me into the bullet-proof vest, which isn't as heavy as I thought it was going to be, and then I zip up my navy jacket, identical in every way to that of some of my FBI mission associates except for the absence of the big letters. As I sit to pull on the boots, I hear a familiar voice and look up to see Pastor Seb Funchess enter, chatting amiably with the officer assigned to assist him. His expression of disdain when he sees me sets the tone for our interaction and from that moment on, we make every effort to avoid eye contact and one another's personal space in that pointed way lovers do after a momentous tiff.

Back upstairs, while waiting to be summoned by Pitcavage, I pour a coffee for myself and Patrick Koper and have to concentrate hard not to spill it because my hand has developed a mild but untamable shake. The uniform feels starchy and I am concerned that the stiff boots are going to chafe as I can already feel a painful pinch on the heel, having only walked up one flight of stairs.

"May I speak with you a moment, Mr. Mignolet?"

The voice of Marge Newlands echoes down the corridor from the door of her office, past Seb Funchess, who is standing sentry-like outside Meeting Room Four.

"Good morning, Marge," he beams, but she shoots him a look of naked antipathy before ushering me in and closing the door. Blinds up, Meeting Room Two is bathed in sunshine and seems much airier than three days before.

She maintains her grip on the door handle as though for support. "We need your help, Mr. Mignolet," she says and I sense immediately that *we* does not refer to Prospero's police force.

"Of course. How can I be—"

"Miranda has gone missing," she blurts. "She won't pick up our calls so we need you to try her in case she might pick up for you. There was a disagreement. Let's call it a family argument. Last night. She slept in the barn, as she often does, but we think she left well before dawn. She took the horse. Can you try calling her?" The sergeant's voice sounds ragged.

"Of course," I say, scrolling quickly to Miranda's name, tagged in my contacts with the selfie she took of the three of us at Shakespeare. "What do you want me to say if she answers?"

"Just … say we're sorry. Ask her to come home. Tell her we can sort everything out and that her father is beside himself with worry. Tell her we have more information … if you can."

I am at pains not to react in the full glare of the painfully personal dilemma facing this woman, who must be cringing internally at the thought of revealing any personal frailty to me, of all people. The ring tone is audible to both of us in the quiet of the office and Marge Newlands shuts her eyes. Midway through the fourth ring, a subdued Miranda answers in a hushed voice as though she has stepped out of an important meeting to take my call.

"Ariel?"

"Miranda. Hi. Where are you?"

"Have you spoken to my mom and dad?"

"Are you nearby? Can we meet up?"

A long pause.

"Have you spoken to my mom?"

It is a game of questions.

"Yes, I—" Before I finish, Marge Newlands pulls my hand, still holding the phone, toward her ear.

"Miranda, honey. It's Mom. Please come home, sweetie.

Or tell us where you are and we'll come get you. Your dad is … Miranda?" The line goes dead.

"Sorry," she says, slowly releasing my hand. "At least she sounds okay. Can you keep trying? Maybe send a text asking her to call you. I know you have to go now anyway so you can tell her I won't interrupt next time. I'm sorry … it's just … I … we're worried. At least she answered."

"Please don't apologize. I understand. I was an only child myself and drove my mother stark crazy as a teenager. I'll try her again now and keep trying all day if necessary. I'm sure it'll be fine." I can't think what else to say as she holds the door open for me to leave and I walk back down the corridor with the phone to my ear under predatory scrutiny from Pastor Funchess. Her number rings out four more times before Paul Pitcavage's clean-shaven head extends out to summon us with his velvety drawl.

"Do step inside, folks. Thank you."

Subgroups have formed along color-coded lines in the seating area of the room as friends and associates within each of the four different law enforcement agencies involved in the operation have coalesced. Having finished a white-board presentation, Pitcavage switches on a few extra overhead lights and points toward me and the pastor with ceremonial flamboyance as though revealing new exhibits in a museum.

"I need y'all to familiarize yourselves with the two civilians traveling with us today, people," he announces. "Ariel Mignolet here is our one and only eyewitness. He was present near the scene of the murder of Officer Argyll and Misters Luiz and Hernandez, and was himself assaulted and chased by our targets when he went to assist. Y'all have on your person a small laminated copy of the identikit Mr. Mignolet helped produce but, having been up close to several of the suspects, he is going to accompany us on this mission to help make reliable identifications on the ground and, hopefully, arrests. Branson, it will be your job to accompany Mr. Mignolet at all times and ensure his safety. He is only to move to advanced positions on my say-so."

I see Officer Branson flashing a characteristically toothy grin in my direction from the back of the room before I cast a glance over my right shoulder at the panel of light switches. A ripple of relief. I had hardly noticed Pitcavage flicking them on. I resolve to call Dr. Carter on my return and tell her the cure for OCD is to distract yourself with something you are scared utterly shitless of.

"Pastor Seb Funchess over here delivered provisions to the target site on many occasions up until about a year ago and has been of huge assistance in the planning of today's operation in conjunction with satellite intel. He is familiar with the senior members of the First Truth Church so will be on hand to help our specialist crisis negotiator if that proves necessary. Officer Fraser, your job is to guide and protect Mr. Funchess throughout the operation today and, once again, please consult me regarding all advances in position. Should anything happen to me, that responsibility will fall to Special Agent in Charge Bob Ensor, sitting back there to the left. Raise your hand for us all, please, Bob."

Pitcavage nods in acknowledgment when Bob, who at about six foot four and two hundred and thirty pounds of well-honed muscle couldn't look inconspicuous if he tried, stands up and makes himself known to everyone.

"Just to quickly acquaint you good gentlemen with the different units participating in today's operation ... first, we have a brave duet in black over near the door. Those are Officers Marsden and Fullcroft, direct from the Department of Homeland Security's counterterrorism training center in nearby Playas, whom, may I add, we are delighted to have with us. Then we have the eleven officers in olive green with yellow armbands and those are a hand-picked subset of the El Paso FBI Hostage Rescue Team SWAT personnel specializing in high-risk raids. Myself and a few other plain-vanilla FBI officers are in navy, like yourselves, and finally we have our nine friends from Biggs Airfield BORTAC here, wearing that particularly fetching shade of sage with no yellow bands. Those guys are gonna stand out anyway because they're all properly fit, unlike the rest of us Quantico lard asses."

A burst of laughter from his audience cements my view that Paul Pitcavage is that rare bird who can both command authority and inspire confidence in those around him while at all times remaining likable, a combination of characteristics I have seldom encountered from Stanford to Wall Street. No doubt there must be hard steel in there, too, for him to have reached this level of seniority and I wonder how much of that I might see over the coming hours.

With the troops chatting among themselves, Pitcavage turns his attention to me and Funchess, giving a condensed summary of what we are to expect. "Once we arrive at target area, approximately thirty-five miles from here, you will wait with your assigned officers near the set-down point while we surround, engage and secure the encampment. On my say-so, you will each be called forward at the appropriate time. The main thing is to listen and stay low and we will take care of the rest. Y'all good with that?"

Satisfied with mute acceptance, he addresses the room again.

"Okay. Y'all know why we are a compact group rather than a full company, folks. In my estimation, we are the perfect number if—and this is a very important if—everybody focuses on the job assigned to them but stays vigilant for the unexpected. It's always the unexpected stuff that causes the trouble. Now this situation will sure as hell not be another Zarephath-Horeb or Waco, but it is bound to have some special twists and turns all of its own and we need to be ready for that. Our intel tells us there is very little to worry about in terms of artillery, but intel can be wrong, so don't assume anything about the target. We will use a combo of live and rubber as per my in-field directions. Let's all make it fast and make it clean. Any last questions?"

His inquiry is met with silence apart from friction noises of Kevlar-clad bodies rustling up helmets and other accessories from under seats in preparation for departure.

"If you would all be so good as to walk past our two civilians here as you exit the room, folks. Take a close look at these faces because I aim to deliver them safe and well back to their loved ones and I'll be relying on all of you to help me in that endeavor."

The nervous energy in the room is palpable as the men and one woman form an orderly line to file out past me and the pastor. Some acknowledge us with perfunctory politeness as they pass but most take only the briefest mental snapshot, clearly too focused on the task ahead of them to be distracted swapping pleasantries with peripheral players.

The weaponry for the whole group is dispensed with stunning efficiency in the parking lot by the two men I had seen earlier, from the back of their white armored vehicle. No time is wasted as automatic weapons, pistols, rifles and a handful of what look like gas canisters are doled out before the armed officers insert themselves and their equipment into the waiting vehicles, perhaps chosen to draw less attention to their cargo than if military-style trucks were deployed.

Branson the BORTAC is polite to a fault and insists on calling me sir despite my protestations. A fully automatic rifle now draped across his shoulder, along with a range of other weaponry belted around his waist, he holds open the door of one of ten Chevy Suburbans for me to squeeze in the back beside Pitcavage, and all my previous comparisons with a ventriloquist's dummy instantly dissolve.

Vehicles queue up to leave once full but deliberately stagger their departure times to avoid traveling in a conspicuous convoy. Within minutes, we have left the town behind and drive southwest at high speed along a bumpy track. With the suspension of the fully loaded SUV being tested to its limits, I have to hold on to the grab handle to prevent my head connecting painfully with the roof for a second time. Conversation is sparse as thoughts are collected and everyone, including myself, looks straight ahead through the front windshield, which frequently requires wipers to sweep aside the fine dusty backwash resettling in the wake of the SUV half a mile ahead. A vibration from my phone in the breast pocket of my shirt alerts me to a text from Sunil: *Copied you on e-mail reply from Chief Detra Antone of the Tohono. Says hasn't seen, spoken to or communicated in any other way with Anegam Cesar for nearly twenty years. Maybe the wrong guy? Let me know and good luck. Su xx*

After a twenty-minute journey off-roading due south from Prospero into remote desert terrain, four helicopters come into view, their idling engines stirring up mini-circular sandstorms around each one. I choose this moment to confide in Branson that my feet are throbbing unbearably and he tells me to remove them immediately. He is confident of finding alternative footwear among the reserve kit in the trunk. It's fifty-two minutes after seven when Branson hands me a pair of standard Border Patrol-issue athletic shoes and, after a short delay on my account, we follow the rest of our group into one of three waiting Bell 412 helicopters.

How can so much be squeezed into fifty-two minutes? My sense of time is being warped by the dizzying velocity at which everyone and everything is moving. Highly trained professionals working to a well-rehearsed plan progress at rates far in excess of standard human pace. Departures and arrivals, ingress and egress of buildings or modes of transport all occur at breakneck speed and I am beginning to feel like an extra in an epic war movie swept along by the action with only minimum direction or understanding of the finer points of the plot.

About a hundred yards to our left, I watch as the landing rails of a Black Hawk helicopter, already loaded up with its eleven yellow-arm-banded cargo, lift off the ground in a billowing swirl of dust. It ascends vertically, about thirty feet, and hovers majestically for a few moments before dipping its nose, as though in salute, and accelerating southward with menace like a giant horned beetle.

During the road journey, Pitcavage had, with no little pride, confided that several modified versions of these dark warbirds had recently been added to the FBI's tactical transportation team's fleet at Quantico. I had nodded dumbly and looked suitably impressed but, on the grounds that this might not be the most appropriate time to chat to him about the importance of fundamental research to investment decisions, I made a deliberate call not to reveal that this is not the first time I have been up close and personal to one of the most notorious instruments of modern warfare.

In 2012, I had occasion to visit the Sikorsky manufacturing plant in West Palm Beach where the Black Hawk is produced. I was there in the company of a small group of other US investment managers, all clients of a hyper-thorough J.T. Carton research analyst who had rightly concluded that grown men love nothing more than ogling large, highly engineered weaponry at close quarters. His hopes of scoring big in commission terms after the trip were realized. Two weeks later, we sold forty million dollars worth of United Technologies stock, Sikorsky's then-mother company, and purchased an equivalent stake in its highly correlated industry peer, Raytheon, after a profit warning in the latter led the share price to nose dive. Never in my wildest imaginings could I have envisioned seeing one in active duty at such close quarters apart, perhaps, from Sunil maneuvering them with his remote in *Delta Force: Black Hawk Down*, a PlayStation favorite of his.

The cabin is an oasis of calm after our sprint beneath the deafening whirr of forty-foot blades, grit whipping our faces as we dashed for the door. Our rendezvous point rapidly disappears from view as we accelerate into a blue sky flecked with millions of evaporating vapor scuds, all that remains of the thick, early-morning mist. My stomach churns in time with the aircraft's vibrations, which feel strongest where the back of my knees hang over the edge of the seat.

I spend most of the fifteen-minute flight scanning the orange-and-putty-colored earth below for signs of life while sending repeat texts to Miranda pleading with her to call me back. Flat, featureless plains regularly give way to craggy hills and vales strewn with lime scrub or sprays of acacia and yellow desert flower, and then jagged rocks like giant fields of sand-locked stepping stones. How long must Blount and his followers have spent trying to pick pathways through and around those barriers all those years ago?

We fly south at first, straight down the Animas Valley, a corridor of Chihuahuan Desert terrain between the Peloncillo Mountains, running north–south along the Arizona border, and the Animas range, whose peaks I have come to know so well. The sun is rising directly behind the majestic 8,500-foot Animas Mountain as we draw closer. At first it appears as a dark pointy shadow, until ten minutes later, after we have veered left in a more southeasterly direction, when it gradually comes into sharper focus and I can make out dark-green crests and peaks. I have heard elevated habitats like this described as sky islands—pockets of high-altitude vegetation, such as piñon pine, which thrive on precipitation falling at high elevations that fails to reach the surrounding desert.

When I inquire as to how much longer he thinks we will be in the air, Branson tells me we are heading for the southern-most foothills of the Animas Mountain Range, a deserted craggy moonscape no more than eight miles from the Mexican border.

"Apt, really, I guess," he adds wistfully, before returning to peering out the window.

"What do you mean?" I ask.

"Animas. It's short for lost souls in Spanish."

Pastor Funchess sits in the cockpit between the two pilots. All three wear shiny green helmets adorned with super-size earphones. He taps the captain on the shoulder and points out the first officer's left-side window toward a circular rocky outcrop studded with thick patches of greenery. From an elevation of two thousand feet, it looks like an emerald island floating in an ocean of barren desert. In a place that enjoys so little rainfall, areas of dense foliage exist only where unusual seeps channel water up from aquifers far below. From the appearance of the area ahead, this is exactly what Blount and his followers found.

All occupants of the helicopter strain to look at the place the pastor is indicating, but there is no detectable trace of human existence until we descend another few hundred feet and, like a mirage, a collection of rectangular metallic roofs become visible within the walls of a circular limestone reef rimmed with thick stands of trees. It is a much bigger area than I had imagined and my first thought is that more troops might be needed to secure an area of this size. Glinting in the sunlight, the dwellings are set alongside each other in a fanlike pattern around what appears to be an inner clearing. We can make out several flat-roofed stone buildings on the other side of the camp and some of these are partially concealed by the branches of mature desert olive, acacia and mesquite.

A long narrow stretch of what appears to be a dried-up river canyon runs due south from the outcrop in the direction of the nearby Mexican border. It is featureless apart from scattered patches of tar bush and creosote. The odd piñon pine and oak tree peek out between the limestone ridges that must have once lined the river's banks, but all evidence of vegetation gradually peters out where the life-giving underground water retreats back to its subterranean tomb hundreds of feet below the surface.

In the moments before we join the other three helicopters

on the ground, some fifty feet or so outside the rocky outer perimeter of the encampment, I catch an eerie glimpse of people scurrying about within its walls.

Chapter Sixteen

The First Truth

Once on the ground, it is quickly evident that every aspect of Paul Pitcavage's plan has been shaped with the benefit of painstaking research of satellite imagery and the guidance of eyewitness information. From above, the limestone walls of the camp appeared to have no obvious breach, but we have managed to land right next to what looks like the main entrance, which the camp occupants have gone to great lengths to disguise with piles of dried brush.

The helicopters retreat back to the skies and Branson guides me to cover behind a dense thicket of juniper. We crouch at the ready. I can make out the backpacks and helmets of officers here and there, moving stealthily forward in a wide wedge-shaped formation to take up positions surrounding the twenty-foot-wide gap in the rock face. Two other smaller teams track wider arcs in opposite directions going around the camp and seem to melt and then reappear fleetingly in a high crawl or crouch, dodging deftly behind what sparse cover the pockets of foliage can provide, before making short, fast rushes to steadily take them away from us to their allocated positions surrounding the entrance. A third grouping, including Pitcavage, hunker down at the base of the jagged limestone rock face waiting to follow in behind the advance party comprising mainly the FBI SWAT team.

Everything happens quickly. Within minutes, all but one or two of the eighteen or so officers actively participating in the advance raid have disappeared through the opening while we are left to wait and another smaller group remains hidden from view in strategic positions around the outer perimeter. The pastor and his assigned officer are outside, too, about twenty feet ahead of us behind a clump of shrubbery. I kneel down because imitating Branson's body position has made my left leg numb. At the outer edge of my personal space, he is crouched and poised to accelerate off his haunches in exactly the pose he adopted the first moment we took cover. "You doing okay, sir?" he whispers, without taking his eyes off the scene.

"Great, thanks," I reply glibly on the basis that I suspect he has little real interest in hearing about nausea and a bothersome itch beneath my unfamiliar headgear.

"Things are real quiet in there. Good sign," he says reassuringly just as a faint electronic crackle fires within his helmet and he responds with a "Yes, sir" into the small black microphone to the side of his mouth, while I watch as Funchess and Fraser steal quietly through the camp's outer entrance.

"Stay down, stay quiet and stay exactly behind me, sir." Branson's tone is professional and calm and as I copy his every move during our dash toward the entrance, I gain some understanding of the merits of the battle-buddy system the US military has been trying so hard to adopt in recent years.

Two BORTAC sentries silently acknowledge us as we

pass through the gap. Ascending a widening path of scree, we are met by one of the men in navy who directs us to take cover behind a ramshackle shed attached to a small fenced-off paddock that may once have corralled small farm animals like goats or pigs but is now in an advanced state of disrepair. There is a foul stench in the air, the source of which is hard to define, but I suspect we must be near raw sewage.

The camp's manmade perimeter fence is at least ten feet high and appears recently reinforced, in a haphazard fashion, using a wide range of materials. Walls of internal stone buildings line up with the boundary to make up part of the defenses and roofs are strewn with broken glass and mesquite thorn to further deter access. All wooden sections of the bulwark have soot streaks, suggesting varying degrees of fire damage. Some char stains reach all the way to the top and, at a glance, look for all the world like narrow cave entrances.

Having by now fanned out, most of the team is no longer visible while Pitcavage, a group of five SWAT personnel, and Seb Funchess kneel in the ready position outside what looks like the front gate. They are surrounded by the truncated torsos of freshly felled trees, the wood from which has been put to use shoring up defenses. Two of the men hold small megaphones and all peer up at a strip of dull white cloth of indecipherable origin flittering forlornly at the end of a whitethorn stick being waved over the top of the gate by an invisible hand.

Pitcavage takes one of the megaphones and speaks slowly and clearly as though he has assumed English is not his audience's first language. "My name is Officer Paul Pitcavage from the United States Federal Bureau of

Investigation. You are surrounded. We are heavily armed but have no violent aims. Pastor Seb Funchess is here with me if you wish to communicate through him. We seek to apprehend a specific group of individuals who we suspect have been involved in a serious crime. If those individuals do not reside here, you have nothing to fear from us. If they do, we intend to bring them to face justice and ask that you surrender them voluntarily once we have entered the camp and identified them. I need all occupants of the camp to assemble immediately in the inner yard and kneel down, keeping their hands where we can see them at all times. Then I request that you open the front gates, very slowly, and send a representative out with their hands raised. If you follow these directions to the letter, I give you my word that no one will get hurt. If we are faced with any resistance of any kind, we will respond with aggression. Do you understand these instructions?"

"Yes, we understand," comes an immediate shout in reply. "You won't find them here." And with that, the invisible hand drops the stick and the makeshift flag of surrender falls, snagging on a nail halfway down the gate where it hangs like a dead sea bird.

For the next five minutes, the sounds of hushed voices and shuffling feet can be heard from behind the bulwark. There is little movement among our ranks apart from the reappearance of a few officers near the front gate to swell our numbers in preparation for entering. I cast a glance at the pastor who, like me, kneels rather than crouches next to Pitcavage, and see an unfamiliar look of anxiety on his face.

Clunk of bolt and clang of chain precede one wing of the gate opening at a glacially slow speed and the emergence of an emaciated face that looks like it never won anything.

The man's lank hair clings to his scalp and he wears a filthy pale-blue shirt held together by a few threads and a pair of dark trousers, ripped short below the knee, above bare feet. He is so painfully undernourished, it is hard to believe he has the strength to stay upright let alone open the heavy gates.

Task complete, he stands forlornly with his hands above his head before a bristling arsenal of sophisticated weaponry and I notice the officers' grip on their rifles loosen as the pathetic face of the enemy is revealed.

"Help us. Please help us," he says breathlessly as though speaking itself requires supreme effort.

Branson and I fall in behind a sixteen-strong team to enter the camp, the officers moving cautiously in formation, vigilant for any new source of peril. We round the corner of a long stone building that brings us into the clearing I had seen from the skies. It is patently obvious from what awaits us that the only real threat in this place is that of starvation. Four lines of skeletal beings dressed in rags, all with pale, patchy skin and thin, matted hair, kneel on the dirt before us. I can't be the only one whose mind springs to footage of POWs and death camps and feels a searing pang of pity. Judging by the strain on their faces, their hands above their heads might as well be sacks of stones and Pitcavage, who has removed his helmet and appears visibly shaken, immediately tells everyone to relax their arms by their sides.

Bedraggled shirts and trousers, perhaps once their Sunday best, hang loosely on the emaciated frames of the men, while the women kneel on long skirts with ragged hems skimming bare feet and plain, dull, high-necked blouses. Their hair is pinned up like school marms from another era.

"Sweet suffering divine Jesus, is this everyone?" Pitcavage asks the camp's emissary, who looks relieved that everything seems to be going smoothly.

"There are three young children in the second RV over there and an old man and woman in the church buildings. Apart from that, we are all that is left. Can we close the gate?"

"What's your name, sir?"

"Stephen," replies the man. "Can we close the gate, sir?"

"Here's what we're gonna do, Stephen. We're going to get these people into the shade, search every inch of this place, document names and see what we can do about sourcing some nutrition. Then I'm gonna find out from y'all what the hell has happened here. I can give you a complete guarantee that you ..."

"We really need to close the gate, sir. Please. They will be back." His plea has a ring of desperation.

"Unless they're packing a few nuclear warheads, Stephen, I can assure you that we are all safe from whoever *they* are. Now I need you to take yourself over to the assembly area there and I look forward to having you brief me on the whole sorry mess, whenever it is that we are ready."

Stephen walks toward his fellow First Truth members, casting several nervous glances behind him as he goes. Pitcavage consults in a huddle with the three team leaders while other officers direct the assembled adults to an area of shade near one of the outbuildings.

Branson and I sit out the next few hours on a bench in the shadow of what seems to be a larder shed, completely empty apart from a few sacks of some kind of musty grain, a bushel of withered mesquite pods and a cloud of flies. It is very hard to imagine spending a week, let alone twenty years, in these antediluvian surroundings. The whole camp encompasses a space approximately the size of two-and-a-half football fields with much of the area behind the semicircle of RVs covered in vigorous creosote bushes, some of which have been burned in an effort to arrest their advance. The smell of feces and rot is only just shy of nausea-inducing, and I notice that several of the SWAT team are already donning face masks. Everything animate and inanimate is covered in a fine layer of dust and, with the teeth of the desert breeze blunted by the fence and the outer rim of trees, a sense of mild suffocation pervades the area.

Arranged like the spokes of a wheel, but far too close for any privacy, the twenty or so old-fashioned RVs, mostly 1970s Airstreams, look like giant silver sardines laid out to dry in the sun, their sheen dulled in places by layers of lichen. One has been completely disassembled and chunks of its skin tacked onto the perimeter fence at various points around the camp. Where these slightly warped aluminum sections face inwards, they appear for all the world like funhouse mirrors and refract the sun's rays at strange angles. Alternative uses have also been found for other segments of the carcass, like the padded seating placed strategically in shady spots around the inner clearing, a shower tray for growing seedlings, and the tires that serve as the legs of a long communal outdoor dining table. It is as though the place, like the starving people, is consuming essential parts of itself to stay alive.

As noon approaches, the heat soars, and the stomach-churning odor and the fly count rise with it. Between unsuccessful attempts to reach Miranda, I take regular sips through the plastic straw attached to a three-liter H2O bag in my backpack to offset the rapid fluid loss. For their own hydration, camp residents traipse back and forth in small groups to replenish a variety of vessels from a water well near the center of the clearing, which is demarcated by a low, circular brick wall and has an upright handle pump that stands proud like a gray stork above a collection of silver water pails strewn about on the dirt like spent cartridges. There is no shortage of these buckets in the encampment, and a batch of them double as chairs for many of the forty-strong group assembled under the trees.

The First Truth faithful sit in eerie silence with only the odd coordinating voice of the interviewing officers to be heard. There is no echo of laughter here, no whispers of happier days gone by. An existence, perhaps a state of penance, is how life here must have been for a long time.

Pitcavage and Funchess emerge from behind an RV and cross the clearing to where Branson and I sit. They have a short discussion before the pastor walks with his minder toward the assembled residents. As he advances toward the group, several of the men rise to greet him, and while I cannot hear the conversation, I can tell from the body language and the tone of the voices receiving him that there is great relief at his presence.

Pitcavage sits down beside Branson. "The pastor's in full-blown shock," he says. "He's never seen anything like this, and I must confess, neither have I. These people are on the verge of death, for Christ's sake. I hardly expect we will be needing your help today, Ariel, unless we find fitter folks hiding under the beds. But I'm fairly sure the group we are looking for are the people responsible for this situation. The three kids in the RV over there are under ten years and not in much better shape than the adults. We're going to finish the search-and-secure and then I'll sit down with the team heads and debrief some of the First Truth folks to find out what exactly has taken place here. You and the pastor should sit in. It will keep you involved while I keep you close.

"Lots of these folks need urgent medical attention so I've already been in touch with El Paso, Las Cruces and even Albuquerque to set up emergency accommodation. Looks like it will be tomorrow morning before they can get the extra birds to airlift people out of here in numbers so, as a stop gap, our choppers are coming back with emergency resources at 1330 hours today. Between now and then, we need to dole out whatever surplus provisions we have in our packs, secure the camp for an overnight and hold a meeting with some of the senior people here to get a better handle on how this has come about. You two should simply stay in the shade for now, although my advice would be to move a bit farther away from the latrine." He smiles and nods knowingly toward an area of brush and swarming flies twenty feet to our right.

"Fucking rancid. No cover. They must have given up draining it when they got too weak. It's basically a cesspit that has overflowed and I already detailed one of the guys to cover it up and dig a temporary pit for us coz I sure as hell wouldn't want to fall into that sucker in the dead of night. Maybe y'all should wait over there in the buildings and pick a room for us to hold the meeting in. I'll call you when it's being convened. All good?" He directs us toward the long stone edifice across the clearing.

"Have they found Blount?" I ask, eager to see the man I have heard so much about.

"Yes. In fact, it turns out Stephen over there is his nephew. You'll probably come across the old geezer in one of the rooms," Pitcavage says, making a circular twirling motion with his index finger at his temple as he walks away.

We have to duck to enter through a simple wooden door. From above, our view of this structure was partially obscured by a particularly tall and dense stand of mesquite trees growing outside the camp fence. The top branches have been trained by prevailing winds to reach over the roof toward the setting sun. Constructed in very basic style from rocks, wood and quicklime, the place is about the size of an average family home, but there is glass in only one of the three small windows facing into the camp, possibly another recycled slice of the disemboweled RV.

We find ourselves in a spacious meeting room set out with rows of pine chairs facing a rudimentary red-brick podium and I assume this must be the First Truth Church's place of worship. The far side of the room is in dark shadow as all five windows have been boarded up so the only source of illumination comes from a flashlight-size beam of sunlight coming in through a hole in one of the makeshift shutters. A doorway behind the pulpit is partially blocked by a stack of oil lamps and leads down a thinly lit corridor with four rooms off it.

The first door is slightly ajar and opens into what is, judging by the cot and assortment of ghoulish instruments and tinctures, a medical examination area the size of a large walk-in closet. The next two lead into larger rooms whose windows are boarded up. The first is completely devoid of furniture apart from a six-foot wooden cross cemented into the center of the floor and, while its function isn't clear, sliding bolts on the outside of the door suggest the room has been used more for enforced confinement than voluntary seclusion. The second is exactly the same but looks like a shabby student dormitory room, crammed with two single beds, piles of clothing and a range of other living essentials. The last door is closed. Branson knocks and we look at each other with surprise when a woman's voice replies "Enter."

Natural light streams into the spacious room through an old window frame that looks out over the stand of trees. The shed I had hidden behind earlier is just visible outside to the left. A long wooden dining table takes up most of the central space and pine planks, which I assume are usually used to board up the window, lie against the wall. A white-haired, bearded man sits in a chair in the wash of early-afternoon sunshine eating lunch from a tray set on what looks like a school desk. He has a fork in one hand and a small spoon in the other and doesn't react in any way to acknowledge our arrival into the room.

The backs of the heads of two BORTAC sentries are visible through the open frame. A peal of laughter at some shared joke and the scent of cigarette smoke infiltrating the room suggests the atmosphere outside has relaxed significantly.

The woman who bade us enter sits on a three-legged stool in the far corner. Her silver hair is tied in a loose ponytail and she wears an ankle-length floral petticoat redolent of those worn by housekeepers long ago. Like everyone else, she is painfully thin but it suits her fine features and delicate bone structure. Her hands are resting quietly on her lap and she does not appear occupied with any task apart from studiously watching the old man eat.

"Do they need me now?" the woman asks in a thin voice, tilting her head sideways like an inquisitive terrier. She is slightly cross-eyed. "Only he hasn't finished yet, you see. I told those nice soldiers our Anthony needs to keep regular, if you know what I mean. Routine and all that. Eat up now, Anthony," she says as though cajoling a small child.

The old man spoons something resembling semolina pudding or very watery rice into his mouth with great effort because his hand shakes violently all the way from the bowl, spilling droplets of white gloop on his lap and down his beard. Having finally connected with the target, the spoon's next, seemingly random destination is the half-eaten plate of brown stew, which I suspect has been sitting there for some time because the rendered fat has begun to congeal.

"It takes him nearly two hours to eat lunch," she says, reading our thoughts. "I always get this job," she adds with a resigned sigh, and it occurs to me from the look of her starved frame that watching her charge eat for all that time must be akin to torture.

"He's our spiritual leader. Did they tell you?" she asks, looking directly at us for the first time and I can see now that her right pupil constantly flickers slightly from side to side, making it hard to maintain eye contact with her for any length of time.

I suspect she will continue to pour words into a one-sided conversation unless we take a turn. "My name is Ariel Mignolet. This is Officer Branson."

"My name is Cora and this is my husband, Anthony Blount. Or, at least, it used to be. You see that man?" She speaks slowly while gesturing gracefully toward her husband like a geisha making formal introductions. "That man is derelict. Like a boarded-up house where squatters have moved in. That is my husband now. Just waiting for our Lord's call, he is. And, as is the way with these things, it falls to me to watch his exterior crumble away until it comes. Isn't that right, Anthony?"

At that moment, a silver object, which I quickly establish is Anthony's spoon, flies across the room and strikes Cora's forehead. She springs from the stool with a screech. It was flung with more force than I thought possible for such a feeble character, and when Branson and I go to assist, her brow is already beginning to swell.

"Bitch," he hisses, his dinner now pushed aside and fork at the ready to launch a second missile. "Wench! Don't talk to her if you know what's good for you," he advises us in a conspiratorial whisper. "She's married to that criminal, Saul Freeth. Know the man?"

He waits for one of us to answer, but I play dumb because I can't figure out if it is better to go along with his demented ravings or to try and pull him up short with the truth and, like Russian roulette, I fear that choosing incorrectly might be disastrous.

"If you try anything like that again, I will have to restrain you, sir," Branson warns Blount.

"Everybody knows Saul's been spreading it around," continues Blount, "and I'd say she likes to spread it around, too, if you know what I mean." A smutty cackle rattles up his throat. "Steer clear, I tell you. Trouble. Bad seeds, those filthy Freeths. Get out, wench!" he barks again across the room at Cora, who is still doubled over, holding her head in her fine-boned hands.

The noise attracts the attention of the sentries outside who, after assessing the scene, ask Branson if we need any assistance.

"He's not really like that," Cora whimpers through her fingers, unfolding herself stiffly back to an upright position.

Branson produces an icepack from his kitbag for Cora Blount and makes radio contact with several of the officers from the tactical unit. In the course of his conversation, I glean that most of that team are now busy pitching tents in and around the encampment. Branson asks the sentries outside to help move Blount to the room next door, which we have now established contains his and Cora's belongings. In a follow-up call to Pitcavage, I hear him say that this room will make an ideal site for a meeting as it is well aired and has less of a stench than the church hall at the other end of the corridor.

Blount grumbles incoherently as he is led away, shuffling stiffly as though his ankles are chained, while we gather up chairs from various rooms and arrange them around the table.

Twenty minutes later, Pitcavage arrives with his other two team leaders followed by Funchess and his minder. On taking his seat, a wordless staring contest develops between the pastor and Cora Blount. Just as it begins to attract the attention of the room, she breaks the deadlock, gets up to leave and almost collides with Stephen the gatekeeper and a man of similar age whom Stephen introduces to us as Tristan, also a nephew of Blount.

"I think maybe Cora should stay, sir," Stephen advises Pitcavage. "If you want the whole story, it might be good to hear her—"

Seb Funchess interrupts, sweeping the appeal aside with a full belt of the authoritative baritone used so effectively from the pulpit. "There is no need for her here, folks. I know what she knows, including the history. All we need is for Stephen here to bring us up to date on what has transpired in the time since our last visit twelve months ago."

"But there are things—" Stephen again fails to complete his sentence when Cora cuts him short.

"I shall stay," she says, clearly angered by the pastor's dismissive tone. "In fact, I insist on staying," she adds and turns to direct her comments to Pitcavage. "Some people might not like what I have to say, but I should be here nonetheless. Give me a moment, if you would. I need to get something."

"Think about this, Cora. Anthony won't be pleased," Funchess shouts.

Her stark reply echoes down the corridor in her wake: "Anthony's gone, Seb. Long gone."

The fuming pastor switches his attention to Pitcavage, whose lead everyone else is following to take their seats.

"Paul, there is no need for that woman to join us. She has a vendetta against me because I wouldn't accept her divorce and remarriage. She's unreliable at best, if not downright untruthful, and I strenuously object to her presence here. Perhaps we could sit down with her at a later stage, in private, after I have given you a more complete picture of her, well, her jaundiced take on things."

"Sit yourself down there, Pastor, please. Mrs. Blount will join the meeting. Now, can we all get some water in here if possible?" Paul Pitcavage gives the man sitting next to him the same subtle smile Marge Newlands was on the receiving end of in Prospero Police Station and the officer departs the room.

The temperature is uncomfortably high, but with the air blowing toward rather than from the main source of the smell, it feels positively fresh in comparison to the interior spaces of the camp. The tabletop is unvarnished, roughly hewn planks of pine and a large splinter pricks my right thigh when I draw my chair up beneath it. Only Pitcavage has the distraction of a phone in front of him and sounds of throat clearing and nervous fidgeting can be heard around the table as we await Cora's return. A few minutes later, she enters carrying an old Sunshine Biscuits tin and takes the seat nearest the door at the head of the table, opposite Pitcavage.

"I'm gonna keep this meeting as short as possible, folks. It's one o'clock now and my aim is to wrap it up in thirty minutes because our air transportation is due back here with a food drop around that time and I need to talk to those folks as a matter of urgency. Now Stephen and I have already spoken briefly about how the members of the First Truth Church here have found themselves in such dire circumstances after so many relatively successful years surviving all the way out here in the desert. It seems like there has been a schism of some kind and an alienated subgroup of, basically, teenagers is keeping the camp under siege. The aim of this meeting is for us all to gain a better understanding of the origins, motives and the general movements of this group so that we can successfully engage with and apprehend those individuals who we now suspect represent a real and present threat to the wider public in this area. Stephen, would you mind beginning at the beginning for us, so to speak. Fill us in a little about the relevant camp history and explain who these people are and why they have broken bad."

Stephen has clearly never held the attention of so many people at once and looks overwhelmed, swallowing hard and gripping his right forearm tightly with his left hand to stem the shaking.

"Take your time, sir. I don't mean to put you under pressure," Pitcavage says kindly.

"Well, I guess it goes all the ways back to the failed coming, sir. That'd be twelve seasons ago now, Tristan, wouldn't I be right in sayin'?"

Tristan, who hasn't yet uttered a syllable and seems content to shrink behind his cousin, leans his long face forward and nods enthusiastically to everyone before retreating again into the back of his chair.

"We were, all of us—that'd be eighty or so back then—doin' well, you could say. We was excited, full of expectations of meetin' our Lord Almighty. So I s'pose you could say we came down fast from that after the End Times came and went. Winter night winds seemed to blow extra hard those next few months. Some folks left, and all that time Anthony wouldn't speak to us. He locked himself away in that cross room for weeks on end and when he eventually came back to preach, he was changed. Much changed and so, too, was Alonso. When Pastor Blount came back, we could all see it weren't going to end good. Ain't that right, Tristan?"

The head of his mute sidekick appears briefly beside him once again to affirm the facts.

"Alonso is Anthony's son. Well, his adopted grandson, really. Seb Funchess there brought him back when he was less than three years old after folks up in Albuquerque rejected him. Too much of a handful, they said."

"Seb, you wanna tell these folks that part?" interjects Pitcavage.

All eyes turn toward the pastor, who takes a moment to collect himself, stealing a quick sip from the Army-issue plastic cup of water as a noisy rustle from the trees outside suggests the wind is rising.

"Stephen is correct. Alonso is the Blounts' grandson. And he is … he has always been … different, if I can put it like that."

"I thought Blount never had children, Seb," Pitcavage says, looking somewhat confused. "Is this Cora Freeth's grandson we are talking about? Caleb Freeth's son?"

Far from the vainglorious evangelist swaggering through

the church aisles, the pastor has assumed the edgy disposition of a chess player who knows he is rapidly running out of moves. His gaze, like his hands, retreats to his lap and all traces of the arrogance so evident in Caleb Freeth's front room are gone. "Yes. He is," he mumbles.

"But I thought … at least Mr. Freeth told us that his kids live with their mother on an Indian reservation in southern Arizona," says Pitcavage. "There was a letter. Is the—?"

"Their mother is buried no more than a thousand feet from where we are sitting, Mr. Pitcavage, sir." Cora's voice has a new note of calm and resolve, of which there was no trace during our earlier encounter. "Take a look for her grave yonder outside the walls. It's the one with a simple *A* etched on a plain wooden cross. Murdered, she was. Murdered by my husband this fourteen years and counting."

"Cora, you simply do not have any evidence that that is what happened," Funchess responds forcefully. "You can't be sure. None of us can."

"I know all right, Seb. I prepared the agave potion for him. He told me he just wanted her sick, but I'm certain he suffocated her once she was too weak to fight back. Acted all surprised when we found her cold body in the nursing room, but I swear to you, he was never happier than those next few months when she was six feet under and he had arranged for the two kids to be taken. Day after she was buried, he disappeared for two weeks, the only time he left camp in all our time here. He confessed to me six months later that he trekked all the way to Arizona, just to post a letter. Faked Anegam's hand to Caleb to tell him she had left to rejoin her tribe."

"So both letters Caleb Freeth told us he received were fakes?" Pitcavage asks. "He mentioned a second one to us, from the chief at the reservation."

With all eyes upon her, Cora opens the box and takes out a yellowing, one-page, hand-written letter and three color photographs about twice the size of typical passport stills, hands each carefully to Branson on her left and indicates that he should pass them around the table.

"That's a first draft of the note Anthony gave Seb during one of his visits here back in two-thousand-three. He dictated it to me same way he does all his letters and sermons. You'll see at the end there that he asked Seb to get it typed up on official-looking Tohono Reservation paper and sign it as if it was from the chief to throw Caleb off the trail, seeing as he wasn't giving up the search for his family too easy. Pastor did a great job with it. Would have passed Internal Revenue muster, it was so authentic looking.

"The photographs. Now those are the only ones of Cehia and Ces before the pastor here took them away. He told us he had found nice half-breed couples to take them but, well, that didn't work out so well for Ces seeing as he was back with us inside six months with a new name and a new personality."

Branson hands me the images, which are a sequence, probably taken seconds apart, of Caleb and Anegam Freeth and their two children, who look to have been toddlers at the time. All the family are laughing and I try and imagine those humor-filled moments before the camera's eye opened. Attempts to squeeze themselves onto a stool in a tiny booth while getting everyone to face forward at the same time. Caleb looks young and handsome and carefree, his hair sandy brown, eyes squinting with mirth. Although her face is creased with humor, Anegam's serene beauty shines up from the image as she touches the right cheek of her pink-clad daughter on her lap, steering the little face toward the lens. My hand ascends slowly, almost involuntarily, to cover my mouth as it opens in a quiet gasp. There, in the space between both sets of laughter-filled eyes, lie pale-pinkish marks the shape of arrowheads, the only blemishes on otherwise immaculate, honey-toned skin.

"Is all this true, Mr. Funchess?" Pitcavage inquires as he takes his turn perusing the exhibits.

"More lies than truths," Funchess replies, his voice shaking with anger. "Firstly, Anthony assured me that Caleb's wife left here of her own volition right after he signed up for the military. He said she only returned from her tribe because she was ill and, with no job and no home, she couldn't look after the children. She died of her illness and, with Caleb having turned his back on the family, we didn't know what else to do. Harsh and all as it sounds, adoption seemed the kindest thing for those kids."

"Did you try to contact him to let him know about his wife and children?" Pitcavage asks.

"You have to understand, Paul, the church here, well, they would have strong views about … about homogeneity … if I can put it like that. Right or wrong, it's just part of their belief system and, in choosing his wife, Caleb flew in the face of that. He flew in the face of it and then he left her behind him. Isn't that so, Stephen?" An imperious note returns to the pastor's voice when he addresses Blount's nephew.

If he appeared nervous at the start of the meeting, Stephen now has the look of a man facing the gallows; his cousin has shimmied so far down in his seat, he is all but invisible. "Caleb brought us a problem, right enough," Stephen whimpers, beads of perspiration glowing on his forehead between long, lank tendrils of hair. "Wasn't part of God's plan for us to be mixed up, Anthony said, and there was no which way one of us was gonna step up to the job of taking those two children ahead of the Rapture. When he came back here looking for his family, we all played dumb. Plain suicide to do anything else."

"But I still don't understand why *you* didn't contact Caleb at that time, Mr. Funchess," Pitcavage persists. "*You* would have been in a position to get a message to him, through military channels, if nothing else. And why play any part in forging the letter?"

"Paul, the last time Anthony and Caleb spoke before Anegam's death was the day he announced he had signed up to fight the A-rabs. As I heard it, that same day he threatened to burn the camp to the ground, with everyone in it, if Anthony was still here when he got back. Told him he no longer believed in the teachings of the First Truth Church and would be taking his family and whoever else he could convince away from this place as soon as he was done fighting," the pastor says. "Look, he wasn't here. The children were motherless and something had to be done. The way I see it, Caleb paid for his decision to leave his family in a very precarious position."

Cora scoffs loudly at the other end of the table. "Anegam was murdered. Caleb was thrown off his children's trail by you and Anthony and then Alonso was never allowed to know the truth of his own roots. We were all in on it and too damned scared of Anthony to say anything." Far from the meek creature we had encountered earlier, Cora Blount now sounds like a lawyer scything through the facts of a complicated case.

"I will never forgive myself for Anegam's death and

not standing up for my grandson, but at least I am telling the God's honest truth now, Seb. At least I will face my Maker having accepted my part in all this. You, on the other hand, seem content to live with the lie while we endure the consequences. Alonso is the pus in a festering old wound finally erupting through the skin."

"Why lie, Cora?" Funchess retorts. "So I helped forge the second letter, but you and I know what Caleb would have been capable of if he managed to dig up the truth at that time. That letter was merely an act of self-defense. You were in danger. All of you. I swear to the Lord Almighty, Mr. Pitcavage, that I knew nothing of any killing of that Indian woman. As far as I'm concerned, she left here herself to return to her own and they delivered her back here a sick woman. Anthony swore it and I believe him. Am I correct, Stephen? That she initially left of her own volition?"

Stephen looks from Cora to the pastor and back, strategically weighing up which way his testimony should fall.

"She never returned to her tribe," I tell the gathering, saving him the stress of taking sides. "She hasn't been seen by her family or any of the Tohono O'odham since she left twenty years ago to marry Caleb."

Nine perplexed faces turn, some trying to work out who I am as Pitcavage had dispensed with introductions in the interests of expediency.

"I made inquiries through official circles, or at least someone I am very close to did. They spoke directly to the Chief Antone, whose signature was forged on the letter Caleb received. He remembered Anegam Cesar very well but says no one there has clapped eyes on her or any children of hers in all the years since she left."

"A proper Poirot, Mr. Mignolet," Pitcavage remarks drily. "Of course, that makes me more inclined to believe Mrs. Blount's version of the whole depressing epic, but at this stage, I think we have spent enough time dissecting history and not enough dealing with the specifics of what has led to the shocking state of the camp here and the other sinister activities we believe this group is responsible for."

"What other sinister activities, sir?" Cora asks tentatively, as though in fear of the answer.

"I can brief you at a later time, ma'am, but right now, if you would be so good as to bring us up to date on the situation facing us here, I would be obliged. Maybe start by giving us some background on your grandson, if you will. I'm still not sure I have a good enough understanding of his motives." A seam of strain is detectable in Pitcavage's normally courteous tone.

"That boy actually started out fine and that's really the worst of it," Cora begins wearily. "I've often wondered about how his sister fared in the end, because they were so alike as babies. Not identical mind, but real similar just the same. I truly believe that our Lord poured that boy's little soul into the mold just perfect, but then it was dented and cracked up so badly over the years that he came out unrecognizable, grotesque. Basically, Alonso, or Ces as we knew him when his mother was alive, was a right happy-go-lucky infant to begin with so don't go believin' anyone who tells you he was born evil or something. But whatever happened to him, with the loss of his mother and then the time he spent with those people Seb Funchess sent him to, he was utterly changed within a matter of months. Came back sullen and cold. No which way of persuading a smile.

"The story we got back through Seb was that the folks

in Albuquerque couldn't stop him crying and no amount of punishment could bend his will so they just tossed him back like a broken toy. The truth is, I was already too tired of life by that stage to cope with a small child, and Anthony, well, he simply wasn't able to love him, so the boy just kinda endured life between hidings.

"Lucky for him, there were lots of children born here within a few years of each other and he took to friends for comfort. A group of them did everything together and it wasn't long before Alonso's one special talent shone through for all the world to see. I'm talking from real young, maybe five or six years old. We could see that boy had a natural primacy over his peers. As effortless as breathing. They never bullied him about his color despite all the preaching about purity. Anthony and the other adults called him names, but the other kids? They adored the ground he walked on."

Branson's radio buzzes and the crackly voice of SAIC Bob Ensor pierces the bubble of rapt attention around the table to report that adequate personnel are now in place outside the outer perimeter to receive the incoming air transportation. I suspect this is where the two men who were earlier stationed outside have gone.

"And so, Ma'am," Pitcavage continues, "the strife that's led to this siege here. Can you enlighten us as to how all that came to a head?"

"It's hard to describe it, really," Cora continues, now gazing dolefully out the window with her one good eye, wisps of silver hair shifting softly around a face on which laughter has left little impression. "I mean it's hard to say exactly when the turning point came, but there was one incident that sticks out in my mind that might help you see the way things shifted … or at least how they … how those boys started to move away.

"Anthony used to hold tournaments every month to prepare for End Times and he kept them up, even after the last day passed. When he came out of hiding, he was hardened somehow. It seemed to me he had become almost immune to the suffering of others and the fights he judged became more brutal as a result. Perhaps I should have seen that was the first real sign of his failing health. At first the duels were hand-to-hand combat, mainly wrestling, but then they started using everything from rocks to wooden rods and over the years it drove Anthony near crazy that none of the kids could beat Caleb's boy. *The half-breed reject*, he used to call him.

"That day, we were out on the cracked flats beyond the river bed and he put one more challenger in front of Alonso, who at that stage was already exhausted after winning three matches. His opponent was no child, more a man, really. In his twenties at least, if I had to guess. Anthony just wanted so bad for Alonso to lose, and lose he did. He went down, eventually, still fighting, mind, but hurt so badly it was hard to watch. I was standing in a circle with Alonso's friends, some of whom he had just defeated, watching as he finally raised his hand in surrender. One of his fingers was crushed to a pulp and his legs were so badly damaged he couldn't stand.

"Despite my pleas, Anthony shouted at the older lad, telling him he wasn't to quit yet and that's when it happened. The teenagers, maybe fifteen of them, walked as a group toward Anthony and stood in silence between him and their friend, facing him down until he turned and walked back toward the camp. He had the good sense not to even try to talk them around and, well, I knew things would never be the same here after that. Next day at church, he railed at everyone from the pulpit about loyalty and the need for unity, but there was no question in my mind that a storm was brewing and it was only a question of when we would all feel its force."

"Can you give me a broad idea of the timeline of all this, Cora? I mean approximate dates of the events you describe in and around the aught-six to the End Times period in 'thirteen?" Pitcavage asks.

"Twins were born in ninety-nine and the final reckoning had come and gone so by the time that first stand-off took place, it must have been, yes, it was two years ago. The river bed dried to stone that summer. Alonso would have been fifteen. Things drifted on for a while, but it was plain to see that Anthony was getting more and more agitated and forgetful. His preaching became unintelligible. He could only remember a few favorite tracts from the Old Testament and it became pathetic, really. Sad. More folks left 'bout then and who'd blame them? Everything was altered. The prophecy dead. Maybe they could see where things were headed. Some even left their children behind because they wouldn't leave Alonso's side. And who can criticize them for it. Seems like a good decision now the way things panned out. We gradually moved from a situation where there was plenty of food from hunting, and the extras Pastor dropped off now and then, to a situation where the grain stores ran empty, and Alonso and the others stopped bringing back food."

Cora's thin fingers fish in the tin once more to extract an almost-translucent blue page, which looks like it has been balled up and smoothed out many times over. I can just make out Caleb's signature when Pitcavage holds the page up to the light. The smooth thith-thith-thith pulse of the helicopters in the distance comes in and out of earshot.

"I don't know why I kept it, really, except it was all I had left of my own son. Caleb asked Clayton Marron to deliver it personally to me all those years ago, and I always did wonder why he trusted it to him rather than the pastor. It sat in that tin for fourteen years. Well hidden, too, and it wasn't Alonso who found it. One of Anthony's young nephews was busy-bodying in my place for food a few weeks after Seb and Clayton's last visit here last year. He found the letter. An hour later, my grandson arrived with an axe in his hand and a look on his face I will never forget. He forced me to confirm, under pain of death, that he was the child, Ces, referred to in Caleb's letter and that Anthony and I had kept his father and sister a secret from him.

"You can guess what happened." She looks at everyone around the table in turn, her voice trembling with emotion. "It was like a human wrecking ball swept through our home. He smashed it into pieces. I'm sure you've seen bits of it scattered round the yard. I thought he would kill us, too, only he couldn't be bothered with Anthony coz he was in a mute phase back then and it would have been like bludgeoning a dumb animal. I told him everything, except the truth of how his mother died. Might as well have stabbed myself in the heart as tell him that. He stuffed the letter and a page of the Bible into my mouth, tied a rope around my neck and dragged me through the camp."

"What page of the Bible?" Pitcavage asks, in keeping with his as-usual forensic attention to detail.

Cora raises her voice to compete with the escalating blare from the sky and tells us Proverbs 19:5. "*A false witness shall not be unpunished, and he that speaketh lies shall not escape.* That day, Alonso's gang loaded up with all manner of weapons and he led them out that gate like the Pied Piper."

Pitcavage offers me the letter over the outstretched expectant hand of the pastor and stands up. "I need to step out here for a few minutes, folks," he announces. "If y'all wouldn't mind staying put here, we will wrap it up real quick when I get back.'

October 2004

Cora,

I won't be back and I don't expect that matters much to folks there. However, I do ask only one favor of you, which I hope you will see your way clear to helping me with.

As you know, Anegam has gone back to the Tohono and taken Ces and Cehia with her. I ask that should she return for whatever reason at whatever moment in time in the future that you give her these instructions about how to find me.

I am living on the Old County Road, about ten miles from Prospero. If they come by day, they will know the house by the giant Cross of Calvary. If they come by night, tell her she will see the brightest lights shining south.

"If we hope for that we see not, then do we with patience wait for it."

I will wait.

Caleb

I hand the letter back to Cora and go to the window to call Miranda. No answer.

Marge Newlands answers at the first ring.

"Sergeant, Ariel here."

"Did you manage to reach her?" The anguish in her voice indicates they have had no success.

"I'm afraid not. I called to see if she had shown up."

Sergeant Newlands emits a weighty sigh. "There are two units and a BORTAC tracker out trawling for her. I'm here myself near the Little Hatchets. It's like she has vanished into thin air."

"It's so out of character for the Miranda I know. I'm struggling to understand what sparked it."

"You're right, Ariel." It's the first time she has called me by my first name. "It's ... the thing is, we gave her some ... some news and she didn't deal with it too well. I'm worried she might do something stupid."

The noise from the helicopters has finally stopped and I think I see movement in the stand of trees. Perhaps the troops who were stationed here earlier have returned.

"News about her college career?" I venture tentatively.

"No. We told her that she was adopted."

It is the kind of deeply personal revelation that might merit an apologetic mumble, but I press on. "Is Miranda Caleb Freeth's daughter?" My question hangs unanswered for so long, I have to check if she is still there. "Sergeant?"

"How ... how did you know?" she says almost under her breath. "I only found that out from Seb Funchess yesterday morning. Caleb doesn't even know."

"I saw some photographs here. Minutes ago. Taken fifteen years ago of Caleb, his wife and their baby twins. Their daughter had that birthmark, you know, Miranda's angel's kiss? And she ... well, she's the living image of her mother."

"I would dearly like to see that," she whispers. "Do you know where her brother is?"

"I have some idea, Sergeant, but ... we are hearing that story now ... from Cora, Caleb's mother."

"Is the pastor there?" she asks before I have a chance to go into any more detail. "Tell the pastor I would very much appreciate if he could call me as soon as possible. Miranda took my keys and security card sometime in the middle of the night. We have her on camera entering the station here at Prospero at five-thirty a.m. and I can tell she went through my desk files, including notes from my meeting with Funchess, Caleb, Operation Granite, the whole sorry mess. I'm really scared she'll do something stupid, Mr. Mignolet."

Paul Pitcavage reenters the room. I hear him in the background telling everyone we have five minutes to wrap up and all eyes turn expectantly toward me.

"I need to go now, Sergeant. I will call and text her again. Don't worry. She'll turn up."

"The photographs?" she prompts.

"I'll see what I can do," I whisper.

Pitcavage asks Cora to pick up where she left off.

"You were telling us about the First Truth subgroup who left the camp almost a year ago. What is the nature of your relationship with them now?"

"All we have seen of them since the day they left has been the whites of their eyes through the trees by day and their shadows by night. When they are around, and we can never predict when that will be, they rain slingshot down on anyone who tries to leave. God, the cruelty. Some who ran the gauntlet paid with their lives and they dumped their broken bodies up here at the gate like cat-kill on a porch. We had to bury two of the dead inside the walls of the camp because it was too risky to venture out front to the graveyard there.

"Sometimes they disappear for long enough to allow hunting parties to gather up provisions, but the fear of being caught is terrible. If you had left it even a few months longer, sir, I promise you there would have been no one left alive here to open the gates. All we have left is the few mesquite pods. Our own hellish End Times would have come and gone and the world none the wiser."

"Would you characterize your grandson as mentally ill, a psychopath or motivated by revenge?"

"Like I said earlier, sir, could be all three. Alonso is the distilled product of relentless brutality and prejudice. His sense of right and wrong is warped, and the young people running with him were ripe for charming, seeing as how they were all so disillusioned after the Lord failed to come. For their entire lives, that one event is what they had been trained for, consumed with."

"In terms of the other crimes we are seeking them in connection with, almost all the victims are non-whites. Given that he is of mixed race himself, why do you think he might view such people as a target?"

"How many other victims?" Cora asks apprehensively.

"They are chief suspects in the murder of eight other persons, Mrs. Blount. Six civilians and two officers of the law. Seven folks of Latino extraction and one Caucasian."

"They were trained long and hard to hate color, Mr. Pitcavage. There's no mystery there. And with Alonso leading them, they would have the will to act on that prejudice, without hesitation."

"What about his twin? The girl?" Pitcavage asks.

"She went to good folk and, I understand, is happy," Funchess interjects. "I believe now it must be that Anthony should never have been given the job of fathering. The Lord had set it that way naturally. Perhaps he was intended only for the flock but not the lamb."

"A bit late for enlightenment about that now, Seb, wouldn't you say? I asked you to take the child back and find a different home when you returned with him. I had seen up-close how Anthony was with Caleb, but you, too, knew of his hate for color. You heard his talk about Anegam. You simply wouldn't listen, Seb. Remember? You had—" The sound of a horse's shrill whinny stops Cora in her tracks. "May the Lord have mercy on us," she recites several times under her breath.

Branson and Ensor vault out the opening and Pitcavage radios for back-up.

"Does the group ever travel on horseback?" Pitcavage asks the three First Truth members among us.

"Never," Cora replies.

Chapter Seventeen

Little Black Snake

"Get some lunch, then oversee the camp detail before waiting with them in the empty cross room," Pitcavage tells Branson, with *them* being myself, the pastor and Mrs. Blount. "The one nearest the hall," he clarifies. "I'll drop in later and give you an update." With that, he and the other FBI officers who had attended the meeting join the clutch of Kevlar helmets flitting back and forth outside since we first heard the horse's whinny.

Branson directs the three of us, along with bewildered cousins Stephen and Tristan, out to the central yard to join the other camp members, most of whom have congregated around a trestle table under the trees. They sit on their buckets, gorging slowly and silently on the recently delivered military rations. Those still waiting in line for their allocation of saltine crackers, peanut butter and bacon-cheddar pocket sandwiches remain remarkably orderly and polite.

Long after I have finished eating, as Branson makes his final inspections of the newly erected tents and sets about establishing a duty roster for the officers' use throughout the night, Cora is still occupied expelling the contents of her foil peanut butter packet. Her face is a mask of intense concentration as she sits, elbows resting on the table, while her arthritic fingers go awkwardly about the serious task of coaxing the salty slick up to her waiting lips. Perhaps due to severely shrunken stomachs, or maybe an inclination to dwell on the sheer pleasure of having plenty, it has taken Cora and many of her fellow camp residents almost three hours to consume the same lunch the operatives gulped down in five minutes. And although they all accept the offer of second helpings, I notice that they stash the precious packets on their person rather than tuck in immediately.

With the sun low in the sky, we reenter the church building and need flashlights to illuminate the back of the now considerably gloomier communal hall. Cora ignites two oil lamps and we wait in the musty corridor for Branson to complete an inspection of the cross room's dark recesses.

"Did someone bring Anthony out to eat?" Cora inquires of me and the pastor in such a way that suggests she thinks this would have been a very bad idea. "They locked him in there earlier," she explains, with a nod toward the open sliding bolt on the door of her living quarters. Handing me one of the lamps, she uses her toe to tentatively nudge the door open like someone long accustomed to less-than-enthusiastic welcomes. Her scream that follows is guttural, like the mournful wail of an Arab woman following her child's coffin up the street.

Branson reacts quickest, urging me to assist with hoisting Anthony Blount upwards so that he can loosen the rope tied around the preacher's neck and cut him free from the cross. Yet it is so obviously hopeless. His face is blue and bloated and his eyeballs bulge to the rim of their sockets like split boiled eggs. Branson radios for help, and then we lay him out on his cot beside the far wall while the pastor recites tracts from the Old Testament, pleading with the Almighty to deliver his old friend's soul into salvation.

"Well, he sure as hell didn't do it to himself, sir," I hear Branson respond drily to some question coming through on his headset. "Yes, sir. We're moving now."

Branson ushers me and Funchess back down the corridor to the open-windowed meeting room but he cannot persuade Cora to leave Blount's side. With her face bathed in the atmospheric glow of the oil lamp, the scene in the dark space might have been rendered by a Dutch Master. Her husband lies long and still on the thin mattress, his pallor now as white as his beard. She, dressed like a Calvinist housemaid, sits on the floor with head resting on the bed and bony fingers gripping his right hand. Her eyes are closed and there is the hint of a smile in her expression as though she has invited some happy memory in.

We see a different side to Agent Pitcavage when he returns. His charm is much less evident and stress notes are detectable in his voice when he summons the team medic to examine Blount's body and tasks Branson with stepping up security. "I need you to take Seb and Ariel to one of the RVs and stand guard until they find whoever it is strung up Anthony in there. Use the ninth one up from the church hall. It's the cleanest. There must be a hidden entrance to this place somewhere, but no one out there seems to have a clue. Blank faces all round. It's a fucking horse for Christ's sake. It wasn't here this morning and it doesn't have wings tucked under its saddle flaps. There must be an entrance you guys missed on the first pass, Branson. A big one."

Branson radios a team called BORTAC 1, who were apparently assigned to security detail earlier that morning, and asks them to take a closer look at areas of dense foliage and inside rocky crags in the southern and western areas of the camp, behind the homes. As his conversation draws to a close, another voice begs our attention from the doorway.

"There's a mine shaft. Silver, I think it was for." Cora must have been listening outside and although she addresses us with the same tone of resolve reserved for the pastor earlier, it is clear from how she grips the door frame that what little life force remains in this woman is rapidly draining away. Her clothes hang off her spindle-thin frame as though draped over a scarecrow's cross and the pupil of her bruised and bloodshot left eye is now fully dilated and frozen in a distant stare. "At least a hundred years old. Where the dried river bed meets the boundary. It's big enough to drive through. They used to pulley the ore up through it to wash and sift so it leads up from the opening of much deeper winzes alongside the river bed. It's Caleb. He's here," she adds, in a voice laden with foreboding.

"She's right," I say, peering out the window toward his bay gelding, now corralled and tethered within the confines of the ramshackle animal pen forty feet away.

"He's the one who blocked it off all those years ago," she continues. "Anthony gave him the project once the church was built. It took him four months and might have taken six only I got someone to fashion him a wheelbarrow. Only a few of them others out there even know it exists so it's not surprising you're getting dumb looks. It's concealed in the bushes and trees behind the fourth home. The only one with white stripes down the side."

Branson wastes no time contacting the team to update them as a crackle of gunfire cuts through the noise of the supply helicopters taking off. The pilot-calm voice of one of the aircrafts' captain fires up Pitcavage's radio.

"Bell 6 to Groundtruth 1. Bell 6 to Groundtruth 1. Do you copy, over?"

"This is Groundtruth 1. Go ahead, Bell 6."

"Came under fire at liftoff, sir, so Guard 2 returned live rounds as instructed. Hard to say what hit us right now, but our instruments are not detecting any significant damage. The shots you're hearing are the guys below still engaging with suspect zone, but we can't see any movement from up here so far and we are hearing they are blind down there, too. Enemy is under good cover in fading light. Sun will set in approximately seventy minutes, sir, at 1903 hours. Our existing orders are to continue on back to base, but would you like us to do a few passes to see if we can spot them? There's a well-camouflaged graveyard about half a klick away and two or three rocky outcrops between here and there. Lots of places for concealment, sir."

"Could it have been gunfire that hit you, Bell 6?" Another burst of gunshot rings out and while Bell 6 is explaining that he's not entirely sure, Branson relays more information from one of his officers on the ground.

"They're fairly sure it was slingshot, Paul. Stones," Branson says, and it's the first time I have heard him address his superior by his first name. "A salvo of rocks shot at high velocity hit one bird's tail as she was lifting off and the same weapons were then directed at Unit 3 near the camp entrance. One casualty on his way in here under his own steam, sir. Not serious. No visual yet on the enemy, but our guys are fairly sure of the suspect zone less than half a klick west and have been returning live fire into a two-hundred-foot area of brush where they think the enemy is concealed. Guard 2 have now retreated to the outer entrance and await further orders right now. Any offensive move will have to take place soon, sir, as light is fading."

Pitcavage takes a seat, removes an iPad Mini from his pack and studies what look like satellite images before making radio contact with the heads of various units of the task force. "Don't engage the enemy in their own territory. Fall back, secure the perimeter, take up sniper positions around the camp area with night vision and pick them off when they show themselves. We can track down and round up any we miss tomorrow when the birds return. The aim here is to maim not claim, folks, so use non-lethal rounds or live only when absolutely necessary to disable. I want to bring this target back alive."

A question-and-answer session commences between the conferencing officers, but that is all we get to hear of Pitcavage's strategy, as the pastor and I are ushered out by Branson while Cora returns to her room, where an exhausted-looking FBI medical officer is taking photographs of the ligature marks on Blount's neck.

As we exit the church hall into rapidly gathering dusk, we pass the walking wounded Branson referred to earlier. Either he was very unlucky or the stone-slinger had unerring aim because the only small area of exposed skin—a patch of cheek below his goggles and above his chin strap—is swollen and split where the missile struck.

If the ninth Airstream RV is the cleanest in the settlement, as Pitcavage advised, I can barely contemplate conditions in the others. When Branson illuminates the interior with some class of military-issue portable lamp, the first things to catch my eye are a pair of psychedelic pink-and-orange paisley cushions on a green upholstered bench beneath a picture of Elvis Presley when he was young and fit. These must be the owner's prized possessions because the rest of the built-in motor home furnishings are a bleak and faded version of their original selves.

The pastor pulls aside a brown corduroy, ringed, separator curtain to reveal the dinette booth behind what was once the driver's cabin. Square windows on two sides overlook the neighboring homes. Yellow felt seat covers are threadbare and coat the legs of my trousers in a thin layer of whitish fungus or mildew that won't rub off. A musty smell of damp replaces the outdoor stench of sewage, which has marginally improved with the advance of nightfall and the earlier cover-up job by the latrine detail.

After a quick inspection of the water closet and sleeping area, Branson suggests we remove our body armor and try and get some rest while he takes up guard outside. He passes by the window every fifteen minutes or so during reconnaissance circuits of the RV, waiting in between times on the steps of its door.

A silent half-hour war of attrition follows between me and the pastor, which finishes when I win the territorial battle and he vacates the dining area in favor of the Elvis Presley lounge, drawing the drapes so we don't have to look at each other. The Airstream's driver's windshield is visible to my left through a gap in a plywood partition. It is opaque with dust except for one semicircular patch that someone has wiped clean with their hand. I can just make out the two large green Army tents and up to ten smaller nylon shelters erected in the central yard to accommodate the sickest of the camp residents and provide for task force members' sleep breaks throughout the night. Illuminated from within, their phosphorescent glow is like the soft warmth of Chinese lanterns.

The flicker of another light catches my attention when

the white eye of the beam of a small flashlight zigzags laser-like in the glass opposite me. When I turn to see its source, it is hastily quenched or concealed and the net curtain in the side window of the RV next door twitches. I turn my back again and, moments later, the light returns, darting back and forth on the wall and window opposite like ham-fisted Morse code. Swiveling around as fast as I can, I am just in time to catch the smiling face of a young child diving for cover, leaving the cotton net to once again drop back into position.

We play at this game for a while and my peek-a-boo partner gives me fractionally more and more face time with each twist until we tire of hide-and-seek and decide to check each other out. There she is now in the glare of the flashlight, the moon and some other wan light source inside her RV. Her mousy bangs frame a thin angelic face and her smile is like a ray of sunshine in these grim surroundings. I mime my inner idiot for her. Haven't done it for years and my eye muscles feel the strain when I force them to meet in the middle above a clown frown. She sees me and raises me by placing the flashlight, similar to the one in my own pack (I figure she has been given it by one of the agents), under her chin to recreate the gaunt visage-of-doom. She dives below again an instant before Branson appears on another one of his circumnavigations. He casts me a knowing smile as he passes and I suspect he is an earlier victim of our little window pixie. She reappears with the white lacy curtain wrapped around her face like a wedding veil and I laugh quietly, loving every minute of our impromptu charades.

What face to try now? I am mulling over a few moves when angel face looks up toward the sky and her expression suddenly darkens. With so little light, it is hard for me to make out what words she is mouthing. There are her two little hands at the window. She has put the flashlight down, but I am pretty sure she is still looking up. Perhaps our game has taken a new twist toward finger puppetry. But her right hand pulls stiffened fingers across her throat in an action devoid of humor and then, in a flutter, she is gone.

My phone has excellent signal, but is beginning to run low on battery. There are six missed calls and a text from Ben that reads *WTF?*, leaving me none the wiser as to whether my Vimeo appearance at the meeting has been a triumph or a disaster.

Miranda's number rings out again and I have just dialed into voice mail when I hear Pastor Funchess rummaging around for the first time in over an hour. I had thought he was fast asleep and envied his ability to switch off in the face of such turmoil. Returning the phone to my ear, a curse-laden tirade from Ben from six o'clock this morning assaults my left ear when I sense a slight shift in the divider drapes quickly followed by the cold snub nose of a pistol pressed to my right temple.

"Switch the phone to silent, hand it to me and give the officer a thumbs up next time he passes," the gunman tells me. Not daring to move my head, I train my eyes' limit right and see thin pale lips and blue eyes, the only body parts exposed in what is otherwise the perfect silhouette. Balaclava, gloves. Head-to-toe black.

My chest feels as if it is about to burst with unexpelled air, as though I have forgotten how to breathe. Locating and flicking the switch at the side of the phone takes me several seconds with shaking fingers misdirected by a racing mind.

"Should I turn now?" I say in a barely audible wheeze before my lungs refill with a noisy gasp.

"Shut up and follow instructions."

Branson takes what feels like an eternity, but probably no longer than four or five minutes, to appear after another turn around the motor home. The gunman stands stock still and says nothing. As the seconds tick by, fear short-circuits my thought processes so that a litany of concerns ignites randomly like neurological napalm. What has become of the pastor? A muffled snort answers my question. Flit to an image of Sunil hugging people at my funeral and dissing those he deems unworthy. Why didn't I listen when he advised against joining the mission? Where is Miranda?

A burst of automatic weapon fire somewhere in the vicinity of the camp jolts me back to lucidity. The snipers have started work. The torchbearers must be out there. The noise acts as a catalyst for Branson to check on his charges. As usual, he looks to catch my eye from a few feet away. Is there no chink in the half-smile accompanying my breezy thumbs up? Does he not see the shadow behind my mask of normality in the way mothers see past their children's *I'm fine* responses? No. He nods and retakes his seat at the door, his weapon at his chest in its usual state of casual readiness.

The instant he disappears from view, a strip of duct tape is slapped over my mouth and my wrists are bound tightly in front of me with cable tie. He drops my phone into a net side pocket in his small backpack before yanking me into the middle section of the home where Seb Funchess sits in a similar state of restraint on the cushioned ledge near the lavatory door. There is just enough light from the moon for me to see the raw terror in his eyes.

"Lie down," the gunman whispers. "Real quiet and keep your face toward me."

Funchess's heavy-duty Army boots are about two feet

from my face when I settle into position on the dirty resin flooring with my back to a set of under-sink kitchen cabinets. Casting my eyes up, I can make out the preacher's face above the silhouetted toe of the boots and then, directly above and behind him, the dusty framed photo of Elvis Presley gyrating in a white suit.

When Caleb removes the balaclava, his hair glows in the moonlight pouring through the open skylight, his point of entry. He returns his gun to its holster across his chest, takes a knife from a belt around his waist and holds its point inches from the pastor while his free hand quietly fishes in a tiny drawer in the cabinet between the bench and curtain. I see him place something small in the other side pocket of his pack before sitting beside the pastor, whose eyes are open so wide now he looks vaguely comical. Muffled murmurs accompany a spasm of resistance by Funchess, who is clearly trying desperately to communicate with Caleb. His greatest weapon thwarted by a swatch of sticky tape.

"Make one more sound and I will kill you now," says Caleb in a low whisper. Then he picks up one of the psychedelically patterned cushions, places it over his nose and smells it long and hard.

I am now sure of it. This was once his home.

He leans closer to the pastor and speaks in hushed tones. My pounding heartbeat and the muted crackling of Branson's radio outside are not loud enough to drown out his words.

"Police showed me a sketch two days ago, Seb, and there he was. The living incarnation of his mother, my son. The son I haven't seen in nearly fifteen years, you bastard. Oh, let me tell you, I heard enough of what was said at that meeting earlier. Enough important stuff, Seb. How two of Satan's serpents poisoned my whole life. Murdered my wife. Stole my kids. You lied to me, you son of a bitch. Lie upon lie upon lie. You. A man of the Bible."

My mind flashes to those noises I heard outside the meeting room. The rustling leaves near the open window and fleeting glimpses of what I had thought were soldiers in the tree line. Caleb.

"To think I bent down and washed your feet to atone for my mother's sins," Caleb adds before leaning in even further and whispering something I cannot hear into the ear of his captive.

For one moment, I suspect he is about to smother Funchess. He holds the cushion out in front of him and examines it as though sizing up its potential. Then, with a shockingly fast thrust of his hand, at once casual and utterly lethal, like a pyromaniac flicking a cigarette butt into a puddle of gas, he slits the pastor's throat.

Soft spatters from the initial spurt of arterial blood land on the sleeve of my shirt. Anticipating the next gush, Caleb deftly stuffs the cushion under Funchess's chin and ties it into place with some kind of rope. The pastor's body shudders and Caleb holds it to make sure it doesn't slide off the bench and make a noise. His big boots jut in front of my face as his body's electric force puts in a final, violent shift to try and jump-start wilting nerve endings. Christ. Oh, Jesus Christ, help me. Such entreaties play on a loop in my head.

Caleb moves on to a new task once the spasms subside, frisking Funchess's clothes for his phone and then rooting in his own backpack. Putting things in. Taking things out. I am watching his every move for signs of my fate.

Blood is dripping from the pastor's shirt sleeve. The thick dark fluid must have found some speedy route down his arm from his neck, little flannel tunnels where his clothing is loose enough to allow liquid to slip over skin. The rivulets amalgamate quickly into a pool on the Formica and seem to want to travel on. Do what they do best. The little stream begins to wend its way toward my face, my taped mouth. The Airstream must be slightly tilted. I have been warned not to move so must lie and wait for the life force of Seb Funchess to reach me. This liquid that fed the brain, the heart, the lungs. This liquid that oiled the vocal cords to deliver such passionate moralisms and impress the minds of his flock is now inching forth to stain my lips.

Caleb pulls the now-stilled body higher into the bench and lays it at an angle toward the corner where the cabinet meets the back of the bench. He sets the head so it rests against the strapped-on pillow as though the pastor is enjoying a longed-for nap. Then, after carefully cleaning the knife on his trouser leg, he crouches down and drags me clear of the crimson tide. Imagine feeling thankful for that. But I do. I do for the briefest of moments before he takes a fist full of my ponytail and yanks my head back to expose my throat. My only view now is of his black trouser leg tucked into black hiking boots. The black baby snake that bit my hand in my dream is poised to exceed all expectations. I am to die like an animal on the floor, my blood blending with that of the pastor's like a leftover soup of virtue and vice.

I wait for the feel of the blade and hope to God it is quick. Thoughts ignite like flash photography in the fraction of time before he makes the cut. Progress to the top of the pile, cum laude, keynote speeches, bonanza bonuses, performance profits, fine dining, five-star hotel trysts. So what? I will die here on a strip of linoleum. For no good reason. And how many will care?

Still breathing (can I even call it that?) and there is a new sound. Oxygen is entering my body in tight little snatches as Caleb works his knife above my head. At my scalp. What must be a razor-sharp blade is scything through my hair, making sounds like the sizzle of burning wool or the rip of parting Velcro. My locks are shorn in a matter of seconds and he casts the blond sheaf aside. It lands in the stream of blood and soaks up some of the slick like the tip of an artist's paintbrush.

Still alive.

He produces a thick blanket from the sleeping quarters and drapes it over the dead man, letting it trail on the floor to hide the blood, before disappearing for a few moments into the water closet, reappearing and urging me to my feet. I move silently through the small door with the knife's point in the small of my back. Another burst of gunfire nearby is followed quickly by three more, and the volleys continue intermittently as the soundtrack to our clandestine exit.

He has removed a square panel from the floor of the WC. I am to drop through the trap door and stay semi-crouched, semi-prone beneath the right rear underbelly of the vehicle while he follows. I see him wait momentarily at the little frosted window, checking for movement outside. But below I can see no sign of Branson's legs so I suspect he is where he has spent most of his time between circuits, sitting on the entrance step of the Airstream tuning in to radio traffic and occasionally joining the conversation.

There is very little headroom and I belly-shimmy along beside Caleb and his knife. Reaching out my tethered wrists, I can prop myself onto forearms and drag my body along like a sniper through long grass. We have about ten feet to cover before clearing the undercarriage and only progress when the talking on Branson's radio is loudest or the gunfire continuous. The space is alive with scuttling creatures, sensed rather than seen. Tiny wells of tepid, foul-smelling water in the uneven muddy ground suggest a leak from a water tank of some kind in the bowels of the old motor home. As we pass the pancake-flat rear right wheel, only feet from the back of the vehicle, I inhale a dense cobweb into one nostril and, almost involuntarily, move to rub it off with my sleeve, causing my elbow to bump off something rusty and hollow above, possibly the exhaust pipe.

It is a nondescript noise, a cross between a swish and a very soft clang, but is enough to move Branson. The knife's point makes a tiny incision through my jacket and into the flesh between my ribs as we watch his pale boots and the circle of light from his flashlight travel around the Airstream.

I hold my breath as the flashlight draws nearer, flitting from side to side along the dust and grass tufts and sometimes throwing its oval gaze over the denser thickets behind the RV or further afield to the home next door. As Branson rounds the rear right corner, the beam threatens to find us each time he pans it left. If he bends down and shines it through the undercarriage, he will see us and, while I have every faith he would be a match for Caleb, I am certain I will not be around to see them fight.

The white stream of light dances back and forth for a few moments inches from the left side of my body. The wheel is helping to hide my pale face, hair and hands. Finally, it moves off and resumes its radar-like progress around the rest of the home. Another volley of shots and, when it passes, we hear the squeak of the Airstream's front door being pulled open. What time is it, I wonder? Maybe eight-thirty? Later?

I didn't feel Caleb move a muscle during Branson's search. Only his head, inches from mine and once again sheathed in black, rotated to follow the officer's progress. Now I feel his free hand reach down toward his pistol. He is coiled for action.

The door closes, Branson's radio fires up and monotone voices again filter through the night. But he does not converse with them. A few shots ring out nearby as usual, but he retakes his sentry's station at the doorstep without checking at my window. Caleb's blanket trick has worked.

We soon clear the back of the RV and steal silently into the thatch of creosote and tar bush that has claimed the stretch of camp between the back of the RVs and the perimeter fence. Caleb checks his watch and doesn't look at me or speak as he carefully picks his way through the jungle of leaves and branches, all the time keeping one hand behind him to hold the cable tie binding my hands. Thin, gnarled stems of the tallest tar bush whip and scrape my face as we edge along. From what I saw of it earlier in the day, I wouldn't have thought there was a way through that wouldn't involve vigorous rustling and branch-hacking, but we reach the fence within minutes without a snap or a crack.

Caleb uses a tiny flashlight to zone in on a particular section of the fence and, within seconds, has removed a flap of wood and we are through to the other side. Light quenched, he pulls me across a path to an area of mesquite trees and boulders that we use as cover as we progress in an easterly direction.

"Stay there and don't move," Caleb breathes in my ear

as he pulls me onto my haunches behind a limestone slab the size of an office desk. He rummages in his backpack again, removing a handkerchief-size cushion of cotton into which he pours a liquid. Even after he has moved away, its pungent, chemical smell lingers in the air.

When we pass the unconscious BORTAC officer, I notice how Caleb has been careful to drag him off the pathway and into a thicket of trees. I am now acutely aware that I am in the company of a highly trained soldier.

A nearby cluster of large boulders marks one of the highest points of the natural rocky barrier surrounding the camp. Caleb pushes aside thickets of brush and we step through a narrow gap into a natural rocky chamber. Overhanging branches cut out the light from the moon. He turns on his flashlight, which illuminates a huge mound of stone rubble in front of us—clearly the remains of the wall Caleb toiled for so long to build many years ago. He must have used his horse to pull it down into the shaft.

We pick our way across the pile. Without free hands as balancing aids, my athletic shoes slip and slide down unseen stone faces into unexpected miniature ravines and crevices, and I struggle to keep up with my captor in the pitch dark. One false step too many and I fall forward onto a reef of sharp shale. The duct tape reduces my resulting yowl to a high-pitched "ehmmmmmmm" and I roll over on my back, groaning loudly. I can't figure out a good way to try to get up. My head is lower down the slope than my legs and I know it will prove difficult to get any purchase with hands or feet. I look toward the torch and wave my bound hands up and down like an upturned crab flailing a pincer. As Caleb makes his way back to help, I track his little light's progress as it flits from tunnel wall to floor. He must have fixed it to his head in some way. Its yellow eye delivers fleeting glimpses of hammock-size cobwebs, ominous inky fissures, spook-infested hanging lanterns, tool handles and rickety tram lines.

"Grab on," he instructs impatiently while shoving a gloved hand in front of me. We latch on to each other's forearms and Caleb hauls me to a standing position, but the treacherously uneven pile of jagged rocks shifts suddenly beneath his feet and we tumble together to the bottom of the slope, sliding to a halt between the wooden trolley tracks, his head propped up on his backpack and my face inches from his like lovers lining up for a kiss.

"Get off me, you filth," Caleb seethes, pushing me off and scrambling to his feet.

We walk the rest of the distance to the base of the shaft between the parallel trolley tracks. The slope is steep, maybe thirty degrees, and very slippery in places where horizontal wooden lats in various states of decrepitude have crumbled away, leaving nowhere for our feet to gain solid ground. A dense ferrous odor intensifies and trickle and drip noises accompany our progress as though the rock vein still weeps from its century-old wounds. The mine's roof varies in height and sometimes our heads snag on reams of web or glance off stray nobs and nails in its surface. It occurs to me that Caleb's horse would have had to remain extremely calm to keep its head down at various points along its trek up through the channel. Why did he ride his horse into camp after it pulled down the wall? Did he want it to be found?

The flashlight beam falls on what appears to be a junction and the tunnel widens to some sort of a chamber. The space houses a line of wine-crate-sized ore trolleys on rusted wheels, now inhabited by spiders and other larger creatures that scurry to the safety of corners as we pass. A black hole to our left appears to be the entrance to the mine proper—a narrow, asymmetrical orifice that could only ever have hosted the brave.

We veer right, behind the mine carts, and through an s-curve of limestone pillars. Away from blackness, toward shades of darkest blue. Emerging into the cool starlit night, Caleb surveys the terrain from beneath a rocky overhang that shields us from watchers above. Once my eyes adjust to the moonlight, outlines are enough to tell me we have arrived where the dry river bed I viewed from the helicopter, about the width of a six-lane highway, meets the highest point of the camp's rocky perimeter.

There isn't suitable shelter here. From the punishing sun. For the horse. And the horse would have needed plenty of water after the long ride from the Old County Road. Caleb cares about his horse and that is why he rode it into camp, I surmise.

The sheer limestone walls of the canyon are highest near the mineshaft's exit and then gradually taper off over a distance of about five hundred yards. In the moonshine, they appear as stark black ridges with the ancient river bed between them a rich cobalt blue. In some places, where desert oaks have eked out an existence among the boulders, the dancing shadows of their leaves bring the channel to life so it looks for all the world like water has returned in a new ghostly incarnation.

Caleb fishes behind a rock and lifts out a fire torch, which he must have concealed there sometime earlier. It is cone shaped, stuffed with dried bark and rags, and smells of kerosene. He produces matches and a pair of scissors from his pack and puts the latter to work cutting off my shirt and tee. Then he removes his own belt and cinches it under my arm pits just above my pectoral muscles, tightening it enough so that it stays up but leaving it loose enough so my breathing is not restricted.

"Nod if you can shoot a gun," he says and when I do, he hands me a revolver while pressing his own weapon to my temple.

"Step out there and shoot five times up at the camp wall. Then drop the gun and run."

My mouth is taped, but my eyes have involuntarily asked him if he is serious.

"Shoot and run or I will cut your throat like the bastard preacher."

When I point the weapon, aiming for the top of the fifty-or-so-foot rock face, I hear Mike. *That's it. Nice strong arms. It's all in the brace and the squeeze.*

Bang, bang, bang, bang, bang. The acoustics in the canyon elevate the explosive sounds to ear-splitting proportions and the kickback into cold flesh vibrates like a tuning fork through every sinew. I must have hit something. Sprays of stone splinters scrape the rocky face as they descend.

"Drop the gun and take the torch."

He hands me the already lighted cone and I set off at a fast pace through the middle of the canyon. With my hands tied, the torch is more of a hindrance than a guide and I struggle to keep it to one side to avoid the stream of sparks it sheds in its wake. A few strides in, I stumble forward onto my knees when the toe of my shoe stubs a smooth half-buried rock. A small thatch of the incendiary material comes away from the main body of the flame and burns on beside me like a miniature bonfire while I pick myself up and progress with more care. I establish some kind of rhythm despite my restraints and it occurs to me rather randomly that I am very glad to be wearing Branson's specially procured sneakers instead of Army-issue boots. Dr. Carter would commend me for such positive thinking at a moment of such hyper-stress.

"Faster," I think I hear, hissed from somewhere to my left beneath the canyon wall.

The first shot zips over my left shoulder and scorches into the dried sandy ground a few feet away with a kind of suck. An electric shiver courses through my body like a supercharged version of a fright-tingle when someone enters a room unexpectedly. I am a decoy. Of course. Caleb is making his way through this exposed alleyway and I am serving as the distraction. To draw fire.

With short hair, naked torso and Olympic flame, I look exactly like one of them. They must be queuing up on the ramparts to take their shot. If they kill me, then they will be focused on retrieving my body, leaving the way clear for Caleb to make good his escape. If I survive?

If I survive …

I veer right, away from the voice. Caleb chose his own route well. The moon is casting a half-shadow across the southeastern side of the river wall and he is using this as cover. Apart from the odd jutting rock face or hardy shrub, the western wall has very little to shield me from the night-vision goggles I know are trained on me from on high. My heart pounds in paroxysms of fear and my nostrils contort in their attempts to keep up with the demand for oxygen.

The canyon walls are lower now. Nearly scalable? What distance have I covered? About three hundred yards? Maybe a bit more. I run in a zigzag pattern to make life more difficult for the shooters. Zip. Another bullet whizzes, splitting the cone of the fire torch and spraying its flaming entrails onto the river bed. When I cast the remaining stump over my shoulder, a last pocket of red-hot embers rains down on my spiky hair and I have to flail my bound hands around my head to snuff them out. If I can just reach the safety of the bank over there, I will be out of the firing line. I try to remove the tape from my mouth but my hands are bound so tightly I find it hard to grab an edge and my efforts slow my pace. I can hardly hear myself think over the impossibly loud noise of my breathing. Swallow, snort, swallow, snort. Thirty more feet and I will have run the gauntlet, once again, and survived.

The bank is definitely low enough over there. Where is Caleb? Snort, swallow, snort. Nearly there. A few more feet.

"Uhhhhmmmm." A bullet hits my lower back. Pain explodes as I tumble forward and face and hands plow me through the dirt to a stop next to the bank. I writhe onto my side. Knees bend and straighten and head lifts to counteract the agony. A wave of vomit is welling up. It occurs to me in the midst of nasally, hummed whimpers that I will choke if it advances to my throat and that might kill me before the wound.

Suddenly, a new pain. Sharp stones sandpapering skin. Caleb is dragging me up the bank using the leather belt around my torso.

"Get up. They're coming," he barks in my ear before ripping off the duct tape and taking at least one layer of lip skin with it. Blood. From my lungs? I wish I could feel my lower back with my fingers. Get a better sense of what class of a wound it is.

"Get up or die, fag," he repeats with manic urgency and thrusts the spout of a water flask into my mouth.

"I've been shot," I groan after gulping several mouthfuls of water.

"It's rubber. Get the fuck up or I swear I will finish you off here and now."

I inhale deeply and struggle to my feet as Caleb cuts the cable tie on my hands at the front and binds them instead behind my back. Then he prepares to reapply the same swatch of adhesive tape.

"One more sip. I beg you," I say, gulping greedily before the gag is slapped back into position.

Caleb leads me through the trees by the leather strap while I slowly release the little well of stored liquid through bloody lips.

Chapter Eighteen

Tempest

We progress stealthily in a wide crescent that initially takes us further from camp before eventually tracking back toward what now, with FBI-issue lamp-lights visible through the rocks and trees, resembles a peaceful hillside hamlet.

A clear sky swathed in a dazzling mantle of stars backdrops a giant autumnal moon whose shades of gray are in spectacular relief. It is cold, maybe forty degrees, and goose bumps persist on my skin despite our frequent sprint-dashes from bush to rock to tree. When cover thins out for longer stretches, Caleb must keep me closer to his blacked-out form than he would like and I notice incremental force in how he shoves me away at each successive pit stop.

About a mile into our excursion, the vegetation begins to change and regular stabs from spear-like yucca leaves supersede the cold and backache as my primary source of discomfort. This is the first time I have seen yucca plants since we arrived in the area this morning—any that might have grown in and around the camp, no doubt, having long since been consumed.

As Miranda explained to me after Mike's funeral, yucca is

a favored plant in cemeteries in this part of the world and that is what Caleb has led me to. It is hard to tell in the dark, but I guess that there are forty or so graves laid out in a rather haphazard manner. Each plot is marked with a pyramid mound of rocks from which wooden crosses protrude like the handles of giant Arthurian swords awaiting extraction. A stand of dense, twenty-foot mesquites, obviously planted once upon a time to delineate the cemetery, act as a screen between us and whoever might be out there scanning the terrain.

Caleb's tiny flashlight is out again. He ignites it into a cupped hand at each cross in order to read the inscriptions, while I follow obediently like a well-trained hound. He pauses at some graves, delaying for a few moments to pay some kind of cursory respects to people he must have once known.

After examining about a dozen and skipping over those where the earth has clearly been recently turned, he finds what he has been looking for. Its mound and cross are significantly smaller than all the others and it is on the edge and slightly apart from its neighbors. Caleb has to push aside the hairy stems of a clump of grama grass to read the simple initial, A, which has been seared into the middle point of the cross. He grabs a handful of the invader's stems and, with an aggressive twist and pull, yanks a huge bunch of it out of the ground, roots and all, casting it aside as though dispensing with a mortal enemy.

A soft breeze shakes the leaves in the tree line and, when it passes, I catch the fresh-soap scent of yucca blossom, always most intense at night. Dramatic, four-foot-long panicles carry bunches of white, bell-shaped blooms—more beautiful than any pimped-up florist's bouquet—that reach out gracefully to bow over the graves. With their starry canvas, these floral boughs waving gently over pale stones and cicadas rehearsing for a part in their next love story, the atmosphere is serene and peaceful. A nice place to rest.

"Lie down," Caleb says gruffly as though he has read my mind. "There, beside that rock."

I lie down on my side in the lee of a craggy granite boulder, about five feet from the foot of Anegam's grave, and he binds my ankles together with cable tie.

The pain in my back is receding, but my body has turned up its cold defenses dial to maximum in the hope that I take the hint that my temperature is dangerously low. After almost an hour of nonstop violent shivering, some involuntary override switch has turned that down to intermittent shudders. It wasn't working, I guess, and the priority now seems to be to conserve energy. Every inch of me is cold apart from one little warm spot where my tongue and lips have stayed busy working spittle onto the increasingly soggy rectangular swatch of tape covering my mouth.

Caleb returns to his wife's graveside. He rips off his balaclava and falls to his knees like a parched man at the wet bank of an oasis. His gloves are off next and he traces the singed lines of the *A* with his index finger before gathering up untidy rocks and stones to return the little cairn to ship shape. Then he runs his hand down the mound in a smoothing, mothering kind of stroke and I hear a tight cough, the kind men make to choke off the advance of tears. When the sound of gunfire again fractures the still night air, I notice that he doesn't flinch, even a fraction, from his business. Next he feels around in a side pocket of his backpack. There. He extracts a small item that I am nearly sure is a ring. His or hers? He kisses it before pushing it gently into a gap in the pile of stones. Back up now into a praying position. He clasps his hands together and begins to recite under his breath.

From this ground-level vantage point, my eye is suddenly drawn to a point beyond two of the most imposing graves, under the arms of a cross at the very back of the site. I think I see something moving about. Not a waving stem or a bird traversing the face of moon. I can barely make it out. Is it human form? Forms?

Caleb's sharp cry of pain when a projectile of some kind knocks him over onto his side answers the first question and I can soon clearly make out six people approaching through the graveyard. They wear dark, three-quarter-length trousers and pale, loose-sleeved shirts in varying states of shabbiness. Even in the dim light, I quickly recognize the point man as Alonso. Mike's murderer. Caleb's son.

Caleb rubs his shoulder and gets to his feet just in time to meet his attackers, who fan out menacingly between graves as though closing off escape routes. Each brandishes an axe and a slingshot either in-hand or wedged into rope belts around their waists. It occurs to me that there is no need for ammunition bags. There are stones everywhere here.

"Ces? Is that you? Alonso? I am Caleb Freeth. Your father."

To my ear, Caleb's tone is that of someone trying to get through to a rabid pet. The palms of his outstretched hands are down and he is inching a slight retreat, clearly the hallmarks of someone hoping for a positive response but expecting a bad one.

"Father." Alonso articulates the word as though trying it on for size.

His comrades, several of whom I recognize from my encounter the night of the murder, look back and forth at each other not as though in search of something to ease their confusion but more to acknowledge proof of a theory.

"Arrrrhhhhh!" Alonso screams the kind of scream that comes during birthing or torture, bending forward to expel every ember of passion from the noise, and I can clearly see the trunks of his neck muscles. "You are nothing to me. Nothing."

Caleb's backward progress transitions from inches to small steps. "I'm sorry. I'm sorry for then. For what happened." He looks down at Anegam's grave. "For it all. I tried …"

I have to draw my knees to my chin very quickly to avoid the onslaught of bodies. Caleb lands heavily after a violent charge by his son. Alonso returns quickly to his feet and makes to strike with his axe but is upended by a swift scissor kick from his adversary on the ground, who then rolls, rises and moves over to a small clearing between the tree line and the first row of graves. He is trying to buy some time, again adopting the palms-up pose of appeaser.

"Don't do this, Ces. I need to … to tell you how things happened. If you just …"

His appeal is cut short as his son springs toward him with weapon in hand. Alonso's right arm and shoulder have emerged through a split seam in his shirt, which now hangs from his body in an off-the-shoulder drape like a Roman senator's toga, adding to his primitive appearance. Caleb's forearm deftly fends off the weapon's handle, and with one swift sidestep he casts his son's body past him onto the dirt. The five henchmen choose this moment to form a loose cordon around the sparring duo in the way they must have done so often during Anthony's monthly tournaments.

Covered now, like Caleb, in a layer of fine pale dust that

appears slightly fluorescent in the moonlight, the younger man gets back to his feet. He drops the small axe into a loop in his rope belt before walking slowly around his father like a circling wolf awaiting an exposed fetlock to sink its teeth into.

It occurs to me that I have so far gone unnoticed, and in a strange twist of fate my survival may now be tied to the outcome of this fight. If Caleb wins, I will probably survive the night. If he loses, I have no doubt that I will be dispensed with in the same way as Mike.

"I thought you were safe with your mother, Ces. They sent me letters. Fakes. Lies. Anthony is responsible for everything, and now he is dead. I killed him this night. Hung him from a cross for the animal he was."

A kind of respectful silence descends on the grouping and Alonso stops his prowl. The five guards once again exchange glances that seem to say, *Did you hear what he just said?*

I no longer feel cold here on my side by the rock. An oddly pleasant numbness has taken hold.

Alonso steps closer to Caleb, to within a foot. They are almost exactly the same height and as they eyeball each other, I can just about make out his son's crushingly succinct response hissed through clenched teeth. "*You.* Left *us.* To *him.*"

He grabs Caleb in a judo wrestler's hold and wrangles him across the clearing. His foot-swipe tackle brings the two men crashing down on a burial plot, snapping the cross at the base so it keels over like a cannon-balled ship's mast. The mound collapses to half its size under their weight and, with the upper hand, Alonso uses the pile to prop up Caleb and attack with his fists. His father shields himself as best he can with his forearms and by writhing and twisting to dodge the blows. But never once do I see him deliver a punch of his own. There is only one fighter in this fight.

Caleb does manage to catch a flailing wrist and wrench it behind Alonso's back, causing the young man to roll back off him in an effort to free himself. With blood flowing freely from his nose, Caleb retreats again, further down the line of trees.

"I left to make a better life, Ces. For the four of us. I had plans."

"Liar!" Alonso's cry accompanies another charge forward. His axe in his hand once again, he wields it in expert circular loops as he advances. He swings it in a short lethal arc toward Caleb's rib cage, but his father shimmies clear. A high-stakes dance continues for several minutes before Alonso launches another full-frontal offensive, charging shoulder first with axe raised menacingly overhead. The two men cover the ground in a deadly embrace, interlocked legs shuffling along with Caleb's left hand holding his son's axe at bay above his head. The cohort move with them to the last of the trees, where Alonso gains a grip under his father's chin and they fall together to the ground in a writhing heap.

Thwack. Thwack. Thwack. Three bullets strike the dirt beside them and seem to be sucked into the earth's crust with a sound similar to the fire that whizzed past me on the river bed. It grabs their attention and they scramble to their feet, retreating swiftly but guardedly back to the shelter of the graveyard. As they regain cover, Alonso immediately launches another offensive, rounding the axe in an upward motion again aimed at his father's torso.

Thwack. At that exact moment, Caleb is hit in the upper

body by a rubber bullet that found its way through the branches, and its impact forces him directly into the path of the rising axe head. "Ughhh!" The sharp adze hits home.

Thwack. Tzing. Crack. Crack. Crack. Crack.

A shower of bullets sprays the area. Those that make it through the trees rip into pockets of foliage, flip over rocks and kick-start mini-landslides that reduce some of the proud, stony pyramids to messy heaps. Many others are buffeted by the mesquite trees whose trunks and branches snap and splinter loudly throughout the course of the attack.

One of the henchmen cries out in pain when he is hit in the arm and Alonso leaves his father, now doubled over in the fetal position. He calls out to the others to leave and they move in my direction, their bare feet covering the ground swiftly and silently. Alonso stops when he sees me in the shadow of the boulder, raising his hand like an Apache chief to draw his followers to a halt. His eyes are as dark and cold as I remember. His face compellingly beautiful. Another volley of shots shakes the trees as he kneels and draws closer to me, bending right down like someone looking for something under the bed, to look directly into my eyes. If it is fear he wants to see, he will see none. I am quite confident of that. Not so much as a shadow. Maybe it is the cold or exhaustion, or perhaps simply an accumulation of terrifying experiences that has somehow plunged me into a shell-shocked state like those children you see in news reports wandering calmly out of war-torn rubble.

He lifts his hand, and for a fleeting moment I think he is reaching for his weapon. I am so numb, I won't even feel it. But he is only bidding the others follow and in a breath they are enveloped by the desert's dark cloak.

Caleb is on the move, too. He shuffles very slowly back

to his wife's graveside, on stubborn legs, seemingly immune to the hail of ammunition. His left hand remains pressed to his side and his face is a mask of agony. Only when he sinks down and leans back against Anegam's grave marker do I see the ominous dark stain on his torn sports shirt, very visible against the pale coating of dust on his clothes. He takes what looks like a T-shirt from his backpack and places it over the wound like a pressure bandage, tying it into place with more of the string he used earlier to attach the cushion to the pastor.

My mind drifts back to the pastor's little bloodstream. And his electrified boots. All of that feels like it happened such a long time ago yet it's only a matter of hours. I am finding it very hard to think clearly here by the rock. I can just about wiggle my fingers but have lost all sensation in my tightly bound feet. Caleb struggles to muster up enough energy to find some pills in his backpack and he washes them down greedily with a swig of water. I presume they are painkillers. Time ticks slowly by. The gunfire has subsided and I tune back in to smaller sounds. Gust of breeze, rustling leaves, cicadas, breathing.

There goes Caleb coughing again and it doesn't sound good at all. It's kind of a half rasp, half gurgle. I look at him closely and see now that he is clearly dying. His breath is coming in short drafts snatched at uneven intervals and his face is startlingly pale. He reclines on the mound in that kind of lifeless hypotonic way that comes only with drunkenness or death. Feet apart, flopping outwards. Palms up and head all the time trying its best to obey gravity and loll to one side.

It is amazing how quickly one can become inured to death. How someone like me, who has attended no more than a handful of closed-casket funerals, can suddenly find himself familiar enough with the gruesome final struggles of a failing body to make trite assessments about how long a mortally wounded man might have left. Perhaps indifference is another symptom of hypothermia. This cloudy, sleepy cold seeping through every fiber.

A sylph-like figure breezes past me. Where did he come from? Or she? I can only see her now from the side. Pronounced cheekbones. Long black hair tied back loosely with … feathers? She wears a mule-colored animal-skin tunic and around her neck are colored beads and more feathers. I don't recall the cutoff jeans and simple sandals you might pick up in Target, but everything else is unmistakably the same. The Native American I saw in Shakespeare is here in the graveyard.

I start shivering again. Not out of control. More like a tremor. I have enough powers of reasoning left to understand that this is actually a good sign. A sign that I am not yet on the verge of freezing to death. I need to sit up to get a better look at this person who is now alongside the stilled form of Caleb and appears to be reaching out.

My coordination is not good. Which … how to … which to do first to get up? I roll onto my knees, using the top of my head as my upper body's prop, but this simple exercise leaves me feeling as though I have run a marathon. Deep breath. And another. I haul myself up to a kneeling position but instantly feel lightheaded and collapse against the boulder. The back of my head and shoulders connects heavily with the rock face, but I shrug off the pain, feeling a ripple of childish delight at my newly elevated perspective.

The ghost lady has vanished. There's no sign of her or any rustle in her wake. Was she there at all? Am I hallucinating?

No. I am absolutely sure of what I saw. The gag feels wet. I open my mouth wide and the segment covering my upper lip gives way and flaps over my chin. I lick my lips and expel the unpalatable stew of blood and adhesive. But even my spit force is weakened so much that the saliva barely clears the remaining swatch of tape and drops in a sticky string onto my bare chest.

A phone is vibrating. A muffled buzz like a bumblebee trapped beneath a picnic blanket. There it is, glowing at me from within the confines of the nylon-net side pocket of Caleb's backpack. A shaking, shining, bright pink beacon six feet from me (it might as well be six miles) but only inches from Caleb's left hand.

"Caleb. Caleb." My voice is weak and croaky. "Caleb," I say with more force. "Wake up."

He doesn't respond, but the rise and fall of his chest tells me he is still alive and I know there can't be too many rings left.

"Caleb!" I shout as loudly as I can muster and he turns his ashen visage toward me. He looks vaguely bewildered initially, as though he had completely forgotten I was there, and then his face reverts to the bedraggled mask of despair he has chosen to die with.

"That's your daughter calling on my phone, Caleb. There in your bag. You need to answer it quickly. Miranda. You know, Miranda from the Cuppa Jo? The sergeant's daughter? She's your daughter, Caleb."

Bzzzz. Bzzzzz.

"You need to answer it or we are both going to die here, Caleb. Please answer the phone. Look at her. She's amazing, your daughter. Please look at her. Reach in and take out the phone. Quickly!"

His brows knit in confusion, but I can tell I have his attention. He looks down and his fingertips tiptoe to the bag and reach into the pocket.

"You need to speed up there, Caleb."

Bzzzz. Bzzzz.

"Just touch the green icon first. You can look at her then. You can talk to her ... Hurry!"

Bzzz ...

Silence descends again, apart from my string of expletives and Caleb's unnatural cough, now a protracted bubbling wheeze that is very hard to listen to.

"Are you sure?" I hear him whisper.

"One hundred percent sure, Caleb. She was adopted by Marge and Gonzalo Vasquez in Silver City in a deal arranged by Pastor Funchess. She's amazing, Caleb. Have a look at her picture on the phone. She is one of the smartest, nicest people I've ever met. Kind and funny. Beautiful. It's all there in her, Caleb. Your daughter."

It requires a massive effort to complete this explanation and I am left short of breath. Does this man even deserve to be offered these crumbs of happiness? My teeth chatter again but only very briefly and I sense that my body is rapidly running out of reserves to fight the cold. Tidal waves of tiredness threaten to sweep me away, but I know I must fight to stay awake and look for distractions in the awesome night sky.

Bzzzzz. Bzzzzz.

Caleb's hand moves faster than I thought possible for someone in his condition and he holds the phone in front of him as though seeing such an object for the first time. Miranda's pink tee stands brightly out between the blue cotton shirts Sunil and I wore that day and I can just about make out the digital clock across her smiling eyes. It reads 00:49, Friday, September 23.

"Touch the green icon," I say urgently and he does.

"Hello? Ariel?" Miranda's voice sounds crisp and clear in the night air. "Ariel, can you hear me?"

"Answer her, for fuck's sake," I growl at Caleb, whose bloodied hand is shaking either with the effort of holding up the phone or the emotion of the moment.

"Is that you?" she asks. She must have heard me in the background.

"Answer her or give me the goddamn phone, Caleb."

He looks skyward and makes a strange noise—like a sigh but more high-pitched—and throws the phone toward me. In a merciful and uncharacteristically serendipitous turn of fate, it lands face up in front of me and I heave myself forward and to the side so I am close enough for her to hear me.

"Miranda. Miran—"

"Ariel? What's going on there? Where are you? I'm sorry for calling so late, but I needed to tell you something."

"Miranda, please listen to me. I can't explain everything, but there are lives at stake here, so please just listen. I need you to listen and do as I ask. Can you do that?"

"Yes, yes, of course. What is it?"

I take several breaths and hear another cough from the mound. It sounds different. Pinched and shallow.

"Please call your mom. Tell her to call Paul Pitcavage and let him know that I am in the graveyard. He will understand. Please call now. Immediately." I relax back onto my side and hear her say my name a few times before the phone goes silent.

Caleb is making a new noise, a whimper. Is he crying? How long will it take, I wonder, for them to get here? A very reasonable line of wondering but one that quickly escalates into an all-consuming obsession involving my phone and my frozen nose. A minute or two after the display darkens, I force myself to roll over again onto my front and nose the screen to check the exact time, deducting a minute or two to get my correct starting point. Up to that moment, I didn't know that iPhones respond to nose tips, but sure enough, they do.

In fairness, this is probably a good way to keep me lucid, but that's not what lies behind it. I have always been consumed with monitoring intervals and events. How long it takes for everyday things to happen. Precisely how many minutes did that taxi take to arrive after I called it up? More or less than they advised? Exactly how long will it take for a medium rare steak to come out of that kitchen after the order going in? How long did they make me wait after the appointment time? I want to be time's keeper, not its passenger. Measuring and logging the periodical subsets that compose my day. This idiosyncrasy is, in fact, a major part of the attraction distance running holds for me. All that clocking and time comparisons? Perfect. Here beside the rock, I will cling to the raft of habit and attempt to make an accurate assessment of how long it is going to take the FBI to respond to my SOS.

Thirteen minutes and seven seconds, I think, significantly shorter than the fifteen I predicted. My nose provides the final reading on hearing the advance of boots and Kevlar. I settle back into a satisfied stupor, musing about the constituent stage times: one minute for Miranda's call to Marge (maybe a bit longer given the situation currently pertaining between those two); another minute for the call between Marge and Pitcavage; three minutes for them to gather themselves up; two to exit the camp with care and then just under six left for them to cover the three hundred yards using their crouch-and-rush method of advance.

It's very impressive, really. Not long at all. But long enough still for Caleb to sink beyond resuscitation. While I am being tucked under foil wrap and blanket on a collapsible gurney, my sense of modesty having remained unruffled by the public placing of a thermometer into my rear end, I catch glimpses of the medical officer working on my neighbor's lifeless body. The doctor appears to have an unending supply of gadgets and sophisticated-looking field equipment but nothing in his armory that can cajole the man back from the dead.

"Keep the warm oxygen flowing over there, but don't let him fall asleep yet. His temp is only marginally above ninety-five degrees. Keep him talking, too, if possible."

I hear the doctor's words but they sound strange, as though they are coming a long way down a warped pipe. Pitcavage's voice, however, is like a warm balm in my ear. "Thought we'd lost you there, Ariel. Like I said, it's the unexpected stuff. Now we're gonna get you home real soon so you can fly off somewhere nice and warm. Tell me. Where do you rich hedge fund folks like to holiday? Come on. I'll wager Monaco or the Caribbean or some such place? Where'd you last take a sun break, Ariel?"

I open my eyes and inhale deeply underneath the Perspex face mask. He is wearing his helmet and his night-vision headset sits up on top like a welder's goggles. I notice he is not wearing his glasses. "Private jet to North Island, Seychelles," I say with a huge grin and he reacts comically as though I have plunged a knife into his heart.

"Tell me. What does one do all day on the North Island, Seychelles? Dive for pearls? Have high tea with English royalty?"

"Can I ask a favor?" Synthesized with the faint hiss of oxygen, my voice sounds distinctly sci-fi.

"Of course. Shoot."

"Those photographs of the twins. Can you get me a—"

A shout from inside the tree line cuts me short. Pitcavage immediately calls out one of the operative's names— "Stapleton" is how it sounds to me. He must have been stationed there as lookout. His cry is quickly followed by fight sounds, groans and rustling leaves. Moments later, Alonso and his five foot soldiers break cover as a single tight-knit group. They all carry loaded slingshots trained on the seven remaining officers, a mix of SWAT and BORTAC, who have arranged themselves into various defensive poses behind grave markers, alongside boulders or just standing, awaiting orders.

Pitcavage points his revolver at Alonso's head and walks toward him. "Surrender or we will shoot," he says in a commanding voice.

Alonso's young comrades look to him for instructions. In the blue light of the moon, their faces look almost angelic, like a small Christmas choir.

"Put down your weapons and surrender," Pitcavage says, only ten feet or so now from his target. "Return fire when fired upon," he instructs his men as he progresses and Alonso takes this as his cue to charge wildly at the officer in a similar way to how he had tackled Caleb earlier.

It takes the FBI officer only minutes to subdue his attacker using the kind of honed fighting techniques that come with years of elite training. His polite and polished veneer had well disguised the skillful brute now on show. He grappled only once with his attacker during that first onslaught. From then on, he ducked, dived and fended off blows, always maneuvering his opponent to a distance where he could deliver his own telling head and body shots.

It finishes when he holds a still-struggling Alonso in a vice-like arm lock so a colleague can cuff him. Once the other attackers are rounded up at gunpoint, Pitcavage and the doctor head into the trees to tend to the officer whose helmet and body armor appear to have saved him from death. Radios fizzle here and there with requests for back-up to help return the prisoners, two stretchers and Caleb's body to camp.

"He *is* the one, right?" Pitcavage asks while dusting himself down and I nod to confirm. "The others?"

"I recognize two or three of them." I have to shout to make myself heard from behind my muzzle. "There were more. At least ten."

"We captured three others over the last eight hours. Sniped them with non-lethal and mopped up. Your ID here is enough to arrest them. We'll get the stragglers at dawn when the birds come back. What happened to Caleb?"

It occurs to me to reply with something cryptic like his dead wife came to take him with her or his past finally caught up with him. "His son killed him," I say, sticking to the safety of facts, but am surprised when the words catch in my throat. I see that Pitcavage notices, but he says nothing, just gives me a respectful nod and walks off to coordinate the return to base.

"You can close your eyes now, sir," the doctor says when we reach camp and my vitals have been taken again. "Sleep is what you need now."

I smile up at him and yield to unfathomable exhaustion.

Chapter Nineteen

HOME

Whirr of chopper blades, whispered questions, the slamming of doors, hospital smells. Semiconscious hours drift past, all within warmth's soothing embrace. And then I wake up in a private, airy room in Deming Hospital to the clatter of a tea cup falling out of its saucer when the tray that is ferrying it is plonked roughly down on the over-bed table.

"Good morning, Mr. Mignolet," breezes the nurse in that no-nonsense, let's-get-this-show-on-the-road voice that hospital staff all eventually perfect. "And a beautiful morning it is out there." She wrenches the blind cord down to prove it. "Are you all right there, my dear? Did you have a good sleep? What can I order you for breakfast?"

Groggily blinking, I hoist myself up a bit on my knuckles and clear my throat. Pain shoots through my lower back.

"I have to confess I preferred your hair the way it was before. Did you get it cut here in Deming?" she asks.

I recognize her now. She is the kind nurse from two weeks ago who didn't take any lip from the sergeant.

"Not enough men grow their locks, if you ask me," she continues. "Except the bikers, of course, but they're not my type. Still, I'd say I'm right in saying you're no biker, Mr.

Mignolet. Am I right about that? How about poached eggs and bacon, hon?" She plumps up my pillows and rolls the table so close to my chin it feels like a wooden bib.

"That would be great," I croak. "Could I get orange juice with that?"

"Orange juice it is," she says and flounces out on squeaking rubber-soled shoes.

Midway through my breakfast, I notice a blue light flashing to my right. I wasn't aware my phone was even in the room so it takes me four more illuminations to locate it in the bedside locker cubby hole where someone has kindly plugged it in to charge. There are twenty-one missed calls and sixty-six unread texts. I sit up on the edge of the bed to take the call and am pleased to discover that, apart from a low-grade backache, I feel pretty good.

"Hello?" I say tentatively. I don't recognize the number so am mentally Rolodexing a long cast of characters.

"Ariel, you sound good. The doctors are happy, but I just wanted to check in with you myself to see how you're recovering and to see that you got the envelope." Pitcavage's tone is at its charming best.

"Paul. Thanks. I'm good. I guess. But what envelope?"

"Your request in the graveyard? You were cut short, but I hope I got the gist of it."

"Actually there is something addressed to me here on the window sill. Yellow? That the one you sent me?"

"Yes, that's it."

"Thanks so much for remembering. Sorry, I've only woken up this minute so I'm a bit slow. It's ... wow, it's Saturday. I appear to have mislaid yesterday."

"I'm surprised you didn't sleep for a week. Hell of a few hours you went through out there and I want to apologize for that, Ariel. Shouldn't have happened. Branson's all chewed up, but like I said to him, he was up against one seriously motivated and well-trained individual in that Caleb Freeth. And, you? You did great. Should be very proud."

I am not sure what to say.

"Thanks, Paul. I appreciate that."

"The mission was a success and I want to personally most sincerely thank you for your contribution. Of course, there's the pastor. I guess that's the biggest fuck-up right there. There'll be an investigation, no doubt about that, but I'm pretty sure the record will show that our procedures were airtight. Still ..."

I notice there is no mention of him having any issue with the deaths of Anthony and Caleb.

"What became of the torchbearers? And the others?" I ask.

"In custody in El Paso and temporary accommodation centers in Albuquerque," he says. "That Alonso character is a most unusual individual. Wild as the west wind. Don't believe incarceration will be of any use to him whatsoever. Still, not my department. Anyway, Ariel, you know you will be needed for the case. As a witness. Different strands of the agency will be in touch on and off over the coming months."

"Sure. That's all fine."

"I'll tell them they need to come here for statements and depositions. You've been inconvenienced enough."

"They'll have to travel a bit farther to find me, Paul. I plan on heading back to San Francisco tomorrow. Going home."

"Well, may I say that, in my humble opinion, that is an excellent decision, Ariel. I wish you best of luck and, please, do give me a thought next time that private jet touches down on the North Island."

"Thanks, Paul. You have restored my faith in US law enforcement."

After a final battery of diagnostic tests, I am wheeled out to a waiting cab, and after a quick pit stop at Prospero Police Station to collect my keys and clothes, I arrive home at one o'clock. At the top of the stairs leading from the front door, I pause to take it all in. The clean, expansive interior and glass walls, as still and serene as ever. That mesmerizing view of vast sandy valleys and purple peaks, all shimmering in today's heat wave. Pensive Letterhead in the middle, keeping a watchful eye on the whole theater.

Everything is exactly as I left it but feels utterly altered. I have always held the view that physical spaces, much like people, emit subliminal auras. Ethereal ambiences that exude a sense of mystery or sanctuary or possibility. Perhaps something happened in the last few days that snuffed out the indefinable appeal this place had for me, and now it feels hollow and unwelcoming.

I text my mother and Sunil and throw my laptop and a few armfuls of clothes into two travel bags. The moving guys can get the rest. I cannot stay another second. The switch for the garage is at the top of the stairs. Laden down with luggage, I flick it on. My hand lingers at the switch for several seconds but the only force I feel is that of habit. The light will stay on. I drive onto the Old County Road for the last time.

Five minutes up the road, Ben calls. "What the fuck, PT?"

"I'm fine, thanks for asking," I reply.

"You were *there*, right? Raiding Camp Loon with the Feds?"

"Yes, Ben. We raided Camp Loon."

"You mad bastard, Ariel. Not bad for a gay boy from Golden Gate. What the hell was that like? The news said three dead, a dozen arrested, and a legion of malnourished nut jobs looking for homes in Albuquerque. Not Waco but, well, an above-average day for an unstable number cruncher. Were you ringside?"

"Ben, can we not talk about it right now? Over dinner maybe? Tuesday? I'm driving back today. Leaving pretty much now."

"Hal-a-fuckin'-looo-ya. He's back to his old self and coming home to Daddy. Hang on a minute. Did you just say you were *driving* home? Actually driving a car? Are you sure you're better?"

"Yeah. Better. But I'll be needing a new nickname."

"Huh?"

"How'd the showdown with Garton go?" I ask.

"Couldn't have been more successful. Now, of course there was all kinds of gnashing of teeth at first when I told them you weren't coming. I guess you got a good understanding of *my* frustration about all that from my voice mail, right?"

"You could say that," I say drily.

"But then … your little video? The America-needs-me speech? Up on the boardroom wall? In your suit? They loved it. And all that stuff about having had time to think out there in the wilderness and the Powell Homes/Lennox idea? The timing on that looks great, by the way. I could see their numbers guys creaming up on the returns potential. The whole thing was genius, Ariel. Bretworth and his cronies were stumped. Where'd you pull the homebuilders' gem out of, anyway?"

"I met a financial guru here in town a few months ago and she put the Powell idea into my head," I reply, but I know I might as well have told him that a turkey had gobbled it in my ear. With no real interest in the origin of things, only their conclusion, Ben will have tuned out the instant the question left his lips.

The mid-afternoon temperature has soared to nearly a hundred degrees by the time I reach the Vasquez home. Their modest front porch offers excellent shade and I am enjoying the fresh scent of potted catmint and thyme when the door opens and Gonzalo smiles and waves me in.

"Is she back?" I ask the back of his head as he leads me through to the kitchen. His demeanor at the door suggests she is, but I ask anyway.

"Indeed she is, thank God. Rode in yesterday morning smelling like stale bread. She was holed up somewhere near Shakespeare apparently. But I suppose there was always a risk that telling her the truth would have consequences, and—no doubt she will tell you this herself—she's now saying she won't go to college next year or maybe any year. Says she wants to find out who she really is first, whatever that means. In fact, we were hoping maybe you would try and talk sense into her. She's out in the barn and she, well, you'll see for yourself. She has put up some walls. Anyway, what a few days *you've* had, Ariel. Marge told me some of the story. I hope the news people don't get wind of any details or you might have to endure the fuss of a hero's mantle having just cast off the villain's."

"Nah. I did nothing. I guess you could say that I was a little bit tied up most of the time, at least, not in a position to help much."

"Coffee?" Gonzalo asks from the kitchen counter while I take a seat at the dining table.

"Yes, please. Black, no sugar. The guy running the show, Paul Pitcavage, he and his team were incredible out there. It's impressive when you see all that training directed at saving lives instead of taking them."

"But the pastor? That was Caleb, right?"

"Yes, sir. Caleb killed him. I … actually, I was there."

Gonzalo pulls up at the table with the coffees and sits quietly for a long time with eyes full of sympathy and a kind of gentle fatherly understanding that I never had the benefit of. If I were younger, I'd swear he would take my hand in his.

"Prospero is a rudderless ship," he says, sipping through steam. "We went into town this morning to see his body laid out in the church. People don't know what to do. Funchess never groomed a proper understudy so there are just a few pale-faced young men in oversized suits fussing about with Bibles under their arms. Can't see how any of them will be able to step into his shoes."

"They'll find someone."

Sergeant Newlands joins our conversation from the hallway door before taking a seat at the table across from me. She wears a peach dress and tiny pearl earrings that render her totally unrecognizable. I would pass her like a stranger on the street.

"Let's just be thankful those thugs are not still roaming out there," she says. "And for all those lives saved. It's hard to contemplate how many would have starved if the mission were delayed even a few weeks. I understand some of them were at death's door. We heard one telling his story on the radio on the way back from town."

"All I can tell you from what I saw is that their entire existence was … it was beyond understanding." I leave it at that and hope they don't ask me to be more specific because I don't feel ready to talk about it all.

"Here, Sergeant, I wanted you guys to have this. It's only a copy, of course. Cora Freeth gave Pitcavage permission to take a photograph with his phone and he had them made up for me."

I slide the envelope across the table and she opens it slowly, tilting it so its precious contents slip out between herself and her husband. The triptych of photo-booth stills of the Freeth family has been reproduced as three separate prints, which they examine together one by one with whispered comments and asides, so absorbed they don't seem to notice when I exit through the sliding door.

The heat has cooked up a stew of stable smells, including the unmistakably acrid whiff of manure. Dust motes and small black flies flit through sunbeams projected at all angles through gaps in the barn's vaulted wooden frame. Dressed in a grime-streaked white vest and blue jeans, Miranda is picking out Pirate's rear hooves in one of four straw-filled stalls. Bent forward with the upturned hoof cupped into her palm and resting against the side of her knee, she works the pick in short strokes away from her to remove debris around the edge. Her tiny tanned shoulder leans into the considerable mass of the horse's chestnut flank while Pirate nonchalantly lips hay strands from a manger.

"Hey," I say quietly from a few feet away.

She looks up, wipes a bead of sweat away from her hairline before returning to her task and replying with a muted "hey" of her own.

"I want to say thank you for reacting so quickly Friday morning. I don't know what possessed you to call in the middle of the night, but it probably saved my life."

She doesn't look up this time but keeps picking away at the creamy-colored underfoot, which, from where I stand, already looks very clean.

"Don't know what possessed me either," she says. "I woke from a dream. A strange woman kept squeezing my hand."

Her words place the final piece in an unfathomably large jigsaw that my subconscious has been busy at for many months. The tingle of nerves I feel might be a momentary rush of satisfaction. I want to ask her was the woman in her dream a Native American. But for some reason I don't.

"I'm not sure how much your mom has told you about Caleb Freeth and the …"

"The real me?" She drops the hoof gently to the ground by the feathers and strokes the silky copper rump with one hand while the other rests on her hip with attitude. I am finding it hard to decipher the look on her face. There is anger there for sure but something else too complex to name.

"Let's see. There's my *real* parents, my crazy twin and the pastor who gave me up for adoption before being murdered by my now-deceased father. Have I missed anything? I think I do know everything *now*, Ariel. The question I have is how long *you* knew about it all?"

"I found out the same day your mother did, Miranda. Thursday. Your grandmother, Cora Blount, showed me photographs that your parents are looking at right now in the house. They show you as an infant with your birth mother, your brother, and Caleb."

My revelation softens her defiant pose and, for a moment, I think she is about to sprint past me to have a look, but she just moves a few feet closer and stands there. I see a shadow of pain in her expression that was never there before and sense that the old Miranda, with all her lightness of being, may be gone forever.

"I am leaving for San Francisco. For good. Today. Now, really. After I leave here. I called in to say goodbye and ask if you would maybe consider coming to visit in the next few weeks. My treat. I could bring you around Stanford and introduce you to some people who can help advise you about courses and colleges. We could even swing by a few art galleries. Do a bit of touristy stuff. Your mom and dad could come, too, if that works. I really think you'd enjoy it and it might help take your mind off things. What do you think?"

She looks down at her feet.

"It won't take my mind off *things*." She says the words almost at the level of a whisper and two wet sniffs betray the welling up of tears.

I move closer and put my hand on her cheek. "Hey, come on."

Moist eyes look up and the tips of her fingers softly trace a line from my hand on her cheek up my arm, past the sleeves of my tee shirt and onto my face where she presses her thumb gently to my lower lip. Then stepping closer, she shakes her head slightly so my hand falls from her face. Setting it free to draw her closer still.

"I think I am in love with you," she breathes and her eyes bore for an immediate response.

Her parted lips. The dew of youth on every honey-toned cell. Unruly tendrils framing an exquisite face. And all the beauty that I know lies beneath. If there were even the tiniest scintilla of heterosexual male lurking in my being, this would be its moment to run riot, to break cover, to seize the day.

"I'm … gay, Miranda. All thirty-four years old and counting. I care deeply about you too, but just not in that way. Never in that way."

How the hell did I not see this coming? I take her two hands in mine and lead her to sit on two straw bales tucked alongside the barn wall. Tears are now streaming down her face. I scramble frantically to recall my own feelings back in St. Patrick's High School when my year-long obsession with an unerringly straight young teacher called Peter Forrester was crushed by seeing him passionately kissing a beautiful woman.

"I am so, so very sorry for any hurt this will cause you, Miranda. God knows the last thing in the world I want to do is cause you pain. You. My amazing, amazing friend. One of the coolest human beings I have ever had the pleasure of knowing. And I can assure you that when you do go to college, you are going to have guys lining up to take you out. I feel so passionately that the whole college idea is perfect for someone like you. To go and ask questions of the world. To get out there and find a role for yourself in the big crazy chorus line."

"Sunil?" Her fluid-filled nose distorts her pronunciation and it takes me a few seconds to work out that she is asking me a question and it has nothing whatsoever to do with my little speech.

"Once upon a time, but now? No," I reply.

The weeping subsides and she wipes her eyes and nose repeatedly with the back of her arm while latching on to me with a scrutinizing gaze, assessing me anew.

"Mike?"

A wrench twists a full turn in my gut. "No, Miranda. Mike was in love with Eliza. He was a good friend. Nothing more."

She picks up a strand of straw, and in a distracted preoccupied kind of way, endeavors to tease it into one of the shoelace holes in her sneakers.

"I'm not going to college, Ariel. Maybe in a few years, but for the time being, I want to stay. To get used to this new person and maybe get to know my family. They say Alonso will be held in El Paso for up to a year."

If she looked up from fidgeting with the straw, she would see my hand move to cover my mouth, that semi-involuntary gesture again that takes over when I get uncomfortable or am not sure what to say. "Alonso is an extremely damaged person, Miranda, and he has a lot of blood on his hands. I saw him kill Mike. I saw him kill Caleb. So I wouldn't want you to get your hopes up. I'm not sure there is a brother left in there to reach."

She looks up at me. "Was that Caleb you were shouting at when I called?"

I nod. "I could see he didn't have long left and had just told him you were his daughter. Dunno … guess I wanted him to have something good to cling on to at the end or maybe it was to get him to answer the damn thing. I'm not sure. But, whatever, he must have been happy something good had come out of the whole mess."

"Please don't go, Ariel. I have nobody. I feel as though my life has been hollowed out at the core."

My chest tightens as though bracing for a punch. I want to take her in my arms and tell her everything is going to be all right.

"Come with me to San Francisco, Miranda. Get out from under Prospero for a while. To think. Come with me today, even for a short break."

She leans back against the wall and looks up to the rafters, fighting back another wave of tears, or perhaps looking for inspiration. It puts her in the line of one of the many beams of light crisscrossing the barn, and she closes her eyes as if to bathe in its glow.

"I can't go. Anywhere. With *you*."

Pirate looks around at us and emits a low whinny as if in support and I take it as my cue to leave.

"I'll call you next week," I offer as my parting shot but regret it immediately as both weak and inappropriate.

My goodbyes to Sergeant Newlands and Gonzalo are more abrupt, bordering on rude, than I would have wished, but I am afraid of what they might infer from my dark demeanor should we get engrossed in any conversation about Miranda.

A cocktail of emotions flows through my mind as I drive to Deming to drop off the keys and sign papers in the Metcalf and Els Real Estate office. Did I not see this coming? Sensed but buried perhaps? At the house there was a wrinkle when she asked me was I ever married. What a monumental waste of talent. Maybe Prospero will improve without Funchess, but if she doesn't escape now, it may well never happen. It occurs to me, depressingly, that, apart from Mike, I haven't cared this much about anything other than a share price in a very long time.

Quick late lunch, real estate agent business squared away and gas tank filled, I reverse out of my parking spot at the mall and enter the final instructions to the GPS system for traffic and weather alerts along the one-thousand-mile journey. I plan to make it over two days, over-nighting in Phoenix before starting the eight-hour stretch home on Sunday morning.

As I edge out onto Cedar Street, a flash of color catches my eye in the rear-view mirror. Sprite Lady is sporting a belted pink mini-dress and black patent flats today. Her bright red locks have been teased into a towering beehive that sways as she runs toward my car and, when she arrives panting at my driver's window, I can see that her lipstick and nail polish match her outfit perfectly.

She taps the glass with the glinting green eye of an enormous costume ring.

"Excuse me, sir. Can I ask you a question?"

As the window hums its way down, I catch the unmistakable whiff of Chanel No. 5. Another car has arrived behind me, but I think there's enough room for it to squeeze past.

"Of course. Shoot," I reply breezily to hide my apprehension.

"I was wondering ... have you ever met Jack Nicholson?"

I quickly cover my mouth to keep from laughing out loud.

"It's just that I'd really like to know what he's like, I mean *really* like. Like in person?"

"I'm sorry, I don't ... or I haven't ever ..."

"Your plates. Beverly Hills, right?" She points to the back of my car and treats me to a puzzled look that suggests my ignorance is a source of profound disappointment. "I was just wondering if maybe your paths might have crossed any time ... in a restaurant or something? I'd love to know what he's like in the flesh. Would he give you the time of day and that kind of thing?"

"Okay. Yes, I get it. Right. Actually, I have *personally* never met the man. You see, I don't actually live in Beverly Hills, only purchased my car there. But I do know someone who invests money for someone who lives very near him on Mulholland Drive and I've heard through that person that he's a good neighbor. Would probably never win husband of the year, but a nice guy."

"Right. So you've never met him in person, then?"

"No, I'm sorry I can't be more helpful."

"Aw, okay, well, that kinda sucks, but thanks anyway," she mutters before turning and walking slowly back toward the wall, shoulders sagging despondently.

The one thousand miles isn't far enough to dim the echo of Sunil's *I told you so* ringing in my head. I check the time and hit the gas. I have a long way to go.

Acknowledgments

Huge thanks go to the following people:

Irene Graham, for her early-stage editorial insights and for the praise and encouragement that gave me the belief to keep writing.

Rosemary Foley, for her super-human attention to detail.

My agent, Elizabeth Trupin-Pulli, at Jet Literary Agency, who championed this story so enthusiastically for so long.

The uber-professional team at Kazoo Independent Publishing Services, including Robert Doran, Chenile Keogh, and Andrew Brown, whose talents combine so effectively to provide a Rolls Royce service to authors.

My earliest critics (including Peg Quinlan, John Stack, Joanne Lawless, and Sharon Ryan) and, especially, my first "proper" readers: Leona Nicholson, Vicky Landy, and Cathy Higgins.

Thanks, Dad, for your precious thesaurus.

My husband, John, for helping me in so many ways to realize this dream.